LARGE
PRINT
EDITION

RANDOM
HOUSE

TICKTOCK

DEAN KOONTZ

Published by Random House Large Print
in association with Ballantine Books
New York   1997

Library of Congress Cataloging-in-Publication Data
Koontz, Dean R. (Dean Ray), 1945–
Ticktock / by Dean Koontz.
p.   cm.
ISBN 0-679-75873-9
1. Large Type Books.
I. Title.
[PS3561.O55T53   1996]
813'.54—dc20   95-36490   CIP

Random House Web Address:
http://www.randomhouse.com/
Printed in the United States of America
FIRST LARGE PRINT EDITION

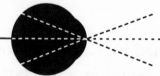

This Large Print Book carries the
Seal of Approval of N.A.V.H.

To Gerda
with the promise
of
sand, surf,
and a Scootie
of our own

To see what we have never seen,
to be what we have never been,
to shed the chrysalis and fly,
depart the earth, kiss the sky,
to be reborn, be someone new:
Is this a dream or is it true?

Can our future be cleanly shorn
from a life to which we're born?
Is each of us a creature free—
or trapped at birth by destiny?
Pity those who believe the latter.
Without freedom, nothing matters.
    —The Book of Counted Sorrows

In the real world
as in dreams,
nothing is quite
what it seems.
    —The Book of Counted Sorrows

ONE

Out of a cloudless sky on a windless November day came a sudden shadow that swooped across the bright aqua Corvette. Tommy Phan was standing beside the car, in pleasantly warm autumn sunshine, holding out his hand to accept the keys from Jim Shine, the salesman, when the fleeting shade touched him. He heard a brief thrumming like frantic wings. Glancing up, he expected to glimpse a sea gull, but not a single bird was in sight.

Unaccountably, the shadow had chilled him as though a cold wind had come with it, but the air was utterly still. He shivered, felt a blade of ice touch his palm, and jerked his hand back, even as he realized, too late, that it wasn't ice but merely the keys to the Corvette. He looked down in time to see them hit the pavement.

He said, "Sorry," and started to bend over.

Jim Shine said, "No, no. I'll get 'em."

Perplexed, frowning, Tommy raised his gaze to the sky again. Unblemished blue. Nothing in flight.

The nearest trees, along the nearby street, were phoenix palms with huge crowns of fronds, offering no branches on which a bird could alight. No birds were perched on the roof of the car dealership, either.

"Pretty exciting," Shine said.

Tommy looked at him, slightly disoriented. "Huh?"

Shine was holding out the keys again. He resembled a pudgy choirboy with guileless blue eyes. Now, when he winked, his face squinched into a leer that was meant to be comic but that seemed disconcertingly like a glimpse of genuine and usually well-hidden decadence. "Getting that first 'vette is almost as good as getting your first piece of ass."

Tommy was trembling and still inexplicably cold. He accepted the keys. They no longer felt like ice.

The aqua Corvette waited, as sleek and cool as a high mountain spring slipping downhill over polished stones. Overall length: one hundred seventy-eight and a half inches. Wheelbase: ninety-six and two-tenths inches. Seventy and seven-tenths inches in width at the dogleg, forty-six and three-tenths inches high, with a minimum ground clearance of four and two-tenths inches.

Tommy knew the technical specifications of this car better than any preacher knew the details of any Bible story. He was a Vietnamese-American, and America was his religion; the highway was his church, and the Corvette was about to become the sacred vessel by which he partook of communion.

Although he was no prude, Tommy was mildly offended when Shine compared the transcendent experience of Corvette ownership to sex. For the moment, at least, the Corvette was better than any bedroom games, more exciting, purer, the very embodiment of speed and grace and freedom.

Tommy shook Jim Shine's soft, slightly moist hand and slid into the driver's seat. Thirty-six and a half inches of headroom. Forty-two inches of legroom.

His heart was pounding. He was no longer chilled. In fact, he felt flushed.

He had already plugged his cellular phone into the cigarette lighter. The Corvette was *his*.

Crouching at the open window, grinning, Shine said, "You're not just a mere mortal any more."

Tommy started the engine. A ninety-degree V-8. Cast-iron block. Aluminum heads with hydraulic lifters.

Jim Shine raised his voice. "No longer like other men. Now you're a *god*."

Tommy knew that Shine spoke with a good-humored mockery of the cult of the automobile—yet he half believed that it was true. Behind the wheel of the Corvette, with this childhood dream fulfilled, he seemed to be full of the power of the car, exalted.

With the Corvette still in park, he eased his foot down on the accelerator, and the engine responded with a deep-throated growl. Five-point-seven liters of displacement with a ten-and-a-half-to-one compression ratio. Three hundred horsepower.

Rising from a crouch, stepping back, Shine said, "Have fun."

"Thanks, Jim."

Tommy Phan drove away from the Chevrolet dealership into a California afternoon so blue and high and deep with promise that it was possible to believe he would live forever. With no purpose except to enjoy the Corvette, he went west to New-port Beach and then south on the fabled Pacific Coast Highway, past the enormous harbor full of yachts, through Corona Del Mar, along the newly developed hills called Newport Coast, with beaches and gently breaking surf and the sun-dappled ocean to his right, listening to an oldies radio station that rocked with the Beach Boys, the Everly Brothers, Chuck Berry, Little Richard, and Roy Orbison.

At a stoplight in Laguna Beach, he pulled up beside a classic Corvette: a silver 1963 Sting Ray with boat-tail rear end and split rear window. The driver, an aging surfer type with blond hair and a walrus mustache, looked at the new aqua 'vette and then at Tommy. Tommy made a circle of his thumb and forefinger, letting the stranger know that the Sting Ray was a fine machine, and the guy replied with a smile and a thumbs-up sign, which made Tommy feel like part of a secret club.

As the end of the century approached, some people said that the American dream was almost extinguished and that the California dream was ashes. Nevertheless, for Tommy Phan on this won-derful autumn afternoon, the promise of his country and the promise of the coast were burning bright.

The sudden swooping shadow and the inexpli-cable chill were all but forgotten.

He drove through Laguna Beach and Dana Point to San Clemente, where at last he turned and, as twilight fell, headed north again. Cruising aimlessly. He was getting a feel for the way the Corvette handled. Weighing three thousand two hundred ninety-eight pounds, it hugged the pavement, low and solid, providing sports-car intimacy with the road and incomparable responsiveness. He wove through a number of tree-lined residential streets merely to confirm that the Corvette's curb-to-curb turning diameter was forty feet, as promised.

Entering Dana Point from the south this time, he switched off the radio, picked up his cellular phone, and called his mother in Huntington Beach. She answered on the second ring, speaking Vietnamese, although she had immigrated to the United States twenty-two years ago, shortly after the fall of Saigon, when Tommy was only eight years old. He loved her, but sometimes she made him crazy.

"Hi, Mom."

"Tuong?" she said.

"Tommy," he reminded her, for he had not used his Vietnamese name for many years. Phan Tran Tuong had long ago become Tommy Phan. He meant no disrespect for his family, but he was far more American now than Vietnamese.

His mother issued a long-suffering sigh because she would have to use English. A year after they arrived from Vietnam, Tommy had insisted that he would speak only English; even as a little kid, he had been determined to pass eventually for a native-born American.

"You sound funny," she said with a heavy accent.

"It's the cellular phone."

"*Whose* phone?"

"The car phone."

"Why you need car phone, Tuong?"

"Tommy. They're really handy, couldn't get along without one. Listen, Mom, guess what—"

"Car phones for big shots."

"Not any more. Everybody's got one."

"I don't. Phone and drive too dangerous."

Tommy sighed—and was slightly rattled by the realization that his sigh sounded exactly like his mother's. "I've never had an accident, Mom."

"You will," she said firmly.

Even with one hand, he was able to handle the Corvette with ease on the long straightaways and wide sweeps of the Coast Highway. Rack-and-pinion steering with power assist. Rear-wheel drive. Four-speed automatic transmission with torque converter. He was *gliding*.

His mother changed the subject: "Tuong, haven't seen you in weeks."

"We spent Sunday together, Mom. This is only Thursday."

They had gone to church together on Sunday. His father was born a Roman Catholic, and his mother converted before marriage, back in Vietnam, but she also kept a small Buddhist shrine in one corner of their living room. There was usually fresh fruit on the red altar, and sticks of incense bristled from ceramic holders.

"You come to dinner?" she asked.

"Tonight? Gee, no, I can't. See, I just—"

"We have *com tay cam.*"

"—just bought—"

"You remember what is *com tay cam*—or maybe forget all about your mother's cooking?"

"Of course I know what it is, Mom. Chicken and rice in a clay pot. It's delicious."

"Also having shrimp-and-watercress soup. You remember shrimp-and-watercress soup?"

"I remember, Mom."

Night was creeping over the coast. Above the rising land to the east, the heavens were black and stippled with stars. To the west, the ocean was inky near the shore, striped with the silvery foam of incoming breakers, but indigo toward the horizon, where a final blade of bloody sunlight still cleaved the sea from the sky.

Cruising through the falling darkness, Tommy *did* feel a little bit like a god, as Jim Shine had promised. But he was unable to enjoy it because, at the same time, he felt too much like a thoughtless and ungrateful son.

His mother said, "Also having stir-fry celery, carrots, cabbage, some peanuts—very good. My *nuoc mam* sauce."

"You make the best *nuoc mam* in the world, and the best *com tay cam,* but I—"

"Maybe you got wok there in car with phone, you can drive and cook at same time?"

In desperation he blurted, "Mom, I bought a new Corvette!"

"You bought phone *and* Corvette?"

"No, I've had the phone for years. The—"

"What's this Corvette?"

"You know, Mom. A car. A sports car."

"You bought sports car?"

"Remember, I always said if I was a big success someday—"

"What sport?"

"Huh?"

"Football?"

His mother was stubborn, more of a traditionalist than was the queen of England, and set in her ways, but she was not thick-headed or uninformed. She knew perfectly well what a sports car was, and she knew what a Corvette was, because Tommy's bedroom walls had been papered with pictures of them when he was a kid. She also knew what a Corvette meant to Tommy, what it symbolized; she sensed that, in the Corvette, he was moving still further away from his ethnic roots, and she disapproved. She wasn't a screamer, however, and she wasn't given to scolding, so the best way she could find to register her disapproval was to pretend that his car and his behavior in general were so bizarre as to be virtually beyond her understanding.

"Baseball?" she asked.

"They call the color 'bright aqua metallic.' It's beautiful, Mom, a lot like the color of that vase on your living-room mantel. It's got—"

"Expensive?"

"Huh? Well, yeah, it's a really good car. I mean, it doesn't cost what a Mercedes—"

"Reporters all drive Corvettes?"

"Reporters? No, I've—"

"You spend everything on car, go broke?"

"No, no. I'd never—"

"You go broke, don't take welfare."

"I'm not broke, Mom."

"You go broke, you come home to live."

"That won't be necessary, Mom."

"Family always here."

Tommy felt like dirt. Although he had done nothing wrong, he felt uncomfortably *revealed* in the headlights of oncoming cars, as though they were the harsh lamps in a police interrogation room and as though he were trying to conceal a crime.

He sighed and eased the Corvette into the right-hand lane, joining the slower traffic. He wasn't capable of handling the car well, talking on the cellular phone, *and* sparring with his indefatigable mother.

She said, "Where your Toyota?"

"I traded it on the Corvette."

"Your reporter friends drive Toyota. Honda. Ford. Never see one drive Corvette."

"I thought you didn't know what a Corvette was?"

"I know," she said, "oh, yes, I know," making one of those abrupt hundred-eighty-degree turns that only a mother can perform without credibility whiplash. "Doctors drive Corvette. You are always

smart, Tuong, get good grades, could have been
doctor."

Sometimes it seemed that most of the Vietnamese-
Americans of Tommy's generation were studying to
be doctors or were already in practice. A medical
degree signified assimilation and prestige, and Vietnamese parents pushed their children toward the
healing professions with the aggressive love with
which Jewish parents of a previous generation had
pushed their children. Tommy, with a degree in journalism, would never be able to remove anyone's
appendix or perform cardiovascular surgery, so he
would forever be something of a disappointment to
his mother and father.

"Anyway, I'm not a reporter any more, Mom, not
as of yesterday. Now I'm a *full-time* novelist, not
just part-time any more."

"No job."

"Self-employed."

"Fancy way of saying 'no job,'" she insisted,
though Tommy's father was self-employed in the
family bakery, as were Tommy's two brothers, who
also had failed to become doctors.

"The latest contract I signed—"

"People read newspapers. Who read books?"

"Lots of people read books."

"Who?"

"*You* read books."

"Not books about silly private detectives with
guns in every pocket, drive cars like crazy maniac,
get in fights, drink whiskey, chase blondes."

"My detective doesn't drink whiskey—"

"He should settle down, marry nice Vietnamese girl, have babies, work steady job, contribute to family."

"Boring, Mom. No one would ever want to read about a private detective like that."

"This detective in your books—he ever marry blonde, he break his mother's heart."

"He's a lone wolf. He'll never marry."

"*That* break his mother's heart too. Who want to read book about mother with broken heart? Too sad."

Exasperated, Tommy said, "Mom, I just called to tell you the good news about the Corvette and—"

"Come to dinner. Clay-pot chicken and rice better than lousy cheeseburgers."

"I can't come tonight, Mom. Tomorrow."

"Too much cheeseburgers and french fries, soon you look like big fat cheeseburger."

"I hardly ever eat cheeseburgers and fries, Mom. I watch my diet, and I—"

"Tomorrow night we have shrimp toast. Pork-stuffed squid. Pot-roasted rice. Duck with *nuoc cham.*"

Tommy's mouth was watering, but he would never admit as much, not even if he were placed in the hands of torturers with countless clever instruments of persuasion. "Okay, I'll be there tomorrow night. And after dinner, I'll take you for a spin in the Corvette."

"Take your father. Maybe he like flashy sports car. Not me. I simple person."

"Mom—"

"But your father good man. Don't put him in fancy sports car and take him out drinking whiskey, fight, chase blondes."

"I'll do my best not to corrupt him, Mom."

"Good-bye, Tuong."

"Tommy," he corrected, but she had hung up.

God, how he loved her.

God, how *nuts* she made him.

He drove through Laguna Beach and continued north.

The last red slash of the sunset had seeped away. The wounded night in the west had healed, sky to sea, and in the natural world, all was dark. The only relief from blackness was the unnatural glow from the houses on the eastern hills and from the cars and trucks racing along the coast. The flashes of headlights and taillights suddenly seemed frenzied and ominous, as though all the drivers of those vehicles were speeding toward appointments with one form of damnation or another.

Mild shivers swept through Tommy, and then he was shaken by a series of more profound chills that made his teeth chatter.

As a novelist, he had never written a scene in which a character's teeth had chattered, because he had always thought it was a cliché; more important, he assumed that it was a cliché without any element of truth, that shivering until teeth rattled was not physically possible. In his thirty years, he had never, for even as much as a day, lived in a cold climate, so he couldn't actually vouch for the effect of a bitter winter wind. Characters in books usually found their teeth chattering from fear, however, and Tommy Phan knew a good deal about fear. As a small boy on a leaky boat on the South China Sea, fleeing from Vietnam with his parents and two brothers and infant sister, under ferocious attack by Thai pirates who would have raped the women and killed everyone if they had been able to get aboard, Tommy had been terrified but had never been so fearful that his teeth had rattled like castanets.

They were chattering now. He clenched his teeth until his jaw muscles throbbed, and that stopped the chattering. But as soon as he relaxed, it started again.

The coolness of the November evening hadn't yet leached into the Corvette. The chill that gripped him was curiously internal, but he switched on the heater anyway.

As another series of icy tremors shook him, he remembered the peculiar moment earlier in the parking lot at the car dealership: the flitting shadow with no cloud or bird that could have cast it, the deep coldness like a wind that stirred nothing else in the day except him.

He glanced away from the road ahead, up at the deep sky, as if he might glimpse some pale shape passing through the darkness above.

What pale shape, for God's sake?

"You're spooking me, Tommy boy," he said. Then he laughed drily. "And now you're even talking to yourself."

Of course, nothing sinister was shadowing him in the night sky above.

He had always been too imaginative for his own good, which was why writing fiction came so naturally to him. Maybe he'd been born with a strong tendency to fantasize—or maybe his imagination had been encouraged to grow by the seemingly bottomless fund of folk tales with which his mother had entertained him and soothed him to sleep when he was a little boy during the war, back in the days when the communists had fought so fiercely to rule Vietnam, the fabled Land of Seagull and Fox. When the warm humid nights in Southeast Asia had rattled with gunfire and reverberated with the distant boom of mortars and bombs, he'd seldom been afraid, because her gentle voice had enraptured him with stories of spirits and gods and ghosts.

Now, lowering his gaze from the sky to the highway, Tommy Phan thought of the tale of Le Loi, the fisherman who cast his nets into the sea and came up with a magical sword rather like King Arthur's shining Excalibur. He recalled "The Raven's Magic Gem" as well, and "The Search for the Land of Bliss," and "The Supernatural Crossbow," in which poor Princess My Chau betrayed her worthy father out of love for her sweet husband and paid a terrible price, and the "Da-Trang Crabs," and "The Child of Death," and dozens more.

Usually, when something reminded him of one of the legends that he had learned from his mother, he could not help but smile, and a happy peace would settle over him as though she herself had just then appeared and embraced him. This time, however, those tales had no consoling effect. He remained deeply uneasy, and he was still chilled in spite of the flood of warm air from the car heater.

Odd.

He switched on the radio, hoping that some vintage rock-'n'-roll would brighten his mood. He must have nudged the selector off the station to which he had been listening earlier, because now there was nothing to be heard but a soft susurration—not ordinary static, but like distant water tumbling in considerable volume over a sloping palisade of rocks.

Briefly glancing away from the road, Tommy pressed a selector button. At once, the numbers changed on the digital readout, but no music came forth, just the sound of water, gushing and tumbling, growling yet whispery.

He pressed another button. The numbers on the display changed, but the sound did not.

He tried a third button, without success.

"Oh, wonderful. Terrific."

He had owned the car only a few hours, and already the radio was broken.

Cursing under his breath, he fiddled with the controls as he drove, hoping to find the Beach Boys,

Roy Orbison, Sam Cooke, the Isley Brothers, or
even someone contemporary like Juliana Hatfield
or maybe Hootie and the Blowfish. Hell, he'd settle
for a rousing polka.

From one end of the radio band to the other, on
both AM and FM, the watery noise had washed
away all music, as if some cataclysmic tide had
inundated broadcast studios the length of the West
Coast.

When he attempted to turn off the radio, the sound
continued undiminished. He was certain that he had
hit the correct button. He pressed it again, to no
effect.

Gradually, the character of the sound had changed.
The splash-patter-gurgle-hiss-roar now seemed less
like falling water than like a distant crowd, like the
voices of multitudes raised in cheers or chants; or
perhaps it was the faraway raging babble of an angry,
destructive mob.

For reasons that he could not entirely define,
Tommy Phan was disturbed by the new quality of
this eerie and tuneless serenade. He jabbed at more
buttons.

Voices. Definitely voices. Hundreds or even thousands of them. Men, women, the fragile voices of
children. He thought he could hear despairing wails,
pleas for help, panicked cries, anguished groans—a
monumental yet hushed sound, as though it was
echoing across a vast gulf or rising out of a black
abyss.

The voices were creepy—but also curiously compelling, almost mesmerizing. He found himself staring at the radio too long, his attention dangerously diverted from the highway, yet each time that he looked up, he was able to focus on the traffic for only a few seconds before lowering his gaze once more to the softly glowing radio.

And now behind the whispery muffled roar of the multitude rose the garbled bass voice of . . . someone else . . . someone who sounded infinitely strange, imperial and demanding. It was a low, wet voice that was less than human, spitting out not-quite-decipherable words as if they were wads of phlegm.

No. Good God in Heaven, his imagination was running away with him. What issued from the stereo speakers was static, nothing but ordinary static, white noise, electronic slush.

In spite of the chill that continued to plague him, Tommy felt a sudden prickle of perspiration on his scalp and forehead. His palms were damp too.

Surely he had pressed every button on the control panel. Nevertheless, the ghostly chorus droned on.

"Damn."

He made a tight fist of his right hand. He thumped the flat of it against the face of the radio, not hard enough to hurt himself, but punching three or four buttons simultaneously.

Second by second, the guttural and distorted words spoken by the weird voice became clearer, but Tommy couldn't quite understand them.

He thumped his fist against the radio once more, and he was surprised to hear himself issue a half-stifled cry of desperation. After all, as annoying as the noise was, it represented no threat to him.

Did it?

Even as he posed that question to himself, he was overcome by the irrational conviction that he must not listen to the susurration coming from the stereo speakers, that he must clamp his hands over his ears, that somehow he would be in mortal danger if he understood even one word of what was being said to him. Yet, perversely, he strained to hear, to wring clarity from the muddle of sound.

"... *Phan* ..."

That one word was irrefutably clear.

"... *Phan Tran* ..."

The repulsive, mucus-clotted voice was speaking flawlessly accented Vietnamese.

"... *Phan Tran Tuong* ..."

Tommy's name. Before he had changed it. His name from the Land of Seagull and Fox.

"... *Phan Tran Tuong* ..."

Someone was calling to him. Far away at first but now drawing closer. Seeking contact. Connection. Something about the voice was ... *hungry.*

The chill, like scurrying spiders, worked deeper into him, weaving webs of ice in the hollows of his bones.

He hammered the radio a third time, harder than before, and abruptly it went dead. The only sounds were the rumble of the engine, the hum of the tires, his ragged breathing, and the hard pounding of his heart.

His left hand, slick with sweat, slipped on the steering wheel, and he snapped his head up as the Corvette angled off the pavement. The right front tire—then the right rear—stuttered onto the rough shoulder of the highway. Sprays of gravel pinged and rattled against the undercarriage. A drainage swale, bristling with weeds, loomed in the headlights, and dry brush scraped along the passenger side of the car.

Tommy grabbed the wheel with both slippery hands and pulled to the left. With a jolt and a shudder, the car arced back onto the pavement.

Brakes shrieked behind him, and he glanced at the rearview mirror as headlights flared bright enough to sting his eyes. Horn blaring, a black Ford Explorer swerved around him, avoiding a rear-end collision with only a few inches to spare, so close that he expected to hear the squeal of tortured sheet steel. But then it was safely past, taillights dwindling in the darkness.

In control of the Corvette again, Tommy blinked sweat out of his eyes and swallowed hard. His vision blurred. A sour taste filled his mouth. He felt disoriented, as if he had awakened from a fever dream.

Although the phlegm-choked voice on the radio had terrified him only moments ago, he was already less than certain that his name had actually been spoken on the airwaves. As his vision rapidly cleared, he wondered if his mind also had been temporarily clouded. It was easier to entertain the possibility that he had suffered something akin to a minor epileptic episode than to believe that a supernatural entity had reached out to touch him through the prosaic medium of a sports-car radio. Perhaps he'd even endured a transient ischemic cerebral attack, an inexplicable but mercifully brief reduction in circulation to the brain, similar to the one that had afflicted Sal Delario, a friend and fellow reporter, last spring.

He had a headache now, centered over the right eye. And his stomach was queasy.

Driving through Corona Del Mar, he stayed below the speed limit, prepared to pull to the curb and stop if his vision blurred . . . or if anything strange began to happen again.

He glanced nervously at the radio. It remained silent.

Block by block, fear drained out of him, but depression seeped in to take its place. He still had a headache and a queasy stomach, but now he also felt hollow inside, gray and cold and empty.

He knew that hollowness well. It was guilt.

He was driving his own Corvette, the car of cars, the ultimate American wheels, the fulfillment of a boyhood dream, and he should have been buoyant, jubilant, but he was slowly sinking into a sea of despondency. An emotional abyss lay under him. He felt guilty about the way he had treated his mother, which was ridiculous because he had been respectful. Unfailingly respectful. Admittedly, he had been impatient with her, and he was pained now to think that maybe she had heard that impatience in his voice. He didn't want to hurt her feelings. Never. But sometimes she seemed so hopelessly stuck in the past, stubbornly and stupidly fixed in her ways, and Tommy was embarrassed by her inability to assimilate into the American culture as fully as he himself had done. When he was with American-born friends, his mother's thick Vietnamese accent mortified him, as did her habit of walking one deferential step behind his father. *Mom, this is the United States*, he had told her. *Everyone's equal, no one better than anyone else, women the same as men. You don't have to walk in anyone's shadow here.* She had smiled at him as though he was a much-loved but dim-witted son, and she'd said, *I not walk in shadow because have to, Tuong. Walk in shadow because want to.* Exasperated, Tommy had said, *But that's wrong.* Still favoring him with that infuriating, gentle smile, she'd said, *In this United States, is wrong to show respect? Is wrong to show love?* Tommy was never able to win one of these debates, but he kept trying: *No, but there are better ways to show it.* She gave him a sly look and ended the discussion with one line: *How better—with Hallmark greeting card?* Now, driving the long-desired Corvette with no more pleasure than if it had been a secondhand rattletrap pickup truck, Tommy was cold and gray inside even as his face flushed hot with shame at his ungrateful inability to accept his mother on her own terms.

Sharper than a serpent's tooth is a thankless child.

Tommy Phan, bad son. Slithering through the California night. Low and vile and unloving.

He glanced at the rearview mirror, half expecting to see a pair of glittery snake eyes in his own face.

He knew, of course, that wallowing in guilt was irrational. Sometimes he had unrealistic expectations of his parents, but he was far more reasonable than his mother. When she wore an *ao dais*, one of those flowing silk tunic-and-pants ensembles that seemed as out of place in this country as a Scotsman's kilts, she looked so diminutive, like a little girl in her mother's clothes, but there was nothing vulnerable about her. Strong-minded, iron-willed, she could be a tiny tyrant when she wished, and she knew how to make a look of disapproval sting worse than the lash of a whip.

Those uncharitable thoughts appalled Tommy even as he indulged in them, and his face grew yet hotter with shame. Taking frightful risks, at tremendous cost, she and Tommy's father had brought him—and his brothers and sister—out of the Land of Seagull and Fox, from under the fist of the communists, to this land of opportunity, and for that he should honor and cherish them.

"I am such a selfish creep," he said aloud. "A real piece of shit, that's what I am."

As he braked to a full stop at an intersection on the border of Corona Del Mar and Newport Beach, he settled deeper in a sea of gloom and remorse.

Would it have killed him to accept her invitation

to dinner? She had made shrimp-and-watercress soup, *com tay cam*, and stir-fried vegetables with *nuoc mam* sauce—three of his favorite dishes when he was a child. Clearly, she had worked hard in the kitchen, hoping to lure him home, and he had rejected her, disappointed her. There was no excuse for turning her down, especially since he hadn't seen her and his father for weeks.

No. Wrong. That was *her* line: *Tuong, haven't seen you in weeks.* On the phone, he had reminded her that this was Thursday and that they had spent Sunday together. But now here he was, minutes later, buying into her fantasy of abandonment!

Suddenly his mother seemed to be all of the stereotypical Asian villains from old movies and books rolled into one: as manipulative as Ming the Merciless, as wily as Fu Manchu.

He blinked at the red traffic light, shocked to have had such a mean-spirited thought about his own mother. This confirmed it: He was a swine.

More than anything, Tommy Phan wanted to be an American—not a Vietnamese-American, just an American, with no hyphen. But surely he didn't have to reject his family, didn't have to be rude and mean to his beloved mother, to achieve that much-desired state of complete Americanization.

Ming the Merciless. Fu Manchu, the Yellow Peril. Dear God, he had become a raging bigot. He seemed to have deceived himself into believing he was a white person.

He looked at his hands on the steering wheel.

They were the color of burnished bronze. In the rearview mirror, he studied the epicanthic folds of his dark Asian eyes, wondering if he was in danger of trading his true identity for one that was a lie.

Fu Manchu.

If he could *think* such unkind things about his mother, he might slip up eventually and say them to her face. She would be crushed. The prospect of it left him breathless with anticipatory fear, and his mouth went as dry as powder, and his throat swelled so tight that he was unable to swallow. It would be more merciful to take a gun and shoot her. Just shoot her in the heart.

So this was the kind of son he had become. The kind of son who shoots his mother in the heart with words.

The traffic light changed from red to green, but he couldn't immediately lift his foot off the brake pedal. He was immobilized by a terrible weight of self-loathing.

Behind the Corvette, another motorist tapped his horn.

"I just want to live my own life," Tommy said miserably as he finally drove through the intersection.

Lately he had been talking aloud to himself far too much. The strain of living his own life and still being a good son was making him crazy.

He reached for the cellular phone, intending to call his mom and ask if the dinner invitation was still open.

Car phones for big shots.

Not any more. Everybody's got one.
I don't. Phone and drive too dangerous.
I've never had an accident, Mom.
You will.

He could hear her voice as clearly as if she were speaking those words now rather than in memory, and he snatched his hand away from the phone.

On the west side of Pacific Coast Highway was a restaurant styled as a 1950's diner. Impulsively, Tommy swung into the lot and parked in the glow of red neon.

Inside, the place was fragrant with the aromas of onions, hamburgers sizzling on a grill, and pickle relish. Ensconced in a tufted red-vinyl booth, Tommy ordered a cheeseburger, french fries, and a chocolate milk shake.

In his mind's ear, his mother's voice replayed: *Clay-pot chicken and rice better than lousy cheeseburgers.*

"Make that *two* cheeseburgers," Tommy amended as the waitress finished taking his order and started to turn away from his booth.

"Skipped lunch, huh?" she asked.

Too much cheeseburgers and french fries, soon you look like big fat cheeseburger.

"And an order of onion rings," Tommy said defiantly, certain that farther north, in Huntington Beach, his mother had just flinched with the psychic awareness of his betrayal.

"I like a man with a big appetite," the waitress said.

She was a slender blue-eyed blonde with a pert nose and rosy complexion—exactly the kind of woman about whom his mother probably had nightmares.

Tommy wondered if she was flirting. Her smile was inviting, but her comment about his appetite might have been innocent small talk. He wasn't as smooth with women as he would have liked to be.

If she had given him an opening, he was incapable of taking it. One rebellion a night was enough. Cheeseburgers, yes, but not both cheeseburgers *and* a blonde.

He could only say, "Give me extra Cheddar, please, and lots of onions."

After slathering plenty of mustard and ketchup on the burgers, he ate every bite of what he ordered. He drained the milk shake so completely that the sucking noises of his straw against the bottom of the glass caused nearby adult diners to glare at him because of the bad example he was setting for their children.

He left a generous tip, and as he was heading toward the door, his waitress said, "You look a lot happier going out than you did coming in."

"I bought a Corvette today," he said inanely.

"Cool," she said.

"Been my dream since I was a little kid."

"What color is it?"

"Bright aqua metallic."

"Sounds pretty."

"It flies."

"I'll bet."

"Like a rocket," he said, and he realized that he was almost lost in the oceanic depths of her blue eyes.

This detective in your books—he ever marry blonde, he break his mother's heart.

"Well," he said, "take care."

"You too," said the waitress.

He went to the entrance. On the threshold, holding the door open, Tommy looked back, hoping that she would still be staring after him. She had turned away, however, and was walking toward the booth that he had vacated. Her slender ankles and shapely calves were lovely.

A breeze had sprung up, but the night was still balmy for November. On the far side of Pacific Coast Highway, at the entrance to Fashion Island Mall, stately ranks of enormous phoenix palms were illuminated by floodlights fixed to their boles. Long green fronds swayed like hula skirts. The breeze was lightly scented with the fecund smell of the nearby ocean; it didn't chill him but, in fact, pleasantly caressed the back of his neck and playfully ruffled his thick black hair. In the wake of his little rebellion against his mother and his heritage, the world seemed to have grown delightfully more sensuous.

In the car, he switched on the radio. It was functioning perfectly again. Roy Orbison was rocking out "Pretty Woman."

Tommy sang along. Lustily.

He remembered the ominous roar of static and the strange phlegmy voice that had seemed to be calling

his name from the radio, but now he found it difficult to believe that the peculiar incident had been as
uncanny as it had seemed at the time. He had been
upset by his conversation with his mother, feeling
simultaneously put-upon and guilty, angry with her
but also with himself, and his perceptions hadn't
been entirely trustworthy. The waterfall-roar of static
had been real enough, but in his pall of guilt, he had
no doubt imagined hearing his name in a meaningless gurgle and squeal of electronic garbage.

All the way home, he listened to old-time rock-
'n'-roll, and he knew the words to every song.

He lived in a modest but comfortable two-story
tract house in the exhaustively planned city of
Irvine. The tract, as was the case with most of those
in Orange County, featured none but Mediterranean
architecture; indeed, the Mediterranean style pre-
vailed to such an extent that it sometimes seemed
restfully consistent but at other times was boring,
suffocating, as if the chief executive officer of Taco
Bell had somehow become an all-powerful dictator
and had decreed that everyone must live not in
houses but in Mexican restaurants. Tommy's place
had an orange barrel-tile roof, pale-yellow stucco
walls, and concrete walkways with brick borders.

Because he'd supplemented his salary from the
newspaper with income from a series of paperback
mystery novels that he'd written during evenings
and weekends, he'd been able to buy the house three
years ago, when he was only twenty-seven. Now his
books were coming out in hardcover first, and his

writing income had gotten large enough to allow him to risk leaving the *Register.*

By any fair assessment, he was more of a success than either of his brothers or his sister. But the three of them had remained deeply involved in the Vietnamese community, so their parents were proud of them. They could never be equally proud of Tuong, who had changed his name as soon as he was legally of an age to do so, and who had eagerly embraced everything American since arriving on these shores at the age of eight.

He supposed that even if he became a billionaire, moved into a thousand-room house on the highest cliff overlooking the Pacific Coast, with solid-gold toilets and chandeliers hung not with mere crystals but with huge diamonds, his mother and father would still think of him as the "failed" son who had forgotten his roots and turned his back on his heritage.

As Tommy swung into his driveway, the bordering beds of white and coral-red impatiens glowed in the headlights as if iridescent. Swift shadows crawled up through the raggedly peeling bark of several melaleucas, swarming into higher branches, where moonlight-silvered leaves shuddered in the night breeze.

In the garage, once the big door closed behind him, he remained in the silent car for a few minutes, savoring the smell of leather upholstery, basking in the pride of ownership. If he could have slept sitting upright in the driver's seat, he would have done so.

He disliked leaving the 'vette in the dark. Because

it was so beautiful, the car should remain under flattering spotlights, as though it were an art object in a museum.

In the kitchen, as he hung the car keys on the pegboard by the refrigerator, he heard the doorbell at the front of the house. Though recognizable, the ringing was different from the usual sound, like a hollow and ominous summons in a dream. The curse of home ownership: Something always needed to be repaired.

He wasn't expecting anyone this evening. In fact, he intended to spend an hour or two in his study, revising a few pages of the current manuscript. His fictional private detective, Chip Nguyen, had been getting wordy in his first-person narration of the story, and the tough but sometimes garrulous gumshoe needed to be edited.

When Tommy opened the front door, ice-cold wind assaulted him, frigid enough to take his breath away. A whirl of dead melaleuca leaves like hundreds of tiny flensing knives spun over him, whispering-buzzing against one another, and he stumbled backward two steps, shielding his eyes with one hand, gasping in surprise.

A dry, papery leaf blew into his mouth. The hard little point pricked his tongue.

Startled, he bit down on the leaf, which had a bitter taste. Then he spit it out.

As suddenly as it had burst through the door, the whirlwind now wound up tight and disappeared into itself, leaving only silence and stillness in its wake. The air was no longer cold.

He brushed leaves out of his hair and off his shoulders, plucked them from his soft flannel shirt and blue jeans. The wood floor of the foyer was littered with crisp brown leaves, bits of grass, and sandy grit.

"What the hell?"

No visitor waited beyond the threshold.

Tommy moved into the open doorway, peering left and right along the dark front porch. It was little more than a stoop—ten feet wide and six feet deep.

No one was on the two steps or on the walkway that cleaved the shallow front lawn, no one in sight who might have rung the doorbell. Under tattered clouds backlighted by a lambent moon, the street was quiet and deserted, *so* hushed that he could half believe that a breakdown in the machinery of the cosmos had brought time to a complete halt for everyone and for all things except for he himself.

Tommy switched on the outside light and saw a strange object on the porch floor immediately in front of him. It was a doll: a rag doll no more than ten inches tall, lying on its back, its stubby arms spread wide.

Frowning, he surveyed the night once more, paying special attention to the shrubbery, where someone might be crouched and watching him. He saw no one.

The doll at his feet was unfinished, covered

entirely with white cotton fabric, unclothed, without facial features or hair. Where each eye should have been, two crossed stitches of coarse black thread dimpled the white cloth. Five sets of crossed black stitches marked the mouth, and another pair formed an X over the heart.

Tommy eased across the threshold onto the porch. He squatted on his haunches beside the doll.

The bitterness of the dry leaf no longer lingered in his mouth, but he tasted something equally unpleasant if more familiar. He stuck out his tongue, touched it, and then looked at the tip of his finger: a small red smear. The point of the leaf had drawn blood.

His tongue didn't hurt. The wound was tiny. Nevertheless, for reasons that he could not fully explain, Tommy was unnerved by the sight of the blood.

In one of the doll's crude, mittenlike hands was a folded paper. It was held firmly in place by a straight pin with a glossy black enamel head as large as a pea.

Tommy picked up the doll. It was solid and sur-prisingly heavy for its size, but loose-jointed and limp—as though it might be filled with sand.

When he pulled the pin out of the doll's hand, the death-still street briefly came alive again. A chilly breeze swept across the porch. Shrubbery rustled, and trees shuddered sufficiently to cause moon-shadows to shimmer across the black lawn. Then all fell quiet and motionless again.

The paper was unevenly yellowed, as though it

might be a scrap of ancient parchment, slightly oily, and splintered along the edges. It had been folded in half, then folded in half again. Opened, it was about three inches square.

The message was in Vietnamese: three columns of gracefully drawn ideograms in thick black ink. Tommy recognized the language but was not able to read it.

Rising to his full height, he stared thoughtfully at the street, then down at the doll in his hand.

After refolding the note and putting it in his shirt pocket, he went inside and closed the door. He engaged the dead-bolt lock. And the security chain.

In the living room, Tommy put the strange blank-faced doll on the end table beside the sofa, propping it against a Stickley-style lamp with a green stained-glass shade so it was sitting with its round white head cocked to the right and its arms straight down at its side. Its mittenlike hands were open, as they had been since he had first seen it on the porch, but now they seemed to be seeking something.

He put the pin on the table beside the doll. Its black enamel head glistened like a drop of oil, and silvery light glinted off the sharp point.

He closed the drapes over each of the three living-room windows. He did the same in the dining room and family room. In the kitchen, he twisted shut the slats on the Levolor blinds.

He still felt watched.

Upstairs in the bedroom that he had outfitted as an office, where he wrote his novels, he sat at the desk

without turning on a lamp. The only light came
through the open door from the hall. He picked up
the phone, hesitated, and then called the home
number of Sal Delario, who was a reporter at the
Register, where Tommy had worked until yesterday.
He got an answering machine but left no message.

He called Sal's pager. After inputting his own
number, he marked it *urgent.*

Less than five minutes later, Sal returned the call.
"What's so urgent, cheesehead?" he asked. "You
forget where you put your dick?"

"Where are you?" Tommy asked.

"In the sweatshop."

"At the office?"

"Wrangling the news."

"Late on another deadline," Tommy guessed.

"You called just to question my professionalism?
You're out of the news racket one day and already
you've lost all sense of brotherhood?"

Leaning forward in his chair, hunched over his
desk, Tommy said, "Listen, Sal, I need to know
something about the gangs."

"You mean the fat cats who run Washington or the
punks that lean on the businessmen in Little
Saigon?"

"Local Vietnamese gangs. The Santa Ana Boys . . ."

". . . Cheap Boys, Natoma Boys. You already
know about them."

"Not as much as you do," Tommy said.

Sal was a crime reporter with a deep knowledge
of the Vietnamese gangs that operated not only in

Orange County but nationwide. While with the newspaper, Tommy had written primarily about the arts and entertainment.

"Sal, you ever hear about Natoma or the Cheap Boys threatening anybody by mailing them an imprint of a black hand or, you know, a skull and crossbones or something like that?"

"Or maybe leaving a severed horse's head in their bed?"

"Yeah. Anything like that."

"You have your cultures confused, boy wonder. These guys aren't courteous enough to leave warnings. They make the Mafia seem like a chamber-music society."

"What about the older gangs, not the teenage street thugs, the more organized guys—the Black Eagles, the Eagle Seven?"

"The Black Eagles have the hard action in San Francisco, the Eagle Seven in Chicago. Here it's the Frogmen."

Tommy leaned back in his chair, which creaked under him. "No horse's head from them, either, huh?"

"Tommy boy, if the Frogmen leave a severed head in your bed, it's going to be your own."

"Comforting."

"What's this all about? You're starting to worry me."

Tommy sighed and looked at the nearest window. Clotting clouds had begun to cover the moon, and fading silver light filigreed their vaporous edges. "That piece I wrote for the 'Show' section last week—I think maybe somebody's threatening to retaliate for it."

"The piece about the little girl figure skater?"

"Yeah."

"And the little boy who's a piano prodigy? What's to retaliate for?"

"Well—"

"Who could've been pissed off by that—some other six-year-old pianist thinks *he* should have gotten the coverage, now he's going to run you down with his tricycle?"

"Well," Tommy said, beginning to feel foolish, "the piece *did* make the point that most kids in the Vietnamese community don't get mixed up in gangs."

"Oooh, yeah, that's controversial journalism, all right."

"I had some hard things to say about the ones who do join gangs, especially the Natoma Boys and Santa Ana Boys."

"One paragraph in the whole piece, you put down the gangs. These guys aren't *that* sensitive, Tommy. A few words aren't going to put them on the vengeance freeway."

"I wonder. . . ."

"They don't care what you think anyway, 'cause to them, you're just the Vietnamese equivalent of an Uncle Tom. Besides, you're giving them a whole lot too much credit. These assholes don't read newspapers."

The dark clouds churned from west to east, congealing rapidly as they moved in from the ocean. The moon sank into them, like the face of a drowner in a cold sea, and the lunar glow on the window glass slowly faded.

"What about the girl gangs?" Tommy asked.

"Wally Girls, Pomona Girls, the Dirty Punks . . . it's no secret they can be more vicious than the boys. But I still don't believe they'd be interested in you. Hell, if they got steamed this easily, they'd have gutted *me* like a fish ages ago. Come on, Tommy, tell me what's happened. What's got you jumpy?"

"It's a doll."

"Like a Barbie doll?" Sal sounded bewildered.

"A little more ominous than that."

"Yeah, Barbie isn't the nasty bitch she used to be. Who'd be afraid of her these days?"

Tommy told Sal about the strange white-cloth figure with black stitches that he had found on the front porch.

"Sounds like the Pillsbury Doughboy gone punk," Sal said.

"It's weird," Tommy said. "Weirder than it probably sounds."

"You don't have a clue what the note says? You can't read any Vietnamese at all, not even a little?"

Taking the paper from his shirt pocket and unfolding it, Tommy said, "Not a word."

"What's the matter with you, cheesehead? You have no respect for your roots?"

"You're in touch with yours, huh?" Tommy said sarcastically.

"Sure." To prove it, Sal spoke swift, musical Italian. Then, reverting to English: "And I write to my *nonna* in Sicily every month. Went to visit for two weeks last year."

Tommy felt more than ever like a swine. Squinting at the three columns of ideograms on the yellowed paper, he said, "Well, this is as meaningless as Sanskrit to me."

"Can you fax it? In maybe five minutes, I can find someone to translate."

"Sure."

"I'll get back to you as soon as I know what it says."

"Thanks, Sal. Oh, hey, you know what I bought today?"

"Do I know what you bought? Since when do guys talk shopping?"

"I bought a Corvette."

"For real?"

"Yeah. An LT1 Coupe. Bright aqua metallic."

"Congratulations."

"Twenty-two years ago," Tommy said, "when I first came through the immigration office with my family and stepped into my first street in this country, I saw a Corvette go by, and that was *it* for me. That said everything about America, that fantastic-looking car, going by so sleek."

"I'm happy for you, Tommy."

"Thanks, Sal."

"Now at last maybe you'll be able to get girls,

won't have to make it any more with Rhonda Rubbergirl, the inflatable woman."

"Asshole," Tommy said affectionately.

"Fax the note."

"Right away," Tommy said, and he hung up.

A small Xerox machine stood in one corner of his office. Without turning on any room lights, he made a photocopy, returned the note to his shirt pocket, and faxed the copy to Sal at the *Register*.

The phone rang a minute later. Sal said, "You put it through the fax wrong-side up, dickhead. All I've got is a blank sheet of paper with your number at the top."

"I'm sure I did it right."

"Even your inflatable woman must be frustrated with you. Send it again."

After switching on a lamp, Tommy returned to the fax machine once more. He was careful to load the page properly. The mysterious ideograms had to be face-down.

He watched as the rollers pulled the single sheet of paper through the machine. The small message window displayed Sal's fax number at the news-paper and the word *sending*. The page of ideograms slid out of the machine, and after a pause, the word in the message window changed to *received*. Then the fax disconnected.

The phone rang. Sal said, "Do I have to drive over there and show you how to do it right?"

"You mean you got a blank page again?"

"Just your sender-ID bar at the top."

"I absolutely loaded it right this time."

"Then something's wrong with your fax," Sal said.

"Must be," Tommy said, although that answer didn't satisfy him.

"You want to bring the note by here?"

"How long will you be there?"

"Couple of hours."

"I might stop by," Tommy said.

"You've got me curious now."

"If not tonight, I'll see you tomorrow."

Sal said, "It might be some little girl."

"Huh?"

"Some other figure skater jealous about the one in your article. Remember that Olympic skater, Tonya Harding? Be careful of your kneecaps, Tommy boy. Some little girl out there may have a baseball bat with your name on it."

"Thank God we don't work in the same building any more. I feel so much cleaner."

"Kiss Rhonda Rubbergirl for me."

"You're a diseased degenerate."

"Well, with Rhonda, *you'll* never have to worry about catching anything nasty."

"See you later." Tommy put down the telephone and switched off the lamp. Once more, the only light was a pale pearlescence that spilled in from the second-floor hallway.

He went to the nearest window and studied the front lawn and the street. The yellowish glow of the streetlamps didn't reveal anyone lurking in the night.

A deep ocean of storm clouds had flooded the sky, entirely submerging the moon. The heavens were black and forbidding.

Tommy went downstairs to the living room, where he discovered the doll slumped on its side on the end table beside the sofa. He had left it propped with its back against the stained-glass lamp, in a sitting position.

Frowning, Tommy stared at it suspiciously. The doll had seemed to be full of sand, well weighted; it should have stayed where he had put it.

Feeling foolish, he toured the downstairs, trying the doors. They were all still securely locked, and there were no signs of visitors. No one had entered the house.

He returned to the living room. The doll might not have been balanced properly against the lamp, in which case the sand could have shifted slowly to one side until the damn thing toppled over.

Hesitant, not sure *why* he was hesitant, Tommy Phan picked up the doll. He brought it to his face, examining it more closely than he had done earlier.

The black sutures that indicated the eyes and the mouth were sewn with heavy thread as coarse as surgical cord. Tommy gently rubbed the ball of his thumb across a pair of crossed stitches that marked one of the doll's eyes . . . then across the row of five that formed its grimly set lips.

As he traced that line of black stitches, Tommy

was startled by a macabre image that popped into his
mind: *the threads abruptly snapping, a real mouth
opening in the white cotton cloth, tiny but razor-
sharp teeth exposed, a quick but savage snap, and
his thumb bitten off, blood streaming from the
stump.*

A shudder coursed through him, and he nearly
dropped the doll.

"Dear God."

He felt stupid and childish. The stitches had not
snapped, and of course no hungry mouth would ever
open in the thing.

It's just a doll, for God's sake.

He wondered what his detective, Chip Nguyen,
would do in this situation. Chip was tough, smart,
and relentless. He was a master of tae kwon do, able
to drink hard all night without losing his edge or suffering a hangover, a chess master who once defeated
Bobby Fischer when they encountered each other in
a hurricane-hammered resort hotel in Barbados, a
lover of such prowess that a beautiful blond socialite
had killed another woman over him in a fit of jealousy, a collector of vintage Corvettes who was able
to rebuild them from the ground up, and a brooding
philosopher who knew that humanity was doomed
but who gamely fought the good fight anyway.
Already, Chip would have obtained a translation of
the note, tracked down the source of the cotton cloth
and the black thread, punched out a thug just for the
exercise, and (being an equal-opportunity lover)
bedded either an aggressive redhead with a glori-

ously pneumatic body or a slender Vietnamese girl with a shy demeanor that masked a profoundly lascivious mind.

What a drag it was to be limited by reality. Tommy sighed and wished that he could step magically through the pages of his own books, into the fictional shoes of Chip Nguyen, and know the glory of being totally self-confident and utterly in control of life.

The evening was waning, and it was too late to drive to the newspaper offices to see Sal Delario. Tommy just wanted to get a little work done and go to bed.

The rag doll was strange, but it wasn't half as menacing as he had tried to pretend that it was. His fertile imagination had been running away with him again.

He was a master of self-dramatization, which, according to his older brother Ton, was the most American thing about him. *Americans*, Ton had once said, *all think the world revolves around them, think each individual person more important than whole society or whole family. But how can each person be most important thing? Can't everyone be the most important thing, all equal but all the most important at same time. Makes no sense.* Tommy had protested that he didn't feel more important than anyone else, that Ton was missing the point about American individualism, which was all about the right to pursue dreams, not about dominating others, but Ton had said, *Then if you don't think you better than us, come*

*work in bakery with your father and brothers, stay
with family, make family dream come true.*

Ton had inherited certain sharp debating skills—
and a useful stubbornness—from their mother.

Now Tommy turned the doll over in his hand, and
the more that he handled it, the less ominous it
seemed. Ultimately, no doubt, the story behind it
would turn out to be prosaic. It was probably just a
prank perpetrated by children in the neighborhood.

The pin with the black enamel head, which had
fastened the note to the doll's hand, was no longer
on the end table where Tommy had left it. Evidently,
when the doll had toppled over, the pin had been
knocked to the floor.

He couldn't see it on the cream-colored carpet,
although the glossy black head should have made it
easy to spot. The vacuum cleaner would get it the
next time he swept.

From the refrigerator in the kitchen, he retrieved a
bottle of beer. Coors. Brewed high in the Colorado
Rockies.

With the beer in one hand and the doll in the
other, he went upstairs to his office once more. He
switched on the desk lamp and propped the doll
against it.

He sat in his comfortable chocolate-brown, leather-
upholstered office armchair, turned on the computer,
and printed out the most recently completed chapter
of the new Chip Nguyen adventure. It was twenty
pages long.

Sipping the Coors from the bottle, he worked on the manuscript with a red pencil, marking changes.

At first the house was deathly silent. Then the incoming storm clouds finally pulled some ground-level turbulence with them, and the wind began to sough in the eaves. An overgrown branch on one of the melaleucas rubbed against an outside wall, a dry-bone scraping sound. From downstairs in the family room came the faint but distinctive creaking of the damper hinge in the fireplace as the wind reached down the flue to play with it.

From time to time, Tommy glanced at the doll. It sat in the fall of amber light from the desk lamp against which it was propped, arms at its sides, mittenlike hands turned palms up as if in supplication.

By the time he finished editing the chapter, he had also drunk the last of the beer. Before entering the red-lined changes in the computer, he went to the guest bathroom off the upstairs hall.

When he returned to his office a few minutes later, Tommy half expected to discover that the doll had toppled onto its side again. But it was sitting upright, as he had left it.

He shook his head and smiled in embarrassment at his *insistence* on drama.

Then, lowering himself into his chair, he saw four words on the previously blank computer screen: THE DEADLINE IS DAWN.

"What the hell . . . ?"

As he settled all the way into the chair, a hot sharp

pain stabbed through his right thigh. Startled, he shot to his feet, pushing the wheeled armchair away from himself.

He clutched his thigh, felt the tiny lance that had pierced his blue jeans, and plucked it out of both the denim and his flesh. He was holding the straight pin with the black enamel head as large as a pea.

Astonished, Tommy turned the pin between thumb and forefinger, his eyes on the glinting point.

Over the soughing of the wind in the eaves and the humming of the laser printer in its stand-by mode, he heard a new sound: a soft *pop* . . . and then again. Like threads breaking.

He looked at the doll in the fall of light from the desk lamp. It was sitting as before—but the pair of crossed stitches over the spot where a person's heart would be had snapped and now hung loose on its white cotton breast.

Tommy Phan didn't realize that he had dropped the pin until he heard it strike—*tink, tink*—the hard plastic mat under his office chair.

Paralyzed, he stared at the doll for what seemed like an hour but must have been less than a minute. When he could move again, he found himself reaching for the damn thing, and he checked himself when his hand was still ten or twelve inches from it.

His mouth was so dry that his tongue had stuck to his palate. He worked up some saliva, but his tongue nevertheless peeled loose as reluctantly as a Velcro fastener.

His frantic heart hammered so hard that his vision

blurred at the edges with each beat, as blood surged through him in artery-stretching quantities. He felt as though he were on the verge of a stroke.

In the better and more vivid world that he inhabited, Chip Nguyen would have seized the doll without hesitation and examined it to determine what device it contained. Perhaps a miniature bomb? Perhaps a fiendishly clever clockwork mechanism that would eject a poisoned dart?

Tommy wasn't half the man that Chip Nguyen was, but he wasn't a complete coward, damn it. Although he was reluctant to pick up the doll, he gingerly extended one index finger and experimentally pressed it against the pair of snapped sutures on the white cotton breast.

Inside the dreadful little manlike figure, directly under Tommy's finger, something twitched, throbbed, and throbbed again. Not as though it were a clockwork mechanism, but as though it were something *alive*.

He snatched his hand back.

At first, what he had felt made him think of a squirming insect: an obscenely fat spider or a frenzied cockroach. Or perhaps a tiny rodent: some God-awful pale and hairless pink mouse like nothing that anyone had ever seen before.

Abruptly the dangling black threads unraveled into the needle holes through which they had been sewn, disappearing into the doll's chest as if something had pulled them from inside.

"Jesus!"

Tommy stumbled backward a step and nearly fell into his office chair. He clutched the arm of it and kept his balance.

Pop-pop-pop.

The stitches over the thing's right eye broke as the cloth under them bulged with internal pressure. Then they, too, raveled into the doll like strands of spaghetti sucked into a child's mouth.

Tommy was shaking his head in denial. He had to be dreaming.

Where the broken sutures had disappeared into the face, the fabric split with a discrete tearing sound.

Dreaming.

The rent in the small blank-white face opened to half an inch, like a gaping wound.

Definitely dreaming. Big dinner, two cheeseburgers, french fries, onion rings, enough cholesterol to kill a horse—and then a bottle of beer. Dozed off at my desk. Dreaming.

From behind the split fabric came a flash of color. Green. A fierce radiant green.

The cotton cloth curled away from the hole, and a small eye appeared in the soft round head. It wasn't the shiny glass eye of a doll, not merely a painted plastic disc, either, but as real as Tommy's own eyes (although infinitely stranger), full of soft eerie light, hateful and watchful, with an elliptical black pupil as in the eye of a snake.

Tommy made the sign of the cross. He had been raised a Roman Catholic, and although he had only rarely attended Mass over the past five years, he was suddenly devout again.

"Holy Mary, Mother of God, hear my plea. . . ."

Tommy was prepared to spend—*happy* to spend—the rest of his life between a confessional and a sacristy railing, subsisting solely on the Eucharist and faith, with no entertainment except organ music and church bingo.

". . . in this my hour of need . . ."

The doll twitched. Its head turned slightly toward Tommy. Its green eye fixed on him.

He felt his gorge rising, tasted a bitter vileness in the back of his throat, swallowed hard, choked it down, and knew beyond doubt that he was not dreaming. He had never before nearly puked in a dream. Dreams weren't this intense.

On the computer screen, the four words began to flash: THE DEADLINE IS DAWN.

The stitches over the doll's second eye popped and raveled into its head. The fabric bulged and began to split again.

The creature's stubby arms twitched. Its small mitten hands flexed. It pushed away from the desk lamp and rose stiffly to its feet, all of ten inches tall but nonetheless terrifying for its diminutive stature.

Even Chip Nguyen—toughest of all private detectives, master of tae kwon do, fearless fighter for truth and justice—would have done precisely what Tommy Phan did then: run. Neither the author nor his creation was a complete fool.

Recognizing that skepticism in this case could get him killed, Tommy spun away from the impossible thing that was emerging from the rag doll. Pushing aside the wheeled office chair, he crashed against the corner of the desk, stumbled over his own feet, maintained his balance, and staggered out of the room.

He slammed the office door behind him so hard that the house—and his own bones—reverberated with the impact. There was no lock on it. Frantically he considered fetching a suitable chair from the master bedroom and bracing it under the knob, but then he realized that the door opened *into* the office beyond and, therefore, could not be wedged shut from the hallway.

He started toward the stairs, but on second thought he dashed into his bedroom, switching on the lights as he went.

The bed was neatly made. The white chenille spread was as taut as a drum skin.

He kept a neat house, and he was distressed to think of it all splattered with blood, especially his own.

What *was* that damn thing? And what did it want?

The rosewood nightstand gleamed darkly from furniture polish and diligent care, and in the top drawer, next to a box of Kleenex, was a pistol that had been equally well maintained.

TWO

The gun that Tommy took from the nightstand drawer was a Heckler & Koch P7 M13. He had purchased it years ago, after the Los Angeles riots sparked by the Rodney King case.

In those days, his merciless imagination had plagued him with vivid nightmares of the violent collapse of civilization. His fear had not been limited to dreams, however. He'd been anxiety-stricken for a month or two and uneasy for at least a year, expecting social chaos to erupt at any moment, and for the first time in a decade, he had flashed back to childhood memories of the bloody carnage that had followed the fall of Saigon in the weeks immediately before he and his family had escaped to sea. Having once lived through an apocalypse, he knew that it could happen again.

Orange County had not been besieged by the rampaging mobs that had chased Tommy through his dreams, however, and even Los Angeles had soon returned to normal, although normal couldn't accurately be called *civility* in the City of Angels these days. He had never needed the pistol.

Until this minute.

Now he desperately needed the weapon—not to hold at bay the expected band of looters, not even to defend his home from a single burglar, but to protect himself from a rag doll. Or from whatever was hidden within the rag doll.

As he hurried out of the bedroom and into the second-floor hallway again, Tommy Phan wondered if he might be losing his mind.

Then he wondered why he was wondering. *Of course* he was losing his mind. He was already past the edge of rationality, plunging off the cliff, on the bobsled of insanity and rocketing down a luge chute that would take him into the cold dark depths of total lunacy.

Rag dolls couldn't become animate.

Ten-inch-tall humanoid creatures with radiant green snake eyes didn't exist.

A blood vessel had popped in his brain. Or maybe a cancerous tumor had grown to that critical stage at which it exerted disabling pressure on the brain cells around it. He was hallucinating. That was the only credible explanation.

The door to his office was closed, as he had left it.

The house was as silent as a monastery full of sleeping monks, without even the murmur of whispered prayers. No wind in the eaves. No tick of clock or creak of floorboards.

Trembling, sweating, Tommy sidled along the carpeted hall, approaching the office door with extreme caution.

The pistol shook in his hand. Fully loaded, it weighed only about two and three-quarter pounds, but under the circumstances it felt enormously heavy.

It was a squeeze cocker, as safe as any double-action piece on the market, but he pointed the muzzle only at the ceiling and kept his finger lightly on the trigger. Chambered for a .40 Smith & Wesson cartridge, the gun could do serious damage.

He reached the closed door, halted, and hesitated.

The doll—or whatever was hiding in the doll—was far too small to reach the knob. Even if it could climb up to the knob, it would not have sufficient strength—or be able to apply enough leverage—to open the door. The thing was trapped in there.

On the other hand, how could he be so confident that it wouldn't have the requisite strength or leverage? This creature was an impossibility to begin with, something out of a science-fiction film, and logic applied to this situation no more than it applied in movies or in dreams.

Tommy stared at the knob, half expecting to see it turn. The polished brass gleamed with a reflection of the hall light overhead. If he peered closely enough, he could discern a weirdly distorted reflection of his own sweat-damp face in the shiny metal: He looked scarier than the thing inside the rag doll.

After a while he put one ear to the door. No sound came from the room beyond—at least none that he could hear over the runaway thudding of his heart.

His legs felt rubbery, and the perceived weight of the Heckler & Koch—more important than its *real* weight—was now twenty pounds, maybe twenty-five, so heavy that his arm was beginning to ache with the burden of it.

What was the creature doing in there? Was it still ripping out of the cotton fabric, like a waking mummy unwinding its burial wrappings?

He tried again to assure himself that this whole incident was a hallucination brought on by a stroke.

His mother had been right. The cheeseburgers, the french fries, the onion rings, the double-thick chocolate milk shakes—those were the culprits that had done him in. Although he was only thirty, his abused circulatory system had collapsed under the massive freight of cholesterol that he forced it to carry. When this terminal episode was finished and the pathologists performed an autopsy on him, they would discover that his arteries and veins were clogged with enough greasy fat to lubricate the wheels on all the trains in America. Standing over his coffin, his weeping but quietly smug mother would say, *Tuong, I try tell you but you not listen, never listen. Too many cheeseburgers, soon you look like big fat cheeseburger, start seeing little snake-eyed monsters, fall dead of shock in upstairs hall with gun in your hand like dumb whiskey-drinking detective in books. Stupid boy, eating like crazy Americans, and now look what happen.*

Inside the office, something rattled softly.

Tommy pressed his ear tighter to the paper-thin crack between the door and the jamb. He heard nothing more, but he was certain that he hadn't imagined the first sound. The silence in that room now had a menacing quality.

On one level, he was frustrated and angry with

himself for continuing to behave as though the snake-eyed minikin was actually inside the office, standing on his desk, shedding its white cotton chrysalis.

But at the same time, instinctively he knew that he was not truly insane, no matter how much he might wish that he were. And he knew that, in fact, he also was not suffering from a stroke or a cerebral hemorrhage, no matter how much more comforting such a condition might be compared with admitting the reality of the rag doll from Hell.

Or wherever it was from. Certainly not from Toys "R" Us. Not from one of the shops at Disneyland.

No delusion. No figment of imagination. It's in there.

Well, all right, if it *was* in the office, then it couldn't open the door to get out, so the smartest thing to do was leave it alone, go downstairs or even get out of the house altogether, and call the police. Find help.

Right away he saw one serious problem with that scenario: The Irvine Police Department didn't have a doll-from-Hell SWAT team that it customarily dispatched upon request. They didn't have an anti-werewolf strike force, either, or a vampire-vice squad. This was Southern California, after all, not darkest Transylvania or New York City.

The authorities would probably write him off as a crackpot akin to those people who reported being raped by Big Foot or who wore homemade aluminum-foil hats to defeat the sinister extraterrestrials who were supposedly attempting to enslave them with microwave beams broadcast from the mothership. The cops wouldn't bother to send anyone in answer to his call.

Or worse, no matter how calmly he described the encounter with the doll, the police might decide that he was suffering a psychotic episode and was a danger to himself and others. Then he could be committed to a hospital psychiatric ward for observation.

Usually a young writer, struggling to build a readership, needed all the publicity he could get. But Tommy wasn't able to imagine how his publisher's promotion of his future novels could be enhanced by a press kit filled with stories about his vacation in a psycho ward and photographs of him in a chic straitjacket. That wasn't exactly a John Grisham image.

His head was pressed so hard against the door that his ear began to ache, but still he heard no further noises.

Moving back one step, he put his left hand on the brass knob. It was cool against his palm.

The pistol in his right hand now seemed to weigh forty pounds. The weapon looked powerful. With its thirteen-round magazine, it should have given him confidence, but he continued to tremble.

Although he would have liked to walk out and never return, he couldn't do that. He was a homeowner. The house was an investment that he couldn't afford to abandon, and bankers seldom canceled mortgages as a result of devil-doll infestations.

He was virtually immobilized, and his indecisiveness deeply shamed him. Chip Nguyen, the hard-boiled detective whose fictional adventures Tommy chronicled, was seldom troubled by doubt. Chip always knew the best thing to do in the most precarious situations. Usually his solutions involved his fists, or a gun, or any blunt instrument close at hand, or a knife wrenched away from his crazed assailant.

Tommy had a gun, a really good gun, a first-rate gun, and his potential assailant was only ten inches tall, but *he could not force himself to open the damn door.* Chip Nguyen's assailants were usually well over six feet tall (except for the demented nun in *Murder Is a Bad Habit*), and frequently they were virtual giants, usually steroid-pumped bodybuilders with massive biceps that made Schwarzenegger look like a sissy.

Wondering how he could ever again write about a man of action if he failed to act decisively in his own moment of crisis, Tommy finally threw off the chains of paralysis and slowly turned the doorknob. The well-lubricated mechanism didn't squeak—but if the doll was watching, it would see the knob rotate, and it might leap at him the moment that he entered the room.

Just as Tommy had turned the doorknob as far as it would go, a thunderous crash shook the house, rattling windowpanes. He gasped, let go of the knob, backed across the hall, and assumed a shooter's stance with the Heckler & Koch gripped in both hands and aimed at the office door.

Then he realized that the crash was thunderous precisely because it *was* thunder.

When the first peal faded to a soft rumble in a distant corner of the sky, he glanced toward the end of the hallway, where pale flickers of lightning played across the window as a second hard explosion shook the night.

He recalled watching the sable-black clouds roll in from the sea and shroud the moon a little earlier in the evening. Soon the rain would come.

Embarrassed by his overreaction to the thunder, Tommy returned boldly to the office door. He opened it.

Nothing leaped at him.

The only light issued from the desk lamp, leaving deep and dangerous shadows throughout the room. Nevertheless, Tommy was able to see that the minikin was not on the floor immediately beyond the doorway.

He stepped across the threshold, fumbled for the wall switch, and turned on the ceiling light. Quicker than a litter of black cats, shadows fled behind and under the furniture.

In the sudden brightness, the minikin was not revealed.

The creature was no longer on the desk—unless it was crouched against the far side of the computer monitor, waiting for him to venture closer.

When he entered the office, Tommy had intended to leave the door open behind him, so he could get out fast should a hasty retreat seem wise. Now, however, he realized that were the doll to escape this room, he would have little chance of locating it when required to search the entire house.

He closed the door and stood with his back against it.

Prudence required that he proceed as though on a rat hunt. Keep the little beast confined to one room. Search methodically under the desk. Under the sofa. Behind the pair of filing cabinets. Search in every cranny where the vermin might be hiding until, at last, it was flushed into the open.

The pistol wasn't the most desirable weapon for a rat hunt. A shovel might have been better. He could have beaten the creature to death with a shovel, but hitting a small target with a round from a pistol might not be easy, even though he was a good marksman.

For one thing, he wouldn't have the leisure to aim carefully and squeeze off a well-calculated shot as he did on the target range. Instead, he would have to conduct himself in the manner of a soldier at war, relying on instinct and quick reflexes, and he wasn't sure that he was adequately equipped with either.

"I am no Chip Nguyen," he admitted softly.

Besides, he suspected that the doll-thing was capable of moving fast. Very fast. Even quicker than a rat.

He briefly considered going down to the garage for a shovel but decided that the pistol would have to be good enough. If he left now, he wasn't confident that he would have the courage to return to the office a second time.

A sudden patter, as of small swift feet, alarmed Tommy. He swung the pistol left, right, left—but then realized that he was hearing only the first fat drops of rain snapping against the clay-tile roof.

His stomach churned with an acidic tide that seemed sufficiently corrosive to dissolve steel nails in an instant if he ate them. Indeed, he felt as though he *had* eaten about a pound of nails. He wished that he'd had *com tay cam* for dinner instead of cheese-burgers, stir-fried vegetables with *nuoc mam* sauce instead of onion rings.

Hesitantly he edged across the room and around the desk. The red-penciled chapter of the latest book and the empty bottle of beer were where he had left them, undisturbed.

The snake-eyed minikin was not hiding on the far side of the computer monitor. It wasn't lurking behind the laser printer, either.

Under the gooseneck desk lamp were two ragged scraps of white cotton fabric. Although somewhat shredded, they had a recognizable mittenlike shape— obviously the cloth that had covered the thing's hands. They appeared to have been torn off—perhaps *chewed* off—at the wrists to free the creature's real hands from confinement.

Tommy didn't understand how there could have been any living creature in the doll when he had first handled it and brought it upstairs. The soft cloth casing had seemed to be filled with sand. He had detected no hard edges whatsoever inside the thing, no indication of a bone structure, no cranium, no cartilage, none of the firmness of flesh, merely a limpness, a loose shifting, an amorphous quality.

THE DEADLINE IS DAWN no longer glowed on the video display terminal. In place of that cryptic yet fearsome message was a single word: TICKTOCK.

Tommy felt as if he had tumbled like poor Alice into a weird alternate world—not down a rabbit hole, however, but into a video game.

He pushed the wheeled office chair out of the way. Holding the pistol in his right hand and thrusting it in front of him, he cautiously stooped to peer into the kneehole of the desk. Banks of drawers flanked that space, and a dark privacy panel shielded the front of it, yet enough light seeped in for him to be sure that the doll-thing was not there.

The banks of drawers were supported on stubby legs, and Tommy had to lower his face all the way to the floor to squint under them as well. He found nothing, and he rose to his feet once more.

To the left of the knee space were one box drawer and a file drawer. To the right was a stack of three box drawers. He eased them open, one at a time, expecting the minikin to explode at his face, but he discovered only his usual business supplies, stapler, cellophane-tape dispenser, scissors, pencils, and files.

Outside, driven by a suddenly fierce wind, rain pounded across the roof, roaring like the marching feet of armies. Raindrops rattled against the windows with a sound as hard as distant gunfire.

The din of the storm would mask the furtive scuttling of the doll-thing if it circled the room to evade him. Or if it crept up behind him.

He glanced over his shoulder, but he wasn't under imminent attack.

As he searched, he strove to persuade himself that the creature was too small to pose a serious threat to him. A rat was a thoroughly disgusting and frightening little beast too, but it was no match for a grown man and could be dispatched without ever having a chance to inflict a bite. Furthermore, there was no reason to assume that this strange creature's intention was to harm him any more than he could have had reason to assume that a rat possessed the strength and power and will to plot the murder of a human being.

Nevertheless, he couldn't convince himself that the threat was less than mortal. His heart continued to race, and his chest was almost painfully tight with apprehension.

He recalled too clearly the radiant green eyes with elliptical black pupils, which had fixed him so threateningly from within the rag face. They were the eyes of a predator.

The brass wastebasket was half filled with crumpled sheets of typing paper and pages from a yellow legal pad. He kicked it to see if he could elicit an alarmed response from anything hiding at the bottom of the trash.

The papers rustled when he kicked the can, but at once they settled again into a silent heap.

From the shallow pencil drawer in the desk,

Tommy withdrew a ruler and used it to stir the papers in the wastebasket. He poked it violently down into the trash a few times, but nothing squealed or tried to wrest the ruler from his hand.

Chain lightning flared outside, and with arachnid frenzy, the turbulent black shadows of wind-shaken trees thrashed across the glass. Thunder boomed, thunder roared, and thunder tumbled down the coal chute of the night.

Across the room from the desk, a sofa stood against the wall, under framed reproductions of movie posters advertising two of his favorite films. Fred MacMurray, Barbara Stanwyck, and Edward G. Robinson in James M. Cain's *Double Indemnity*. Bogart and Bacall in *Dark Passage*.

Occasionally, when his writing wasn't going well, especially when he was stuck for an engaging plot twist, Tommy stretched out on the sofa, his head elevated on the two decorative red pillows, did some deep-breathing exercises, let his mind drift, and gave his imagination a chance to work. Often he solved the problem within an hour and went back to work. More often he fell asleep—and woke with a flush of shame at his laziness, sticky with perspiration and excessive guilt.

Now Tommy gingerly moved the two red throw pillows. The minikin wasn't hiding behind either of them.

The sofa was built to the floor rather than supported on legs. Consequently, nothing could be hiding under it.

The doll-thing might be behind the sofa, however, and to move such a heavy piece away from the wall, Tommy needed both hands. He would have to put aside the pistol; but he was reluctant to let go of it.

He worriedly surveyed the room.

The only movement was the vaguely phosphorescent wriggle of the rain streaming down the windows.

He placed the gun on a cushion, within easy reach, and dragged the sofa away from the wall, sure that something hideous, half clothed in torn cotton rags, would come at him, shrieking.

He was uneasily aware of how vulnerable his ankles were to sharp little teeth.

Furthermore, he should have tucked the legs of his jeans into his socks or clamped them shut with rubber bands, as he would have done in an actual rat hunt. He shuddered at the thought of something squirming up the inside of a pant leg, clawing and biting him as it ascended.

The minikin had not taken refuge behind the sofa.

Relieved but also frustrated, Tommy left the cumbersome piece standing away from the wall and picked up the pistol.

He carefully lifted each of the three square sofa cushions. Nothing waited under them.

Perspiration stung the corner of his right eye. He blotted his face on the sleeve of his flannel shirt and blinked frantically to clear his vision.

The only place left to search was a mahogany credenza to the right of the door, in which he stored reams of typing paper and other supplies. By standing to one side of the cabinet, he was able to peer into the narrow space behind it and satisfy himself that nothing lurked between it and the wall.

The credenza had two pairs of doors. He considered firing a few rounds through them before daring to look inside, but at last he opened them and poked among the supplies without finding the tiny intruder.

Standing in the middle of the office, Tommy turned slowly in a circle, trying to spot the hiding place that he had overlooked. After making a three-hundred-sixty-degree sweep, he was as baffled as ever. He seemed to have searched everywhere.

Yet he was certain that the doll-thing was still in this room. It could not have escaped during the short time that he had been gone to fetch the pistol. Besides, he sensed its hateful presence, the coiled energy of its predatory patience.

He felt something watching him even now.

But watching from where?

"Come on, damn you, show yourself," he said.

In spite of the perspiration that sheathed him and the tremor that periodically fluttered through his belly, Tommy was gaining confidence by the minute. He felt that he was handling this bizarre situation with remarkable aplomb, conducting himself with sufficient courage and calculation to impress even Chip Nguyen.

"Come on. Where? Where?"

Lightning flashed at the windows, and tree shadows

ran spider-quick over glass and streaming rain, and like a warning voice, the tolling thunder seemed to call Tommy's attention to the drapes.

The drapes. They didn't extend all the way to the floor, hung only an inch or two below the bottoms of the windows, so he hadn't thought that the minikin could be hiding behind them. But perhaps somehow it had climbed two and a half feet of wall—or had leaped high enough—to snare one of the drapes, and then had pulled itself upward into concealment.

The room had two windows, both facing east. Each window was flanked by panels of heavy fabric—a faux brocade in shades of gold and red, probably polyester, backed by a white lining—which hung from simple brass rods without concealing valances.

All four drapery panels hung in neat folds. None appeared to be pulled out of shape by a rat-size creature clinging to the back.

The fabric was heavy, however, and the doll-thing might have to weigh even more than a rat before it noticeably distorted the gathered pleats.

With the pistol cocked and his finger taut on the trigger, Tommy approached the first of the two windows. Using his left hand, he took hold of one of the drapery panels, hesitated, and then shook it vigorously.

Nothing fell to the floor. Nothing snarled or scrambled for a tighter hold on the fabric.

Although he spread the short drape and lifted it away from the wall, Tommy had to lean behind it to inspect the liner, to which the intruder might be clinging. He found nothing.

He repeated the process with the next panel, but no snake-eyed minikin hung from the back of it, either.

At the second window, his colorless reflection in the rain-sheathed glass caught his attention, but he averted his gaze when he glimpsed such stark fear in his own eyes that it belied the confidence and courage on which he had so recently congratulated himself. He didn't feel as terrified as he looked—but maybe he was successfully repressing his terror in the urgent interest of getting the job done. He didn't want to think too much about it, because if he acknowledged the truth of what he saw in his eyes, he might be paralyzed again by indecision.

Cautious inspection revealed that nothing unnatural was behind the drape to the left of the second window.

One panel of faux brocade remained. Gold and red. Hanging heavy and straight.

He shook it without effect. It felt no different from the other three panels.

Spreading the material, lifting it away from the wall and the window, Tommy leaned in, looked up, and immediately saw the minikin hanging above him, not from the liner of the drape, but from the brass rod, suspended upside-down by an obscenely glistening black tail that had sprouted from the white cotton fabric, which had once seemed to contain nothing other than the inert filler of a doll. The thing's two hands, no longer like mittens, sprouting from ragged white cotton sleeves, were mottled black and sour yellow, curled tightly against its cotton-covered chest: four bony fingers and an opposable thumb, as well defined as the hands of a human being, but also exhibiting a reptilian quality, each digit tipped with tiny but wickedly pointed claws.

During two or three eerily and impossibly attenuated seconds of stunned immobility, when it seemed as though the very flow of time had nearly come to a stop, Tommy had an impression of hot green eyes glaring from a loose white sack rather like the headgear worn by the Elephant Man in the old David Lynch movie, numerous small yellow teeth that evidently had chewed open the five sets of crossed black sutures with which the mouth had been sewn shut, and even a pebbled black tongue with a flickering forked tip.

Then a blaze of lightning thawed that moment of heart-freezing confrontation. Time had crept as ponderously as a glacier, but suddenly it was a floodtide surge.

The minikin hissed.

Its tail unwound from the brass rod.

It dropped straight at Tommy's face.

He ducked his head, pulled back.

As thunder crashed in the wake of the lightning, he fired the pistol.

But he had squeezed the trigger in blind panic. The bullet must have torn harmlessly through the top of the drape and lodged in the ceiling.

Hissing, the doll-thing landed on Tommy's head. Its tiny claws scrabbled determinedly through his thick hair and pierced his scalp.

Howling, he swiped at the creature with his left hand.

The minikin held fast.

Tommy clutched it by the back of the neck and, mercilessly squeezing its throat, tore it off his head.

The beast squirmed ferociously in his grip. It was stronger and more supple than any rat could have been, writhing and flexing and twisting with such shocking power that he could barely hold it.

He was caught in the drape. Tangled somehow. Jesus. The front sight on the Heckler & Koch was not prominent, barely more than a nubbin, but it was snagged in the liner, caught as securely as a fishhook.

A wet guttural snarl issued from the minikin, and it gnashed its teeth, trying to bite his fingers, striving to sink its claws into him again.

With a zipperlike sound, the liner material tore away from the gun sight.

The creature's cold, slick tail slithered around Tommy's wrist, and the feel of it was so singularly repulsive that he gagged with disgust.

Frantically he flailed out from beneath the entangling drape, and with all of his might, he threw the beast as though firing off a killer pitch in a baseball game.

He heard it shrieking as it was hurled across the room, and then heard the shriek cut off abruptly as the thing thudded hard against the far wall, perhaps hard enough to snap its spine. But he didn't see it hit the plaster, because in the process of freeing himself from the drape, he pulled the brass rod out of its supports, and the entire assemblage—rod and two panels of material, trailing cords—fell on him.

Cursing, he tossed the blinding cowl of faux brocade off his head and thrashed loose of the drapery cords, feeling like Gulliver resisting capture in the land of Lilliput.

The hideous minikin was crumpled on the carpet against the baseboard at the far side of the room, near the door. For an instant Tommy thought the thing was dead or at least badly stunned. But then it shook itself, moved.

Thrusting the pistol in front of him, Tommy took a step toward the intruder, intending to finish it off. The mound of fallen drapes snared his feet. He stumbled, lost his balance, and slammed to the floor.

With his left cheek flat against the carpet, he now shared the murderous minikin's plane of view, though from a tilted perspective. His vision blurred for a second when his head hit the floor, but it cleared at once. He was staring at his diminutive adversary, which had risen to its feet.

The creature stood as erect as a man, trailing its six-inch black tail, still dressed in—and mostly concealed by—the rags of the doll's skin in which it had hidden.

Outside, the storm was reaching a crescendo, hammering the night with a greater barrage of lightning and thunder than it had produced thus far. The ceiling light and the desk lamp flickered but did not go out.

The creature sprinted toward Tommy, white cotton cloth flapping like tattered banners.

Tommy's right arm was stretched out in front of him, and the pistol was still firmly in his grip. He raised the weapon perhaps four inches off the floor, squeeze-cocked it, and fired two shots in quick succession.

One of the rounds must have hit the minikin, because it flew off its feet. It tumbled backward all the way to the wall against which Tommy had thrown it earlier.

Proportionately, the slug from the .40 Smith & Wesson cartridge was to this beast what a shell from a major piece of battlefield artillery would be to a human being; the damn thing should have been as devastated—as stone dead—as any man would have been after taking a massive mortar round in the chest. It should have been smashed, shattered, blown to bits.

Instead, the small figure appeared to be intact. Sprawled in a tangle of limbs and scorched white cotton cloth. Racked by spasms. Tail slithering back and forth on the floor. Wisps of smoke rising from it. But intact.

Tommy raised his throbbing head for a better view. He didn't see any splatters of blood on the carpet or on the wall. Not one drop.

The beast stopped shuddering and rolled onto its back. Then it sat up and sighed. The sigh was one not of weariness but of pleasure, as though being shot point-blank in the chest had been an interesting and gratifying experience.

Tommy pushed up onto his knees.

Across the office, the minikin put its black-and-
yellow-mottled hands on its scorched, smoking
abdomen. No . . . it actually reached *into* its abdomen, digging with its claws, and wrenched something out of itself.

Even from a distance of fifteen feet, Tommy was
pretty sure that the lumpish object in the beast's
hands was the misshapen slug from the .40-caliber
cartridge. The minikin tossed the chunk of lead aside.

Shaky, weak-kneed, slightly nauseated, Tommy
got to his feet.

He felt his scalp, where the puncture wounds from
the thing's claws still stung. When he checked his
fingertips, he saw only tiny dots of blood.

He hadn't been seriously hurt.

Yet.

His adversary rose to its feet as well.

Although he was seven times taller than the
minikin and perhaps thirty times its weight, Tommy
was so terrified that he felt as though he might pee in
his pants.

Chip Nguyen, hard-boiled detective, would never
lose control of himself in that fashion, humiliate
himself to that extent, but Tommy Phan no longer
gave a damn what Chip Nguyen would do. Chip
Nguyen was an idiot, a whiskey-drinking fool who
put too much faith in guns, martial arts, and tough
talk. The most precisely executed and powerfully
delivered tae kwan do kick wouldn't stop a super-
naturally animated devil doll that could take a .40-
caliber round in its guts and keep on ticking.

Now, *there* was an indisputable truth. Not the kind of truth you would hear on the evening news or read in the newspaper. Not a truth they taught in school or church. Not a truth that would be acclaimed by Carl Sagan or the scientific establishment. Truth nonetheless, from Tommy's point of view, truth even if the only forum that might report it was a rag like the *National Enquirer* in a story about the ominous rise of demonic presences in our apocalyptic age and the inevitable forthcoming battle between Satan Incarnate and Saint Elvis on the eve of the new millennium.

Pointing the P7 at the minikin, Tommy felt a mad laugh swelling in him, but he choked it down. He wasn't insane. He had gotten past that fear. It was God Himself who must be mad—and the universe a lunatic asylum—if He made room in Creation for something like this predatory gremlin in a rag-doll disguise.

If the minikin was a supernatural presence, as it seemed to be, resistance to it might be stupid and pointless, but Tommy couldn't very well throw the gun aside, bare his throat, and wait for the killing bite. At least the round from the pistol had knocked the thing down and temporarily stunned it. He might not be able to kill it with the gun, but at least he could fend it off.

Until he ran out of ammunition.

He had fired three rounds. One when the thing dropped from the drapery rod onto his head. Two more when he was lying on the floor.

Ten rounds remained in the thirteen-shot magazine. And in his bedroom closet was a box of ammunition, which would buy more time if he could get to it.

The doll-thing cocked its rag-swaddled head and regarded him with a fierce green-eyed hunger. The strips of cotton hanging over its face looked like white dreadlocks.

Thus far the gunfire had probably been pretty much masked by the peals of thunder. Eventually, however, the neighbors in this peaceful city of Irvine would realize that a battle was being waged next door, and they would call the cops.

The doll-thing hissed at him.

God in Heaven, what is this—Showdown at the Twilight Zone Corral?

When the police arrived, he would have to tell them what was happening, even though he would sound like a poster boy for paranoid dementia. Then the minikin would either brazenly reveal itself, and the rest of the world would plummet into this nightmare along with Tommy—or the cunning little demon would hide and let the police transfer their raving ward to a windowless but well-lighted room with rubber wallpaper.

At this moment, Tommy almost didn't care which of the two scenarios played out. In either case, the immediate terror would be over, and he would be able to avoid peeing in his pants. He'd have time to catch his breath, think, maybe even puzzle out an explanation for what had happened here—although that seemed no more likely than his arriving at an understanding of the meaning of life.

The fiend hissed again.

A new possibility occurred to Tommy, and it wasn't a good one. Maybe the hateful little thing would secretly follow him to the psychiatric ward and continue to torment him there for the rest of his life, cleverly avoiding being seen by the physicians and attendants.

Instead of charging again, the minikin abruptly darted toward the sofa, which still stood away from the wall where Tommy had left it during the search.

With the pistol sight, Tommy followed the creature, but he wasn't able to track it closely enough to justify squeezing off one of his remaining shots.

The thing disappeared behind the sofa.

Buoyed slightly by his adversary's retreat, Tommy dared to hope that the .40-caliber round had done some damage after all, at least enough to make the little beast cautious. Seeing the minikin run from him, he regained a degree of perspective regarding the indisputable advantage of size that he enjoyed. A modest measure of his lost confidence returned to him.

Tommy eased across the room to peer around the sofa. The far end of it still touched the wall, so the space behind it was a V-shaped dead end, yet the minikin wasn't there.

Then he saw the torn flaps of fabric and the ragged hole in the upholstery. The creature had burrowed into the sofa and was now hiding inside it.

Why?

Why ask why?

From the moment the stitches had pulled out of the doll's face and the first monstrous eye had blinked at him through the tear in the cloth, Tommy had been beyond all the *why* questions. They were more suitable for a sane universe where logic ruled, not for this place in which he currently found himself. The main issue now was *how*—how could he stop the beast, how could he save himself? And he also had to ask *what next?* Even if the utter irrationality of these events made it impossible to anticipate where the night would lead before dawn, he had to try to puzzle out the purpose behind the doll, the course of the plot.

THE DEADLINE IS DAWN.

He didn't understand that message at all. What deadline, for God's sake? Who had established it? What did he have to do to *meet* the deadline?

TICKTOCK.

Oh, he understood *that* message well enough. Time was running out. The night was passing as fast as the rain was falling outside, and if he didn't get his act together, then he was going to be toast before sunrise.

TICKTOCK.

Toast for the hungry minikin.

TICKTOCK.

Munch, munch. Crunch, crunch.

His head was spinning—and not simply because he had thumped it hard against the floor when he fell.

He circled the sofa, studying it as he moved.

Fire. Maybe a roaring fire could achieve better results than a bullet.

While the creature was building a nest—or doing whatever the hell it was doing in there—Tommy might be able to sneak down to the garage, siphon a quart of gasoline out of the Corvette, grab a pack of matches from a drawer in the kitchen, and return to set the sofa on fire.

No. No, that would take too long. The repulsive little creepozoid would realize that he was gone, and when he came back, the thing probably wouldn't be inside the sofa any more.

Now the minikin was quiet, which didn't mean that it was taking a nap. It was scheming at something.

Tommy needed to scheme too. Desperately.

Think, think.

Because of the light-beige carpet, Tommy kept one can of spot remover downstairs and another upstairs in the master bathroom, so he would be able to attack an accidental spill of Pepsi or whatever before it became a permanent stain. The can contained approximately one pint of fluid, and in bold red letters the label warned HIGHLY FLAMMABLE.

Highly flammable. That had a pleasant ring to it. *Highly flammable, hugely flammable, spectacularly flammable, explosively flammable*—no words in the English language sounded sweeter than those.

And on the hearth of the small fireplace in the master bedroom was a battery-sparked butane match he used to light the gas under the ceramic logs. He should be able to leave the office, grab the spot remover, pluck the match off the hearth, and return here in a minute, maybe less.

One minute. Even as clever as it seemed to be, the minikin probably wouldn't realize that Tommy was out of the room for that brief time.

So now who's going to be toast?

Tommy smiled at the thought.

From deep in the mysterious creature's upholstered haven came a creaking and then a sharp *twang*.

Tommy flinched—and lost his smile.

The beast fell silent once more. It was up to something, all right. But what?

If Tommy retrieved the spot remover and set the sofa on fire, the flames would spread across the carpet and swiftly to the walls. The house might burn down, even if he telephoned the fire department immediately after setting the blaze.

He was fully insured, of course, but the insurance company would refuse to pay if arson was suspected. The fire marshal would probably investigate and discover traces of an accelerant—the spot remover—in the rubble. Tommy would never be able to convince them that he had set the fire as an act of self-defense.

Nevertheless, he was going to ease open the door, step quietly into the hallway, sprint for the can of spot remover, and take his chances with—

From the minikin's lair came the sound of fabric ripping, and one of the seat cushions was dislodged by the beast as it tore out of the sofa directly in front of Tommy. In one dark bony hand it held a six-inch length of a broken seat spring: a spiral of gleaming eighth-inch steel wire.

Shrieking with rage and mindless hatred, its piercing voice as shrill as an electronic oscillation, the creature flung itself off the sofa and at Tommy with such force and velocity that it almost seemed to fly.

He scrambled out of its way, reflexively firing—and wasting—one more round from the P7.

The beast hadn't been attacking, after all. The lunge had been a feint. It dropped to the carpet and streaked past Tommy, across the office, around the corner of the desk, and out of sight, moving at least as fast as a rat, although running on its hind feet as if it were a man.

Tommy went after it, hoping to corner it and jam the muzzle of the Heckler & Koch against its head and squeeze off one-two-three rounds at zero range, smash its brain if, indeed, it had a brain, because maybe that would devastate it as a single bullet in the guts had failed to do.

When Tommy followed the minikin around the desk, he discovered it at an electrical outlet, looking back and up at him. The creature appeared to be grinning through its mask of rags as it jammed the steel spring into the receptacle.

Power surged through bare steel—*cracklesnap*—and outside in the fuse box, a breaker tripped, and all the lights went out except for a shower of gold and blue sparks that cascaded over the minikin. Those fireworks lasted only an instant, however, and then darkness claimed the room.

THREE

Depleted by distance and filtered by trees, the yellowish glow of the streetlamps barely touched the windows. Rain shimmered down the glass, glimmering with a few dull-brass reflections, but none of that light penetrated to the room.

Tommy was frozen by shock, effectively blind, unable to see anything around him and trying not to see the fearsome images that his imagination conjured in his mind.

The only sounds were the rataplan of rain on the roof and the moaning of wind in the eaves.

Undoubtedly the doll-thing was alive. The electricity hadn't fazed it any more than a .40-caliber bullet in the midsection.

Tommy clutched the P7 as if it possessed magical power and could protect him from all the known and unknown terrors of the universe, whether physical or spiritual. In fact, the weapon was useless to him in this saturant darkness. He couldn't stun the minikin with a well-placed shot if he couldn't see it.

He supposed that by now it had dropped the twisted piece of steel spring and had turned away from the electrical outlet. It would be facing him in the gloom. Grinning through its mummy rags.

Maybe he should open fire, squeeze off all nine

shots remaining in the magazine, aiming for the general area where the creature had been when the lights went out. He was almost sure to get lucky with one or two rounds out of *nine*, for God's sake, even if he wasn't any Chip Nguyen. With the minikin stunned and twitching, Tommy could run into the second-floor hallway, slam the door between them, leap down the stairs two at a time, and get out of the house.

He didn't know what the hell he would do after that, where he would go in this rain-swept night, to whom he would turn for help. All he knew was that to have any chance of survival whatsoever, he had to escape from this place.

He was loath to squeeze the trigger and empty the gun.

If he didn't stun the minikin with a blind shot, he would never get to the door. It would catch him, climb his leg and his back with centipede-like quickness, bite the nape of his neck, slip around to his throat, and burrow-for-chew-at-tear-out his carotid artery while he flailed ineffectively—or it would scramble straight over his head, intent upon gouging out his eyes.

He wasn't just letting his imagination carry him away this time. He could vividly sense the thing's intentions, as though on some level he was in psychic contact with it.

If the attack came after the pistol magazine was empty, Tommy would panic, stumble, crash into furniture, fall. Once he fell, he would never have a chance to get to his feet again.

Better to conserve ammunition.

He backed up one step, two, but then he halted, overcome by the awful certainty that the little beast was not, after all, in front of him, where it had been when the lights failed, but behind him. It had circled him as he had dithered; now it was creeping closer.

Spinning around a hundred and eighty degrees, he thrust the pistol toward the suspected threat.

He was facing into a portion of the room that was even blacker than the end with the windows. He might as well have been adrift at the farthest empty edge of the universe to which the matter and the energy of Creation had not yet expanded.

He held his breath.

He listened but could not hear the minikin.

Only the rain.

The rain.

The rattling rain.

What scared him most about the intruder was not its monstrous and alien appearance, not its fierce hostility, not its physical spryness or speed, not its rodentlike size that triggered primal fears, not even the fundamental mystery of its very existence. What sent chills up the hollow of Tommy's spine and squeezed more cold sweat from him was the new realization that the thing was highly *intelligent.*

Initially he had assumed that he was dealing with an animal, an unknown and clever beast but a beast nonetheless. When it thrust the steel spiral into the electrical outlet, however, it revealed a complex and frightening nature. To be able to adapt a simple sofa spring into an essential tool, to understand the electrical system of the house well enough to disable the office circuit, the beast not only was able to think but was possessed of sophisticated knowledge that no mere animal could acquire.

The worst thing Tommy could do was trust his own animal instincts when his adversary was stalking him with the aid of cold reason and logical deliberation. Sometimes the deer *did* escape the rifleman by natural wiles, yes, but far more often than not, higher intelligence gave the human hunter an advantage that the deer could never hope to overcome.

So he must carefully think through each move before he made it. Otherwise he was doomed.

He might be doomed anyway.

This was no longer a rat hunt.

The minikin's strategic imposition of darkness revealed that this was a contest between equals. Or at least Tommy hoped it was a contest between equals, because if they weren't equals, then this was a rat hunt after all, and *he* was the rat.

By opting for darkness, had the creature merely been trying to minimize Tommy's size advantage and the threat of the gun—or did it gain an advantage of its own from the darkness? Perhaps, like a cat, it could see as well at night as it could in daylight.

Or maybe, like bloodhound, it could track him by his scent.

If the thing benefited from both the superior intelligence of a human being and the more acute senses of an animal, Tommy was screwed.

"What do you want?" he asked aloud.

He would not have been surprised if a small whis-pery voice had responded. Indeed, he almost hoped it would speak to him. Whether it spoke or only hissed, its reply would reveal its location—maybe even clearly enough to allow him to open fire.

"Why me?" he asked.

The minikin made no sound.

Tommy would have been astonished if such a creature had crawled out of the woodwork one day or squirmed from a hole in the backyard. He might have assumed that the thing was extraterrestrial in nature or that it had escaped from a secret genetic-engineering laboratory where a scientist with a con-science deficit had been hard at work on biological weapons. He had seen all the applicable scary movies: He had the requisite background for such speculation.

But how much *more* astonishing that this thing had been placed on his doorstep in the form of a nearly featureless rag doll out of which it had either burst or swiftly metamorphosed. He had never seen any movie that could provide him with an adequate explanation for *that*.

Swinging the Heckler & Koch slowly from side to side, he tried again to elicit a telltale response from the tiny intruder: "What are you?"

The minikin, in its original white cotton skin, brought to mind voodoo, of course, but a voodoo doll was nothing like this creature. A voodoo doll was simply a crude fetish, believed to have magical potency, fashioned in the image of the person meant to be harmed, accessorized with a lock of his hair, or a few of his nail clippings, or a drop of his blood. Solemnly convinced that any damage done to the fetish would befall the real person as well, the torturer then stuck it full of pins, or burned it, or "drowned" it in a bucket of water. But the doll was never actually animate. It never showed up on the doorstep of the intended victim to bedevil and assault him.

Nevertheless, into the gloom and the incessant drumming of the rain, Tommy said, "Voodoo?"

Whether this was voodoo or not, the most important thing he had to learn was who had made the doll. Someone had scissored the cotton fabric and sewn it into the shape of a gingerbread man, and someone had stuffed the empty form with a substance that felt like sand but proved to be a hell of a lot stranger than sand. The dollmaker was his ultimate enemy, not the critter that was stalking him.

He was never going to find the dollmaker by waiting for the minikin to make the next move. Action, not reaction, was the source of solutions.

Because he had established a dialogue with the little beast, even if its every response was the choice not to respond, Tommy was more confident than at any time since he'd felt the insectoid squirming of the creature's heartbeat beneath his index finger. He was a writer, so using words gave him a comforting sense of control.

Perhaps the questions he tossed into the darkness

diminished the minikin's confidence in direct pro-
portion to the degree that they increased his own.
If phrased crisply and spoken with authority, his
questions might convince the beast that its prey
wasn't afraid of it and wasn't likely to be easily
overpowered. Anyway, he was reassured to think
this might be the case.

His strategy was akin to one he would have used
if confronted by a growling dog: Show no fear.

Unfortunately, he had already shown more than
a little fear, so he needed to rehabilitate his image.
He wished he could stop sweating; he wondered
whether the thing could smell his perspiration.

Behind his armor of forcefully stated questions,
he found the courage to move toward the center of
the wall opposite the windows, where the door
should be. "What are you, damn it? What right do
you have to come into my house? Who made you,
left you on the porch, rang the bell?"

Tommy bumped into the door, fumbled for the
knob, found it—and still the minikin did not attack.

When he yanked open the door, he discovered
that the lights were also off in the upstairs hall,
which shared a circuit with his office. Lamps were
aglow on the first floor, and pale light rose at the
stairs.

As Tommy crossed the threshold, leaving the
office, the minikin shot between his legs. He didn't
see it at first, but he heard it hiss and felt it brush
against his jeans.

He kicked, missed, kicked again.

A scuttling sound and a snarl revealed that the creature was moving away from him. Fast.

At the head of the stairs, it appeared in silhouette against the rising light. It turned and fixed him with its radiant green eyes.

Tommy squeeze-cocked the P7.

The rag-entwined minikin raised one gnarly fist, shook it, and shrieked defiantly. Its cry was small but shrill, piercing, and utterly unlike the voice of anything else on earth.

Tommy took aim.

The creature scrambled down the stairs and out of sight before Tommy could squeeze off a shot.

He was surprised that it was fleeing from him, and then he was relieved. The pistol and his new strategy of showing no fear seemed to have given the beast second thoughts.

As quickly as surprise had given way to relief, however, relief now turned to alarm. In the gloom and at a distance, he could not be certain, but he thought that the creature had still been holding the six-inch length of spring steel, not in the fist that it had raised but in the hand held at its side.

"Oh, shit."

His newfound confidence rapidly draining away, Tommy ran to the stairs.

The minikin wasn't in sight.

Tommy descended the steps two at a time. He almost fell at the landing, grabbed the newel post to keep his balance, and saw that the lower steps were deserted too.

Movement drew his attention. The minikin streaked across the small foyer and vanished into the living room.

Tommy realized that he should have gone to the master bedroom for the flashlight in his nightstand drawer. It was too late to go back for it. If he didn't move fast, he was going to be in an increasingly untenable position: either trapped in a pitch-black house where all the electrical circuits were disabled or driven on foot into the storm where the minikin could repeatedly attack and retreat with the cover of darkness and rain.

Though the thing was only a tiny fraction as strong as he was, its supernatural resilience and maniacal relentlessness compensated for its comparative physical weakness. It was not merely pretending to be fearless, as Tommy had pretended to be while talking his way out of his office. Though the creature was of Lilliputian dimensions, its reckless confidence was genuine; it expected to win, to chase him down, to *get* him.

Cursing, Tommy raced down the last flight. As he came off the bottom step, he heard a hard crackle-snap, and the lights went out in the living room and the foyer.

He turned right, into the dining room. The brass-and-milk-glass chandelier shed a pleasant light on the highly polished top of the maple table.

He glimpsed himself in the ornately framed mirror above the sideboard. His hair was disarranged. His eyes were wide, whites showing all the way around. He looked demented.

As Tommy pushed through the swinging door into the kitchen, the minikin squealed behind him. The familiar sound of an electric arc snapped again, and the dining-room lights went out.

Fortunately, the kitchen lights were on a different circuit from those in the dining room. The overhead fluorescent tubes were still bright.

He snatched the car keys off the pegboard. They jangled, and though their ringing was flat and unmusical and utterly unlike bells, Tommy was reminded of the bells that were rung in church during Mass: *Through my fault, through my fault, through my most grievous fault.* For an instant, instead of feeling like the potential victim that he was, he felt a terrible weight of guilt, as though the extraordinary trouble that had befallen him this night was of his own making and was merely what he deserved.

The easy-action pivot hinges on the door to the dining room swung so smoothly that even the ten-inch minikin was able to squeeze into the kitchen close behind Tommy. With the keys ringing in his hand, with the remembered scent of incense as strong and sweet as it had ever been when he had served as an altarboy, he didn't dare pause to look back, but he could hear the thing's tiny clawed feet click-click-clicking against the tile floor.

He stepped into the laundry room and slammed the door behind him before the creature could follow.

No lock. Didn't matter. The minikin wouldn't be able to climb up and turn the knob on the other side. It couldn't follow him any farther.

Even as Tommy turned away from the door, the lights failed in the laundry room. They must have been on the same circuit as those in the kitchen, which the creature evidently had just shorted. He groped forward through the blackness.

At the end of this small rectangular space, past the washer and dryer, opposite the door that he had just closed, was the connecting door to the garage. It featured a deadbolt lock with a thumb-turn on this side.

In the garage, the lights still functioned.

On this side, the deadbolt on the laundry-room door could be engaged only with a key. He didn't see any point in taking the time to lock it.

The big overhead door began to rumble upward when Tommy tapped the wall switch, and storm wind chuffed like a pack of dogs at the widening space at the bottom.

He hurriedly circled the Corvette to the driver's side.

The garage lights blinked out, and the roll-up door stopped ascending when it was still half blocking the exit.

No.

The minikin could not have gotten through two closed doors and into the garage to cause a short circuit. And there hadn't been time for it to race out of the house, find the electric-service panel, climb the conduit on the wall, open the fuse box, and trip a breaker.

Yet the garage was as black as the darkest hemisphere of some strange moon never touched by the sun. And the roll-up door was only half open.

Maybe power had been lost throughout the neighborhood because of the storm.

Frantically Tommy pawed at the darkness overhead until he located the dangling release chain that disconnected the garage door from the electric motor that operated it. Still clutching the pistol, he rushed to the door and manually pushed it up, all the way open.

A noisy burst of November wind threw shatters of cold rain in his face. The balminess of the afternoon was gone. The temperature had plummeted at least twenty degrees since he left the Corvette dealership in his new car and headed south along the coast.

He expected to see the minikin in the driveway, green eyes glaring, but the sodium-yellow drizzle from a nearby streetlamp revealed that the thing was not there.

Across the street, warm welcoming lights shone in the windows of other houses. The same was true at the homes to the left and right of his own.

The loss of power in his garage had nothing to do with the storm. He had never really believed that it did.

Although he was convinced he would be attacked before he reached the Corvette, he got behind the steering wheel and slammed the door without encountering the minikin.

He put the pistol on the passenger seat, within easy reach. He had been gripping the weapon so desperately and for so long that his right hand remained curled to the shape of it. He was forced to concentrate on flexing his half-numb fingers in order to relax them and regain use of them.

The engine started with no hesitation.

The headlights splashed against the back wall of the garage, revealing a workbench, neatly racked tools, a cool forty-year-old sign from a Shell service station, and a framed poster of James Dean leaning against the 1949 Mercury that he drove in *Rebel Without a Cause*.

Backing out of the garage, Tommy expected the minikin to ravel down from the rafters on a web of its own making, directly onto the windshield. Still largely concealed by the increasingly soiled and ragged fabric that had been the skin of its doll phase, the creature had appeared to be partly reptilian, with the scales and the eyes of a serpent, but Tommy had perceived insectile qualities to it as well, features and capabilities not yet fully revealed.

He reversed into the driveway, into torrents of rain, switched on the windshield wipers, and continued into the street, leaving the garage door open, other doors unlocked.

At worst, what might get into the house during his absence? A stray cat or dog? Maybe a burglar? A couple of dim-witted, doped-up kids with a can of red spray paint and vandalism on their minds?

After escaping from the devil doll, Tommy was ready and able to deal with any number of *ordinary* uninvited guests.

But as he shifted the Corvette out of reverse and drove away from his house, he was stricken by an unsettling premonition: *I'll never see this place again.*

He was driving too fast for a residential neighborhood, almost flying, casting up ten-foot-high wings of white water as he raced through a flooded intersection, but he was unwilling to slow down. He felt that the gates of Hell had been flung open and that each creature among the legion of monstrosities seething out of those portals was intent on the same prey: Tommy Phan.

Maybe it was foolish to believe that demons existed, and it was *certainly* foolish to believe—if they did exist—that he could outrun them by virtue of owning a sports car with three hundred horsepower. Nevertheless, he drove as if pursued by Satan.

A few minutes later, on University Drive, passing the Irvine campus of the University of California, Tommy realized that he was squinting at the rearview mirror every few seconds—as if one of the cars far behind him on the rain-washed, tree-lined avenue might be driven by the minikin. The absurdity of that thought was like a hammer that broke some of the chains of his anxiety, and he finally eased up on the accelerator.

Still damp with cold sweat and with the slanting rain that had blown through the open garage door, Tommy shivered violently. He switched on the car heater.

He was half dazed, as though the dose of terror he had taken was a potent drug with a lingering narcotic effect. His thinking was cloudy. He couldn't focus on what needed to be done next, on deciding where—and to whom—he should turn.

He wanted to be Chip Nguyen and live in the world of detective fiction, where blazing guns and hard fists and sardonic wit always led to satisfactory resolutions. Where the motives of adversaries were simple greed, envy, and jealousy. Where angst was *fun*, and where amused misanthropy was a sure sign of a private investigator's superior moral character. Where bouts of alcoholic melancholy were comforting rather than dispiriting. Where the villains, by God, *never* had serpent eyes, or sharp little yellow teeth, or ratlike tails.

Living in Chip's world was impossible, however, so Tommy was willing to settle for a nap. He wanted to pull off the road, lie down, curl into the fetal position, and go to sleep for a few hours. He was exhausted. His limbs felt weak. As though the earth were suddenly rotating at a much higher speed than before, a heavier gravity oppressed his mind and heart.

In spite of the hot air streaming from the heater vents, he was not getting warmer. The chill that afflicted him didn't come from the November night or from the rain; it arose from deep within him.

The metronomic thump of the windshield wipers lulled him, and more than once he came out of a sort of waking dream to find that he was in a different neighborhood from the one he last remembered. He relentlessly cruised residential streets, as if searching for the address of a friend, although every time that he ascended from his strange daze, he was never on a street where anyone of his acquaintance had ever lived.

He understood what was wrong. He was a well-educated man with an unshakably rational viewpoint; he had always assumed that he could clearly read the big map of life and that he had both hands firmly on the controls of his destiny as he cruised confidently into the future. From the moment that the two black sutures had popped and the green eye had glared at him out of the doll's torn face, however, his world had begun to collapse. It was collapsing still. Forget the great laws of physics, the logic of mathematics, the dissectible truths of biology that, as a student, he had struggled so hard to grasp. They might still apply, but they didn't explain *enough*, not any more. Once he had thought that they explained everything, but everything that he believed was proving to be only half the story. He was confused, lost, and dispirited, as only a rationalist of utter conviction could be upon encountering irrefutable evidence that something supernatural was at play in the universe.

He might have accepted the devil doll with greater equanimity if he had still been in Vietnam, the Land of Seagull and Fox, where his mother's folk tales were set. In that Asian world of jungles, limpid waters, and blue mountains like mirages, it was easier to believe in the fantastic, such as the story of the mandarin named Tu Thuc, who had climbed Mount Phi Lai and, at the top, had found the Land of Bliss, where the immortals lived in perfect happiness and harmony. On humid nights along the banks of the Mekong River or on the shores of the South China Sea, the air seemed thickened by magic, which Tommy could remember even after twenty-two years, and in that far place, one could give some credit to the tale of the good genie of medicine, Tien Thai, and his flying mountain, or to the story of beautiful Nhan Diep, the faithless wife who, after her death, returned to earth in the form of the first buzzing cloud of mosquitoes ever seen, initially to afflict her husband and then all of humankind. If Tommy were in Vietnam again—and returned to childhood—he might be able to believe in devil dolls too, although Vietnamese folk tales were generally gentle in nature and featured no monsters like the shrieking, sharp-toothed minikin.

But this was the United States of America, the land of the free and the brave, the land of Big Business and Big Science, from which men had gone to the moon and back, where movies and television had been invented, where the atom had first been split, where scientists were rapidly mapping the human genome and developing nanotechnology and shining light into the deepest mysteries of existence—where eighty-five percent of the citizenry declared themselves deeply religious, yes, but where fewer than three in ten attended church. This was America, damn it, where you could solve any problem with a screwdriver and a wrench, or with a computer, or with fists and a handgun, or at worst with the help of a therapist and a twelve-step program to effect personal enlightenment and change.

Screwdrivers, wrenches, computers, fists, guns, and therapists weren't going to help him cope with the minikin if he returned to his house and found the creature still in residence. And it *would* be there; he had no doubt about that.

It would be waiting.

It had a job to finish.

It had been sent to kill him.

Tommy didn't know how he could be so sure of the minikin's ultimate purpose, but he knew that what he intuited was true. Little assassin.

He could still feel a vaguely sore spot on his tongue where he had been pricked by the windblown melaleuca leaf when he opened the front door of his house and discovered the doll lying on the porch.

Holding the steering wheel with only his left hand, he pressed his right hand to his thigh. He had no difficulty locating the spot where the pin with the black enamel head had pierced his flesh.

Two wounds. Both small but clearly symbolic.

Now Tommy cruised Spyglass Drive, piloting the Corvette along ridges stippled with million-dollar houses that overlooked Newport Beach, past graceful California-pepper trees thrashing in the wind, and his thoughts were as chaotic as his driving was aimless. Cold drowning tides of rain came off the black Pacific, and although the torrents couldn't touch him now, they seemed to wash confidence and reason out of him, leaving him limp with doubt and feverish with superstitious speculations.

He wanted to go to his parents' cozy house in Huntington Beach, take refuge in the bosom of his family. His mother was the person most likely to believe his story. Mothers were required by law— not the law of men, but natural law—to be able to discern the truth when their children told it to them, to be quick to defend them against the disbelief of others. If he stared directly into his mother's eyes and explained about the devil doll, she would know that he was not lying. Then he would no longer be alone in his terror.

His mother would convince his father that the threat, although outlandish, was real, whereupon his father would convince Tommy's two brothers and his sister. Then there would be six of them—an entire family—standing against the unnatural power that had sent the hateful minikin to him. Together they could triumph as they had triumphed so long ago against the communists in Vietnam and against the Thai pirates on the South China Sea.

But instead of turning the Corvette toward Huntington Beach, Tommy swung left on El Capitan and drove higher into the night and the storm. He wove from street to street across Spyglass Hill, past the houses of strangers who would never in this lifetime believe him if he rang their doorbells and told them his incredible story.

He was reluctant to go to his parents for fear that he had put too much emotional distance between them and himself to warrant the unconditional acceptance that they once would have given him. He might babble out the story of the devil doll only to see his mother's face pinch with disapproval and hear her say, *You drink whiskey like your silly detective?*

No whiskey, Mom.

I smell whiskey.

I had one beer.

One beer, soon whiskey.

I don't like whiskey.

You carry guns in every pocket—

One gun, Mom.

—drive car like crazy maniac, chase blondes—

No blondes.

—drink whiskey like it only tea, then surprised when see demons and dragons—

No dragons, Mom.

—demons and ghosts—
No ghosts, Mom.
—demons, dragons, ghosts. You better come home
to stay, Tuong.
Tommy.
Better start living right way, Tuong.
Tommy.
Better stop drinking whiskey like tough guy, stop
trying always to be so American, too American.

Tommy groaned aloud in misery.

Still letting the imaginary conversation play out in his head, he cautiously steered the Corvette around an immense branch from a coral tree that had blown down in the storm and blocked half the street.

He decided not to go home to Huntington Beach, because he was afraid that, once he got there, he would find that it wasn't really home any more. Then, having discovered that he didn't belong in the Phan house in quite the way that he had once belonged, and not being able to return to his own minikin-haunted house in Irvine, what place would he be able to call *home*? Nowhere. He would be homeless in a deeper sense than were those vagrants who wandered the streets with all their worldly goods in a shopping cart.

That was a discovery he was not yet prepared to make—even if he had to deal with the minikin alone.

Deciding that he should at least call his mother, he picked up the car phone. But he put it down again without punching in her number.

Car phones for big shots. You big shot now? Phone and drive too dangerous. Gun in one hand, whiskey bottle in other, how you hold phone anyway?

Tommy reached to the passenger seat and briefly put his right hand on the Heckler & Koch. The shape of the pistol, the sense of godlike power cast in steel, did not comfort him.

Minutes later, after the rhythmic thump of the windshield wipers had once more half hypnotized him, he came out of his daze and saw that he was on MacArthur Boulevard, on the southern end of Newport Beach. He was traveling west in light traffic.

According to the dashboard clock, the time was 10:26 p.m.

He couldn't go on like this, driving aimlessly through the night until he ran out of fuel. Preoccupied as he was, he might become so inattentive that he'd skid on the rain-slick pavement and crash into another car.

He decided to seek family help after all, but not from his mother and father. He would go to his older and beloved brother Gi Minh Phan.

Gi had changed his name too—from Phan Minh Gi, merely reversing the order to place the surname last. For a while he had considered taking an American name, as Tommy had done, but he decided against it, which earned points with their parents, who were far too conservative to adopt new names themselves. Gi had given American names to his four children—Heather, Jennifer, Kevin, and Wesley; however, that was all right with Mom and Dad because all four had been born in the United States.

The oldest of the three Phan brothers, Ton That, eight years Tommy's senior, had five children, all born in the U.S.A., and each of them enjoyed both a Vietnamese and an American name. Ton's first-born was a daughter whose legal name was Mary Rebecca but who was also known as Thu-Ha. Ton's kids called one another by their Vietnamese names when they were around their grandparents and other traditionalist elders, used their American names when with friends of their own age, and used either with their parents as the situation seemed to require, yet not one of them had an identity crisis.

In addition to a nagging inability to define his own identity in a way that fully satisfied him—and compared with his brothers—Tommy suffered from an offspring crisis: He didn't have any. To his mother, this was worse than a crisis; this was a tragedy. His parents were still Old World enough to think of children neither as mere responsibilities nor as hostages to fortune, but primarily as wealth, as blessings. In their view, the larger that a family grew, the better chance it had to survive the turmoil of the world and the more successful it would inevitably become. At thirty, unmarried, childless, with no prospects—except the prospect of a successful career as a novelist writing silly stories about a whiskey-guzzling maniac detective—Tommy was undermining his parents' dreams of a sprawling Phan empire and the security that, to them, sheer numbers ensured.

His brother Ton, sixteen when they had fled Vietnam, was still sufficiently mired in the ways of the Old World that he shared some of the elder Phans' frustration with Tommy. Ton and Tommy had been reasonably close as brothers, but they had never been the kind of brothers who were also friends. Gi, on the other hand, though six years older than Tommy, was a brother and a friend and a confidant—or once had been—and if anyone in this world would give the devil-doll story a fair hearing, it would be Gi.

As Tommy crossed San Joaquin Hills Road, less than a mile from Pacific Coast Highway, he was planning the easiest route north to the family bakery in Garden Grove, where Gi managed the graveyard shift, so he didn't immediately react to the peculiar noise that rose from the Corvette's engine compartment. When he finally took note of it, he realized that he'd been dimly aware of the noise on a subconscious level for a couple of minutes: underlying the monotonous squeak-and-thump of the windshield wipers—a soft rattling, a whispery scraping as of metal abrading metal.

He was at last warm. He turned off the heater in order to hear the sound better.

Something was loose . . . and working steadily looser.

Frowning, he leaned over the steering wheel, listening closely.

The noise persisted, low but troubling. He thought he detected an *industrious* quality to it.

He felt a queer vibration through the floorboards. The noise grew no louder, but the vibration increased.

Tommy glanced at the rearview mirror. No traffic was close behind him, so he eased his foot off the accelerator.

As the sports car gradually slowed from fifty-five to forty miles per hour, the noise did not diminish in relation to the speed, but continued unabated.

The shoulder on his side of the highway was narrow, with a slope and then a dark field or a gully beyond, and Tommy didn't want to be forced to pull off here in the blinding downpour. The Newport Beach Library lay in the near distance, looking deserted at this hour, and the lights of the high-rise office buildings and hotels in Fashion Island loomed somewhat farther away through the silvery veils of rain, but in spite of being in a busy commercial and residential area, this stretch of MacArthur Boulevard was less of a boulevard than its name implied, with no sidewalks or streetlamps along its westbound lanes. He wasn't sure that he would be able to pull off the pavement far enough to eliminate the risk of being sideswiped—or worse—by passing traffic.

Abruptly the noise stopped.

The vibration ceased as well.

The 'vette purred along as smoothly as the dream machine that it was supposed to be.

Tentatively, he increased his speed.

The rattling and scraping didn't resume.

Tommy leaned back in his seat, letting out his pent-up breath, somewhat relieved but still concerned.

From under the hood came a sharp *twang* as of metal snapping under tremendous stress.

The steering wheel shuddered in Tommy's hands. It pulled hard to the left.

"Oh, God."

Traffic was headed upslope in the eastbound lanes. Two cars and a van. They were not moving as fast in the rain-slashed night as they would have been in better weather, but they were coming too fast nonetheless.

With both hands, Tommy pulled the wheel to the right.

The car responded—but sluggishly.

The oncoming vehicles began to swerve to their right as the drivers saw him cross over the center line. Not all of them were going to be able to get out of his way. They were restricted by a sidewalk and by the concrete-block wall surrounding a housing development.

The catastrophic *twang* under the hood was immediately followed by a clattering-pinging-clanking-grinding that instantly escalated into cacophony.

Tommy resisted the powerful urge to stomp the brake pedal flat to the floorboard, which might cast the Corvette into a deadly spin. Instead he eased down on it judiciously. He might as well have stood on the pedal with both feet, because he had no brakes. None. Nada. Zip. Zero. No stopping power whatsoever.

And the accelerator seemed to be stuck. The car was picking up speed.

"Oh, God, no."

He wrenched at the steering wheel so forcefully that he felt as though he would dislocate his shoulders. At last the car angled sharply back into the westbound lanes where it belonged.

Over in the eastbound lanes, the wildly sweeping glimmer of headlights on the wet pavement reflected the other drivers' panic.

Then the Corvette's steering failed altogether. The wheel spun uselessly through his aching hands.

The 'vette didn't arc toward oncoming traffic again, thank God, but shot off the highway, onto the shoulder, kicking up gravel that rattled against the undercarriage.

Tommy let go of the spinning steering wheel before the friction between it and his palms could burn his skin. He shielded his face with his hands.

The car flattened a small highway-department sign, tore through tall grass and low brush, and rocketed off the embankment. It was airborne.

The engine was still screaming, demanding acceleration.

Tommy had the crazy notion that the Corvette would sail on like an aircraft, rising instead of descending, soaring gracefully above a cluster of phoenix palms at the corner of MacArthur and Pacific Coast Highway, then over the businesses and houses that lay in the last couple of blocks before the coast, out across the black waters of the vast Pacific, head-on into the storm, eventually up-up-up and beyond the rain and the turbulence, into a tranquil realm of silence with an eternity of stars above and deep clouds below, with Japan far to the west but growing nearer. If the genie of medicine, Tien Thai, could fly around the world on his own engineless mountain, then surely it was possible to do so even more easily in a Corvette with three hundred horse-power at five thousand rpm.

He had been nearing the end of MacArthur Boulevard when he ramped off the embankment, and the drop from the highway was not as drastic here as it would have been if he had lost control just a quarter of a mile earlier. Nevertheless, having been launched at an angle, the car was in the air long enough to tilt slightly to the right; therefore, it came down only on the passenger-side tires, one of which exploded.

The safety harness tightened painfully across Tommy's chest, cinching the breath out of him. He wasn't aware that his mouth was open—or that he was screaming—until his teeth clacked together hard enough to crack a walnut.

Like Tommy, the big engine stopped screaming on impact too, so as the Corvette rolled, he was able to hear the fearsome and familiar shriek of the minikin. The beast's shrill cry was coming through the heating vents from the engine compartment. *Gleeful* shrieking.

With a hellish clatter to rival the sound of an 8.0

earthquake shaking through an aluminum-pot fac-
tory, the sports car rolled. The laminated glass of the
windshield webbed with a million fissures and
imploded harmlessly, and the car tumbled through
one revolution and started another, whereupon the
side windows shattered. The hood buckled with a
skreeeeek, started to tear loose, but then was cracked
and crunched and twisted and jammed into the
engine compartment during the second roll.

With one headlight still aglow, the Corvette
finally came to rest on the passenger side, after two
and a quarter revolutions. Or maybe it was three. He
couldn't be sure. He was anxious and disoriented
and as dizzy as if he had spent the past hour on a
roller coaster.

The driver's side of the car was where the roof
should have been, and only the web of the safety
harness prevented him from falling into the passenger seat, which was now where the floor should
have been.

In the comparative stillness of the aftermath,
Tommy could hear his own panicky breathing, the
hot tick of overheated engine parts, the tinkle-clink
of falling bits of glass, the whistle of pressurized
coolant escaping through a punctured line, and rain
drumming against the wreckage.

The minikin, however, was silent.

Tommy didn't delude himself that the demon had
been killed in the crash. It was alive, all right, and
eagerly wriggling toward him through the wreckage.
At any moment, it would kick out a vent grill or

climb in through the empty windshield frame, and in the confines of the demolished car, he would not be able to get away from it fast enough to save himself.

Gasoline fumes. The chill wind brought him the last thing he wanted to smell: the astringent odor of gasoline fumes so strong that he was briefly robbed of his breath.

The battery still held a charge. The possibility of shorting wires, a spark, was all too real.

Tommy wasn't sure which fate was worse: having his eyes clawed out by the hissing minikin and his carotid artery chewed open—or being immolated in his dream car on the very day that he had bought it. At least James Dean had *enjoyed* his Porsche Spyder for nine days before he had been killed in it.

Although dizzy, Tommy found the release button for the safety harness. Holding on to the steering wheel with one hand to avoid dropping down into the passenger's seat, he disentangled himself from the straps.

Tommy located the door handle, which seemed to work well enough. But the lock was shattered or the door was torqued, and no matter how he strained against it, the damn thing wouldn't open.

The side window had broken out in the crash, leaving not even a fragment of glass stuck in the frame. Cold rain poured through the hole, soaking Tommy.

After pulling his legs out from under the dashboard, he squirmed around to brace his feet against the gear console between the seats. He thrust his head through the window, then his shoulders and arms, and levered himself out of the wreckage.

He rolled off the side of the tipped Corvette into matted brown grass soaked with rain, into a cold puddle, into mud.

The stink of gasoline was stronger than ever.

Pushing onto his feet, swaying unsteadily, he saw that the car had tumbled across a parcel of bare land that was the site of a future shopping center at the highly desirable corner of MacArthur Boulevard and Pacific Coast Highway. In recent years, this field had been used as a Christmas-tree lot every December, sometimes as a pumpkin patch at Halloween, but had served no substantial commercial purpose. He was damn lucky that it was early November and that he had rolled the car through an empty field instead of through happily chattering families in a holiday mood.

Because the Corvette was turned on its side, he was standing next to the undercarriage. From out of the mechanical guts of the machine, the minikin issued a shriek of rage and *need.*

Tommy stumbled back from the car, splashing through another puddle, and nearly fell on his ass.

As the bone-piercing shriek trailed into a snarl and then into an industrious grumble, Tommy heard the demon pounding-straining-clawing, and metal creaked against metal. He couldn't see into the dark undercarriage, but he sensed that the minikin was temporarily trapped in the tangled wreckage and struggling furiously to pry itself free.

The fiberglass body of the Corvette was a mess. His dream car was a total loss.

He was fortunate to have gotten out unscathed. In the morning, of course, he would be crippled by whiplash and a thousand smaller pains—if he lived through the night.

The deadline is dawn.

Ticktock.

Crazily, he wondered what the per-hour cost of his brief ownership had been. Seven thousand dollars? Eight thousand? He looked at his watch, trying to calculate the number of hours since he had made the purchase and been handed the keys, but then he realized that it didn't matter. It was only money.

What mattered was survival.

Ticktock.

Get moving.

Keep moving.

When he circled around the front of the tipped car, passing through the beam of the sole functioning headlight, he couldn't see the engine compartment, either, for the hood had compacted into it. But he could hear the demon battering frantically against the walls of its prison.

"Die, damn you," Tommy demanded.

In the distance, someone shouted.

Shaking his head to cast off his remaining dizziness, blinking through the rain, Tommy saw that two cars had stopped along MacArthur Boulevard to the south, near the place where he had run the Corvette off the roadway.

A man with a flashlight was standing at the top of the low embankment about eighty yards away. The guy called again, but the meaning of his words was swallowed by the wind.

Traffic had slowed and a few vehicles were even stopped on Pacific Coast Highway as well, although no one had gotten out of them yet.

The guy with the flashlight started to descend the embankment, coming to offer assistance.

Tommy raised one arm and waved vigorously, encouraging the good Samaritan to hurry, to come hear the squawking demon trapped in the smashed machinery, to see the impossible doll-thing with his own eyes if it managed to break loose, to marvel at its existence, *to be a witness.*

Gasoline, which was evidently pooled under the length of the Corvette, ignited. Blue and orange flames geysered high into the night, vaporizing the falling rain.

The great hot hand of the fire slapped Tommy with such fury that his face stung, and he was stag-gered backward by the force of the blow. There had been no explosion, but the heat was so intense that he surely would have been set afire in that instant if his hair and his clothes had not been thoroughly soaked.

An unearthly squealing rose from the trapped minikin.

At the foot of the embankment, the good Samari-tan had halted, startled by the fire.

"Hurry! *Hurry!*" Tommy shouted, although he

knew that the roar of rain and wind prevented the man with the flashlight from hearing either him or the demon.

With a boom and a splintery crack like bone breaking, the battered and burning hood exploded off the engine compartment and tumbled past Tommy, spewing sparks and smoke as it clattered toward the stand of phoenix palms.

Like a malevolent genie freed from a lamp, the minikin flung itself out of the inferno and landed upright in the mud, no more than ten feet from Tommy. It was ablaze, but the streaming cloaks of fire that had replaced its white fabric shroud did not seem to disturb it.

Indeed, the creature was no longer shrieking in mindless rage but appeared to be exhilarated by the blaze. Raising its arms over its head as if joyfully exclaiming *hallelujah*, swaying almost as if in a state of rapture, it fixed its attention not on Tommy but on its own hands, which, like tallow tapers on some dark altar, streamed blue fire.

"Bigger," Tommy gasped in disbelief.

Incredibly, the thing had grown. The doll on his doorstep had been about ten inches long. This demon swaying rapturously before him was approximately eighteen inches tall, nearly twice the size that it had been when he had last seen it streaking across his foyer into the living room to short-circuit the lights. Furthermore, its legs and arms were thicker and its body heavier than they had been earlier.

Because of the masking fire, Tommy could not

see details of the creature's form, although he thought he detected wickedly spiky protrusions extending the length of its spine—which had not been there before. Its back seemed to be more hunched than it had been previously, and perhaps its hands were becoming disproportionately large for the length of its arms. Whether he perceived these details correctly or not, Tommy was certain that he could not be mistaken about the beast's greater size.

Having expected the minikin to wither and collapse in the consuming flames, Tommy was dangerously mesmerized by the sight of it thriving instead.

"This is nuts," he muttered.

The falling rain captured the light of the wildly leaping fire, carrying it into puddles on the ground, which glimmered like pools of melting doubloons and flickered with the shadow of the capering minikin.

How could it possibly have grown so fast? And to add this much body weight, it would have required nourishment, fuel to feed the feverish growth.

What had it eaten?

The good Samaritan was approaching again, behind the bobbling beam of his flashlight, but he was still more than sixty yards away. The burning Corvette was between him and the demon, which he wouldn't be able to see until he had come virtually to Tommy's side.

What had it eaten?

Impossibly, the rhapsodic minikin appeared to swell larger even as the flames seethed from it.

Tommy began to back slowly away, overcome by the urgent need to flee but reluctant to turn and run. Any too-sudden movement on his part might shatter the demon's ecstatic fascination with the fire and remind it that its prey was nearby.

The guy with the flashlight was forty yards away. He was a heavyset man in a hooded raincoat that flared behind him. Lumbering through the puddles, slipping in the mud, he resembled a cowled monk.

Suddenly Tommy was afraid for the Samaritan's life. At first he had wanted a witness; but that was when he thought the minikin would perish in the flames. Now he sensed that it wouldn't *allow* a witness.

He would have shouted at the stranger to stay away, even at the risk of drawing the minikin's attention, but fate intervened when a gunshot cracked through the rainy night, then a second and a third.

Evidently recognizing the distinctive sound, the heavyset stranger skidded to a halt in the mud. He was still thirty yards away, with the ruined car intervening, so he couldn't possibly have seen the blazing demon.

A fourth shot boomed, a fifth.

In the scramble to get out of the Corvette after the crash, Tommy had not remembered the pistol. He wouldn't have been able to locate it anyway. Now the intense heat was detonating the ammunition.

Reminded that he lacked even the inadequate protection of the Heckler & Koch, Tommy stopped

backing away from the demon and stood in tremu-
lous indecision. Although he was drenched by the
storm, his mouth was as dry as the sun-scorched
sand on an August beach.

The rain washed parching panic through him, and
his fear was like a fever burning in his brow, in his
eyes, in his joints.

He turned and ran for his life.

He didn't know where he was going, didn't know
if he had any hope of escaping, but he was propelled
by sheer survival instinct. Maybe he could outrun
the minikin in the short term, but he didn't have high
expectations of being able to stay beyond its reach
for the next six or seven hours, until dawn.

It was growing.

Getting stronger.

Becoming a more formidable predator.

Ticktock.

Mud sucked at Tommy's athletic shoes. Tangles
of dead grass and creeping lantana vines almost
snared him, almost brought him down. A palm frond
like the feather from a giant bird, torn loose by the
wind, spun out of the night and lashed his face as it
flew past him. Nature herself seemed to be joined in
a conspiracy with the minikin.

Ticktock.

Tommy glanced over his shoulder and saw that
the flames at the Corvette, although brightly whip-
ping the night, were subsiding. The smaller confla-
gration that marked the burning demon was fading
much faster than the blaze at the car, but the beast

continued to be entranced and was not yet giving chase.

The deadline is dawn.

Tomorrow's sunrise hung out there just a few minutes this side of eternity.

Almost to the street, Tommy dared to glance back again through the obscuring gray curtains of rain. Flames still sputtered from the minikin, but only fitfully. Apparently, most of the gasoline saturating the creature had burned off. Too little fire remained—mere wisps of yellow—to allow Tommy to see the thing well: just well enough to be certain that it was on the move again and coming after him.

It was not pursuing as fast as it had been before, maybe because it was still inebriated from its infatuation with the flames. But it was coming nonetheless.

Having crossed the empty lot on the diagonal, Tommy reached the corner of Pacific Coast Highway and Avocado Street, skidded across the last stretch of mud like an ice-skater on a frozen pond, and plunged off the curb into the calf-deep water that overflowed the gutters at the intersection.

A car horn blared. Brakes screeched.

He hadn't checked oncoming traffic because he had been looking over his shoulder and then watching the treacherous ground ahead of him. When he snapped his head up in surprise, an astonishingly colorful Ford van was *there*, blazing yellow-red-gold-orange-black-green, as if appearing magically—*poof!*—from another dimension. The dazzling van stopped an instant before Tommy reached it, rocking on its springs, but he couldn't prevent himself from running into it full tilt. He bounced off the fender, spun around to the front of the vehicle, and fell to the pavement.

Clutching the van, he immediately pulled himself up from the blacktop.

The extravagant paint job wasn't psychedelic, as it had appeared on first impression, but, rather, was an attempt to transform the van into an Art Deco jukebox: images of leaping gazelles amid stylized palm fronds, streams of luminous silver bubbles in bands of glossy black, and more luminous gold bubbles in bands of Chinese-red lacquer. As the driver's door opened, the night swung with Benny Goodman's big-band classic "One O'clock Jump."

As Tommy regained his feet, the driver appeared at his side. She was a young woman in white shoes, what might have been a nurse's white uniform, and a black leather jacket. "Hey, are you all right?"

"Yeah, okay," Tommy wheezed.

"You're really okay?"

"Yeah, sure, leave me alone."

He squinted at the rain-swept vacant lot.

The minikin was no longer afire, and the flashing red emergency lights at the back of the van didn't penetrate far into the gloom. Tommy couldn't see where the creature was, but he knew it was closing the gap between them, perhaps moving sluggishly but closing the gap.

"Go," he told her, waving her away with one hand.

The woman insisted, "You must be—"

"Go, hurry."

"—hurt. I can't—"

"Get out of here!" he said frantically, not wanting to trap her between him and the demon.

He pushed away from her, intending to continue across all six lanes of Pacific Coast Highway. At the moment, there was no traffic except for a few vehicles that had stopped half a block to the south, where their drivers were watching the burning Corvette.

The woman clutched tenaciously. "Was that your car back there?"

"Jesus, lady, it's coming!"

"What's coming?"

"*It!*"

"What?"

"*It!*" He tried to wrench loose of her.

She said, "Was that your new Corvette?"

He realized that he knew her. The blond waitress. She had served cheeseburgers and fries to him earlier this evening. The restaurant was across this highway.

The place had closed for the night. She was on her way home.

Again Tommy had the queer sensation that he was riding the bobsled of fate, rocketing down a luge chute toward some destiny he could not begin to understand.

"You should see a doctor," she persisted.

He wasn't going to be able to shake her loose.

When the minikin arrived, it wouldn't want a witness.

Eighteen inches tall and growing. A spiky crest along the length of its spine. Bigger claws, bigger teeth. It would rip her throat out, tear her face off.

Her slender throat.

Her lovely face.

Tommy didn't have time to argue with her. "Okay, a doctor, okay, get me out of here."

Holding his arm as if he were a doddering old man, she started to walk him around to the passenger door, which was the side of the van closest to the vacant lot.

"Drive the fucking thing!" he demanded, and at last he tore loose of her.

Tommy went to the passenger door and yanked it open, but the waitress was still standing in front of her jukebox van, stupefied by his outburst.

"Move or we'll *both* die!" he shouted in frustration.

He glanced back into the vacant lot, expecting the minikin to spring at him out of the darkness and rain, but it wasn't here yet, so he clambered into the Ford.

The woman slid into the driver's seat and slammed her door an instant after Tommy slammed his.

Switching off "One O'clock Jump," she said, "What happened back there? I saw you come shooting off MacArthur Boulevard—"

"Are you stupid or deaf or both?" he demanded, his voice shrill and cracking. "We gotta get out of here *now*!"

"You've no right to talk to me that way," she said quietly but with visible anger in her crystalline-blue eyes.

Speechless with frustration, Tommy could only sputter.

"Even if you're hurt and upset, you can't talk to me that way. It isn't nice."

He glanced out the side window at the vacant lot next to them.

She said, "I can't abide rudeness."

Forcing himself to speak more calmly, Tommy said, "I'm sorry."

"You don't sound sorry."

"Well, I am."

"Well, you don't sound it."

Tommy thought maybe he would kill her rather than wait for the minikin to do it.

"I'm genuinely sorry," he said.

"Really?"

"I'm truly, truly sorry."

"That's better."

"Can you take me to a hospital," he asked, merely to get her moving.

"Sure."

"Thank you."

"Put on your seatbelt."

"What?"

"It's the law."

Her hair was honey-dark and lank with rain, pasted to her face, and her uniform was saturated. He reminded himself that she had gone to some trouble for him.

As he unreeled the shoulder harness and locked it across his chest, he said as patiently as possible:

"Please, miss, please, you don't understand what's happening here—"

"Then explain. I'm *neither* stupid nor deaf."

For an instant the improbability of the night left him without words again, but then suddenly they exploded in a long hysterical gush: "This thing, this doll, on my doorstep, and then the stitches pulled out and it had a real eye, green eye, rat's tail, dropped on my head from behind the drape, and it pretty much eats bullets for breakfast, which is bad enough, but then it's also *smart*, and it's growing—"

"What's growing?"

Frustration pushed him dangerously close to the edge of rudeness once more: "The doll snake rat-quick little monster thing! It's growing."

"The doll snake rat-quick little monster thing," she repeated, eyeing him suspiciously.

"Yes!" he said exasperatedly.

With a wet *thunk*, the shrieking minikin hit the window in the passenger door, inches from Tommy's head.

Tommy screamed.

The woman said, "Holy shit."

The minikin was growing, all right, but it was also changing into something less humanoid than it had been when it first began to emerge from the doll form. Its head was proportionately larger than before, and repulsively misshapen, and the radiant green eyes bulged from deep sockets under an irregular bony brow.

The waitress released the emergency brake. "Knock it off the window."

"I can't."

"Knock it off the window!"

"*How*, for God's sake?"

Although the minikin still had hands, its five digits were half like fingers, half like the spatulate tentacles of a squid. It held fast to the glass with pale suckerpads on both its hands and its feet.

Tommy wasn't going to roll down the window and try to knock the thing off. No way.

The blonde shifted the Ford into drive. She stomped on the accelerator hard enough to punch the van into warp speed and put them on the far side of the galaxy in maybe eighteen seconds.

As the engine shrieked louder than the minikin, the tires spun furiously on the slick pavement, and the Ford didn't go across the galaxy or even to the end of the block, but just hung there, kicking up sprays of dirty water from all four wheels.

The minikin's mouth was open wide. Its glistening black tongue flickered. Black teeth snapped against the glass.

The tires found traction, and the van shot forward.

"Don't let it in," she implored.

"Why would I let it in?"

"Don't let it in."

"Do you think I'm insane?"

The Ford van was a rocket, screaming north on Pacific Coast Highway. Tommy felt as if he were

pulling enough g's to distort his face like an astro-
naut in a space-shuttle launch, and rain was hitting
the windshield with a clatter almost as loud as sub-
machine-gun fire, but the stubborn minikin was
glued to the glass.

"It's trying to get in," she said.

"Yeah."

"What does it want?"

He said, "Me."

"Why?"

"For some reason, I just piss it off."

The beast was still mostly black mottled with
yellow, but its belly was entirely pus yellow, pressed
against the glass. A slit opened the length of its underside, and obscenely wriggling tubes with suckerike
mouths slithered out of its guts and attached themselves to the window.

The light inside the van wasn't good enough to
reveal exactly what was happening, but Tommy saw
the glass begin to smoke.

He said, "Uh-oh."

"What?"

"It's burning through the glass."

"Burning?"

"Eating."

"What?"

"Acid."

Barely braking for the turn, she hung a hard right
off the highway into the entrance drive of the Newport Beach Country Club.

The van canted drastically to the right, and centrifugal force threw Tommy against the door, pressing his face to the window, beyond which the minikin's extruded guts wriggled on the smoking glass.

"Where are you going?"

"Country club," she said.

"Why?"

"Truck," she said.

She turned sharply to the left, into the parking lot, a maneuver that pulled Tommy away from the door and the dissolving window.

At that late hour the parking lot was mostly deserted. Only a few vehicles stood on the blacktop. One of them was a delivery truck.

Aiming the van at the back of the truck, she accelerated.

"What're you doing?" he demanded.

"Detachment."

At the last moment she swung to the left of the parked truck, roaring past it so close that she stripped the elaborate custom paint job off the front fender and tore off the van's side mirror. Showers of sparks streamed from tortured metal, and the minikin was jammed between the van window and the flank of the big truck. The rocker panel peeled off the side of the van, but the minikin seemed tougher than the Ford—until its suckers abruptly popped loose with a sound Tommy could hear even above all the other noise. The window in the passenger door burst, and tempered glass showered across Tommy, and he thought the beast was falling into his lap, Jesus, but then they were past the parked truck, and he realized that the creature had been torn away from the van.

"Want to circle back and run over the damn thing a few times?" she shouted over the howling of the wind at the broken-out window.

He leaned toward her, raising his voice. "Hell, no. That won't work. It'll grab the tire as you pass over it, and this time we'll never shake it loose. It'll crawl up into the undercarriage, tear through, squeeze through, get at us one way or another."

"Then let's haul ass out of here."

At the end of the country-club drive, she turned right onto the highway at such high speed that Tommy expected the Ford to blow a tire or roll, but they came through all right, and she put the pedal to the metal with less respect for the speed limit than she had shown, earlier, for the seatbelt law.

Tommy half expected the minikin to explode out of the storm again. He didn't feel safe until they crossed Jamboree Road and began to descend toward the Newport harbor.

Rain slashed through the missing window and snapped against the side of his head. It didn't bother him. He couldn't get any wetter than he already was.

At the speed they were making, the hooting and gibbering of the wind was so great that neither of them made an effort to engage in conversation.

As they crossed the bridge over the back-bay channel, a couple of miles from the parking lot where they had left the demon, the blonde finally reduced speed. The noise of the wind abated somewhat.

She looked at Tommy in a way that no one had ever looked at him before, as though he were green, warty, with a head like a watermelon, and had just stepped out of a flying saucer.

Well, in fact, his own mother had looked at him that way when he first talked about being a detective-story writer.

He cleared his throat nervously and said, "You're a pretty good driver."

Surprisingly she smiled. "You really think so?"

"Actually, you're terrific."

"Thanks. You're not bad yourself."

"Me?"

"That was some stunt with the Corvette."

"Very funny."

"You went airborne pretty straight and true, but you just lost control of it in flight."

"Sorry about your van."

"It comes with the territory," she said cryptically.

"I'll pay for the repairs."

"You're sweet."

"We should stop and get something to block this window."

"You don't need to go straight to a hospital?"

"I'm okay," he assured her. "But the rain's going to ruin your upholstery."

"Don't worry about it."

"But—"

"It's blue," she said.

"What?"

"The upholstery."

"Yeah, blue. So?"

"I don't like blue."

"But the damage—"

"I'm used to it."

"You are?"

She said, "There's frequently damage."

"There is?"

"I lead an eventful life."

"You do?"

"I've learned to roll with it."

"You're a strange woman," he said.

She grinned. "Thank you."

He felt disoriented again. "What's your name?"

"Deliverance," she said.

"Yeah?"

"Deliverance Payne. P-A-Y-N-E. It was a hard birth, and my mom has a weird sense of humor."

He didn't get it. And then he did. "Ah."

"People just call me Del."

"Del. That's nice."

"What's your name?"

"Tuong Phan." He startled himself. "I mean Tommy."

"Tuong Tommy?"

"Tuong nothing. My name's Tommy Phan."

"Are you sure?"

"Most of the time."

"You're a strange man," she said, as if that pleased her, as if returning a compliment.

"There really is a lot of water coming in this window."

"We'll stop soon."

"Where'd you learn to drive like that, Del?"

"My mom."

"Some mother you have."

"She's a hoot. She races stock cars."

"Not *my* mother," Tommy said.

"And powerboats. And motorcycles. It has an engine, my mom wants to race it."

Del braked at a red traffic light.

They were silent for a moment.

Rain poured down as if the sky were a dam that had just broken.

Finally Del said, "So . . . back there . . . That was the doll snake rat-quick little monster thing, huh?"

FOUR

As they drove, Tommy told Del about the doll on his doorstep, everything up to the moment when it had shorted out the lights in his office. She never gave the slightest indication that she found his story dubious or even, in fact, particularly astonishing. From time to time she said "uh-huh" and "hmmmm" and "okay," and—two or three times—"yeah, that makes sense," as if he were telling her about nothing more incredible than what she might have heard on the nightly TV news.

Then he paused in his tale when Del stopped at a twenty-four-hour supermarket. She insisted on getting a few things to clean the van and close off the shattered window, and at her request, Tommy went shopping with her. He pushed the cart.

So few customers prowled the enormous market that it was almost possible for Tommy to believe that he and Del were in one of those 1950's science-fiction movies, in which all but a handful of people had vanished from the face of the earth as the result of a mysterious apocalypse that had left buildings and all other works of humanity undisturbed. Flooded with glary light from the overhead fluorescent panels, the long wide aisles were uncannily empty and silent but for the ominous low-pitched hum of the compressors for the refrigerated display cases.

Striding purposefully through these eerie spaces in her white shoes, white uniform, and unzipped black leather jacket, with her wet blond hair slicked straight back and tucked behind her ears, Del Payne looked like a nurse who might also be a Hell's Angel, equally capable of ministering to a sick man or kicking the ass of a healthy one.

She selected a box of large plastic garbage bags, a wide roll of plumbing tape, a package containing four rolls of paper towels, a packet of razor blades, a tape measure, a bottle of one-gram tablets of vit-amin C, a bottle of vitamin-E capsules, and two twelve-ounce bottles of orange juice. From an early-bird display of Christmas decorations, she snatched up a conical, red flannel Santa hat with a fake white fur trim and white pom-pom.

As they were passing the dairy-and-deli section, she stopped and pointed at a stack of containers in one of the coolers and said, "Do you eat tofu?"

Her question seemed so esoteric that Tommy could only repeat it in bafflement: "Do I eat tofu?"

"I asked first."

"No. I don't like tofu."

"You should."

"Why," he asked impatiently, "because I'm Asian? I don't eat with chopsticks, either."

"Are you always so sensitive?"

"I'm not sensitive," he said defensively.

"I didn't even think about your being Asian until you brought it up," she said.

Curiously, he believed her. Though he didn't know her well, he already knew that she was different from other people, and he was willing to believe that she had just now noticed the slant of his eyes and the burnt-brass shade of his skin.

Chagrined, he said, "I'm sorry."

"I was only asking if you ate tofu because if you eat it five times a week or more, then you'll never have to worry about prostate cancer. It's a homeopathic preventative."

He had never met anyone whose conversation was as unpredictable as Del Payne's. "I'm not worried about prostate cancer."

"Well, you should be. It's the third-largest cause of death among men. Or maybe fourth. Anyway, for men, it's right up there with heart disease and crushing beer cans against the forehead."

"I'm only thirty. Men don't get prostate cancer until they're in their fifties or sixties."

"So one day, when you're forty-nine, you'll wake up in the morning, and your prostate will be the size of a basketball, and you'll realize you're a statistical anomaly, but by then it'll be too late."

She plucked a carton of tofu from the cooler and dropped it into the shopping cart.

"I don't want it," Tommy said.

"Don't be silly. You're never too young to start taking care of yourself."

She grabbed the front of the cart and pulled it along the aisle, forcing him to keep pace with her, so he didn't have an opportunity to return the tofu to the cooler.

Hurrying after her, he said, "What do you care whether I wake up twenty years from now with a prostate the size of Cleveland?"

"We're both human beings, aren't we? What kind of person would I be if I didn't care what happens to you?"

"You don't really know me," he said.

"Sure I do. You're Tuong Tommy."

"Tommy Phan."

"That's right."

At the checkout station, Tommy insisted on paying. "After all, you wouldn't have a broken window or all the mess in the van if not for me."

"Okay," she said as he took out his wallet, "but just because you're paying for some plumbing tape and paper towels doesn't mean I have to sleep with you."

Chip Nguyen would have replied instantly and with a playful witticism that would have charmed her, because in addition to being a damn fine private detective, he was a master of romantic repartee. Tommy, however, blinked stupidly at Del, racked his brain, but could think of nothing to say.

If he could just sit down at his computer for a couple of hours and polish up a few gems of dialogue, he would develop some repartee that would have Ms. Deliverance Payne begging for mercy.

"You're blushing," she said, amused.

"I am not."

"Yes, you are."

"No, I'm not."

Del turned to the cashier, a middle-aged Hispanic woman wearing a tiny gold crucifix on a gold chain at her throat, and said, "Is he blushing or isn't he?"

The cashier giggled. "He's blushing."

"Of course he is," said Del.

"He's cute when he blushes," said the cashier.

"I'll bet he knows that," Del said, mischievously delighted by the woman's comment. "He probably uses it as a tool for seduction, can blush any time he wants to, the way some really good actors can cry on cue."

The cashier giggled again.

Tommy let out a long-suffering sigh and surveyed the nearly deserted market, relieved that there were no other customers close enough to hear. He was blushing so intensely that his ears felt as though they were on fire.

When the cashier ran the carton of tofu across the bar-code scanner, Del said, "He worries about pro-state cancer."

Mortified, Tommy said, "I do not."

"Yes, you do."

"No, I don't."

"But he won't listen to me, won't believe that tofu can prevent it," Del told the cashier.

After hitting the key to total their order, the cashier frowned at Tommy, and in a matronly voice with no trace of the former musical giggle, almost as if speaking to a child, she said, "Listen here, you better believe it, 'cause it's true. The Japanese eat it every day, and they have almost no prostate cancer."

"You see?" Del said smugly.

Tommy shook his head. "What do you do when you aren't waiting tables—run a medical clinic?"

"It's just widely known, that's all."

"We sell a lot of tofu to Japanese customers, Koreans," said the cashier as she finished bagging their purchases and accepted payment from Tommy. "You must not be Japanese."

"American," Tommy said.

"Vietnamese-American?"

"American," he repeated stubbornly.

"A lot of Vietnamese-Americans eat tofu too," said the cashier as she counted out his change, "though not as much as our Japanese customers."

With a grin that now seemed demented, Del said, "He's going to wind up with a prostate the size of a basketball."

"You listen to this girl and take care of yourself," the cashier instructed.

Tommy stuffed the change into a pocket of his jeans and grabbed the two small plastic sacks that contained the purchases, desperate to get out of the market.

The cashier repeated her admonition: "You listen to the girl."

Outside, the rain chilled him again, sluicing away the warmth of the blush. He thought of the minikin, which was still out there in the night—and not as mini as it had once been.

For a few minutes, in the market, he had actually forgotten the damn thing. Of all the people he had ever met, only Del Payne could have made him forget, even briefly, that he had been under attack by something monstrous and supernatural less than half an hour earlier.

"Are you nuts?" he asked as they neared the van.

"I don't think so," she said brightly.

"Don't you realize that thing is out there somewhere?"

"You mean the doll snake rat-quick little monster thing?"

"What *other* thing would I mean?"

"Well, the world is full of strange stuff."

"Huh?"

"Don't you watch *The X-Files*?"

"It's out there and it's looking for me—"

"Probably looking for me too," she said. "I must've pissed it off."

"I'd say that's a safe bet. So how can you be going on about my prostate, the benefits of tofu—when we've got some demon from *Hell* trying to track us down?"

She went to the driver's door, and Tommy hurried around to the other side of the jukebox van. She didn't answer his question until they were both inside.

"Regardless of what other problems we have just

now," she said, "they don't change the fact that tofu is good for you."

"You *are* nuts."

Starting the engine, she said, "You're so sober, serious, so straight-arrow. How can I resist tweaking you a little?"

"Tweaking me?"

"You're a hoot," she said, putting the van in gear and driving away from the supermarket.

He looked down glumly at the pair of plastic sacks on the floor between his legs. "I can't believe I paid for the damn tofu."

"You'll like it."

A few blocks from the market, in a district of warehouses and industrial buildings, Del parked the van under a freeway overpass, where it was sheltered from the rain.

"Bring the stuff we bought," she said.

"It looks awful lonely here."

"Most of the world is lonely corners."

"I'm not sure it's safe."

"Nowhere is safe unless you want it to be," she said, having entered her cryptic mode once more.

"What does that mean exactly?"

"What *doesn't* it mean?"

"You're putting me on again."

"I don't know what you mean," she said.

She was not grinning now. The merriness that had

brightened her when she conducted the tofu torture was gone.

Leaving the engine running, she got out from behind the wheel and went around to the back of the Ford—which wasn't a recreational vehicle, but a delivery van of the kind commonly used by florists and other small businesses—and she opened the rear door. She took the supermarket bags from Tommy and emptied the contents on the floor of the cargo hold.

Tommy stood watching her, shivering. He was wet through and through, and the temperature, as midnight approached, must have been in the low fifties.

She said, "I'll put together a cover for the broken window. While I'm doing that, you use the paper towels to soak up as much water as you can from the front seat and the floor, get rid of the glass."

With no residential or commercial structures in the area to draw traffic, the street seemed to be another set from that same science-fiction movie about a depopulated, post-apocalyptic world that Tommy had remembered in the supermarket. A rumble overhead was the sound of trucks on the freeway above, but because those vehicles could not be seen from here, it was easy to imagine that the source of the noise was colossal machinery of an alien nature engaged in the fulfillment of a meticulously planned holocaust.

Considering his overactive imagination, he probably should have tried writing a type of fiction more colorful than detective stories.

In the cargo hold was a cardboard carton full of smaller boxes of dog biscuits. "I went shopping this afternoon for Scootie," she explained as she removed the packages of biscuits from the larger container.

"Your dog, huh?"

"Not just my dog. *The* dog. The essence of all dogginess. The coolest canine on the planet. No doubt in his last incarnation before Nirvana. That's my Scootie."

With the new tape measure, she got the accurate dimensions of the broken-out window, and then she used one of the razor blades to cut a rectangle of that precise size from the cardboard carton. She slid the panel of cardboard into one of the plastic garbage bags, folded the bag tightly around that insert, and sealed it with lengths of the waterproof plumbing tape. More tape secured the rectangle, inside and out, to the glassless window frame in the passenger's door.

While Del made the rain shield, Tommy worked around her to purge the front seat of water and sparkling fragments of tempered glass. As he worked, he told her what had happened from the moment when the minikin had shorted out the office lights until it had erupted from the burning Corvette.

"Bigger?" she asked. "How much bigger?"

"Almost double its original size. And different.

The thing you saw clinging to the van window . . . that's a hell of a lot weirder than it was when it first began to emerge from the doll."

Not one vehicle drove through the underpass as they worked, and Tommy was increasingly concerned about their isolation. Repeatedly he glanced toward the open ends of the concrete shelter, where heavy rain continued to crash down by the ton weight, bracketing the dry space in which they had taken refuge. He expected to see the radiant-eyed demon—swollen to greater and stranger dimensions—approaching menacingly through the storm.

"So what do you think it is?" she asked.

"I don't know."

"Where does it come from?"

"I don't know."

"What does it want?"

"To kill me."

"Why?"

"I don't know."

"There's a lot you don't know."

"I know."

"What do you do for a living, Tuong Tommy?"

He ignored the purposeful misstatement of his name and said, "I write detective stories."

She laughed. "So how come, in this investigation, you can't even find your own butt?"

"This is real life."

"No, it's not," she said.

"What?"

With apparent seriousness, she said, "There's no such thing."

"No such thing as real life?"

"Reality is perception. Perceptions change. Reality is fluid. So if by 'reality' you mean reliably tangible objects and immutable events, then there's no such thing."

Having used two rolls of paper towels to clean the passenger's seat and the leg space in front of it, heaping the last of them on the sodden little pile that he had created against the wall of the underpass, he said, "Are you a New Age type or something— channel spirits, heal yourself with crystals?"

"No. I merely said reality is perception."

"Sounds New Age," he said, returning to watch her finish her own task.

"Well, it's not. I'll explain someday when we have more time."

"Meanwhile," he said, "I'll wander aimlessly in the wilderness of my ignorance."

"Sarcasm doesn't become you."

"Are you about finished here? I'm freezing."

Del stepped back from the open passenger-side door, the roll of plumbing tape in one hand and the razor blade in the other, surveying her work. "It'll keep the rain out well enough, I guess, but it's not exactly the latest thing in aesthetically pleasing motor-vehicle accessories."

In the poor light, Tommy couldn't clearly see the elaborate Art Deco, jukebox-inspired mural on the van, but he could discern that a substantial portion of it had been scraped off the passenger side. "I'm really sorry about the paint job. It was spectacular. Must have cost a bundle."

"Just a little paint and a lot of time. Don't worry about it. I was thinking of redoing it anyway."

She had surprised him again. "You painted it yourself?"

"I'm an artist," she said.

"I thought you were a waitress."

"Being a waitress is what I *do*. An artist is what I *am*."

"I see."

"Do you?" she said, turning away from the door.

"You said it yourself earlier—I'm a sensitive guy."

On the freeway overhead, the airbrakes of a big truck screeched like the cry of a scaly behemoth raging through a Jurassic swamp.

Tommy was reminded of the demon. He glanced nervously at one end of the short concrete tunnel, then at the other end, but he saw no monster, large or small, approaching through the rain.

At the back of the van, Del handed one of the two bottles of orange juice to Tommy and opened the other for herself.

His teeth were chattering. Rather than a swig of cold orange juice, he needed a mug of steaming coffee.

"We don't have coffee," she said, startling him, as though she had read his mind.

"Well, I don't want juice," he said.

"Yes, you do." From the two vitamin bottles, she counted out ten one-gram tablets of C and four gelatin capsules of E, took half for herself, and handed the rest to him. "After all that fear and stress, our bodies are totally flooded with dangerous free radicals. Incomplete oxygen molecules, tens of thousands of them, ricocheting through our bodies, damaging every cell they encounter. You need antioxidants, vitamins C and E as a minimum, to bond with the free radicals and disarm them."

Though Tommy wasn't much concerned about maintaining a healthy diet or vitamin therapy, he remembered having read about free-radical molecules and antioxidants, and there seemed to be medical validity to the theory, so he washed down the pills with the orange juice.

Besides, he was cold and weary, and he could save a lot of energy by cooperating with Del. She was indefatigable, after all, while he was merely fatigued.

"You want the tofu now?"

"Not now."

"Maybe later with some chopped pineapple, maraschino cherries, a few walnuts," she suggested.

"That sounds nice."

"Or just a slight sprinkle of shredded coconut."

"Whatever."

Del picked up the red flannel Santa hat with the white trim and white pom-pom, which she had found in the display of Christmas items at the supermarket.

"What's that for?" Tommy asked.

"It's a hat."

"But what are you going to use it for?" he asked, since she'd had such specific uses for everything else they had picked up at the market.

"Use it for? To cover my head," she said, as if he were daft. "What do *you* use hats for?"

She put it on. The weight of the pom-pom made the peak of the cap droop to one side.

"You look ridiculous."

"I think it's cute. Makes me feel good. Puts me in a holiday mood." She closed the back door of the van.

"Do you see a therapist regularly?" he asked.

"I dated a dentist once, but never a therapist."

Behind the wheel of the van again, she started the engine and switched on the heater.

Tommy held his trembling hands in front of the dashboard vents, relishing the gush of hot air. With the broken window covered, he might be able to dry out and get warm.

"Well, Detective Phan, do you want to start this investigation by trying to find it?"

"Find what?"

"Your butt."

"Just before I totaled the Corvette, I'd decided to go see my brother Gi. Could you drop me off there?"

"Drop you off?" she said disbelievingly.

"It's the last thing I'll ask you for."

"Drop you off—and then what? Just go home and

sit and wait for the doll snake rat-quick little monster thing to come tear out my liver and eat it for
dessert?"

Tommy said, "I've been thinking—"

"Well, it doesn't show."

"—and I don't think you're in any danger from it—"

"You don't *think* I am."

"—because, according to the message that the
thing apparently typed on my computer, the deadline
is dawn."

"How exactly am I to take comfort from this?"
she asked.

"It's got until dawn to get me—and I've got until
dawn to stay alive. At that point the game ends."

"Game?"

"Game, threat, whatever." He squinted through
the windshield at the silvery skeins of rain falling
beyond the underpass. "Could we get moving?
Makes me nervous to sit here so long."

Del released the handbrake and put the van in
gear. But she kept her foot on the brake pedal and
didn't drive out from under the freeway. "Tell me
what you mean—game."

"Whoever made the doll is willing to play by
rules. Or maybe they have to, maybe that's what the
magic requires."

"Magic?"

He locked his door. "Magic, sorcery, voodoo,
whatever. Anyway, if I make it to dawn, maybe I'm
safe." He reached across Del and locked her door

too. "This creature . . . it isn't going to come after you if it's been sent to get me and if it has only a limited amount of time to make the kill. The clock is ticking for me, sure, but it's also ticking for the assassin."

Del nodded thoughtfully. "That makes perfect sense," she said, and she sounded sincere, as though they were discussing the laws of thermodynamics.

"No, it's insane," he corrected. "Like the whole situation. But there's a certain nutty logic to it."

She drummed her fingers on the steering wheel. "One thing you've overlooked."

He frowned. "What's that?"

She checked her wristwatch. "It's now seven minutes past midnight."

"I hoped it was later. Still a lot of time to get to the finish line." He looked over his shoulder, across the cargo hold, at the back door of the van, which wasn't locked.

"And dawn is in . . . probably five and a half or, at most, six hours," Del said.

"So?"

"Tommy, at the rate you're going, the creepy-crawler will catch you by one o'clock, tear your head off—and still have four or five hours of spare time on its hands. If it has hands. Then it'll come for me."

He shook his head. "I don't think so."

"*I* think so."

"It doesn't know who you are," he said patiently. "How would it find you?"

"It wouldn't need to hire your silly detective," she said.

Tommy winced because she sounded like his mother, and he never wanted this woman, of all women, *ever* to remind him of his mother. "Don't call him silly."

"The damn thing will track me the same way it's tracking *you* right this very minute."

"Which is how?"

She tilted her head in thought. The fluffy white pompom dangled. "Well . . . by the pattern of your psychic emanations, telepathy. Or if each of us has a soul that emits a sound . . . or maybe a radiance that's visible in some spectrum beyond those that ordinary humans are able to sense, a radiance as unique as a fingerprint . . . then this thing could home in on it."

"Okay, all right, maybe it could do something like that if it was a supernatural entity—"

"*If* it was a supernatural entity? *If?* What else do you think it is, Tommy? A shape-changing robot they send out from MasterCard to teach you a lesson when your monthly payment is overdue?"

Tommy sighed. "Is it possible that I'm insane, tenderly cared for in some pleasant institution, and all this is happening only in my head?"

At last Del pulled back into the street and drove out from under the freeway, switching on the windshield wipers as heavy volleys of rain exploded across the van.

"I'll take you to see your brother," she said, "but

I'm not just dropping you off, tofu boy. We're in this together, all the way . . . at least until dawn."

In Garden Grove, the New World Saigon Bakery operated in a large tilt-up concrete industrial building surrounded by a blacktop parking lot. It was painted white, with the name of the company in simple peach-colored block letters, a severe-looking structure softened only by a pair of ficus trees and two clusters of azaleas that flanked the entrance to the company offices at the front. Without the guidance of the sign, a passerby might have thought the company was engaged in plastic injection molding, retail-electronics assembly, or other light manufacturing.

On Tommy's instructions, Del drove around to the back of the building. At this late hour, the front doors were locked, and one had to enter through the kitchen.

The rear parking area was crowded with employees' cars and more than forty sizable delivery trucks.

"I was picturing a mom-and-pop bakery," Del said.

"Yeah, that's what it was twenty years ago. They still have two retail outlets, but from here they supply breads and pastries to lots of markets and restaurants, and not just Vietnamese restaurants, in Orange County and up in L.A. too."

"It's a little empire," she said as she parked the

van, doused the headlights, and switched off the engine.

"Even though it's gotten this big, they keep up the quality—which is why they've grown in the first place."

"You sound proud of them."

"I am."

"Then why aren't you in the family business too?"

"I couldn't breathe."

"The heat of the ovens, you mean?"

"No."

"An allergy to wheat flour?"

He sighed. "I wish. That would have made it easy to opt out. But the problem was . . . too much tradition."

"You wanted to try radical new approaches to baking?"

He laughed softly. "I like you, Del."

"Likewise, tofu boy."

"Even if you are a little crazy."

"I'm the sanest person you know."

"It was family. Vietnamese families are sometimes so tightly bound, so structured, the parents so strict, traditions so . . . so like chains."

"But you miss it too."

"Not really."

"Yes, you do," she insisted. "There's a deep sadness in you. A part of you is lost."

"Not lost."

"Definitely."

"Well, maybe that's what growing up is all about—losing parts of yourself so you can become something bigger, different, better."

She said, "The thing from inside the doll is becoming bigger and different too."

"Your point?"

"Different isn't always better."

Tommy met her gaze. In the dim light, her blue eyes were so dark that they might as well have been black, and they were even less readable than usual.

He said, "If I hadn't found a different way, one that worked for me, I would have died inside—more than I have by losing some degree of connection with the family."

"Then you did the right thing."

"Whether it was or not, I did it, and it's done."

"The distance between you and them is a gap, not a gulf. You can bridge it."

"Never quite," he disagreed.

"In fact, it's no distance at all compared to the light-years we've all come from the Big Bang, all the billions of miles we've crossed since we were just primal matter."

"Don't go strange on me again, Del."

"What strange?"

"I'm the Asian here. If anyone's supposed to be inscrutable, it's me."

"Sometimes," Deliverance Payne said, "you listen but you just don't hear."

"That's what keeps me sane."

"That's what gets you in trouble."

"Come on, let's go see my brother."

As they hurried through the rain, between two rows of delivery trucks, Del said, "How do you expect Gi to be able to help you?"

"He's had to deal with the gangs, so he knows about them."

"Gangs?"

"Cheap Boys. Natoma Boys. Their kind."

The New World Saigon Bakery operated in three eight-hour shifts. From eight in the morning until four in the afternoon, Tommy's father served as the shift manager while also conducting corporate business from his front office. From four o'clock until midnight, the oldest of the Phan brothers, Ton That, was the chief baker and the shift manager, and from midnight until eight in the morning, Gi Minh filled those same positions.

Organized gangs, intent on extortion, were active around the clock. But when they used sabotage to get their way, they preferred the cover of deep darkness, which meant that Gi, by virtue of running the graveyard shift, had been on duty during some of the nastier confrontations.

For years, all three men had worked seven days a week, a full fifty-six hours each, because most of the bakery's customers needed fresh merchandise on a daily basis. When one of them needed to have a weekend off, the other two split his time between them and worked sixty-four-hour weeks without complaint. Vietnamese-Americans with an entrepreneurial bent were among the most industrious people in the country and could never be faulted for failing to carry their own weight. Sometimes, however, Tommy wondered how many of Ton and Gi's generation—former refugees, boat children highly motivated to succeed by early memories of poverty and terror in Southeast Asia—would live long enough to retire and enjoy the peace that they had struggled so hard to earn.

The family was finally training a cousin—the American-born son of Tommy's mother's younger sister—to serve as a shift manager on a rotating basis that would allow everyone at the management level to work approximately forty-hour weeks and, at last, have normal lives. They had resisted bringing in the cousin, because for too long they had stubbornly waited for Tommy to return to the fold and take the job himself.

Tommy suspected that his parents had believed he'd eventually be overwhelmed with guilt as he watched his father and brothers working themselves half to death to keep all the principal management positions in the immediate family. Indeed, he had lived with such guilt that he'd had dreams in which he'd been behind the wheel of a car with his father and brothers as passengers, and he'd recklessly driven it off a high cliff, killing them all while he miraculously survived. Dreams in which he had been flying a plane filled with his family, had crashed, and had walked away as the sole survivor, his clothes red with their blood. Dreams in which a whirlpool sucked down their small boat at night on the South China Sea, drowning everyone but the youngest and most thoughtless of all the Phans, he himself, the son who was sharper than a serpent's tooth. He had learned to live with the guilt, however, and to resist the urge to give up his dream of being a writer.

Now, as he and Del stepped through the back door of the New World Saigon Bakery, Tommy was conflicted. Simultaneously he felt at home yet on dangerous ground.

The air was redolent of baking bread, brown sugar, cinnamon, baker's cheese, bitter chocolate, and other tantalizing aromas less easily identifiable in the fragrant mélange. This was the smell of his childhood, and it plunged him into a sensory river of wonderful memories, torrents of images from the past. This was also the smell of the future that he had firmly rejected, however, and underneath the mouthwatering savor, Tommy detected a cloying sweetness that, by virtue of its very intensity, would in time sour the appetite, nauseate, and leave the tongue capable of detecting only bitterness in any flavor.

Approximately forty employees in white uniforms and white caps were hard at work in the large main room—pastry chefs, bread bakers, assistant bakers, clean-up boys—amid the assembly tables, dough-mixing machines, cooktops, and ovens. The whir of mixer blades, the clink-clank of spoons and metal spatulas, the scrape-rattle of pans and cookie sheets being slid across baking racks, the muffled roar of gas flames in the hollow steel shells of the minimally insulated commercial ovens: This noise was music to Tommy, although like everything else about the place, it had two conflicting qualities—a cheerful and engaging melody, but an ominous underlying rhythm.

The hot air immediately chased away the chill of the night and the rain. But almost at once, Tommy felt that the air was too hot to breathe comfortably.

"Which one's your brother?" Del asked.

"He's probably in the shift manager's office." Tommy realized that Del had removed the Santa hat. "Thanks for not wearing the stupid hat."

She withdrew it from a pocket in her leather jacket. "I only took it off so the rain wouldn't ruin it."

"Please don't wear it, don't embarrass me," he said.

"You have no sense of style."

"Please. I want my brother to take me seriously."

"Doesn't your brother believe in Santa?"

"Please. My family are very serious people."

"Please, please," she mocked him, but teasingly and without malice. "Maybe they should have become morticians instead of bakers."

Tommy expected her to don the frivolous red flannel chapeau with characteristic defiance, but she crammed it back into her jacket pocket.

"Thank you," he said gratefully.

"Take me to the somber and humorless Gi Minh Phan, infamous anti-Santa activist."

Tommy led her along one side of the main room, between the equipment-packed baking floor and the stainless-steel doors to a series of coolers and storerooms. The place was brightly lighted with banks of suspended fluorescent fixtures, and everything was nearly as well scrubbed as a hospital surgery.

He had not visited the bakery in at least four years, during which time its business had grown, so he didn't recognize many of the employees on the graveyard shift. They all appeared to be Vietnamese, and the great majority were men. Most of them were concentrating so intensely on their work that they didn't notice they had visitors.

The few who looked up tended to focus on Del Payne and give Tommy only scant attention. Even rain-soaked—again—and bedraggled, she was an attractive woman. In her wet and clinging white uniform and black leather jacket, she possessed an irresistible air of mystery.

He was glad she wasn't wearing the Santa hat. That would have been too much novelty to ignore, even for a roomful of industrious Vietnamese fixated on their work. Everyone would have been staring at her.

The manager's office was in the right front corner of the room, elevated four steps above the main floor. Two walls were glass, so the shift boss could see the entire bakery without getting up from his desk.

More often than not, Gi would have been on the floor, working elbow to elbow with the bakers and their apprentices. At the moment, however, he was at his computer, with his back to the glass door at the top of the steps.

Judging by the tables of data on the monitor, Tommy figured his brother was putting together a computer model of the chemistry of a new recipe. Evidently some pastry hadn't been coming out of the ovens as it should, and they hadn't been able to identify the problem on the floor, with sheer baker's instinct.

Gi didn't turn around when Tommy and Del entered, closing the door behind them. "Minute," he said, and his fingers flew across the computer keyboard.

Del nudged Tommy with one elbow and showed him the red flannel cap, half out of her pocket.

He scowled.

She grinned and put the cap away.

When Gi finished typing, he spun around in his chair, expecting to see an employee, and gaped wide-eyed at his brother. "Tommy!"

Unlike their brother Ton, Gi Minh was willing to use Tommy's American name.

"Surprise," Tommy said.

Gi rose from his chair, a smile breaking across his face, but then he registered that the person with Tommy wasn't an employee, either. As he turned his full attention to Del, his smile froze.

"Merry Christmas," Del said.

Tommy wanted to tape her mouth shut, not because her greeting was completely off the wall—

after all, Christmas was only seven weeks away, and supermarkets were already selling decorations—but because she almost made him laugh, and laughter was not going to help him convince Gi of the seriousness of their plight.

"Gi," Tommy said, "I would like you to meet a friend of mine. Miss Del Payne."

Gi inclined his head politely toward her, and she held out her hand, and Gi took it after only a brief hesitation. "Miss Payne."

"Charmed," she said.

"You're terribly wet," Gi told her.

"Yes. I like it," Del said.

"Excuse me?"

"Invigorating," she said. "After the first hour of a storm, the falling rain has scrubbed all the pollution from the air, and the water is so pure, so healthy, good for the skin."

"Yes," Gi said, looking dazed.

"Good for the hair too."

Tommy thought, *Please, God, stop her from warning him about prostate cancer.*

At five-feet-seven, Gi was three inches shorter than Tommy, and though as physically trim as his brother, he had a round face utterly unlike Tommy's. When he smiled, he resembled Buddha, and as a child he had been called "little Buddha" by certain members of the family.

His smile, though stiff, remained on his face until he let go of Del's hand and looked down at the puddles of rainwater both she and Tommy were leaving on his office floor. When he raised his gaze and met Tommy's eyes, he wasn't smiling any more, and he didn't look anything at all like Buddha.

Tommy wanted to hug his brother. He suspected that Gi would return his embrace, after a moment of stiffness. Yet neither of them was able to display affection first—perhaps because they both feared rejection.

Before Gi could speak, Tommy hurriedly said, "Brother, I need your advice."

"My advice?" Gi's stare was disconcertingly direct. "My advice hasn't meant much to you for years."

"I'm in deep trouble."

Gi glanced at Del.

She said, "I'm not the trouble."

Clearly, Gi doubted that assertion.

"In fact," Tommy said, "she saved my life earlier tonight."

Gi's face remained clouded.

Beginning to worry that he was not going to be able to make this connection, Tommy found himself babbling: "Really, she did, she saved my life, just put herself on the line for me, a total stranger, got her van bashed up because of me, she's the reason I'm even standing here, so I'd appreciate if you'd invite us to sit down and—"

"Total stranger?" Gi asked.

Tommy had been plunging forward so rapidly that he had lost track of what he had said, and he didn't understand his brother's reaction. "Huh?"

"Total stranger?" Gi repeated.

"Well, yes, up to an hour and a half ago, and *still* she put her life on the line—"

"He means," Del explained to Tommy, "that he thought I was your girlfriend."

Tommy felt a blush, as hot as oven steel, rising in his face.

Gi's somber expression brightened slightly at the prospect that this was *not* the long-anticipated blonde who would break Mama Phan's heart and divide the family forever. If Del was not dating Tommy, then there was still a chance that the youngest and most rebellious of the Phan boys would one day do the right thing after all and take a lovely Vietnamese girl as his wife.

"I'm not his girlfriend," Del said to Gi.

Gi appeared willing to be convinced.

Del said, "We've never dated. In fact, considering that he doesn't like my taste in hats, I don't see how we ever *could* date. I couldn't go out with any man who was critical of my taste in hats. A girl has to draw the line somewhere."

"Hats?" Gi said, confused.

"Please," Tommy said, speaking as much to Del as to Gi, "can we just sit down and talk about this?"

"About what?" Gi asked.

"About someone trying to kill me, that's what!"

Stunned, Gi Minh Phan sat with his back to his computer. With a wave of his hand, he indicated the two chairs on the other side of his desk.

Tommy and Del sat, and Tommy said, "I think I'm in trouble with a Vietnamese gang."

"Which?" Gi asked.

"I don't know. Can't figure it out. Neither can Sal Delario, my friend at the newspaper, and he's an expert on the gangs. I'm hoping you'll recognize their methods when I tell you what they've done."

Gi was wearing a white shirt. He unbuttoned the left cuff, rolled up the sleeve, and showed Del the underside of his muscular forearm, which bore a long ugly red scar.

"Thirty-eight stitches," Gi told her.

"How awful," she said, no longer flippant, genuinely concerned.

"These worthless scum creep around, saying you have to pay them to stay in business, insurance money, and if you don't, then you and your employees might get hurt, have an accident, or some machinery could break down, or your place could catch fire some night."

"The police—"

"They do what they can—which often amounts to nothing. And if you pay the gangs what they ask, they'll want more, and more, and more still, like politicians, until one day you wind up making less out of your business than *they* do. So one night they came around, ten of them, those who call themselves the Fast Boys, all carrying knives and crowbars, cut our phone lines so we couldn't call the cops, figuring they could just walk through the place and smash

things while we would run and hide. But we surprised them, let me tell you, and some of us got hurt,
but the gang boys got hurt worse. A lot of them were
born here in the States, and they think they're tough,
but they don't know suffering. They don't know
what *tough* means."

Able to repress her true nature no longer, Del
couldn't resist saying, "It *never* pays to go up
against a bunch of angry bakers."

"Well, the Fast Boys know that now," Gi said with
utmost seriousness.

To Del, Tommy said, "Gi was fourteen when we
escaped Vietnam. After the fall of Saigon, the communists believed that young males, teenagers, were
potential counterrevolutionaries, the most dangerous
citizens to the new regime. Gi and Ton—that's my
oldest brother—were arrested a few times and held a
week or two each time for questioning about supposed anti-communist activities. *Questioning* was a
euphemism for *torture*."

"At fourteen?" Del said, appalled.

Gi shrugged. "I was tortured when I was twelve.
Ton That, my brother, was fourteen the first time."

"The police let them go each time," Tommy continued, "—but then my father heard from a reliable
source that Gi and Ton were scheduled to be arrested
and sent upcountry to a reeducation camp. Slave
labor and indoctrination. We put to sea in a boat with
thirty other people the night before they would have
been taken away."

"Some of our employees are older than me," said Gi. "They went through much worse . . . back home."

Del turned in her chair to look out at the men on the bakery floor, all of whom appeared deceptively ordinary in their white caps and white uniforms. "Nothing's ever what it seems," she said softly, thoughtfully.

To Tommy, Gi said, "Why would the gangs be after you?"

"Maybe something I wrote when I still worked at the newspaper."

"They don't read."

"But that has to be it. There's no other reason."

"The more you write about how bad they are, the more they would like it if they *did* read it," Gi said, still doubtful. "They want the bad-boy image. They thrive on it. So what have they done to you?"

Tommy glanced at Del.

She rolled her eyes.

Although Tommy had intended to tell Gi every incredible detail of the night's bizarre events, he was suddenly reluctant to risk his brother's disbelief and scorn.

Gi was far less of a traditionalist and more under-standing than Ton or their parents. He might even have envied Tommy's bold embrace of all things American and, years ago, might have secretly har-bored similar dreams for himself. Nevertheless, on another level, faithful son in the fullest Vietnamese sense, he disapproved of the path that Tommy had taken. Even to Gi, choosing self over family was ultimately an unforgivable weakness, and his respect for his younger brother had declined steadily in recent years.

Now Tommy was surprised by how desperately he wanted to avoid sinking further in Gi's esteem. He had thought that he'd learned to live with his family's disapproval, that they could not hurt him any more by reminding him how much he had disappointed them, and that what they thought of him was less important than what kind of person he knew himself to be. But he was wrong. He still yearned for their approval and was panicky at the prospect of Gi's dismissing the tale of the doll-thing as the ravings of a drug-addled mind.

Family was the source of all blessings—and the home of all sadness. If that wasn't a Vietnamese saying, it should have been.

He might have risked speaking of the demon anyway, if he had come here alone. But Del Payne's presence already prejudiced Gi against him.

Therefore, Tommy thought carefully before he spoke, and then he said, "Gi, have you ever heard of the Black Hand?"

Gi looked at Tommy's hands, as if expecting to be told that he had contracted some hideous venereal disease affecting the upper extremities, if not from this blonde-who-was-nearly-a-stranger, then from some other blonde whom he knew far better.

"*La Mano Nera,*" Tommy said. "The Black Hand. It was a secret Mafia organization of blackmailers and assassins. When they marked you for murder, they sometimes warned you by sending a white piece of paper with the black-ink imprint of a hand. Just to scare the crap out of you and make you suffer for a while before they finally popped you."

"This is ridiculous detective-story stuff," Gi said flatly, rolling down the sleeve of his white shirt and buttoning the cuff.

"No, it's true."

"Fast Boys, Cheap Boys, Natoma Boys, the Frogmen, their types—they don't send a black hand first," Gi assured him.

"No, I realize they don't. But have you ever heard of any gang that sends ... something else as a warning?"

"What else?"

Tommy hesitated, squirmed in his chair. "Well ... say, like a doll."

Frowning, Gi said, "Doll?"

"A rag doll."

Gi looked at Del for illumination.

"Ugly little rag doll," she said.

"With a message on a piece of paper pinned to its hand," Tommy explained.

"What was the message?"

"I don't know. It was written in Vietnamese."

"You once could read Vietnamese," Gi reminded him in a tone of voice thick with disapproval.

"When I was little," Tommy agreed. "Not now."

"Let me see this doll," Gi said.

"It's . . . well, I don't have it now. But I have the note."

For a moment Tommy couldn't recall where he had stashed the message, and he reached for his wallet. Remembering, he slipped two fingers into the pocket of his flannel shirt and withdrew the sodden note, dismayed by its condition.

Fortunately, the parchmentlike paper had a high oil content, which prevented it from dissolving entirely into mush. When Tommy carefully unfolded it, he saw that the three columns of ideograms were still visible, though badly faded and smeared.

Gi accepted the note and held it in his cupped palm as if he were providing a perch for a weary and delicate butterfly. "The ink has run."

"You can't read it?"

"Not easily. So many ideograms are alike but with one small difference. Not like English letters, words. Each small difference in the stroke of the pen can create a whole new meaning. I'd have to dry this out, use a magnifying glass, study it."

Leaning forward in his chair, Tommy said, "How long to decipher it—if you can?"

"A couple of hours—if I can." Gi raised his gaze from the note. "You haven't told me what they did to you."

"Broke into my house, vandalized it. Later . . . ran me off the road, and the car rolled twice."

"You weren't hurt?"

"I'll be sore as hell in the morning, but I got out of the car without a cut."

"How did this woman save your life?"

"Del," said Del.

Gi said, "Excuse me?"

"My name is Del."

"Yes," said Gi. To Tommy, he said, "How did this woman save your life?"

"I got out of the car just in time, before it caught fire. Then . . . they were coming after me and—"

"They? These gangsters?"

"Yes," Tommy lied, certain that every deception was transparent to Gi Minh. "They chased me, and I ran, and just when they might have nailed me for good, Del here pulled up in her van and got me out of there."

"You haven't gone to the police?"

"No. They can't protect me."

Gi nodded, not in the least surprised. Like most Vietnamese of his generation, he did not fully trust the police even here in America. In their homeland, before the fall of Saigon, the police had been mostly corrupt, and after the communist takeover, they had been worse—sadistic torturers and murderers licensed by the regime to commit any atrocity. Even more than two decades later, and half a world away from that troubled land, Gi was wary of all uniformed authorities.

"There's a deadline," Tommy said, "so it's really important that you figure out what that note says as soon as possible."

"Deadline?"

"Whoever sent the doll also sent a message to me by computer. It said, 'The deadline is dawn. Ticktock.' "

"Gangsters using computers?" Gi said disbelievingly.

"Everyone does these days," said Del.

Tommy said, "They mean to get me before sunrise . . . and from what I've seen so far, they'll stop at nothing to keep to that timetable."

"Well," Gi said, "you can stay here while I work on the message, until we figure this out—what it is they want, or why they're out to get you. Meanwhile, no one can hurt you here, not with all those men down on the floor to stand with you."

Tommy shook his head and rose from his chair. "I don't want to draw these . . . these gangsters here." Del got to her feet as well and moved to his side. "I don't want to cause you trouble, Gi."

"We can handle them like before."

Tommy was sure that the pastry and bread artists of New World Saigon Bakery could hold their own against any group of human thugs. But if it chose to reveal itself in order to get at Tommy, the demon-from-the-doll would be as unfazed by bakers as it was by bullets. It would cut through them like a buzz saw through a wedding cake—especially if it had grown and had continued its apparent evolution into ever more predatory forms. He didn't want anyone to be harmed because of him.

He said, "Thank you, Gi. But I think I'd better

keep moving, so they can't find me. I'll call you in a couple of hours to see if you've been able to translate the note."

Gi rose from his chair but did not step out from behind his desk. "You came for advice, you said, not just to have this message translated. Well, my advice is . . . you're safer trusting in family."

"I do trust in you, Gi."

"But you trust a stranger more," Gi said pointedly, although he did not look at Del.

"It saddens me to hear you say that, Gi."

"It saddens me to have to say it," his brother replied.

Neither of them moved one inch toward the other, though Tommy sensed a yearning that matched his own.

Gi's face was worse than angry, worse than hard. It was placid, almost serene, as if Tommy could no longer touch his heart for better or worse.

"I'll call you," Tommy finally said, "in a couple hours."

He and Del left the office and went down the steps into the enormous bakery.

Tommy felt profoundly confused, petty, stubborn, stupid, guilty, and miserable—all emotions that the legendary private detective, Chip Nguyen, had never felt, had never been *capable* of feeling.

The aromas of chocolate, cinnamon, brown sugar, nutmeg, yeasty baking bread, and hot lemon icing were no longer appealing. Indeed, he was half sickened by the stench. Tonight the smell of the bakery was the smell of loss and loneliness and foolish pride.

As he and Del passed the coolers and storerooms, heading toward the back of the building and the door through which they had entered, she said, "Well, thanks for preparing me."

"For what?"

"For the glorious reception I received."

"I told you how it was with me and the family."

"You made it sound strained between you and them. It's more like the Capulets and Montagues and the Hatfields and McCoys all thrown together and named Phan."

"It's not that dramatic," he disagreed.

"Seemed pretty dramatic to me, quiet but dramatic, like both of you were ticking and liable to explode at any second."

Halfway across the room from the shift manager's office, Tommy stopped, turned, and looked back.

Gi was standing at one of the big windows in that managerial roost, watching them.

Tommy hesitated, raised a hand, and waved. When Gi didn't return the wave, the bakery stench seemed to intensify, and Tommy walked faster toward the rear exit.

Lengthening her stride to keep up with him, Del Payne said, "He thinks I'm the whore of Babylon."

"He does not."

"Yes, he does. He disapproves of me even if I did

save your life. Severely disapproves. He thinks I'm
a succubus, a wicked white temptress who's leading
you straight into the fiery pit of eternal damnation."

"Well, you're lucky. Just imagine what he'd think
if you'd worn the Santa hat."

"I'm glad to see you still have a sense of humor
about this family stuff."

"I don't," he said gruffly.

"What if I was?" she asked.

"Was what?"

"A wicked white temptress."

"What are you talking about?"

They reached the rear exit, but she put a hand on
Tommy's arm, halting him before he could open the
door. "Would you be tempted?"

"You *are* nuts."

She pretended to pout as if hurt. "That's not as
flattering a response as I'd hoped for."

"Have you forgotten the issue here?"

"What issue is that?" she asked.

Exasperated, he said, "Staying alive."

"Sure, sure. The doll snake rat-quick little monster thing. But listen, Tommy, you're a pretty attractive guy in spite of all your glowering, all your deep
angst, all your playing at being Mr. Mysterious East.
A girl could fall for you—but if she did, would you
be available?"

"Not if I'm dead."

She smiled. "That's a definite *yes*."

He closed his eyes and counted to ten.

When Tommy was at four, Del said, "What're you doing?"

"Counting to ten."

"Why?"

"To calm down."

"What number are you at?"

"Six."

"What number now?"

"Seven."

"What number now?"

"Eight."

When he opened his eyes, she was still smiling. "I *do* excite you, don't I?"

"You *scare* me."

"Why scare?"

"Because how are we going to manage to keep this supernatural *thing* from killing us if you keep acting this way?"

"What way?"

He took a deep breath, started to speak, decided there was no adequate reply, exhaled explosively, and said only, "Have you ever been in an institution?"

"Does the post office count?"

Muttering a curse in Vietnamese, the first words he had spoken in that language in at least twenty years, Tommy pushed open the metal door. He stepped into the skirling wind and the rain—and he immediately regretted doing so. In the bakery heat, he had gotten warm for the first time since scrambling out of the wrecked Corvette, and his clothes had begun to dry. Now he was instantly chilled to the marrow once more.

Del followed him into the storm, as ebullient as any child. "Hey, did you ever see Gene Kelly in *Singin' in the Rain?*"

"Don't start dancing," he warned.

"You need to be more spontaneous, Tommy."

"I'm very spontaneous," he said, tucking his head down to keep the rain out of his eyes. He bent into the wind and headed toward the battered, mural-bright van, which stood under a tall lamppost.

"You're about as spontaneous as a rock."

Splashing through ankle-deep puddles, shivering, poised on the slippery slope of self-pity, he didn't bother to answer.

"Tommy, wait," she said, and grabbed his arm again.

Spinning to face her, cold and wet and impatient, he demanded, "Now what?"

"It's here."

"Huh?"

No longer flirtatious or flippant, as alert as a deer scenting a wolf in the underbrush, she stared past Tommy: "*It.*"

He followed the direction of her gaze. "Where?"

"In the van. Waiting for us in the van."

FIVE

Oil-black rain briefly blazed as bright as molten gold, down through lamplight, drizzled over the van, and then puddled black again around the tires.

"Where?" Tommy asked, blinking rain out of his eyes, studying the murkiness beyond the van's windshield, searching for some sign of the demon. "I don't see it."

"Neither do I," she said. "But it's there, all right, in the van. I sense it."

"You're psychic all of a sudden?"

"Not all of a sudden," she said, her voice thickening, as though sleep was overcoming her. "I've always had strong intuition, very reliable."

Thirty feet away, the Ford van was exactly as it had been when they left it to go into the bakery. Tommy didn't feel what Del felt. He perceived no sinister aura around the vehicle.

He looked at Del as she stared intently at the van. Rain streamed down her face, dripped off the end of her nose and the point of her chin. Her eyes weren't blinking, and she seemed to be sinking into a trance. Her lips began to move, as though she were speaking, but no sound escaped her.

"Del?"

After a moment her silently moving lips produced

a wordless murmur, and then she began to whisper: "Waiting . . . cold as ice . . . dark inside . . . a dark cold thing . . . ticktock . . . ticktock . . ."

He shifted his attention to the van again, and now it seemed to loom as ominously as a hearse. Del's fear had infected him, and his heart raced as he was overwhelmed by a sense of impending assault.

The woman's whisper faded into the susurration of the raindrops dissolving against the puddled pavement. Tommy leaned closer. Her voice was hypnotically portentous, and he didn't want to miss anything that she said.

". . . ticktock . . . so much bigger now . . . snake's blood and river mud . . . blind eyes see . . . dead heart beats . . . a need . . . a need . . . a need to feed . . ."

Tommy wasn't sure which frightened him more at the moment: the van and the utterly alien creature that might be crouching within it—or this peculiar woman.

Abruptly she emerged from her mesmeric state. "We have to get out of here. Let's take one of these cars."

"An employee's car?"

She was already moving away from the van, among the more than thirty vehicles that belonged to the workers at New World Saigon Bakery.

Glancing warily back at the van, Tommy hurried to keep up with her. "We can't do that."

"Sure we can."

"It's stealing."

"It's survival," she said, trying the door of a blue Chevrolet, which was locked.

"Let's go back into the bakery."

"The deadline is dawn, remember?" she said, moving on to a white Honda. "It won't wait forever. It'll come in after us."

She opened the driver's door of the Honda, and the dome light came on, and she slipped in behind the steering wheel. No keys dangled in the ignition, so she searched under the seat with one hand to see if the owner had left them there.

Standing at the open door of the Honda, Tommy said, "Then let's just walk out of here."

"We wouldn't get far on foot before it caught us. I'm going to have to hot-wire this crate."

Watching as Del groped blindly for the ignition wires under the dashboard, Tommy said, "You can't do this."

"Keep a watch on my Ford."

He glanced over his shoulder. "What am I looking for?"

"Movement, a strange shadow, anything," she said nervously. "We're running out of time. Don't you sense it?"

Except for the wind-driven rain, the night was still around Del's van.

"Come on, come on," Del muttered to herself, fumbling with the wires, and then the Honda engine caught, revved.

Tommy's stomach turned over at the sound, for he

seemed to be sliding ever faster down a greased
slope to destruction—if not at the hands of the
demon, then by his own actions.

"Hurry, get in," Del said as she released the
handbrake.

"This is car theft," he argued.

"I'm leaving whether you get in or not."

"We could go to jail."

She pulled the driver's door shut, forcing him to
step back, out of the way.

Under the tall sodium-vapor lamp, the silent van
appeared to be deserted. All the doors remained
closed. The most remarkable thing about it was the
Art Deco mural. Already its ominous aura had
faded.

Tommy had allowed himself to be infected by
Del's hysteria. The thing to do now was get control
of himself, walk over to the van, and show her that it
was safe.

Del put the Honda in gear and drove forward.

Quickly stepping in front of the car, slapping his
palms down flat on the hood, Tommy blocked her
way, forcing her to stop. "No. Wait, wait."

She shifted into reverse and started to back out of
the parking space.

Tommy ran around to the passenger's side, caught
up with the car, pulled open the door, and jumped
inside. "Will you just wait a second, for God's
sake?"

"No," she said, braking and shifting out of reverse.

As she tramped the accelerator, the car shot forward across the parking lot, and the door beside Tommy was flung shut.

They were briefly blinded by the rain until Del found the switch for the windshield wipers.

"You're not thinking this through," he argued.

"I know what I'm doing."

The engine screamed, and great plumes of water sprayed up from the tires.

"What if the cops stop us?" Tommy worried.

"They won't."

"They will if you keep driving like this."

At the end of the large building, before turning the corner, Del braked hard. The car shrieked, fishtailing as it slid to a full stop.

Studying her rearview mirror, she said, "Look back."

Tommy turned in his seat. "What?"

"The van."

Under the tall lamppost, falling rain danced on empty pavement.

For a moment Tommy thought he was looking in the wrong place. There were three other lampposts behind the bakery. But the van was not under any of those, either.

"Where'd it go?" he asked.

"Maybe out to the alley, or maybe around the other side of the building, or maybe it's just behind those delivery trucks. I can't figure why it didn't come straight after us."

She drove forward, around the corner, along the side of the bakery, toward the front.

Bewildered, Tommy said, "But who's driving it?"

"Not a who. A what."

"That's ridiculous," he said.

"It's a lot bigger now."

"It would have to be. But still—"

"It's changed."

"And it got a driver's license, huh?"

"It's very different from what you've seen before."

"Yeah? What's it like now?"

"I don't know. I didn't see it."

"Intuition again?"

"Yeah. I just know . . . it's different."

Tommy tried to envision a monstrous entity, something like one of the ancient gods from an old H. P. Lovecraft story, with a bulbous skull, a series of mean little scarlet eyes across its forehead, a sucking hole where the nose should be, and a wicked mouth surrounded by a ring of writhing tentacles, comfortably ensconced behind the steering wheel of the van, fumbling with a clumsy tentacle at the heater controls, punching the radio selector buttons in search of some old-fashioned rock-'n'-roll, and checking the glove box to see if it could find any breath mints.

"Ridiculous," he repeated.

"Better belt up," she said. "We might be in for a bumpy ride."

As Tommy buckled the safety harness across his chest, Del drove speedily but warily from the shadow of the bakery and across the front parking lot. Clearly, she expected the Art Deco van to bullet out of the night and crash into them.

A debris-clogged storm drain had allowed a small lake to form at the exit from the lot. Leaves and paper litter swirled across the choppy surface.

Del slowed and turned right into the street, through the dirty water. Theirs was the only vehicle in sight.

"Where did it go?" Del Payne wondered. "Why the hell isn't it following us?"

Tommy checked his luminous wristwatch. Eleven minutes after one o'clock.

Del said, "I don't like this."

Ticktock.

Half a mile from the New World Saigon Bakery, in the stolen Honda, Tommy broke a three-block silence. "Where did you learn to hot-wire a car?"

"My mom taught me."

"Your mom."

"She's cool."

"The one who likes speed, races stock cars and motorcycles."

"Yep. That's the one. The only mom I've got."

"What is she—a getaway driver for the mob?"

"In her youth, she was a ballet dancer."

"Of course. All ballet dancers can hot-wire a car."

"Not all of them," Del disagreed.

"After she was a ballet dancer . . . ?"

"She married Daddy."

"And what does he do?"

Checking the rearview mirror for any sign of a pursuer, Del said, "Daddy plays poker with the angels."

"You're losing me again."

"He died when I was ten."

Tommy regretted the sarcastic tone he had adopted. He felt coarse and insensitive. Chastened, he said, "I'm sorry. That's tough. Only ten."

"Mom shot him."

Numbly, he said, "Your mother the ballerina."

"Ex-ballerina by then."

"She shot him?"

"Well, he asked her to."

Tommy nodded, feeling stupid for having regretted his sarcasm. He slipped comfortably back into it: "Of course he did."

"She couldn't refuse."

"It's a marital obligation in your religion, is it? To kill one's spouse upon request?"

"He was dying of cancer," Del said.

Tommy felt chastened again. "Jesus, I'm sorry."

"Pancreatic cancer, one of the most vicious."

"You poor kid."

They were no longer in an industrial district. The broad avenue was lined with commercial enterprises. Beauty salons. Video stores. Discount electronics and discount furniture and discount glassware stores. Except for an occasional 7-Eleven or twenty-four-hour coffee shop, the businesses were closed and dark.

Del said, "When the pain got so bad Daddy

couldn't concentrate on the cards any more, he was ready to go. He loved cards, and without them he just didn't feel he had any purpose."

"Cards?"

"I told you—Daddy was a professional poker player."

"No, you said he now plays poker with the angels."

"Well, why would he be playing poker with them if he wasn't a professional poker player?"

"Point taken," Tommy said, because sometimes he was smart enough to know when he had been defeated.

"Daddy traveled all over the country, playing in high-stakes games, most illegal, though he played a lot of legal games in Vegas too. In fact, he twice won the World Championship of Poker. Mom and I went with him everywhere, so by the time I was ten, I'd seen most of this country three times or more."

Wishing he could just keep his mouth shut but too fascinated to resist, Tommy said, "So your mother shot him, huh?"

"He was in the hospital, pretty bad by then, and he knew he was never getting out."

"She shot him right there in the hospital?"

"She put the muzzle of the gun against his chest, positioned it very carefully right over his heart, and Daddy told her he loved her more than any man had ever loved a woman before, and she said she loved him and would see him on the Other Side, and then she pulled the trigger, and he died instantly."

Aghast, Tommy said, "You weren't there at the time, were you?"

"Heavens, no. What kind of person do you think Mom is? She'd never have put me through something like that."

"I'm sorry. I should have—"

"She told me all about it an hour later, before the cops came by the house to arrest her, and she gave me the expended cartridge from the round that killed him."

Del reached inside her wet uniform blouse and fished out a gold chain. The pendant suspended at the end of the chain was an empty brass shell casing.

"When I hold this," Del said, wrapping her hand around the shell casing, "I can feel the love—the *incredible* love—they had for each other. Isn't it the most romantic thing ever?"

"Ever," Tommy said.

She sighed and tucked the pendant inside her blouse once more. "If only Daddy hadn't gotten cancer until I was closer to puberty, then he wouldn't have had to die."

For a while Tommy struggled to understand that one, but at last he said, "Puberty?"

"Well, it wasn't to be. Fate is fate," she said cryptically.

Half a block ahead of them, on the far side of the wide street, a police cruiser was just starting to turn out of the westbound lane into the parking lot at an all-night diner.

"Cops," Tommy said, pointing.

"I see them."

"Better slow down."

"I'm really in a hurry to get back to my place."

"You're doing twenty over the speed limit."

"I'm worried about Scootie."

"We're in a stolen car," he reminded her.

They breezed past the police cruiser without slowing.

Tommy twisted in his seat to look through the back window.

"Don't worry about him," Del said. "He won't come after us."

The squad car had braked when they shot past it.

"Who's Scootie?" Tommy asked, still watching the patrol car behind them.

"I told you before. My dog. Don't you ever listen?"

After a hesitation, the squad car continued to pull into the parking lot at the diner. The lure of coffee and doughnuts was apparently stronger than the call of duty.

As Tommy let out a sigh of relief and faced front again, Del said, "Would you shoot me if I asked you to?"

"Absolutely."

She smiled at him. "You're so sweet."

"Did your mother go to jail?"

"Only until the trial was over."

"The jury acquitted?"

"Yeah. They deliberated only fourteen minutes, and they were all crying like babies when the foreman read the verdict. The judge was crying too, and the bailiff. There wasn't a dry eye in the courtroom."

"I'm not surprised," Tommy said. "After all, it's an extremely touching story." He wasn't sure whether he was being sarcastic or not. "Why are you worried about Scootie?"

"There's some weird *thing* driving around in my van, you know, so maybe it knows my address now and even knows how much I love my Scootie."

"You really think it stopped chasing us just so it could go kill your dog?"

She frowned. "You're saying that's unlikely?"

"It's *me* that's cursed, *me* that it's been sent to get."

Glancing at him disapprovingly, she said, "Well, look who's all of a sudden turned into Mr. Ego. You're not the center of the universe, you know."

"I am as far as this demon is concerned! I'm its whole reason for existence!"

"Whatever, I'm not taking any chances with my Scootie," she said stubbornly.

"He's safer at home than with us."

"He's safest with me."

She turned south on Harbor Boulevard. Even at that hour and in the rain, there was a steady flow of traffic.

"Anyway," she said, "as far as I can see, you don't

exactly have any clever plan for survival that we have to put into action right this minute."

"Just keep moving, I think. When we stop, it's easier for the thing to find us."

"You can't know that for sure."

"I have intuition too, you know."

"Yeah, but it's mostly bogus."

"It is not," he disagreed. "I'm very intuitive."

"Then why did you bring this devil doll into your house?"

"It *did* make me uneasy."

"Later, you thought you'd gotten away from your house clean. You didn't know the creature was hitching a ride in the Corvette's engine compartment."

"No one's intuition is *totally* reliable."

"Now, honey, face it. Back there at the bakery, you would've gotten in the van."

Tommy chose not to respond. With a computer—or even a pencil and paper—and enough time, he could have crafted a reply to refute her, to humble her with logic and penetrating insights and dazzling wit. But he had neither a computer nor (with dawn rolling inexorably toward them out of the now-black east) enough time, so he would have to spare her the punishing experience of his devastating verbal virtuosity.

Placatingly, Del said, "We'll stop at my place just long enough to pick up Scootie, and then we'll hit the road again, cruise around until it's time to call your brother and see if he's been able to translate the note."

*   *   *

Newport Harbor, home to one of the largest
armadas of private yachts in the world, was enclosed
on the north by the curve of the continental shoreline
and on the south by a three-mile-long peninsula that
extended west to east and separated the hundreds of
protected boat docks and moorings from the surges
of the Pacific.

The homes on the shoreline and on the five
islands within the harbor were among the priciest in
Southern California. Del lived not in a less expensive home on one of the landlocked blocks of
Balboa Peninsula, but in a sleek three-story contemporary house that faced the harbor.

As they approached the place, Tommy leaned forward, staring out of the windshield in astonishment.

Because she had left her garage-door opener in
the van, Del parked the stolen Honda on the street.
The police wouldn't be looking for it yet—not
until the shifts changed at the bakery.

Tommy continued to stare through the blurring rain
after Del switched off the windshield wipers. In the
burnishing glow of the landscape lighting that underlit
the queen palms, he could see that every corner of the
house was softly rounded. The patinated-copper windows were rectangular with radius corners, and the
white stucco was troweled so smoothly that it
appeared to be as slick as marble, especially when wet
with rain. It was less like a house than like a small,
gracefully designed cruise ship that had run aground.

"You live *here*?" he asked wonderingly.

"Yeah." She opened her door. "Come on. Scootie's wondering where I am. He's worried about me."

Tommy got out of the Honda and followed her through the rain to a gate at one side of the house, where she entered a series of numbers—the disarming code—into a security keypad.

"The rent must be astronomical," he said, dismayed to think that she might not be a renter at all but might be living here with the man who owned the place.

"No rent. No mortgage. It's mine," she said, unlocking the gate with keys that she had fished from her purse.

As he closed the heavy gate behind them, Tommy saw that it was made of geometric patinated-copper panels of different shapes and textures and depths. The resultant Art Deco pattern reminded him of the mural on her van.

Following her along a covered, pale-quartzite walkway in which flecks of mica glimmered like diamond chips under the light from the low path lamps, he said, "But this must've cost a fortune."

"Sure did," she said brightly.

The walkway led into a romantic courtyard paved with the same quartzite, sheltered by five more dramatically lighted queen palms, softened with beds of ferns, and filled with the scent of night-blooming jasmine.

Bewildered, he said, "I thought you were a waitress."

"I told you before—being a waitress is what I *do*. An artist is what I *am*."

"You sell your paintings?"

"Not yet."

"You didn't pay for this from tips."

"That's for sure," she agreed, but offered no explanation.

Lamps glowed warmly in one of the downstairs rooms facing onto the courtyard. As Tommy followed Del to the front door, those windows went dark.

"Wait," he whispered urgently. "The lights."

"It's okay."

"Maybe the thing got here ahead of us."

"No, that's just Scootie playing with me," she assured him.

"The dog can turn off the lights?"

She giggled. "Wait'll you see." She unlocked the front door and, stepping into the foyer, said, "Lights on."

Responding to her vocal command, the overhead fixture and two sconces glowed.

"If my cell phone wasn't in the van," she said, "I could've called ahead to the house computer and turned on any combination of lights, the spa, the music system, the TV. The place is totally auto-mated. I also had the software customized so Scootie can turn the lights on in any room with just one bark and turn them off with two."

"And you could train him to do that?" Tommy asked, closing the door behind him and engaging the thumb-turn deadbolt.

"Sure. Otherwise he never barks, so he can't confuse the system. Poor thing, he's here alone for hours at a time in the evening. He should be able to have it dark if he wants to nap—and light if he's feeling lonely or spooked."

Tommy had expected the dog to be waiting at the door, but it was not in sight. "Where is he?"

"Hiding," she said, putting her purse on a foyer table with a black granite top. "He wants me to find him."

"A dog that plays hide-and-seek?"

"Without hands, it's too frustrating to play Scrabble."

Tommy's wet shoes squished and squeaked on the honed-travertine floor. "We're making a mess."

"It's not Chernobyl."

"Huh?"

"It'll clean up."

At one end of the generous foyer, a door stood ajar. Del went to it, leaving wet shoe prints on the marble.

"Is my naughty little furball in the powder room?" she asked in an annoyingly cute, coddling tone of voice. "Hmmmm? Is my bad boy hiding from his mommie? Is my bad boy hiding in the powder room?"

She opened the door, manually switched on the lights, but the dog wasn't there.

"I didn't think so," she said, leading Tommy into the living room. "That was too easy. Though sometimes he knows easy works because it's not what I'm expecting. Lights on."

The large travertine-floored living room was furnished with J. Robert Scott sofas and chairs upholstered in platinum and gold fabrics, blond-finished tables in exotic woods, and bronze Art Deco lamps in the form of nymphs holding luminous crystal balls. The enormous Persian carpet boasted such an intricate design and was so softly colored, as if exquisitely faded by time, that it must have been an antique.

Del's vocal command had switched on mood lighting that was low enough to minimize reflection on the glass wall and allow Tommy to see outside to the patio and the boat dock. He also had a glimpse of rain-dimmed harbor lights.

Scootie was not in the living room. He wasn't in the study or the dining room, either.

Following Del through a swinging door, Tommy stepped into a large, stylish kitchen with clear-finished maple cabinets and black granite counter tops.

"Oh, him not here, either," Del said, cooing again as if talking to a baby. "Where could my Scootie-wootums be? Did him turn off the lights and quick-like-a-bunny run upstairs?"

Tommy was riveted by a wall clock with a green neon rim. It was 1:44 in the morning. Time was running out, so the demon was sure to be seeking them with increasing fury.

"Let's find the damn dog and get out of here quick," he said nervously.

Pointing to a tall narrow section of cabinetry next

to which Tommy was standing, Del said, "Get me the broom out of there, would you, please?"

"Broom?"

"It's the broom closet."

Tommy opened the door.

Squeezed into the broom closet was a huge midnight-black creature with teeth bared and fat pink tongue lolling, and Tommy bolted backward, slipped in his own wet shoe prints, and fell on his butt before he realized that it wasn't the demon leering out at him. It was a dog, an enormous black Labrador.

Del laughed delightedly and clapped her hands. "I *knew* you were in there, you naughty little furball!"

Scootie grinned out at them.

"I knew you'd give Tommy a good scare," she told the dog.

"Yeah, just what I needed," Tommy said, getting to his feet.

Panting, Scootie came out of the closet. The space was so narrow and the dog so large that it was like a cork coming out of a wine bottle, and Tommy half expected to hear a *pop*.

"How'd he get in there?" Tommy wondered.

Tail wagging furiously, Scootie went directly to Del, and she dropped to her knees so she could pet him and scratch behind his ears. "Him miss mommie, did him? Hmmmmm? Was him lonely, my fuzzy-wuzzy baby, my cutie Scootie?"

"He couldn't step in there and turn around," Tommy said. "Not enough room."

"He probably backed into it," Del said, hugging Scootie.

"Dogs don't back into things any more than motorcycles do. Besides, how did he get the door shut after he was in there?"

"It falls shut on its own," Del said.

Indeed, the broom-closet door had slowly closed after the Labrador had squeezed out of confinement into the kitchen.

"Okay, but how did he open it in the first place?" Tommy persisted.

"Pawed it open. He's clever."

"Why did you teach him this?"

"Teach him what?"

"To play hide-and-seek."

"Didn't teach him. He's always liked to do it."

"It's weird."

Del puckered her lips and made kissing sounds. The dog took the cue and began to lick her face.

"That's disgusting," Tommy said.

Giggling, Del said, "His mouth is cleaner than yours."

"I seriously doubt that."

As if quoting from a medical journal, she pulled back from the Labrador and said, "The chemical composition of a dog's saliva makes its mouth a hostile environment for the spectrum of bacteria that are harmful to people."

"Bullshit."

"It's true." To Scootie, she said, "He's just jealous, because *he* wants to lick my face."

Nonplussed, blushing, Tommy looked at the wall clock. "Okay, we have the dog, so let's get out of here."

Rising to her feet, heading out of the kitchen with the dog at her heels, Del said, "A waitress's uniform isn't suitable gear for a girl on the lam. Give me five minutes to change clothes, get into jeans and a sweater, and then we can split."

"No, listen, the longer we stay in one place, the quicker it's going to find us."

In a train—woman, dog, and man—they crossed the dining room as Del said, "Relax, Tommy. There's always enough time if you think there is."

"What's that mean?"

"Whatever you expect is what will be, so simply change your expectations."

"I don't know what that means, either."

"It means what it means," she said, enigmatic once more.

In the living room, he said, "Damn it, wait a minute!"

Del turned to look at him.

The dog turned to look at him.

Tommy sighed, gave up. "Okay, change your clothes. But hurry."

To the dog, Del said, "You stay here and get acquainted with Tuong Tommy." Then she went into the foyer and up the stairs.

Scootie cocked his head, studying Tommy as if he were a strange and amusing form of life never seen before.

"Your mouth is *not* cleaner than mine," Tommy said.

Scootie pricked one ear.

"You heard me," Tommy said.

He crossed the living room to the large glass sliding doors and gazed out toward the harbor. Most of the houses on the far shore were dark. Where dock and landscape lamps glowed, attenuated reflections of gold and red and silver light glimmered hundreds of feet across the black water.

After a few seconds, Tommy became aware of being watched—not by someone outside, but by someone inside.

He turned and saw the dog hiding behind the sofa, only its head revealed, observing him.

"I see you," Tommy said.

Scootie pulled his head back, out of sight.

Along one wall was a handsome entertainment center and library unit made from a wood with which Tommy was unfamiliar. He went to have a closer look, and he discovered that the beautiful grain was like rippled ribbons that appeared to undulate as he shifted his head from one side to the other.

He heard noises behind him and knew that Scootie was on the move, but he refused to be distracted from his examination of the entertainment center. The depth of the glossy lacquer finish was remarkable.

From elsewhere in the room came the sound of a fart.

"Bad dog," he said.

The sound repeated.

Finally Tommy turned.

Scootie was sitting on his hindquarters in one of the armchairs, staring at Tommy, both ears pricked, holding a large rubber hotdog in his mouth. When he bit down on the toy, it made that sound again. Perhaps the rubber hotdog had once produced a squeak or a whistle, but now only a repulsive flatulence issued from it.

Checking his watch, Tommy said, "Come on, Del."

Then he went to an armchair that directly faced that in which the dog sat, with only the coffee table between them. The chair was upholstered in leather, in a sealskin shade, so he didn't think his damp jeans would harm it.

He and Scootie stared at each other. The Labrador's eyes were dark and soulful.

"You're a strange dog," Tommy said.

Scootie bit the hotdog again, producing the blatty noise.

"That's annoying."

Scootie chomped on the toy.

"Don't."

Another faux fart.

"I'm warning you."

Again the dog bit the toy, again, and a third time.

"Don't make me take it away from you," Tommy said.

Scootie dropped the hotdog on the floor and barked twice.

The room was plunged into darkness, and Tommy was startled out of his chair before he remembered that two closely spaced barks was the signal that told the computer to switch off the lights.

Even as Tommy was bolting to his feet, Scootie was coming across the coffee table in the dark. The dog leaped, and Tommy was carried backward into the leather armchair.

The dog was all over him, chuffing in a friendly way, licking his face affectionately, licking his hands when he raised them to cover his face.

"Stop, damn it, stop, get off me."

Scootie scrambled off Tommy's lap, onto the floor—but seized the heel of his right shoe and began to worry at it, trying to gain possession of it.

Not wanting to kick at the mutt, afraid of hurting it, Tommy reached down, trying to get hold of its burly head.

The Rockport suddenly slipped off his foot.

"Ah, shit."

He heard Scootie hustling away through the darkness with the shoe.

Getting to his feet, Tommy said, "Lights!" The room remained dark, and then he remembered the complete command. "Lights on!"

Scootie was gone.

From the study, adjacent to the living room, came a single bark, and light appeared beyond the open door.

"They're both crazy," Tommy muttered as he went around the coffee table and picked up the rubber hotdog from beside the second armchair.

Scootie appeared in the study doorway, without the shoe. When he saw that he'd been seen, he retreated.

Limping across the living room to the study, Tommy said, "Maybe the dog wasn't always crazy. Maybe she made it crazy, the same way she'll make me crazy sooner or later."

When he entered the study, he found the dog standing on the bleached-cherry desk. The mutt looked like an absurdly oversized decorative accessory.

"Where's my shoe?"

Scootie cocked his head as if to say, *What shoe?*

Holding up the toy hotdog, Tommy said, "I'll take this outside and throw it in the harbor."

With his soulful eyes focused intently on the toy, Scootie whined.

"It's late, I'm tired, my Corvette blew up, some damn *thing* is after me, so I'm in no mood for games."

Scootie merely whined again.

Tommy circled the desk, searching for his shoe.

Atop the desk, Scootie turned, following him with interest.

"If I find it without your help," Tommy warned, "then I won't give the hotdog back."

"Find what?" Del asked from the doorway.

She had changed into blue jeans and a cranberry-red turtleneck sweater, and she was holding two big guns.

"What the hell are those?" Tommy asked.

Hefting the weapon in her right hand, she said,

"This is a short-barreled, pump-action, pistol-grip, 12-gauge Mossberg shotgun. Excellent home-defense weapon." She raised the gun in her left hand. "This beauty is a Desert Eagle .44 Magnum pistol, Israeli-made. It's a real door-buster. A couple of rounds from this baby will stop a charging bull."

"You run into a lot of charging bulls?"

"Or the equivalent."

"No, seriously, why do you keep heavy artillery like that?"

"I told you before—I lead an eventful life."

He remembered how easily she had dismissed the damage to her van earlier in the evening: *It comes with the territory.*

And when he had worried about the rain ruining the upholstery, she had shrugged and said, *There's frequently damage . . . I've learned to roll with it.*

Tommy sensed a *satori*, a sudden profound insight, looming like a tidal wave, and he waited breathlessly for it to wash over him. This woman was not what she appeared to be. He had thought of her as a waitress, but had discovered she was an artist. Then he had thought of her as a struggling artist who worked as a waitress to pay the rent, but she lived in a multimillion-dollar house. Her eccentricities and her habit of peppering her conversation with cryptic babble and non sequiturs had convinced him that she had a few screws loose in the cranium, but now he suspected that the worst mistake he could make with her would be to write her off as a flake. There were depths to her that he was only beginning to perceive—and swimming in those depths were some strange fish that would surprise him more than anything that he had seen to date.

He recalled another fragment of their conversation, and it seemed to have new import: *Reality is perception. Perceptions change. Reality is fluid. So if by "reality" you mean reliably tangible objects and immutable events, then there's no such thing. . . . I'll explain someday when we have more time.*

He sensed that every screwball statement she made was not, in fact, half as screwball as it seemed. Even in her most airheaded statements, an elusive truth was lurking. If he could just step back from her, put aside the conception of her that he had already formed, he would see her entirely differently from the way that he saw her now. He thought of those drawings by M. C. Escher, which played with perspective and with the viewer's expectations, so a scene might appear to be only a drift of lazily falling leaves until, suddenly, one saw it anew as a school of fast-swimming fish. Within the first picture was hidden another. Within Del Payne was hidden a different person—someone with a secret—who was cloaked by the ditsy image that she projected.

The *satori*, tidal wave of revelation, loomed, loomed, loomed—and then began to recede without bringing him understanding. He had strained too hard. Sometimes enlightenment came only when it wasn't sought or welcomed.

Del stood in the doorway between the study and the living room, a gun in each hand, meeting

Tommy's gaze so directly that he half suspected she knew what he was thinking.

Frowning, he said, "Who *are* you, Del Payne?"

"Who is any of us?" she countered.

"Don't start that again."

"Don't start what?"

"That inscrutable crap."

"I don't know what you're talking about. What're you doing with Scootie's rubber hotdog?"

Tommy glared at the Labrador on the desk. "He took my shoe."

In an admonishing tone, she said to the dog, "Scootie?"

The mutt met her eyes almost defiantly, but then he lowered his head and whined.

"Bad Scootie," she said. "Give Tommy his shoe."

Scootie studied Tommy, then chuffed dismissively.

"Give Tommy his shoe," Del repeated firmly.

Finally the dog jumped down from the desk, padded to a potted palm in one corner of the room, poked his head behind the celadon pot, and returned with the athletic shoe in his mouth. He dropped it on the floor at Tommy's feet.

When Tommy bent down to pick up his shoe, the dog put one paw on it—and stared at the rubber hotdog.

Tommy put the hotdog on the floor.

The dog looked at the hotdog and then at Tommy's hand, which was only a few inches away from the toy.

Tommy withdrew his hand.

The Labrador picked up the hotdog with his mouth—and only then lifted his paw off the shoe. He padded into the living room, biting on the toy to produce the farting sound.

Staring thoughtfully after Scootie, Tommy said, "Where did you get that mutt?"

"At the pound."

"I don't believe it."

"What's not to believe?"

From the living room came a veritable symphony of rubber-hotdog flatulence.

"I think you got him from a circus."

"He's clever," she agreed.

"Where did you really get him?"

"At a pet store."

"I don't believe that, either."

"Put on your shoe," she said, "and let's get out of here."

He hobbled to a chair. "Something's strange about that dog."

"Well, if you must know," Del said flippantly, "I'm a witch, and he's my familiar, an ancient super-natural entity who helps me make magic."

Untying the knot in his shoelace, Tommy said, "I'd believe that before I'd believe you found him at the pound. He's got a demonic side to him."

"Oh, he's just a little jealous," Del said. "When he gets to know you better, he'll like you. The two of you are going to get along famously."

Slipping his foot into the shoe, Tommy said, "What about the house. How can you afford this place?"

"I'm an heiress," she said.

He tied the shoelace and got to his feet. "Heiress? I thought your father was a professional poker player."

"He was. A damned good one. And he invested his winnings wisely. When he died, he left an estate worth thirty-four million dollars."

Tommy gaped at her. "You're serious, aren't you?"

"When am I not?"

"That's the question, all right."

"You know how to use a pump-action shotgun?"

"Sure. But guns aren't going to stop it."

She handed the Mossberg to him. "They might slow it down—like your pistol did. And these pack a lot more punch. Come on, let's hit the road. I think you're right about being safe only when we're on the move. Lights out."

Following her out of the now dark study, Tommy said, "But . . . for God's sake, when you're already a multimillionaire, why do you work as a waitress?"

"To understand."

"Understand what?"

Moving toward the foyer, she said, "Lights out," and the living room went dark. "To understand what the average person's life is like, to keep my feet on the ground."

"That's ridiculous."

"My paintings wouldn't have any soul if I didn't live part of my life the way most people do." She opened the door to the foyer closet and slipped a blue nylon ski jacket off a hanger. "Labor, hard work, is at the center of most people's lives."

"But most people *have* to work. You don't. So in the end, if it's only a choice for you, how can you really understand the necessity the rest of us feel?"

"Don't be mean."

"I'm not being mean."

"You are. I don't have to be a rabbit and get myself torn to pieces in order to understand how a poor bunny feels when a hungry fox chases it through a field."

"Actually, I suspect you *do* have to be the rabbit to really *know* that kind of terror."

Shrugging into the ski jacket, she said, "Well, I'm not a rabbit, never have been a rabbit, and I'm not going to become a rabbit. What an absurd idea."

"What?"

"If you want to know what that kind of terror feels like, then *you* become a rabbit."

Befuddled, Tommy said, "I've lost track of the conversation, the way you keep twisting things around. We aren't talking about rabbits, for God's sake."

"Well, we certainly weren't talking about squirrels."

Trying to get the discussion back on track, he said, "Are you really an artist?"

Sorting through the other coats in the closet, she said, "Is any of us really anything?"

Exasperated with Del's preference for speaking in cryptograms, Tommy indulged in one himself: "We're anything in the sense that we are everything."

"You've finally said something sensible."

"I have?"

Behind Tommy, as if by way of comment, Scootie bit the rubber hotdog: *tthhhpphhtt.*

Del said, "I'm afraid none of my jackets will fit you."

"I'll be okay. I've been cold and wet before."

On the granite-topped foyer table, beside Del's purse, were two boxes of ammunition: cartridges for the Desert Eagle and shells for the 12-gauge Mossberg that Tommy carried. She put down the pistol and began to fill the half dozen zippered pockets of her ski jacket with spare rounds for both weapons.

Tommy studied the painting that hung above the table: a bold work of abstract art in primary colors. "Are these your paintings on the walls?"

"That would be tacky, don't you think? I keep all my canvases in my studio, upstairs."

"I'd like to see them."

"I thought you were in a hurry."

Tommy sensed that the paintings were the key that would unlock the mysteries of this strange woman—

—tthhhpphhtt—

—and her strange dog. Something about her style or her subject matter would be a revelation, and upon seeing what she had painted, he would achieve the *satori* that had eluded him earlier.

"It'll only take five minutes," he pressed.

Still jamming spare ammo into her pockets, she said, "We don't have five minutes."

"Three. I really want to see your paintings."

"We've got to get out of here."

"Why are you suddenly so evasive?" he asked.

Zipping shut a pocket bulging with shotgun shells, she said, "I'm not being evasive."

"Yes, you are. What the hell have you been painting up there?"

"Nothing."

"Why are you so nervous all of a sudden?"

"I'm not."

"This is weird. Look me in the eyes, Del."

"Kittens," she said, avoiding his gaze.

"Kittens?"

"That's what I've been painting. Stupid, tacky, sentimental crap. Because I'm not really very talented. Kittens with big eyes. Sad little kittens with big sorrowful eyes and happy little kittens with big laughing eyes. And moronic scenes of dogs playing poker, dogs bowling. That's why I don't want you to see them, Tommy. I'd be embarrassed."

"You're lying."

"Kittens," she insisted, zipping shut another pocket.

"I don't think so." He started toward the stairs. "Two minutes is all I need."

She snatched the Desert Eagle .44 Magnum off the foyer table, swung toward him, and pointed the weapon at his face. "Stop right there."

"Jesus, Del, that gun's loaded."

"I know."

"Don't point it at me."

"Get away from the stairs, Tommy."

There was nothing frivolous about her now. She was cold and businesslike.

"I'd never point this at you," he said, indicating the shotgun in his right hand.

"I know," she said flatly, but she didn't lower her weapon.

The muzzle of the Desert Eagle was only ten inches from Tommy and aligned with the bridge of his nose.

He was looking at a new Deliverance Payne. Steely.

His heart thudded hard enough to shake his entire body. "You won't shoot me."

"I will," she said with such icy conviction that she could not be doubted.

"Just to keep me from seeing some paintings?"

"You're not ready to see them yet," she said.

"Meaning . . . someday you *will* want me to see them."

"When the time is right."

Tommy's mouth was so dry that he had to work up some saliva to loosen his tongue. "But I won't *ever* see them if you blow my brains out."

"Good point," she said, and she lowered the gun. "So I'll shoot you in the leg."

The pistol was aimed at his right knee.

"One round from that monster would blow my whole damn leg off."

"They make excellent prosthetic limbs these days."

"I'd bleed to death."

"I know first aid."

"You're a total fruitcake, Del."

He meant what he said. To one extent or another, she *had* to be mentally unbalanced, even though she had told him earlier that she was the sanest person he knew. Regardless of what mysteries she guarded, what secrets she held, nothing she ultimately revealed to him would ever be sufficiently exculpatory to prove her behavior was reasoned and logical. Nevertheless, though she scared him, she was enormously appealing as well. Tommy wondered what it said about his own sanity to acknowledge that he was strongly attracted to this basketcase.

He wanted to kiss her.

Incredibly, she said, "I think I'm going to fall in love with you, Tuong Tommy. So don't make me blow your leg off."

Astonished into a blush, conflicted as never before, Tommy reluctantly turned away from the stairs and went past Del to the front door.

She tracked him with the Desert Eagle.

"Okay, okay, I'll wait until you're ready to show them to me," he said.

At last she lowered her weapon. "Thank you."

"But," he said, "when I finally do see them, they damn well better be worth the wait."

"Just kittens," she said, and she smiled.

He was surprised that her smile could still warm him. Seconds ago, she had threatened to shoot him, but already he felt a pleasant tingle when she favored him with a smile.

"I'm as crazy as you are," he said.

"Then you've probably got what it takes to make it till dawn." Slinging her purse over one shoulder, she said, "Let's go."

"Umbrellas?" he wondered.

"Hard to handle an umbrella and a shotgun at the same time."

"True. Do you have another car besides the van?"

"No. My mom has all the cars, quite a collection. If I need something besides the van, I borrow it from her. So we'll have to use the Honda."

"The *stolen* Honda," he reminded her.

"We're not criminals. We just borrowed it."

As he opened the front door, Tommy said, "Lights off," and the foyer went dark. "If a cop stops us in our stolen Honda, will you shoot him?"

"Of course not," she said, following him and Scootie into the courtyard. "That would be wrong."

"That would be wrong?" Tommy said, still capable of being amazed by her. "But it would've been right to shoot *me*?"

"Regrettable but right," she confirmed as she locked the door.

"I don't understand you at all."

"I know," she said, tucking the keys in her purse.

Tommy checked the luminous dial of his watch. Six minutes past two o'clock.

Ticktock.

While they were inside the house, the wind had died away completely, but the power of the storm had not diminished. Although no thunder or lightning had disturbed the night for hours, cataracts still crashed down from the riven sky.

The queen palms hung limp, drizzling from the tip of every blade of every frond. Under the merciless lash of the rain, the lush ferns drooped almost to the point of humble prostration, their lacy pinnae glimmering with thousands upon thousands of droplets that, in the low landscape lighting, appeared to be incrustations of jewels.

Scootie led the way, padding through the shallow puddles in the courtyard. In the quartzite paving, specks of mica glinted around the dog's splashing paws, almost as if his claws were striking sparks from the stone. That phantom fire marked his path along the walkway beside the house as well.

The Art Deco panels of copper were cold against Tommy's hand as he pushed open the gate to the street. The hinges rasped like small whispering voices.

On the sidewalk in front of the house, Scootie abruptly halted, raised his head, and pricked his ears. He dropped his rubber hotdog and growled softly.

Alerted by the dog, Tommy brought up the shotgun, gripping it with both hands.

"What is it?" Del asked. She held the gate open behind them to prevent it from falling shut, automatically locking, and inhibiting their retreat if they needed to go back to the house.

But for the splatter-splash-gurgle-plink of water, the lamplit street was silent. The houses were all dark. No traffic approached from either east or west.

Nothing moved except the rain and those things that
the rain disturbed.

The white Honda stood fifteen feet to Tommy's
right. Something could be crouched along the far
side of it, waiting for them to draw nearer.

Scootie was not interested in the Honda, however,
and Tommy was inclined to trust the Labrador's
senses more than his own. The dog was riveted by
something directly across the street.

At first Tommy could not see anything threatening—or even out of the ordinary. In the storm, the
slumbering houses huddled, and the blackness of
their blind windows revealed not even a single pale
face of any neighborhood insomniac. Palms, ficuses,
and canopied carrotwoods stood solemnly in the
windless downpour. Through the cone of amber
light cast by the streetlamp, skeins of rain unraveled
off the spool of night above, weaving together into a
stream that nearly overflowed the gutter.

Then Scootie stiffened and flattened his ears
against his skull and growled again, and Tommy
spotted the man in the hooded raincoat. The guy was
standing near one of the large carrotwoods across
the street, beyond the brightest portion of the lightfall from a streetlamp but still vaguely illumined.

"What's he doing?" Del asked.

Although Tommy couldn't see the stranger's
shadowed face, he said, "Watching us."

Del sounded as if she had seen something else
that surprised her: "Tommy . . . ?"

He glanced at her.

She pointed east.

Half a block away, on the far side of the street, her battered van was parked at the curb.

Something about the imposing figure under the carrotwood tree was anachronistic—as though he had stepped through a time warp, out of the medieval world into the late twentieth century. Then Tommy realized that the hooded raincoat was the source of that impression, for it resembled a monk's robe and cowl.

"Let's get to the Honda," Del said.

Before they could move toward the car, however, the observer stepped away from the carrotwood, into the glow of the streetlamp. His face remained hidden under the hood, as if he were Death engaged in his nightly collections of those poor souls who perished in their sleep.

Nevertheless, faceless though he was, the stranger was naggingly familiar to Tommy. Tall. Heavyset. The way he moved . . .

He was the good Samaritan from earlier in the night, the man who had clumsily descended the embankment from MacArthur Boulevard and crossed the muddy field where the Corvette had crashed. He had been approaching the blazing car when Tommy turned and ran from the fire-enraptured demon.

"Let's see what he wants," Del said.

"No."

How the thing-from-the-doll could now be riding the Samaritan, or hiding inside him, or posing as him—this was a mystery that Tommy was not able to fathom. But the fat man in that muddy field no longer existed; he had been either slaughtered and devoured or conquered and controlled. Of that much, Tommy was certain.

"It's not a man," he said.

The Samaritan moved ponderously through the lamplight.

Scootie's growl escalated into a snarl.

The Samaritan stepped off the curb and splashed through the deep, fast-moving water in the gutter.

"Get back," Tommy said urgently. "Back to the house, inside."

Although his growl had been menacing and he had seemed prepared to attack, Scootie needed no further encouragement to retreat. He whipped around, shot past Tommy, and streaked through the gate that Del was holding open.

Del followed the dog, and Tommy backed through the gate as well, holding the Mossberg in front of him. As the patinated-copper panel fell shut, Tommy saw the Samaritan in the middle of the street, still heading toward them but not breaking into a run, as if confident that they could not escape.

The gate clacked shut. The electric security lock would buy no more than half a minute, because the Samaritan would be able to climb over the barrier with little trouble.

The portly man would no longer be hampered by his less-than-athletic physique. He would have all the strength and agility of the supernatural entity that had claimed him.

When Tommy reached the courtyard, Del was at the front entrance to the house.

He was surprised that she had been able to fish her keys out of her purse and get the door open so quickly. Evidently Scootie was already inside.

Following Del into the house, Tommy heard the gate rattle out at the street.

He closed the door, fumbled for the thumb-turn, and engaged the deadbolt. "Leave the lights off."

"This is a house, not a fortress," Del said.

"Ssshhh," Tommy cautioned.

The only sounds from the courtyard were rain splattering against quartzite pavers, rain chuckling through downspouts, rain snapping against palm fronds.

Del persisted: "Tommy, listen, we can't expect to defend this place like a fort."

Wet and chilled yet again, weary of running, taking some courage from the power of the Mossberg and from the door-buster pistol that Del carried, Tommy hushed her. He remembered a night of terror long ago on the South China Sea, when survival had come only after those refugees in the boat had stopped trying to run from the Thai pirates and had fought back.

Twelve-inch-wide, six-foot-tall sidelights flanked the front door. Through those rain-spotted panes, Tommy was able to see a small portion of the courtyard: wetly glimmering light, blades of darkness that were palm fronds.

The flow of time seemed suspended.

No tick.

No tock.

He was gripping the shotgun so tightly that his hands ached, and the muscles began to twitch in his forearms.

Remembering the green reptilian eye in the torn cotton face of the doll, he dreaded meeting the demon again, now that it was no longer merely ten inches tall.

A moving shadow, swift and fluid and less geometric than those cast by the palm trees and ferns, swooped across one pane of glass.

The fat man didn't knock, didn't ring the bell, didn't leave a note and quietly depart, because he wasn't a *good* Samaritan any more. He slammed into the door, which shook violently in its frame, slammed into it again so hard that the hinges creaked and the lock mechanism made a half-broken rattling noise, and slammed into it a third time, but still the door held.

Tommy's hammering heart drove him across the dark foyer and nailed him against the wall opposite the door.

Although the sidelights were too narrow to admit the fat man, he smashed his fist through one of them. Shattered glass rang across the travertine floor.

Tommy squeezed the trigger. Flame flared from the muzzle of the Mossberg, and the deafening roar of gunfire rebounded from the walls of the foyer.

Even though the shotgunned Samaritan reeled back from the broken sidelight, he didn't scream in pain. He wasn't a man any more. Pain meant nothing to him.

Her voice hollow and strange in the shivery echo of the blast, Del shouted, "No, Tommy, no, this place is just a trap! Come on!"

With tremendous force, the fat man slammed into the door again. The deadbolt *skreeked* against the striker plate, and the squeal of shearing metal rose from the tortured hinges, and wood splintered with a dry cracking sound.

Reluctantly Tommy had to admit that this was not the South China Sea and that their inhuman adversary was not as vulnerable as a mere Thai pirate.

The fat man hit the door again. It would not hold much longer.

Tommy followed Del across the dark living room, able to see her only because she was silhouetted against the wall of glass that faced the harbor lights. Even in the gloom, she knew the place well enough to avoid the furniture.

One of the large sliding glass doors was already open when they reached it. Apparently, Scootie had rolled it aside, because he was waiting for them on the patio.

Tommy wondered how the dog, even as clever as he was, could have managed that feat. Then he heard the front door crash open at the other end of the house, and that frightful sound knocked all of the curiosity out of him.

For some reason, Tommy had thought that Del intended to escape by water, across the harbor to the far shore. But the back-glow from the pier light that shone on her rain-soaked flag was bright enough to reveal that no boat was tied at her private dock. In the empty slip was only rain-stippled black water.

"This way," she said, hurrying not toward the harbor but to the left across the patio.

Then he expected her to turn left once more into the serviceway between her house and the one next door, go out to the street again, to the Honda, and try to split before the Samaritan found them. But when she didn't choose that route, he understood why she avoided it. The passage was narrow, flanked by the two houses, with a gate at the far end; once they had entered it, their options would have been danger-ously limited.

The homes along the harbor were set close to-gether on narrow lots, because the land on which they stood was enormously valuable. To preserve the multimillion-dollar views, the property lines between neighbors' patios and backyards were de-lineated neither by high walls nor by dense masses of foliage, but by low shrubs, or planter boxes, or fences only two to three feet high.

Scootie bounded over a foot-high planter wall that overflowed with vine geraniums. Del and Tommy followed him onto the brick patio of the neighboring Cape Cod–style house.

A security lamp on the nearby dock revealed cushionless teak outdoor furniture left to weather through the winter, terra-cotta pots full of stalk primrose, and a massive built-in barbecue center now covered with a tailored vinyl rain shield.

They leaped over a low plum-thorn hedge that delineated another property line, squished through a muddy flower bed, crossed another patio behind a stone and mahogany house that seemed inspired by Frank Lloyd Wright, and clambered over more plum-thorn that snagged at the legs of Tommy's jeans and pricked through his socks to puncture the skin at his ankles.

As they headed west along the peninsula, sprinting past the back of a brooding Spanish colonial home with deep balconies on three levels, a formidable dog penned in a narrow run between houses began to bark savagely at them and throw itself against a restraining gate. The hound sounded as eager to rend and kill as any German shepherd or Doberman ever trained by the Gestapo. Ahead, still more barking arose from other dogs anticipating their approach.

Tommy didn't dare look back, for fear that the Samaritan was at his heels. In his mind's eye, he could see five fat fingers, as pale and cold as those of a corpse, reaching toward him, inches from the nape of his neck.

Behind a three-story ultramodern house that was all angled glass and polished-limestone cladding, blinding banks of floodlights came on, evidently triggered by motion detectors in a security system that was more aggressive than anything protecting

the other houses. The shock of this sudden glare
caused Tommy to stumble, but he kept his balance
and maintained his grip on the shotgun. Gasping for
breath, he plunged forward, with Del, across a massive cast-stone balustrade onto the unlighted patio of
a Mediterranean-style house, where a TV glowed in
the family room and where a startled old man peered
out at them as they raced past.

The night seemed to be filled with uncountable
barking dogs, all close but out of sight, as though they
were falling with the rain, coming down through the
black sky, soon to land in packs on all sides.

Three houses beyond the ultramodern pile with
the floodlamps, the beam of a big flashlight suddenly speared out of the darkness and the rain,
fixing on Del.

The man behind the light shouted, "Stop right
there!"

Without any cry of warning, another guy erupted
from the gloom and blindsided Tommy, as if they
were professional football players and this were the
Super Bowl. They both skidded and went down on
the slick concrete decking, and Tommy landed so
hard that his breath was knocked out of him. He
rolled into some patio chairs that tumbled over with
a tubular-steel ringing. Stars swarmed behind his
eyes, and he cracked his left elbow squarely on the
ulnar nerve—the ill-named funny bone—sending a
disabling painful tingle the length of his arm.

To the man with the flashlight, Del Payne said,

"Back off, you asshole, I've got a gun, back off, back off!"

Tommy realized that he had dropped the Mossberg. In spite of the numbing pain in his left arm, wheezing noisily as he struggled to get some air into his lungs, he pushed onto his hands and knees. He was desperate to find the weapon.

The foolhardy tackle was sprawled facedown, groaning, apparently in even worse shape than Tommy. As far as Tommy was concerned, the stupid son of a bitch deserved to have a broken leg, two broken legs, and maybe a skull fracture for good measure. At first he had assumed that the men were cops, but they hadn't identified themselves as policemen, and now he realized that they evidently lived here and fancied themselves to be natural-born heroes ready to take on a pair of fleeing burglars.

As Tommy crawled past the groaning man, he heard Del say, "Get that damn light out of my eyes right now, or I'll shoot it out and take you with it."

The other would-be hero's courage wavered, and so did his flashlight.

By a stroke of luck, the nervous beam quivered across the patio, revealing the shotgun.

Tommy crawled to the Mossberg.

The man who'd tackled him had managed to sit up. He was spitting out something—possibly teeth— and cursing.

Clutching at another patio table, Tommy pulled

himself to his feet just as Scootie began to bark loudly, urgently.

Tommy glanced to the east and saw the fat man two properties away, silhouetted against the bright backdrop of the floodlamps at the ultramodern house. As the Samaritan raced toward them, leaping a low fence into the property next door, he was no longer the least bit clumsy but as graceful as a panther in spite of his size, his raincoat billowing like a cape behind him.

Snarling, Scootie moved to intercept the fat man.

"Scootie, no!" Del shouted.

Assuming a shooter's stance as naturally as if she had been born with a gun in her hands, she opened fire with the Desert Eagle when the Samaritan cleared a hedge and splashed onto this patio, where they were apparently going to be forced to make their last stand. She squeezed off three rounds with what seemed to be calm deliberation. The evenly timed explosions were so thunderous that Tommy thought the recoil of the powerful handgun would knock her flat, but she stood tall.

She was an excellent shot, and all three rounds appeared to hit their target. With the first *boom*, the Samaritan stopped as if he'd run head-on into a brick wall, and with the second *boom*, he was half lifted off his feet and sent staggering backward, and with the third, he spun and swayed and almost fell.

The hero with the flashlight had thrown it aside and had fallen to the deck to get out of the line of fire.

The tooth-spitter was still sitting on the puddled

concrete, legs splayed in an infantile posture, hands clasped to his head. He was apparently frozen in terror.

Edging away from the patio table, toward Del and Scootie, Tommy remained riveted by the wounded Samaritan, who was turned half away from them, who had taken three rounds from the .44 Magnum, who swayed but did not drop, did not drop.

Did. Not. Drop.

The hood was no longer over the fat man's head, but the darkness still masked the side of his face. Then he slowly turned toward Tommy and Del, and though his features remained obscure, his extraordinary eyes fixed on them and on the growling Labrador. They were radiant, green, inhuman eyes.

Scootie's growl degenerated into a whimper, and Tommy knew exactly how he felt.

With admirable calm, made of sterner stuff than either Tommy or Scootie, Del squeezed off shot after shot with the Desert Eagle. The explosions crashed across the harbor and echoed off the far shore, and they were still echoing back and forth after she had emptied the magazine.

Every round appeared to hit the fat man, because he jerked, twitched, doubled over, but then snapped upright as if in response to the impact of another slug, executed a limb-flapping, marionette-like spin, and at last went down. He landed on one side, knees drawn up in the fetal position, and the frosty beam of the would-be hero's flashlight, which lay discarded on the patio, illuminated one of the Samaritan's

white, thick-fingered hands. He seemed to be dead,
but certainly was not.

"Let's get out of here," Del said.

Scootie was already leaping across a hedge, into
the backyard of the next house to the west.

The roar of the .44 Magnum had been so daunting
that most of the barking dogs along the harbor had
fallen silent, no longer eager to escape their pens.

In the silvery beam of the flashlight, the Samaritan's plump white hand lay cupped, palm up, filling
with rain. Then it spasmed, and the pale flesh grew
mottled and dark.

"Oh, shit," Tommy said.

Impossibly, the fingers metamorphosed into spatulate tentacles and then into spiky insectile digits with
wicked chitinous hooks at each knuckle.

The entire shadowed mass of the fallen Samaritan
seemed to be shifting, pulsating. Changing.

"Seen enough, outta here," Del declared, and she
hurried after Scootie.

Tommy searched for the courage to approach the
creature and fire the shotgun point-blank into its
brain. By the time he could reach the beast, however, it might have transformed itself so radically it
would have nothing that was recognizably a head.
Besides, intuitively he knew that no number of
rounds from the Mossberg—or any other gun—
would destroy it.

"Tommy!" Del called frantically from the patio of
the house next door.

"Run, get out of here," Tommy advised the home-owner who was prone on the concrete deck.

The man seemed traumatized by all the gunfire, confused. He started to push onto his knees, but then he must have glimpsed the shotgun, because he pleaded, "No, don't, Jesus, don't," and pressed flat to the deck again.

"Run, for God's sake, run, before it recovers from the shots," Tommy urged the second man, the tooth-spitter, who continued to sit in a daze. "Please, run."

Heeding his own advice, he followed Del, grateful that he had not broken a leg when he'd been tackled.

In the distance, a siren wailed.

When Tommy, Del, and the dog were two properties away from the scene of the confrontation, one of the would-be heroes screamed in the night behind them.

Tommy skidded to a halt on a slate patio at a Tudor house and looked toward the cries.

Not much could be seen in the rain and murk. Shadows thrashed against the backdrop of security lights from the ultramodern house farther east. Some were decidedly strange shadows, huge and quick, jagged and jittering, but he would have been indulging his fevered imagination if he had claimed to see a monster in the night.

Now two men were screaming. Terrible screams. Blood-freezing. They shrieked as though they were being wrenched limb from limb, slit open, torn apart.

The demon would allow no witnesses.

Perhaps a sound reached Tommy of which he was only subliminally aware, a voracious chewing, or perhaps some quality of the two men's soul-curdling screams spoke to him on a primitive level and inspired racial memories of a prehistoric age when human beings had been easy prey to larger beasts, but somehow he knew that they were not merely being slaughtered; they were being devoured.

When the police arrived, they might not find much left of the victims on that patio. Perhaps nothing other than a little blood—and not even blood after a few more minutes of cleansing rain. The two men would seem to have vanished.

Tommy's stomach twisted with nausea.

If his arm hadn't still been tingling from the blow to his funny bone, if his muscles and joints hadn't ached from the fall and burned with fatigue, if he had not been shivering from the cold, he might have thought that he was in a nightmare. But he was suffering enough discomfort and pain that he had no need to pinch himself to determine if he was awake.

More than one siren cleaved the night, and they were rapidly drawing nearer.

Scootie ran, Del ran, Tommy ran once more, as one of the men stopped screaming, stopped being *able* to scream, and then the second man's cries choked off as well, and not a single dog was barking any more, all silenced by the scent of something otherworldly, while the harbor gradually filled with an incoming tide and the earth rotated inexorably toward dawn.

SIX

Under the roof of the silent and unmoving carousel, among the herd of colorful horses frozen in mid-gallop, Tommy and Del found a two-person chariot with carved eagles on the sides. They were glad to be out of the rain and to have a chance, however brief, to rest.

Ordinarily the perimeter of the carousel was covered when it was not in use, but this night it stood open to the elements.

Scootie quietly prowled among the horses, circling the elevated platform, apparently on sentry duty, ready to warn them if the demon approached in either its Samaritan guise or any other.

The Balboa Fun Zone, arguably the heart of the peninsula's important tourist business, extended for a few blocks along Edgewater Avenue, a pedestrian mall that did not admit vehicular traffic west of Main Street. Numerous gift shops, Pizza Pete's, ice-cream stands, restaurants, Balboa Saloon, arcades offering video games and pinball and skee-ball, boat-rental operations, bumper cars, a Ferris wheel, the carousel on which Tommy and Del sat, Lazer Tag, docks for various companies offering guided-tour cruises, and other diversions lined Edgewater, with views of the dazzling harbor and its islands to be glimpsed between the attractions on the north side.

In spring, summer, and autumn—or on any warm day in the winter—tourists and sun lovers strolled this promenade, taking a break from the Pacific surf and from the beaches on the opposite side of the narrow peninsula. Newlyweds, elderly couples, spectacular-looking young women in bikinis, lean and tanned young men in shorts, and children walked-skated-Rollerbladed among veterans in wheelchairs and babies in strollers, enjoying the glitter of sunlight on water, eating ice-cream cones, roasted corn from Kountry Corn, Popsicles, cookies. Laughter and happy chatter mingled with the music from the carousel, the putter of boat engines, and the ceaseless ring-beep-pong-bop from the game arcades.

At two-thirty on this stormy November morning, the Fun Zone was deserted. The only sounds were those made by the rain as it drummed hollowly on the carousel roof, pinged off the brass poles on the outer circle of horses, snapped against festoons of limp vinyl pennants, and drizzled through the fronds of the queen palms along the harbor side of the promenade. This was a lonely music, the forlorn and tuneless anthem of desolation.

The shops and other attractions were shuttered and dark but for an occasional security lantern. On summer evenings, when augmented by the neon and the sparkling Tivoli lights of the arcades and rides, the old bronze lampposts with frosted-glass globes—some round, most in the form of urns with finials—provided an appealing and romantic glow; then everything glimmered, including the great mirror that was the harbor, and the world was scintillant, effervescent. But now the lamplight was strangely bleak, cold, too feeble to prevent the crushing weight of the November night from pressing low over the Fun Zone.

Extracting a shotgun shell from a pocket in her ski jacket, Del spoke in a murmur that would not carry beyond the carousel: "Here. You only fired one round, I think."

"Yeah," Tommy said, matching her soft tone.

"Keep it fully loaded."

"Those poor damn guys," he lamented as he slid the shell into the magazine tube on the Mossberg. "What horrible deaths."

"It's not your fault," she said.

"They wouldn't have been there, the *thing* wouldn't have been there, if *I* hadn't been there."

"It's upsetting," she agreed. "But you were only trying to stay alive, running for your life, and they stepped in."

"Still."

"Obviously, they were marked for an unnatural extraction."

"Extraction?"

"From this world. If the thing in the fat man hadn't gotten them, then they would have been taken

in some other unusual way. Like spontaneous com-
bustion. Or an encounter with a lycanthrope."

"Lycanthrope? Werewolf?" He wasn't able to deal
with her weirdness just now, so he changed the subject. "Where the hell did you learn to shoot like that?
Your mother again?"

"Daddy. He taught Mom and me, wanted us to be
prepared for anything. Pistols, revolvers, rifles, shotguns. I can handle an Uzi as if I were born with it,
and—"

"Uzi?"

"Yeah. And when it comes to—"

"Submachine guns?"

"—when it comes to knife throwing—"

"*Knife* throwing?" Tommy said, and realized that
he had raised his voice.

"—I'm good enough to put together a stage act
and make a living with it in Vegas or even the circus,
if I ever had to," Del continued in a murmur as she
unzipped another pocket and took from it a handful
of cartridges for the Desert Eagle. "Unfortunately,
I'm not half as good at fencing as I'd like to
be, though I'll admit to being first-rate with a
crossbow."

"He died when you were ten," Tommy said. "So
he taught you all this when you were just a little
kid?"

"Yeah. We'd go out in the desert near Vegas and
blow the crap out of empty soda bottles, tin cans,
posters of old movie monsters like Dracula and the
creature from the Black Lagoon. It was a lot of fun."

"What in the name of God was he preparing you for?"

"Dating."

"Dating?"

"That was his joke. Actually he was preparing me for the unusual life he knew I was going to have."

"How could he know?"

Rather than answer the question, Del said, "But the truth is, because of the training Daddy gave me, I've never been on a date with any guy who intimidated me, never had a problem."

"I guess not. I think you'd have to be dating Hannibal Lecter before you'd feel uneasy."

Pressing the last two rounds into the .44 magazine, she said, "I still miss Daddy. He truly understood me—and not many people ever do."

"I'm trying," Tommy assured her.

Passing by on his sentry duties, Scootie came to Del, put his head in her lap, and whimpered as though he had heard the regret and the sense of loss in her voice.

Tommy said, "How could a little girl hold and fire a gun like that? The recoil—"

"Oh, of course, we started with an air rifle, an air pistol, and then a .22," she said, slamming the loaded magazine into the Israeli pistol. "When we practiced with rifles or shotguns, Daddy padded my shoulders, crouched behind to brace me, and held the gun with me. He was only familiarizing me with the more powerful weapons, so I'd feel comfortable with them from an early age, wouldn't be afraid of them when the time came to actually handle them. He died before I *really* got good with the bigger stuff, and then Mom continued the lessons."

"Too bad he never got around to teaching you how to make bombs," Tommy said with mock dismay.

"I'm comfortable with dynamite and most plastic explosives, but they really aren't particularly useful for self-defense."

"Was your father a terrorist?"

"Furthest thing from it. He thought all politics were stupid. He was a gentle man."

"But he just usually had some dynamite laying around to practice making bombs."

"Not usually."

"Just at Christmas, huh?"

"Basically, I learned explosives not to make bombs but to disarm them if I had to."

"A task we're all faced with every month or so."

"No," she said, "I've only had to do it twice."

Tommy wanted to believe that she was kidding, but he decided not to ask. His brain was overloaded with new discoveries about her, and in his current weariness, he did not have the energy or the mental capacity to contemplate more of her disconcerting revelations. "And I thought *my* family was strange."

"Everyone thinks his family is strange," Del said, scratching Scootie behind the ears, "but it's just that . . . because we're closer to the people we love, we tend to see them through a magnifying glass, through a thicker lens of emotion, and we exaggerate their eccentricities."

"Not in the case of *your* family," he said. "Magnifying glass or no magnifying glass, it's a strange clan."

Scootie returned to his patrol, padding quietly away through the motionless stampede of wooden horses.

As Del zipped shut the pocket from which she had taken the ammunition, she said, "The way I see it, your family might have a prejudice against blondes, but when they see how much I've got to offer, they'll learn to like me."

Grateful that she couldn't see him blush in this gloom, Tommy said, "Never mind expertise with guns. Can you cook? That's a big deal in my family."

"Ah, yes, the family of fighting bakers. Well, I've picked up a lot from my folks. Daddy won several prizes in chili-cooking contests all across Texas and the Southwest, and Mom graduated from Cordon Bleu."

"Was that *while* she was a ballerina?"

"Right after."

He checked his watch—2:37. "Maybe we better get moving again."

Another siren rose in the distance.

Del listened long enough to be sure that the siren was drawing nearer rather than receding. "Let's wait a while. We're going to have to find new wheels and hit the road again, but I don't want to be hot-wiring a car when the streets around here are crawling with cops."

"If we stay too long in one place—"

"We're okay for a while. You sleepy?"

"Couldn't sleep if I tried."

"Eyes itchy and burning?"

"Yeah," he said. "But I'll be okay."

"Your neck aches so bad you can hardly hold up your head," she said, as if she could feel his discomfort.

"I'm alert enough. Don't worry about me," he said, and with one hand he squeezed the nape of his neck as if he could pull the pain out of his flesh.

She said, "You're weary to the bone, poor baby. Turn away from me a little. Let me work on you."

"Work on me?"

"Move your butt a little, tofu boy, come on," she said, nudging him with her hip.

The chariot was narrow, but he was able to turn enough to allow her to massage his shoulders and the back of his neck. Her slender hands were surprisingly strong, but though she pressed hard at times, she relieved rather than caused pain.

Sighing, he said, "Who taught you this?"

"It's just a thing I know. Like my painting."

They were both quiet for a minute, except for Tommy's occasional groan as Del's fingers found another coil of tension and slowly unwound it.

The diligent Scootie passed, out at the edge of the platform, as black as the night itself and as silent as a spirit.

As she worked her thumbs up and down the nape of Tommy's neck, Del said, "Have you ever been abducted by aliens?"

"Oh, boy."

"What?"

"Here we go again."

"You mean you *have*?"

"Been abducted? Of course not. I mean, here *you* go again, getting weird."

"You don't believe in extraterrestrial intelligences?"

"I believe the universe is so big that there's got to be lots of other intelligent species in it."

"So what's weird?"

"But I *don't* believe they come all the way across the galaxy to kidnap people and take them up in flying saucers and examine their genitals."

"They don't just examine the genitals."

"I know, I know. Sometimes they take the abductee to Chicago for beer and pizza."

She lightly, chastisingly slapped the back of his head. "You're being sarcastic."

"A little."

"It's not becoming to you."

"Listen, an alien species, vastly more intelligent than we are, creatures millions of years more evolved than we are, probably wouldn't have any interest in us at all—and certainly wouldn't be interested enough to spend so much manpower harassing a bunch of ordinary citizens."

Massaging his scalp now, Del said, "Personally, I believe in alien abductions."

"I am not surprised."

"I believe they're worried about us."

"The aliens?"

"That's right."

"Why would they be worried about us?"

"We're such a troubled species, so confused, self-destructive. I think the aliens want to help us achieve enlightenment."

"By examining our genitals? Then those guys sitting ringside at nude-dancing clubs only want to help the girls on the stage to achieve enlightenment."

From behind him, she reached around to his forehead, drawing light circles on his brow with her fingers. "You're such a wise guy."

"I write detective novels."

"Maybe you've even been abducted," she said.

"Not me."

"You wouldn't remember."

"I'd remember," he assured her.

"Not if the aliens didn't want you to."

"Just a wild shot in the dark here—but I bet you think *you've* been abducted."

She stopped massaging his brow and pulled him around to face her again. Her murmur fell to a conspiratorial whisper: "What if I told you there are a few nights when I've had missing hours, blank spots, where I just seem to have blacked out, gone into a fugue state or something. All abductees report these missing hours, these holes in their memories where their abduction experiences have been erased or suppressed."

"Del, dear sweet loopy Del, please don't be offended, please understand that I say this with affection: I wouldn't be surprised to hear that you had a couple of these missing hours every day of the week."

Puzzled, she said, "Why would I be offended?"

"Never mind."

"Anyway, I don't have them every day of the week—only one or two days a year."

"What about ghosts?" he asked.

"What about them?"

"Do you believe in ghosts?"

"I've even met a few," she said brightly.

"What about the healing power of crystals?"

She shook her head. "They can't heal, but they *can* focus your psychic power."

"Out-of-body experiences?"

"I'm sure it can be done, but I like my body too much to want to leave it even for a short time."

"Remote viewing?"

"That's easy. Pick a town."

"What?"

"Name a town."

"Fresno," he said.

With bubbly confidence, she said, "I could describe any room in any building in Fresno—where I've never been in my life, by the way—and if we drove up there tomorrow, you'd see it was just like I said."

"What about Big Foot?"

She put a hand over her mouth to stifle her giggle.

"You're such a goof, Tuong Tommy. Big Foot is bullshit, invented by the tabloids to sell newspapers to gullible fools."

He kissed her.

She kissed him too. She kissed him better than he had ever been kissed before. She had a talent for it, like throwing knives.

When at last he pulled back from her, Tommy said, "I've never met anyone remotely like you, Deliverance Payne—and I'm not sure if that's good or bad."

"One thing's for sure. If it had been any other woman who picked you up from your burning car, you wouldn't have lived half this long."

That was inarguably true. No other woman—no other *person*—he had ever met would have reacted with such equanimity when the demon had slammed against the window and fastened itself to the glass with its hideous suckerpads. No one else could have done the stunt driving necessary to detach the repulsive beast from the van—and perhaps no one else, even having seen the creature, would have accepted Tommy's devil-doll story so unequivocally.

"There is such a thing as fate," she told him.

"I suppose there might be."

"There *is*. Destiny. It's not written in stone, however. On a spiritual level, completely unconsciously, we make our destinies for ourselves."

Bewilderment and joy swelled in Tommy, and he felt as though he were a child just beginning to unwrap a wonderful gift. "That doesn't sound as totally crazy to me as it would have an hour or two ago."

"Of course it doesn't. I suspect that while I wasn't looking, I've made you my destiny, and it's beginning to seem as if you've made me yours."

Tommy had no answer to that. His heart was pounding. He had never felt this way before. Even if he'd had a computer keyboard in front of him and time to think, he would not easily have been able to put these new feelings into words.

Abruptly his joyful mood and sense of impending transcendence were diminished when a strange slithering sensation crept up the hollow of his spine. He shivered.

"Cold?" she asked.

"No."

As sometimes happens along the coast, the air temperature had bottomed out after midnight; it was rising again. The sea was an efficient heat sink that stored up the warmth of the sun during the balmy day and gradually released it after darkness fell.

The slithering in the spine came again, and Tommy said, "It's just a weird feeling. . . ."

"Oooh, I like weird feelings."

". . . maybe a premonition."

"Premonition? You're getting more interesting by the moment, Tuong Tommy. Premonition of what?"

He looked around uneasily at the tenebrous forms of the carousel horses. "I . . . don't quite . . . know. . . ."

Then he suddenly became aware that his neck and

shoulders were no longer sore. His headache had passed too.

Astonished, he said, "That was an incredible massage."

"You're welcome."

In fact, no pain lingered in any muscle in his body, not even in those that he had bruised when he had been tackled on the concrete patio. He was not sleepy, either, and his eyes no longer itched and burned as before. Indeed, he felt wide-awake, energetic, and better than he had felt before this entire pursuit had begun.

Frowning at Del in the gloom, he said, "Hey, how did—"

Scootie interrupted, thrusting his head between them and whining fearfully.

"It's coming," Del said, rising from the chariot.

Tommy snatched the Mossberg off the carousel floor.

Already Del was easing between the horses, using them for cover but moving closer to the edge of the platform for a better view of the promenade.

Tommy joined her behind a great black stallion with bared teeth and wild eyes.

Standing almost on point and utterly still, like a hunting dog in a field where a pheasant had been spotted in the brush, Scootie stared east along lamp-lit Edgewater Avenue, past Anchors Away Boat Rentals and Original Harbor Cruises toward Balboa Beach Treats. Except for his smaller size, he might have been one of the carved animals waiting in mid-stampede for sunshine and for the riders who would come with it.

"Let's get out of here," Tommy whispered.

"Wait."

"Why?"

"I want to see it better," she said, indicating the three-globe streetlamp past which the fat man would have to come. Her words were almost as faint as exhalations.

"*I* have no desire to see it better."

"Anyway, we have the guns. We can knock it down again."

"We might not be lucky this time."

"Scootie can try to misdirect it."

"You mean lead it away from us?"

Del didn't reply.

Ears pricked, head held high, Scootie was clearly ready to do whatever his mistress demanded of him.

Maybe the dog *could* outrun the creature. Although the thing posing as the portly Samaritan apparently was a supernatural entity, immortal and ultimately unstoppable, it too seemed bound by some of the laws of physics, which was why the hard impact of high-caliber ammunition could halt it, knock it down, delay it; consequently, there was no reason to assume that it could move as fast as Scootie, who was smaller, lower to the ground, and designed by nature for speed.

"But the thing won't be lured away by the dog," Tommy whispered. "Del, it isn't interested in the dog. It only wants me . . . and maybe you now."

"Hush," she said.

In the wintry light from the frosted globes on the nearest lamp, the falling rain appeared to be sleet. The concrete walkway glistened as though coated with ice.

Beyond the light, the rain darkened to tarnished silver and then to ash gray, and out of the grayness came the fat man, walking slowly along the center of the deserted promenade.

At Tommy's side, Scootie twitched but made no sound.

Holding the shotgun in both hands, Tommy hunched lower behind the carousel stallion. In the windless night, he stared out at the promenade past the perpetually wind-tossed tail of the carved horse.

At the other end of the leaping stallion, Del shrank herself too, watching the Samaritan from under the horse's neck.

Like a dirigible easing along the ground toward its berth, the fat man advanced as if he were drifting rather than walking, making no splashing sounds on the puddled pavement.

Tommy felt the night grow chillier, as though the demon moved in clouds of cold sufficiently powerful to damp the effect of the harbor's slow release of the day's stored heat.

At first the Samaritan-thing was only a gray mass in the gray static of the rain, but then its image cleared as it came forth into the lamplight. It was slightly larger than before, but not as large as it should have been if, indeed, it had devoured two men, every scrap of flesh and splinter of bone.

Realizing how absurd it was to try to rationalize the biology of a supernatural entity, Tommy wondered again if his sanity had fled sometime earlier in the night.

The Samaritan-thing still wore the raincoat, though that garment was punctured and torn, apparently by gunfire. The hood lay rumpled at the back of its neck, and its head was exposed.

The thing's face was human but inhumanly hard and perhaps no longer capable of gentler expressions, and at a distance the eyes seemed to be human as well. Most likely this was the moon-round face of the fat man who had stopped to lend assistance at the scene of the Corvette crash. The mind and soul of the fat man were long gone, however, and the thing wearing his form was an entity of such pure hatred and savagery that it could not prevent its true nature from darkling through even the soft features of a face well suited to smiles and laughter.

As the thing moved more directly into the pale light, no more than forty feet away, Tommy saw that it cast *three* distinct shadows, when he might have expected that, like a vampire, it would cast none. For a moment he thought that the shadows were a freakish effect of the three globes on the old street-lamp, but then he noted that they stretched across the wet pavement at angles unrelated to the source of illumination.

When he returned his attention to the creature's face, he saw its pudgy features change. A far leaner and utterly different face metamorphosed on the rotund body; the nose became more hawkish, the jawline jutted, and the ears flattened tighter to the skull. The rain-soaked mop of thick black hair crinkled into lank blond curls. Then a third countenance replaced the second: that of a slightly older man with brush-cut, iron-gray hair and the square features of the quintessential army drill sergeant.

As he watched the Samaritan's moon-round visage reappear, Tommy suspected that the other two faces were those of the unlucky men whom the creature had slaughtered a short while ago on the patio behind that harborside house. He shuddered— and feared that the demon would hear the chattering of his teeth even at a distance of forty feet, even through the screening tattoo of the rain.

The beast stepped to the center of the lightfall from the lamp, where it stopped. Its eyes were dark and human one moment, radiant green and unearthly the next.

Because Scootie's flank was against Tommy's left leg, he felt the dog shiver.

From the center of the promenade, the creature surveyed the Fun Zone around it, beginning with the carousel, which was elevated two feet above the public walkway and partially screened by a low, green wrought-iron fence. The terrible eyes, serpent bright and serpent mean, seemed to fix on Tommy, and he could sense the beast's hellish hunger.

The old carousel was crowded with shadows that outnumbered the riders who, for decades, had mounted its tail-chasing steeds, so it seemed unlikely that Tommy and Del and Scootie could be seen in such blackish shelter, as long as they remained still. Yet the hateful demon looked upon the world through extraordinary eyes, and Tommy became convinced that it had spotted him as easily as it would have if he had been standing in noontime sun.

But the creature's gaze slid away from him. The demon studied Bay Burger to the west, then looked north across the promenade to the dark Ferris wheel and the Fun Zone Boat Company.

It knows we're nearby, Tommy thought.

Opposite the elevated carousel were lush palm trees gracing an open-air dining terrace with views of boat docks and the harbor beyond. Turning its back to the horses, the demon slowly surveyed the fixed tables, benches, trash containers, empty bicycle racks, and dripping trees.

On the terrace, two additional three-globe lampposts shed more of the icy light that seemed, in this strange night, to reveal less than it should. The area was well-enough illuminated, however, for the creature to ascertain, at a glance, that its prey was not hiding there. Nevertheless, it spent an inordinate amount of time studying the terrace, as if doubting its own eyes, as if it thought that Tommy and Del were able, chameleon-like, to assume the visual character of any background and effectively disappear.

Finally the beast looked west again along the

promenade and then focused once more on the carousel. Its radiant gaze traveled over the shadowed horses only briefly before it turned to stare east, back the way it had come, as if it suspected that it had passed their hiding place.

It seemed confused. Indeed, its frustration was almost palpable. The thing sensed that they were close, but it could not catch their scent—or whatever more exotic spoor it tracked.

Tommy realized that he was holding his breath. He let it out and inhaled slowly through his open mouth, half convinced that even a breath drawn too sharply would instantly attract the hunter's attention.

Considering that the creature had tracked them many miles across the county to the New World Saigon Bakery and later had found them again at Del's house, its current inability to detect them from only forty feet away was baffling.

The creature turned to the carousel.

Tommy held his breath again.

The serpent-eyed Samaritan raised its plump hands and moved its flattened palms in circles in the rain-filled air, as though wiping off a dirty pane of glass.

Seeking psychic impressions, some sign of us, trying to get a clearer view, Tommy thought.

He tightened his grip on the Mossberg.

Round and round, round and round, the pale hands moved, like radar dishes, seeking signals.

Tick.

Tock.

Tommy sensed that their time and luck were rapidly running out, that the demon's inhuman senses would lock onto them at any second.

Sailing down from the night above the harbor, wings thrumming, as ethereal as an angel but as swift as a flash of light, a large sea gull swooped past the demon's pale hands and arced up into the darkness from which it had come.

The Samaritan-thing lowered its hands.

The gull plummeted once more, wings cleaving the chilled air and the rain in a breathtaking display of graceful aerobatics. As radiant as a haunting spirit in the frost-white light, it swept past the demon's upraised hands again, and then rocketed heavenward in a spiral.

The Samaritan-thing peered up at the bird, turning to watch it as it wheeled across the sky.

Something important was happening, something mysterious and profound, which Tommy could not comprehend.

He glanced at Del for her reaction, but her attention remained riveted on the demon, and he could not see her face.

At Tommy's side, flank pressed against his leg, the Labrador quivered.

The sea gull circled back across the harbor and swooped down into the Fun Zone again. Flying only a few feet above the surface of the promenade, it sailed past the demon and disappeared between the shops and arcades to the east.

The serpent-eyed Samaritan stared intently after

the gull, clearly intrigued. Its arms hung at its sides, and it repeatedly flexed and fisted its plump hands as though working off the excess energy of rage and frustration.

From overhead and west near the stilled Ferris wheel came the thrumming of many wings, as eight or ten sea gulls descended in a flock.

The demon swung around to face them.

Breaking out of their steep dive only a few feet above the ground, the gulls streaked after the first bird, swarming straight toward the demon and then parting into two groups that swept around it, disappearing east on Edgewater Avenue. None of them cawed or shrieked in their characteristic manner; but for the air-cutting whoosh of their wings, they passed in eerie silence.

Captivated, curious, the Samaritan-thing faced east to watch them depart.

It took a step after them, another step, but then halted.

Through the wintry lamplight fell sleet-white rain.

The demon took another step east. Stopped. Stood swaying.

At the nearby docks, boats creaked on the rising tide, and a halyard clink-clink-clinked against a steel mast.

The Samaritan-thing directed its attention once more to the carousel.

Out of the west came a drumming different from—and louder than—the rain.

The beast turned toward the Ferris wheel, tilting its face up, peering into the bottomless black sky, raising its plump white hands, as though either seeking the source of the drumming or preparing to fend off an assault.

Out of the swarming darkness above the harbor, birds descended once more, not merely eight or ten, but a hundred birds, two hundred, three hundred, sea gulls and pigeons and sparrows and blackbirds and crows and hawks, even several enormous and startlingly prehistoric-looking blue herons, beaks open but producing no sound, a river of feathers and small shiny eyes, pouring down over the Ferris wheel, along the promenade, splitting into two streams to pass the demon, and then rejoining in a single surging mass to disappear east between the shops and arcades, and still they came, a hundred more and then a hundred behind them, and hundreds arcing down after them, as though the sky would disgorge birds forever, the drumming of frantic pinions reverberating off every hard surface with such formidable volume that it was reminiscent of the freight-train rumble of a medium-magnitude earthquake.

On the carousel, Tommy *felt* the vibration of the wings, waves of pressure against his face and against his marveling eyes, and his tympanic membranes began to flutter in sympathy, so that it felt as though the wings themselves, not merely the sound of them, were in his ears. The humid air carried the faint ammonia scent of damp feathers.

He remembered something that Del had said earlier in the night: *The world is full of strange stuff.
Don't you watch* The X-Files?

Although the spectacle of the birds left Tommy as
clueless as he was wonderstruck, he suspected that
Del understood what was happening, that what was
deepest mystery to him was as clear as rainwater
to her.

With the apparently infinite flock swooping
around the demon, it turned away from the Ferris
wheel and stared east toward where the birds disappeared into the night past the Balboa Pavilion. It
hesitated. Took a step in that direction. Stopped.
Took another step.

As though finally interpreting the winged visita-
tion as a sign that it could not ignore, the beast broke
into a run, drawn by the birds in the night ahead of
it, encouraged by the birds rocketing past on both
sides of it, harried by the birds behind it. The torn
raincoat flapped like great tattered wings, but the
Samaritan-thing remained earthbound, borne east by
birds and bird shadows.

For perhaps a minute after the Samaritan-thing
passed out of sight, the birds continued to descend
from the stormy sky above the Ferris wheel to the
west, sail along Edgewater Avenue past the carousel,
and disappear to the east. Gradually the flock grew
thinner, until it ended with a few blackbirds, two
gulls, and a single blue heron at least three feet tall.

The blackbirds abruptly broke from their pell-mell eastward flight, spiraled over the dining terrace as if battling one another, and then fell to the promenade, where they fluttered on the wet concrete as though stunned.

The two sea gulls landed on the pavement, stumbled forward, flopped on their sides, squawked in distress, sprang to their feet, and wobble-walked in circles, bobbing their heads, apparently dazed and confused.

Stalk-legged and ungainly in appearance, the giant blue heron was nevertheless a graceful creature—except in this instance. It tottered off the promenade onto the dining terrace, weaving around the boles of the palm trees, curling and bending its long neck as if the muscles were so loose that it couldn't hold its head up, in general performing as if inebriated.

One by one the blackbirds stopped flopping on the concrete, hopped onto their feet, shook themselves, spread their wings, and soared into the air.

The pair of gulls regained their composure. They also took wing and disappeared into the deep-black sky above the harbor.

Having regained its equilibrium, the heron sprang onto one of the tables on the dining terrace and stood erect, its head held high, surveying the night on all sides, as if surprised to find itself in this place. Then it, too, departed.

Tommy sucked in a deep cool breath and blew it out and said, "What the hell was *that*?"

"Birds," Del said.

"I know they were birds, even a blind man would know they were birds, but what were they doing?"

The dog shook itself, whined, and padded to Del, rubbing against her as if for comfort.

"Good Scootie," she said, crouching to scratch the dog behind the ears. "Him were so quiet, so still. Him good baby, him is, mommy's little Scootie-wootums."

Scootie wagged his tail happily and chuffed.

To Tommy, Del said, "We better get out of here."

"You haven't answered my question."

"You have so *many* questions," she said.

"Right now, only this one about the birds."

Rising from beside the dog, she said, "Will you feel better if I scratch behind *your* ears too?"

"Del, damn it!"

"They were just birds. Agitated about something."

"More than that," he disagreed.

"Everything is more than it seems, but nothing is as mysterious as it appears to be."

"I want a *real* answer, not metaphysics."

"Then you tell me."

"What the hell is going on here, Del, what have I gotten into the middle of, what is this all about?"

Instead of answering, she said, "It might come back. We better get moving."

Frustrated, he followed her and Scootie off the carousel and into the rain. They went down the steps to Edgewater Avenue along which the thousands of birds had flocked.

At the end of the wall and the iron railing that

defined the raised area where the carousel stood, they stopped and peeked out warily along the Fun Zone, east to where the demon had disappeared. The beast was nowhere to be seen. All of the birds were gone as well.

Scootie led them onto the promenade.

A few dozen feathers in different hues were stuck to the wet concrete or floated in the puddles. Otherwise, it would have been easy to believe that the birds had not been real, but a phenomenal and phantasmagoric illusion.

"This way," Del said, and she headed briskly west, the opposite direction from that in which the Samaritan-thing had gone.

"*Are* you a witch?" Tommy asked.

"Certainly not."

"That's suspicious."

"What?" she asked.

"Such a direct answer. You never give them."

"I always give direct answers. You just don't listen to them properly."

As they passed between the Fun Zone Game Room and the Fun Zone Boat Company, between Mrs. Fields Cookies and the deserted Ferris wheel, Tommy said exasperatedly, "Del, I've been listening all night, and I still haven't heard anything that makes sense."

"That just proves what bad ears you have. You better make an appointment to see a good audiologist. But you sure do kiss a lot better than you hear, tofu boy."

He had forgotten the kiss that they had shared on the carousel. How could he possibly have forgotten the kiss? Even with the sudden arrival of the Samaritan-thing followed by the astonishing flock of birds, how could he have forgotten that kiss?

Now his lips burned with the memory of her lips, and he tasted the sweetness of her darting tongue as though it were still in his mouth.

Her mention of the kiss left him speechless.

Maybe that had been her intention.

Just past the Ferris wheel, at the intersection of Edgewater Avenue and Palm Street, Del stopped as if not sure which way to go.

Directly ahead, Edgewater was still a pedestrian promenade, though they were nearing the end of the Fun Zone.

Palm Street entered from the left. Though no parking was allowed along it, the street was open to vehicular traffic because it terminated at the boarding ramp to the Balboa Ferry.

At this hour no traffic moved on Palm, because the ferry was closed for the night. In the docking slip at the foot of the ramp, one of the barge-type, three-car ferries creaked softly, wallowing on the high tide.

They could turn left on Palm and leave the Fun Zone for the next street to the south, which was Bay Avenue. In the immediate vicinity, it was not a residential street, but they might still find a parked car or two that Del could hot-wire.

Tommy was thinking like a thief. Or at least he was thinking like a thief's apprentice. Maybe blondes—at least this blonde—were every bit the corrupting influence that his mother had always believed them to be.

He didn't care.

He could still taste the kiss.

For the first time, he felt as tough and adaptable and suave as his detective, Chip Nguyen.

Beyond Bay Avenue was Balboa Boulevard, the main drag for the length of the peninsula. With police no doubt still coming and going from the scene of the shooting farther east, Tommy and Del would be too noticeable on the well-lighted boulevard, where at this hour they would probably be the only pedestrians.

Scootie growled, and Del said, "It's coming back."

For an instant Tommy didn't understand what she meant, and then he understood too well. Bringing up the shotgun, he spun around to face east. The promenade was deserted as far as he could see, and even at night in the rain he could see past the carousel and as far as the Balboa Pavilion at the entrance to the Fun Zone.

"It doesn't know exactly where we are yet," she said, "but it's coming back this way."

"Intuition again?" he asked sarcastically.

"Or whatever. And I don't think we can outrun it."

"So we've got to find a car," he said, still keeping a watch on the east end of the Fun Zone, expecting the Samaritan-thing to come racing toward them, birdless and furious.

"Car, no. That's too dangerous. That means going

out toward the boulevard where a cop might pass by and see us and think we're suspicious."

"Suspicious? What's suspicious about two heavily armed people and a big strange black dog on the street at three in the morning in the middle of a storm?"

"We'll steal a boat," Del said.

Her announcement drew his attention away from the promenade. "A boat?"

"It'll be fun," she said.

Already she and Scootie were on the move, and Tommy glanced east along the deserted amusement area once more before scrambling after the woman and the dog.

Past the entrance ramp to the ferry was Balboa Boat Rentals, a business that offered a variety of sailing skiffs, small motorboats, and kayaks to the tourist trade.

Tommy didn't know how to sail, wasn't sure that he would be able to operate a motorboat, and didn't relish paddling out onto the rain-lashed harbor in a kayak. "I'd prefer a car."

Del and Scootie ran past the shuttered rental facility and departed the open promenade. They passed between a couple of dark buildings and went to the sea wall.

Tommy followed them through a gate and along a pier. Though he wore rubber-soled shoes, the rain-soaked planks were slippery.

They were in what appeared to be a small marina area where docking space could be rented, though some of the docks to the west were evidently private. A line of boats—some commercial party boats, some charter-fishing craft, and a few private craft big enough to be classified as full-blown yachts—were tied up side by side in the pounding rain, dimly revealed by the pier security lamps.

Del and Scootie hurried along a dock head serving several slips and moorings, looking over ten boats before stopping at a sleek white double-deck cruiser. "This is good," she said as Tommy joined them.

"Are you kidding? You're going to take *this*? It's huge!"

"Not so big. Bluewater 563, fifty-six-foot length, fourteen-foot beam."

"We can't handle this—how could we ever handle this?—we need a whole crew to handle this," Tommy babbled, wishing that he didn't sound so panicky.

"I can handle it just swell," she assured him with her usual ebullience. "These Bluewater yachts are sweet, really sweet, about as easy as driving a car."

"I can drive a car, but I can't drive one of these."

"Hold this." She handed him the .44 Magnum and moved out along the finger of the dock to which the Bluewater was tied.

Following her, he said, "Del, wait."

Pausing briefly to untie the bowline from a dock cleat, she said, "Don't worry. This baby's got less than two feet of draft, a windage-reducing profile, and the hull's after sections are virtually flat—"

"You might as well be talking alien abductions again."

"—two deep, wide-spaced propeller pockets give it a whole lot more turning leverage," she continued as she passed three smaller lines and went to the back of the craft, where she untied the stern line from another dock cleat, coiled it, and tossed it aboard. "You have real shaft-angle efficiency with this sweetheart. Twenty-one tons, but I'll make it pirouette."

"Twenty-one tons," he worried, following her back to midships. "Where are you planning on taking this—Japan?"

"No, it's a coastal cruiser. You wouldn't want to take this too far out on the open sea. Anyway, we're just going across the harbor to Balboa Island, where the police aren't all agitated. We can get a car there without being spotted."

As Del unzipped her ski jacket and stripped out of it, Tommy said, "Is this piracy?"

"Not if no one's aboard. Ordinary theft," she assured him brightly, handing her jacket to him.

"What're you doing?"

"I'm going to have my hands full with the boat, so you're our only line of defense. The jacket pockets are full of spare ammo. You might need it. Position yourself on the bow deck, and if the damn thing shows up, do what's necessary to keep it from getting aboard."

As the skin crawled on the nape of his neck, Tommy looked back across the dock, along the pier and east to the gate through which they had come from the Fun Zone. The Samaritan-thing was not yet in sight.

"It's getting close," she assured him.

Her voice was no longer at his side, and when he turned to her, he saw that she had already climbed aboard the yacht through the gap in the port railing.

Scootie was also aboard, ascending the port-side steps to the open upper deck.

"What about these lines?" Tommy asked, indicating the three dock ties that she had not cast off.

"Forward spring, after spring, and breast line. I'll take care of them. You just get in position on the bow."

He shoved the Desert Eagle under the waistband of his jeans, praying to God he wouldn't stumble and fall and accidentally blow off his manhood. Draping Del's jacket over the shotgun in his left hand, he grabbed the railing with his right hand, and pulled himself aboard.

As he started forward, another worry occurred to him, and he turned to Del. "Hey, don't you need keys or something to start it?"

"No."

"For God's sake, it can't be like an outboard motor with a pull cord."

"I have my ways," she assured him.

In spite of the deep gloom, he could see that her smile was even more enigmatic than any with which she had previously favored him.

She leaned toward him, kissed him lightly on the mouth, and then said, "Hurry."

He went forward to the open bow deck. At the foremost point of the yacht, he stepped into the slightly depressed well in which the anchor winch was mounted. He dropped the jacket, which wasn't going anywhere because it weighed about ten pounds with all the ammo in its pockets.

With a sigh of relief at not having been neutered, he gingerly withdrew the pistol from his waistband and placed it on top of the jacket, where he could easily get hold of it if the need arose.

The rain-swept docks were still deserted.

A halyard rattled mutedly against a mast on a sail-boat. Dock rollers creaked and rasped over concrete pilings, and jammed rubber fenders squeaked between a boat hull and a dock.

The water was oil black and had a faint briny smell. In the detective novels he wrote, this was the cold, murky, secret-keeping water into which villains sometimes dropped chain-wrapped victims in concrete boots. In other writers' books, such water was home to great white sharks, giant killer squid, and sea serpents.

He looked back at the dark windows of the enclosed lower deck, immediately behind him, wondering where Del had gone.

The smaller top deck began farther aft, and as he raised his gaze to it, soft amber light appeared at the windshield of what might have been an upper helm station. Then he glimpsed Del as she slipped behind the wheel and looked over the instrumentation.

When Tommy checked the docks again, nothing moved on them, although he wouldn't have been surprised to see policemen, harbor policemen, Coast

Guardsmen, FBI agents, and so many other officers of one law-enforcement agency or another that the Samaritan-thing, if it showed up, would be unable to shoulder its way through the crowd. He had probably broken more laws tonight than in his entire previous thirty years combined.

The Bluewater's twin diesel engines chugged, coughed, and then turned over with a hard rumble of power. The foredeck vibrated under Tommy's shoes.

He looked toward the top-deck helm again and saw, beside Del, Scootie's head, ears pricked. The Labrador was apparently standing with his forepaws on the instrument board, and Del was patting his big head as if to say, *Good dog.*

For some reason he couldn't grasp, Tommy was reminded of the swarming birds. He flashed back, as well, to the courtyard of Del's house, when they had entered from the street with the Samaritan in pursuit of them, and the previously locked front door had seemed to be open before she could have reached it. Abruptly he felt poised on the brink of a *satori* again, but then the moment passed without bringing him enlightenment.

This time, when he turned his attention to the docks, he saw the Samaritan-thing hurtling through the gate at the sea wall, no more than two hundred feet away, raincoat billowing like a cape behind it, no longer dazzled by birds, its eyes on the prize.

"Go, go!" Tommy urged Del as the yacht began to ease backward out of its slip.

The demon descended to the dock head and raced

westward along the base of the sea wall, passing all of the boats that Del had rejected.

Standing in the anchor well, Tommy held the Mossberg in both hands, hoping the creature would never get close enough to require the use of the shotgun.

The yacht was halfway out of the slip and moving faster by the second.

Tommy heard the thudding of his own heart, and then he heard an even louder pounding: the hollow booming of the demon's footfalls on the dock planks.

The yacht was three-quarters of the way out of the slip, and waves of black water rolled in where it had been, slapping the dock.

Skidding on the wet planks, the fat-man-that-wasn't-a-fat-man reached the head of the slip and sprinted onto the port-side finger, desperately trying to catch them before they reversed all the way into the channel.

The beast was close enough for Tommy to see its radiant green eyes, as improbable and frightening in the pale face of the Samaritan as in that of the rag doll.

The Bluewater reversed all the way out of the slip, churning hard through water now festooned with garlands of phosphorescent foam.

The demon sprinted to the end of the port-side finger of the slip just as the yacht pulled away. It didn't stop, but leaped across the six-foot gap between the end of the dock and the boat, slammed into the pulpit only three feet in front of Tommy, and seized the railing with both hands.

As the thing tried to pull itself over the railing and aboard, Tommy squeezed off a round from the shotgun, point-blank in its face, flinching at the roar and at the gout of flame that spurted from the muzzle of the Mossberg.

In the pearlescent glow of the running lights, he saw the fat man's face vanish in the blast, and he gagged in revulsion at the grisly spectacle.

But the Samaritan-thing didn't let go of the pulpit railing. It should have been torn loose by the powerful hit that it had taken, but the relentless beast still hung from the bow and continued trying to drag-heave-roll itself onto the foredeck.

Out of the raw, oozing mass of torn flesh left by the shotgun blast, the fat man's glistening white face at once miraculously re-formed, utterly undamaged, and the green serpent eyes blinked open, radiant and vicious.

The thick-lipped mouth yawned wide, gaping silently for a moment, and then the Samaritan-thing screamed at Tommy. The piercing voice was not remotely human, less like an animal sound than like an electronic shriek.

Cast back on the faith of his youth, pleading with the Holy Virgin, Mother of God, to save him, Tommy pumped another round into the breach, fired, worked the pump action again, and fired a third round, both from a distance of only three feet.

The hands on the railing were not human any

more. They had metamorphosed into chitinous pincers with serrated edges and were locked so fiercely
that the stainless-steel tubing actually appeared to be
bending in the creature's grip.

Tommy pumped, fired, pumped, squeezed the
trigger, pumped, squeezed the trigger, and then realized that he was dry-firing. The magazine of the
Mossberg was empty.

Shrieking again, the beast hauled itself higher on
the pulpit railing as the bow of the reversing yacht
came around to port and away from the dock.

Tommy dropped the empty shotgun, snatched up
the Desert Eagle, slipped, and fell backward. He
landed on his butt on the bow deck with his feet still
in the anchor well.

The gun was beaded with rain. His hands were
wet and shaking. But he didn't drop the weapon
when he landed.

Clambering over the railing, shrieking in triumph,
the serpent-eyed Samaritan loomed over Tommy.
The moon-round, moon-pale visage split open from
chin to hairline, as if it weren't a skull at all but a
strained sausage skin, and the halves of the bifur-
cated face peeled apart, with the demented green
eyes bulging at either side, and out of the sudden
gash sprouted an obscene mass of writhing, segmented, glossy-black tentacles as thin as whips,
perhaps two feet long, and as agitated as the append-
ages of a squid in a feeding frenzy. At the base of the
squirming tentacles was a wet sucking hole full of
clashing teeth.

Two, four, five, seven times Tommy fired the .44 Magnum. The pistol bucked in his hands and the recoil slammed through him hard enough to rattle his vertebrae. At such close quarters, he didn't have to be as first-rate a marksman as Del was, and every round seemed to strike home.

The creature shuddered with the impact of the shots and pitched backward over the pulpit railing. Pincers flailed, grabbed, and one of them locked tightly on the steel tubing. Then the eighth and ninth rounds found their mark, and simultaneously a section of railing gave way with a gonglike *clang*, and the beast plunged backward into the harbor.

Tommy scrambled to the damaged railing, slipped, almost pitched through the gap, clutched a firmly anchored section tightly with one hand, and searched the black water for some sign of the creature. It had vanished.

He didn't believe that it was really gone. He anxiously scanned the water, waiting for the Samaritan-thing to surface.

The yacht was cruising forward now, east along the channel, past the other boats in the moorings and the small marina. A speed limit was in effect in the harbor, but Del wasn't obeying it.

Moving aft along the short bow deck, clutching at the starboard railing, Tommy searched the waters on that side, but soon the area where the creature had disappeared was well behind them and receding rapidly.

The crisis wasn't over. The threat wasn't gone. He

was not going to make the mistake of taking another breather. He wasn't safe until dawn.

If then.

He returned to the pulpit to retrieve the shotgun and the ski jacket full of ammunition. His hands were shaking so badly that he dropped the Mossberg twice.

The yacht was cruising fast enough to stir up a wind of its own in the windless night. Although the skeins of rain still fell as straight as the strands of a glass-bead curtain, the speed at which the boat surged forward made it seem as if the droplets were being flung at Tommy by the fury of the storm.

Carrying both of the guns and the ski jacket, he retreated along the narrow port-side passway and hurriedly climbed the steep stairs to the upper deck.

The aft portion of the open-air top deck contained a built-in table for alfresco dining and an enormous elevated sunbathing pad across the entire stern. Toward starboard, an enclosed stairwell led to the lower deck.

Scootie was standing on the sunbathing pad, gazing down at the foaming wake that trailed away from the stern. He was as focused on the churning water as he might have been on a taunting cat, and he didn't look up at Tommy.

Forward on the top deck, the upper helm station had a hardtop roof and a windshield, but the back of it was meant to be open in good cruising weather. Currently a custom-sewn vinyl enclosure was snugged to the supporting rear framework of the hardtop, forming a weatherproofed cabin of sorts, but Del had unsnapped the center vent to gain access to the wheel.

Tommy pushed through the loose flaps, into the dim light beyond, which arose only from the control board.

Del was in the captain's seat. She glanced away from the rain-streaked windshield. "Nice job."

"I don't know," he said worriedly, putting the guns down on the console behind her. He began to unzip pockets on the ski jacket. "It's still out there somewhere."

"But we're outrunning it now, on the move and safe."

"Yeah, maybe," he said as he added nine rounds of ammo to the Desert Eagle magazine, replenishing the thirteen-shot capacity as quickly as his trembling hands could cope with the cartridges. "How long to cross the harbor?"

Bringing the Bluewater sharply and expertly around to port, she said, "We're starting the run right now. Going so fast, I'll have to throttle back just a little, but it should still take like maybe two minutes."

At various points down the center of the broad harbor, clusters of boats bobbled at permanent moorings, gray shapes in the gloom that effectively divided the expanse of water into channels. But as far as could be seen in the rain, theirs was the only craft currently making way.

Del said, "Problem is—when we get to Balboa Island, I need to find an empty slip, a suitable dock to tie up to, and that might take some time. Thank God, it's high tide and this baby has such a low draft, 'cause we can slide in almost anywhere."

Reloading the Mossberg, he said, "How'd you start the engines without keys?"

"Hot-wired the sucker."

"I don't think so."

"Found a key."

"Bullshit."

"Well," she said airily, "those are your choices."

Outside on the open top deck, Scootie began to bark ferociously.

Tommy's stomach fluttered nervously, and his heart swelled with dread. "Jesus, here we go already."

Armed with both the shotgun and the pistol, he pushed through the vinyl flaps, into the night and rain.

Scootie still stood vigilant on the sunbathing pad, staring down at the churning wake.

Balboa Peninsula was swiftly receding.

Tommy stepped quickly past the dining table and the upholstered horseshoe bench that encircled it, to the platform on which the dog stood.

No railing encircled the outer edge of the sunbathing pad, only a low wall, and Tommy didn't want to risk standing on it and perhaps pitching over the stern. He wriggled forward on his belly, across the wet canvas-upholstered pad, beside the Labrador, where he peered down at the turbulent wake.

In the murk, he couldn't see anything out of the ordinary.

The dog barked more savagely than ever.

"What is it, fella?"

Scootie glanced at him and whined.

He could see the wake but nothing of the boat's stern, which was recessed beneath the top deck. Easing forward, his upper body extended over the low sun-deck wall, Tommy squinted down and back at the lower portion of the yacht.

Under Tommy, behind the enclosed first deck, was a back-porch-type afterdeck. It was overhung by the sunbathing platform on which he lay, and was therefore largely concealed.

Sans raincoat, the fat man was climbing out of the harbor and over the afterdeck railing. He disappeared under the overhang before Tommy could take a shot at him.

The dog scrambled to a closed stairhead hatch immediately starboard of the sunbathing platform.

Joining the Labrador, Tommy put down the pistol. Holding the Mossberg in one hand, he opened the hatch.

A small light glowed at the bottom of molded-fiberglass steps, revealing that the Samaritan-thing was already clambering upward. Its serpent eyes flashed, and it shrieked at Tommy.

Grasping the shotgun with both hands, Tommy pumped the entire magazine into the beast.

It grasped at a rail and held on tenaciously, but the last two blasts tore it loose and hurled it to the bottom of the steps. The thing rolled out of the stairwell, onto the afterdeck again, out of sight.

The indomitable creature would be stunned, as before. Judging by experience, however, it wouldn't

be out of action for long. There wasn't even any
blood on the steps. It seemed to absorb the buckshot
and bullets without sustaining any real wounds.

Dropping the shotgun, Tommy retrieved the .44
pistol. Thirteen rounds. That might be enough ammunition to knock the beast back down the stairs twice
more, but then there would be no time to reload.

Del appeared at his side, looking gaunt and more
worried than she had been before. "Give me the
gun," she said urgently.

"Who's driving?"

"I locked the wheel. Give me the gun and go forward, down the port stairs to the foredeck."

"What are you going to do?" he demanded, reluctant to leave her there even if she had the Desert
Eagle.

"I'll start a fire," she said.

"What?"

"You said fire distracted it."

He remembered the enraptured minikin at the
blazing Corvette, lost to all sensation except the
dancing flames. "How're you going to start a fire?"

"Trust me."

"But—"

Below, the recuperated Samaritan-thing shrieked
and entered the bottom of the stairwell.

"Give me the damn gun!" she snarled, and virtually tore it out of Tommy's grip.

The Desert Eagle bucked in her hands—once,
twice, three times, four times—and the roar echoed
back at them out of the stairwell, like cannonfire.

Squealing, spitting, hissing, the creature crashed down to the afterdeck again.

To Tommy, Del shouted, "Go, damn it, *go!*"

He stumbled across the open top deck to the port stairs farther forward, beside the helm station.

More gunfire erupted behind him. The beast had come back at her faster this time than before.

Clutching at the railing, Tommy descended the open port-side stairs, up which he had climbed earlier. At the bottom, the narrow railed passway led forward to the bow but didn't lead back toward the stern, so there was no easy route by which the Samaritan-thing could make its way to him directly from the afterdeck—unless it broke into the enclosed lower deck, rampaged forward through the state-rooms, and smashed out at him through a window.

More gunfire crashed above and aft, and the hard sound slapped across the black water, so it seemed as though Newport had gone to war with neighboring Corona Del Mar.

Tommy reached the bow deck, where only a few minutes ago he'd taken a stand against the Samaritan-thing when it had first tried to board the vessel.

In the night ahead, Balboa Island loomed.

"Holy shit," Tommy said, horrified by what was about to happen.

They were approaching Balboa Island at considerable speed, on a line as direct and true as if they were being guided by a laser beam. With the wheel locked and the throttles set, they would pass

between two large private docks and ram the sea
wall that surrounded the island.

He turned, intending to go back to the helm and
make Del change course, but he halted in astonishment when he saw that the aft end of the yacht was
already ablaze. Orange and blue flames leaped into
the night. Shimmering with reflections of the fire,
the falling rain looked like showers of embers from
a celestial blaze.

Scootie padded along the port-side passway and
onto the bow deck.

Del was right behind the Labrador. "The damn
thing's in the stairwell, burning in ecstasy, like you
said. Creepy as hell."

"How did you set it on fire so quick?" Tommy
demanded, half shouting to be heard above the
drumming rain and the engines.

"Diesel fuel," she said, raising her voice as well.

"Where'd you get diesel fuel?"

"There's six hundred gallons aboard."

"But in tanks somewhere."

"Not any more."

"And diesel fuel doesn't burn *that* fiercely."

"So I used gasoline."

"Huh?"

"Or napalm."

"You're lying to me again!" he fumed.

"You're making it necessary."

"I *hate* this crap."

"Sit on the deck," she instructed.

"This is so *nuts*!"

"Sit down, grab hold of the railing."

"You're some crazy gonzo Amazon witch or something."

"Whatever you say. Just brace yourself, 'cause we're going to crash, and you don't want to be thrown overboard."

Tommy looked toward Balboa Island, which was clearly defined by the streetlamps along the sea wall and the dark shapes of houses beyond. "Dear God."

"As soon as we run aground," she said, "get up, get off the boat, and follow me."

She crossed to the starboard flank of the bow deck, sat with her legs splayed in front of her, and grabbed hold of the railing with her right hand. Scootie clambered into her lap, and she put her left arm around him.

Following Del's example, Tommy sat on the deck, facing forward. He didn't have a dog to hug, so he gripped the port railing with *both* hands.

Sleek and swift, the yacht cruised through the rainy darkness toward doom.

If Del had set the fuel tanks on fire, the engines wouldn't be running. Would they?

Don't think, just hold on.

Maybe the fire had come from the same place as the seething flock of birds. Which was—where?

Just hold on.

He expected the boat to explode under him.

He expected the flaming Samaritan-thing to shake off its rapture and, still ablaze, leap upon him.

He closed his eyes.

Just hold on.

If he had just gone home to his mother's for *com tay cam* and stir-fried vegetables with *nuoc mam* sauce, he might not have been home when the door-bell rang, might never have found the doll, might now be in bed, sleeping peacefully, dreaming about the Land of Bliss at the peak of fabled Mount Phi Lai, where everyone was immortal and beautiful and deliriously happy twenty-four hours every day, where everyone lived in perfect harmony and never said one cross word to anyone else and never suffered an identity crisis. But *nooooo*, that wasn't good enough for him. *Nooooo*, he had to offend his mother and make a statement about his independence by going instead to a diner for cheeseburgers, cheeseburgers and french fries, cheeseburgers and french fries and onion rings and a chocolate milk shake, Mr. Big Shot with his own car phone and his new Corvette, intrigued by the blond waitress, flirting with her, when the world was filled with beautiful and intelligent and charming Vietnamese girls—who were perhaps the most lovely women in the world—who never called you "tofu boy," never hot-wired cars, didn't think they had been abducted by aliens, didn't threaten to blow your head off when you wanted to look at their paintings, never stole yachts and set them on fire, *gorgeous* Vietnamese women who never talked in riddles, never said things like "reality is what you think it is," didn't have any expertise with throwing knives, hadn't been taught by their fathers to use high explosives, didn't wear father-killing bullets as necklace pendants, didn't run around with big black smartass hounds from hell with farting rubber hotdogs. He couldn't go home and eat *com tay cam*, had to write stupid detective novels instead of becoming a doctor or a baker, and now as payment for his selfishness and his arrogance and his bullheaded determination to be what he could never be, he was going to *die*.

Just hold on.

He was going to die.

Just hold.

Here came the big sleep, the long good-bye.

Hold.

He opened his eyes.

Shouldn't have done that.

Balboa Island, where no structure was taller than three stories, where half the houses were bungalows and cottages, seemed as large as Manhattan, *towering*.

Screws turning furiously, the fifty-six-foot, merrily blazing Bluewater yacht came into the island at extreme high tide, drawing less than two feet, virtually *skimming* like a cigarette racing boat, for God's sake, in spite of its size, came in between two docks (one of which was already decorated for Christmas), and struck the massive steel-reinforced concrete sea wall with a colossal shattering-ripping-screeching booming noise that made Tommy cry out in fear and that would have awakened the dead if perhaps any of the islanders had perished in their sleep this night. At the water line, the hull, although as strong as any, was crushed and torn open at the bow. The impact dramatically slowed the yacht, but the diesel engines were so powerful and the screws provided such enormous thrust that the vessel surged forward, striving to climb the sea wall, heaving across the top of it, angling up at the bow, up, over the wide public promenade that ringed the island, up, as though it might churn all the way out of the harbor and sail through the front of one of the large houses that lined the island's waterfront. Then at last it shuddered to a halt, securely hung up on the sea wall and badly weighed down by the tons of sea water pouring through the broken hull into the lower holds.

Tommy had been bounced against the deck and slammed sideways against the low port sill, but he had held fast to the railing, even though at one point he thought that his left arm was going to be dislocated at the shoulder. He came through the wreck without serious injury, however, and when the yacht was fully at rest, he let go of the railing, rose into a crouch, and crabbed sideways across the bow to Del.

She was on her feet by the time he reached her. "Let's get the hell out of here."

The stern of the yacht burned brighter than ever. The fire was spreading forward, and there were flames behind the windows of the lower-deck staterooms.

An eerie and chilling ululation arose from deep within the crackling blaze. It might have been steam venting or hydraulic fluid singing through a pierced steel line—or the crooning of the enraptured demon.

The bow deck was canted three or four degrees because the boat was ramped up on the sea wall.

They walked uphill to the pulpit, which thrust out of the water and was suspended over the deserted pedestrian promenade.

All along the recently slumbering waterfront, lights began to blink on in the closely spaced houses.

Scootie hesitated at the gap in the pulpit railing, but only briefly, then leaped down onto the concrete sward on the island side of the sea wall.

Del and Tommy followed him. From the pulpit to the sidewalk was about a ten-foot drop.

The dog sprinted west along the promenade, as if he knew where he was going.

Del followed the Labrador, and Tommy followed Del. He glanced back once and, in spite of all the outrageous incidents of the night, which should have inured him to spectacle, he was awestruck at the sight of the enormous boat balanced on the sea wall, overhanging the public walkway, as if it were the Ark washed ashore after the Great Flood.

As worried faces began to appear at upstairs windows but before any front doors flew open, before frightened voices rose in the night, Tommy and Del and the dog found the nearest street leading away from the promenade. They headed toward the center of the island.

Although Tommy looked over his shoulder from time to time, expecting a serpent-eyed fat man or worse, no creature swaddled in fire pursued them.

SEVEN

Hundreds of houses crowded the small lots on Balboa Island, and because of inadequate garage space, both sides of the narrow streets were lined with the parked cars of residents and visitors. Shopping for a set of wheels to steal, Del had a daunting variety of choices. Rather than settle for a Buick or Toyota, however, she was attracted to a fire-engine-red Ferrari Testarossa.

They stood under the cloaking boughs of an old podocarpus while she admired the sports car.

"Why not that Geo?" Tommy asked, pointing to the vehicle parked in front of the Ferrari.

"The Geo's okay, but it's not cool. The Ferrari is cool."

"It costs as much as a house," Tommy objected.

"We're not buying it."

"I'm acutely aware of what we're doing."

"We're just borrowing it."

"We're stealing it," he corrected.

"No. Bad guys steal stuff. We're not bad guys. We're the good guys. Ergo, we can't be stealing it."

"Actually, that's a defense that might work with a California jury," he said sourly.

"You keep a lookout while I see if it's unlocked."

"Why not destroy a cheaper car?" he argued.

"Who said anything about destroying it?"

"You're hard on machinery," he reminded her.

From the far end of the island came the sirens of fire engines. Above the silhouettes of the tightly packed houses, the night sky to the south was brightened by the glow of the burning yacht.

"Keep a lookout," she repeated.

The street was deserted.

With Scootie, she stepped off the sidewalk and went boldly to the driver's side of the Ferrari. She tried the door, and it was unlocked.

"Surprise, surprise," Tommy muttered.

Scootie entered the car ahead of her.

The Ferrari started even as Del settled behind the wheel and pulled the driver's door shut. The engine sounded powerful enough to ensure that the car would be airborne if Del decided that she wanted it to fly.

"Two seconds flat. A true master criminal," Tommy murmured to himself as he went to the car and opened the other door.

"Scootie is willing to share the passenger seat."

"He's a sweetheart," Tommy said.

After the dog leaped out into the rain, Tommy climbed into the low-slung car. He resisted the temptation to close the door before the mutt could reenter.

Scootie sat with his rump in Tommy's lap, his hind legs on the seat, and his forepaws on the dashboard.

"Put your arms around him," Del said as she switched on the headlights.

"What?"

"So he doesn't go through the windshield if we stop suddenly."

"I thought you weren't going to destroy the car?"

"You never know when you might have to stop suddenly."

Tommy put his arms around the Labrador. "Where are we going?"

"Mom's house," Del said.

"How far is that?"

"Fifteen minutes tops. Maybe ten in this baby."

Scootie turned his head, made eye contact, licked Tommy from chin to forehead, and then faced forward again.

"It's going to be a long drive," Tommy said.

"He's decided he likes you."

"I'm flattered."

"You should be. He doesn't lick just anyone."

Scootie chuffed as if to confirm that statement.

As Del pulled the Ferrari away from the curb and into the street, she said, "We'll leave this crate at Mom's place, and she can have it brought back here. We'll borrow one of her cars for the rest of the night."

"You've got an understanding mother."

"She's a peach."

"How'd you get the car started so quickly?" he asked.

"The keys were in it."

With the big dog in his lap, Tommy couldn't see much of the street ahead of them, but he certainly could see the ignition, in which no key was inserted.

"Where are they now?" he asked.

"Where are what?"

"The keys?"

"What keys?"

"The ones you started the car with."

"I hot-wired it," she said, grinning.

"It started while you were pulling your door shut."

"I can hot-wire one-handed."

"In two seconds flat?"

"Cool, huh?"

She turned left onto a divided street that led to Marine Avenue, the island's main drag.

"We're so soaked, we're ruining the upholstery," he worried.

"I'll send the owner a check."

"I'm serious. This is expensive upholstery."

"I'm serious too. I'll send him a check. You're such a *nice* man, Tommy. Such a straight arrow. I like that about you."

Emergency beacons flashing, a police car turned the corner ahead and passed them, no doubt heading toward the burning boat.

"What do you think it cost?" Tommy asked.

"A thousand bucks ought to cover it."

"For an entire yacht?"

"I thought you meant the upholstery damage. The Bluewater cost about seven hundred and fifty thousand."

"Those poor people."

"What people?"

"The poor people whose boat you trashed. Are you going to write them a check too?"

"Don't have to. It's my boat."

He gaped at her. Since encountering Deliverance Payne, staring agape had become his most-used expression.

As she stopped at the Marine Avenue intersection, she smiled at him and said, "Only owned it since July."

He managed to rehinge his jaw to ask, "If it's your boat, why wasn't it docked at your house?"

"It's so big it blocks my view. So I rent that slip where it was tied up."

Scootie thumped one paw repeatedly against the dashboard, as though expressing his impatience to get moving.

Tommy said, "So you blew up your own boat."

Turning left on Marine Avenue, which was the commercial center of the island, Del said, "Didn't blow it up. You have a tendency to exaggeration, Tommy. I hope your detective novels aren't full of hyperbole."

"Okay, you set it on fire."

"Big difference, I think. Blow up, set on fire—there's a big difference."

"At this rate, even *your* inheritance won't last long."

"Oh, you're such a goof, Tommy. I don't set yachts on fire every day, you know."

"I wonder."

"Besides, I'll never have money worries."

"You're a counterfeiter too?"

"No, silly. Daddy taught me to play poker, and I'm even better than he was."

"Do you cheat?"

"Never! Cards are sacred."

"I'm glad to hear you think *something*'s sacred."

"I think a lot of things are sacred," she said.

"Like the truth?"

With a coy look, she said, "Sometimes."

They were reaching the end of Marine Avenue. The bridge across the back channel to the mainland lay less than a block ahead.

He said, "Truth—how did you start this car?"

"Didn't I say? The keys were in the ignition."

"That's one of the things you said. How did you start the fire on the boat?"

"Wasn't me. Was Mrs. O'Leary's cow, kicked over a lantern."

Scootie made a weird chuffing, wheezing sound. Tommy could have sworn it was doggy laughter.

Another police cruiser appeared on the arched bridge ahead of them, entering the island from the mainland.

"Truth—where did the birds come from?" Tommy asked.

"Well, it's the eternal mystery, isn't it: Which came first, the chicken or the egg?"

The oncoming patrol car stopped at the foot of the bridge and flashed its headlights at them.

"Thinks we might be bad guys," Del said.

"Oh, no."

"Relax."

Del stopped beside the cruiser.

Tommy said, "Don't turn him into a cat or a crow or something."

"I was thinking—a goose."

The electric window purred down.

The cop had already lowered his window. He sounded surprised when he said, "Del?"

"Hi, Marty!"

"I didn't realize it was you," the cop said, smiling at her from behind the wheel of his cruiser. "New car?"

"You like it?"

"A real beauty. Yours or your mom's?"

"You know Mom."

"Don't *you* go breaking any speed limits."

"If I do, will you personally paddle me?"

Marty, the cop, laughed. "I'd be delighted."

"What's all the hubbub?" Del asked innocently.

"You won't believe this. Some fool rammed a big damn boat high speed into the sea wall."

"Must've been having a great party on board. Why do I never get invited to the great parties?"

Apparently uninterested in Tommy, Marty said, "Hi, Scootie."

Craning his burly head to look past Del, out the side window, the Labrador grinned, tongue lolling.

To Del, Marty said, "Tell your mom we'll be watching for her in that car."

"You might not see her," Del said, "but you'll sure hear the sonic boom."

Laughing, Marty drove away, and Del continued onto the bridge, over the back channel, to the mainland.

Tommy said, "What happens when he discovers the yacht on the sea wall is yours?"

"He won't know. It's not in my name. It's registered to our offshore corporation."

"Offshore corporation? How far off? Mars?"

"Grand Cayman, in the Caribbean."

"What happens when this car is reported stolen?"

"It won't be. Mom'll have it brought back before it's missed."

"Scootie smells."

"It's only his wet coat."

"It better be," Tommy said. "Truth—was it just chance that you happened to be driving by that vacant lot when I rolled the Corvette, or did you know I was going to be there?"

"Of course I didn't know. Like I said, though, we're clearly each other's destiny."

"God, you're infuriating!" Tommy said.

"You don't mean that."

"Yes, I do."

"Poor confused Tommy."

"Infuriating."

"Actually, you mean to say *interesting*."

"Infuriating."

"Interesting. In fact, you're *enthralled* with me."

He sighed.

"Aren't you?" she teased. "Enthralled."

He sighed again.

"Aren't you?" she insisted.

"Yes."

"You're so sweet," she said. "Such a sweet man."

"Want me to shoot you?"

"Not yet. Wait till I'm dying."

"That's not going to be easy."

Del's mother lived in a private guard-gated community on a hill overlooking Newport Beach. The guardhouse was finished in mottled-pastel stucco with cast-stone wainscot and cast-stone quoins at the corners, and it stood under several enormous, theatrically lighted phoenix palms.

Because no resident sticker adorned the Ferrari windshield, the young guard had to open the gatehouse door and lean out to ask whom Del was visiting. He was slack-faced and sleepy-eyed when he first appeared, but the moment he saw her, his face tightened and his eyes brightened.

"Miss Payne!"

"Hi, Mickey."

"New car?"

She said, "Maybe. We're test-driving it."

The guard came out of the gatehouse, into the rain, and stooped beside Del's open window to be at her level. "Quite a machine."

"My mom could make it go to the moon."

"If she had this," the guard said, "the community would have to put in speed bumps the size of garbage Dumpsters to slow her down."

"How's Emmy?"

Although Mickey was not wearing a raincoat, he seemed to be oblivious to the downpour, as though Del so completely commanded his awareness that he simply didn't have the capacity also to notice the inclement weather—or anything else, for that matter. Tommy knew exactly how the poor guy felt.

"Emmy's great," Mickey said. "She's in total remission."

"That's wonderful, Mickey."

"The doctors can't believe it."

"I told you not to lose hope, didn't I?"

"If the tests keep coming back as clear as they do now, they'll probably release her from the hospital in about three days. I just pray to God she'll never . . . never have to . . . go back."

"She'll be fine, Mickey."

"It's so nice of you to go visit her the way you do."

"Oh, I adore her, Mickey. She's an absolute angel. It's no trouble at all."

"She thinks the world of you, Miss Payne. She sure loved that storybook you brought her." Looking past Del, he said, "Hi, Scootie."

The Labrador chuffed.

Del said, "Mickey, this is my friend, Tommy Tofu."

Mickey said, "Glad to meet you, Mr. Tofu."

Peering between Del and the dog, Tommy said, "Likewise. You're getting soaked, Mickey."

"Am I?"

"Yes, you are," Del said. "You better get back inside, dear. Tell Emmy I'll see her the day after tomorrow. And after she's been out of the hospital a while and put on a little weight, maybe she can come to my studio on the peninsula and sit for me. I'd like to paint her portrait."

"Oh, she'd love that, Miss Payne. Getting her portrait done—she'd feel like a princess."

Dripping, Mickey returned to the gatehouse, and Del put up the car window.

In front of them, a massive iron gate ornamented with gilded balls rolled out of the way, admitting them to the private community.

As Del piloted the Ferrari through the open gate, Tommy said, "Who's Emmy?"

"His little girl. Eight years old, cute as a button."

"She's in total remission from what?"

"Cancer."

"That's tough—eight years old and hit with cancer."

"She'll be absolutely fine now. Won't she, Scootie-wootums?"

The Labrador leaned over to nuzzle and lick her neck, and she giggled.

They cruised along winding streets lined with enormous houses behind deep and lushly landscaped grounds.

"I'm sorry we have to wake your mother at three-thirty in the morning," Tommy said.

"You're just so delightfully thoughtful and polite,"

Del said, reaching over to pinch his cheek. "But don't worry yourself. Mom will be awake and busy."

"She's a night person, huh?"

"She's an around-the-clock person. She never sleeps."

"Never?"

"Well, not since Tonopah," Del amended.

"Tonopah, Nevada?"

"Actually, outside Tonopah, close to Mud Lake."

"Mud Lake? What're you talking about?"

"That was twenty-eight years ago."

"Twenty-eight years?"

"Approximately. I'm twenty-seven."

"Your mother hasn't slept since before you were born?"

"She was twenty-three then."

"Everyone has to sleep," Tommy said.

"Not everyone. You've been up all night. Are you sleepy?"

"I was earlier, but—"

"Here we are," she said happily, turning a corner and driving into a cul-de-sac.

At the end of the short street stood a grove of palm trees and behind them a stone estate wall illuminated by landscape lighting so subtle that Tommy couldn't always discern the source.

Set in the wall was a tall bronze gate with two-inch-square pickets. In an eighteen-inch-deep cast header across the top of the gate were what appeared to be hieroglyphics. The massive portal made the main gate to the community look, by comparison, like a tin-foil construction.

Del stopped, put down her window, and pushed a call button on an intercom box set in a stone post.

From the speaker came a solemn male voice with a British accent. "Who's calling, please?"

"It's me, Mummingford."

"Good morning, Miss Payne," said the voice on the intercom.

The gate rolled open ponderously.

"Mummingford?" Tommy asked.

As she put up her window, Del said, "The butler."

"He's on duty at this hour?"

"Someone's always on duty. Mummingford prefers the night shift, actually, because it's usually more interesting here," Del explained as she drove forward through the gateway arch.

"What're those hieroglyphics on the gate?"

"It says, 'Toto, we're not in Kansas any more.' "

"I'm serious."

"So am I. Mom has a whimsical side."

Looking back at the gate as they passed through the wall, Tommy said, "What language is it written in?"

"The Great Pile," Del said.

"That's a language?"

"No, that's the name of the house. Look."

The Payne mansion, standing on perhaps three acres of grounds behind the estate wall, was easily the largest in the neighborhood. It was an enormous, sprawling, wildly romantic Mediterranean villa with deep loggias behind colonnades, arches upon arches, lattice panels dripping with the white blossoms of night-blooming jasmine, balustraded balconies shaded by trellises groaning under the weight of red-flowering bougainvillaea, bell towers and cupolas, so many steeply pitched barrel-tile roofs hipping into one another that Tommy might have been looking down on an entire Italian village rather than at a single structure. The scene was so cunningly and romantically lighted that it could well have been the most insanely ornate stage setting in the most mania-cally extravagant Andrew Lloyd Webber musical that the singular British genius of Broadway kitsch had ever created.

The driveway descended slightly into a spacious, stone-paved motor court at the center of which stood a four-tiered fountain featuring fifteen life-size marble maidens in togas, pouring water from vases.

As she drove the Ferrari around the astonishing fountain to the front door, Del said, "Mom wanted to build a more modern place, but the community's architectural guidelines specified *Mediterranean*, and the architectural committee had a very narrow definition of the word. She became so frustrated with the approval process that she designed the most ridiculously exaggerated Mediterranean house the world had ever seen, thinking they'd be appalled and reconsider her previous plans—but they loved it. By then it seemed a good joke to her, so she built the place."

"She built all this as a joke?"

"My mom's nothing if not cool. Anyway, some people in this neighborhood have named their houses, so Mom called this place The Great Pile."

She parked in front of an arched portico supported by marble columns featuring carved vines and bunches of grapes.

Warm amber and rose-colored light seemed to glow behind every beveled pane of every leaded-glass window in the house.

"Is she having a party at this hour?"

"Party? No, no. She just likes the place to be lit up like, as she puts it, 'a cruise ship on a dark sea.' "

"Why?"

"To remind herself that we're all passengers on an endless and magical journey."

"She actually said that?"

"Isn't it a pretty thought?" Del said.

"She sure sounds like your mother."

The limestone front walk was bordered by inlaid mosaic patterns created with terra-cotta and yellow ceramic tiles. Scootie raced ahead of them, tail wagging.

The ornate surround at the twelve-foot-high door consisted of sixteen highly embellished scenes intricately carved in limestone, all depicting a haloed monk in different poses but always with the same beatific expression, surrounded by joyous crowds of smiling and capering animals with their own haloes—dogs, cats, doves, mice, goats, cows, horses, pigs, camels, chickens, ducks, raccoons, owls, geese, rabbits.

"Saint Francis of Assisi, talking to the animals," Del said. "They're antique carvings by an unknown sculptor, taken out of a fifteenth-century Italian monastery that was mostly destroyed in World War Two."

"Is it the same order of monks that produces all those Elvis paintings on velvet?"

Grinning at him, she said, "Mom's going to like you."

The massive mahogany door swung open as they reached it, and a tall silver-haired man in a white shirt, black tie, black suit, and mirror-polished black shoes stood just beyond the threshold. A fluffy white beach towel was folded precisely over his left arm, as a waiter might carry a linen bar towel to wrap a champagne bottle.

With a reverberant British accent, he said, "Welcome to The Great Pile."

"Is Mom still making you say that, Mummingford?"

"I shall never tire of it, Miss Payne."

"Mummingford, this is my friend, Tommy Phan."

Tommy was surprised to hear her say his name correctly.

"Honored to meet you, Mr. Phan," Mummingford said, half bowing from the waist as he stepped back from the doorway.

"Thank you," Tommy said, nodding in acknowledgment of the bow and almost giving the words a crisp British accent.

Scootie preceded them through the doorway.

Mummingford led the dog aside, dropped to one knee, and began to dry the mutt and blot its paws with the beach towel.

As Del closed the door, Tommy said, "I'm afraid we're as soaked as Scootie. We're going to make a mess."

"Alas, you are," said Mummingford drily. "But I must tolerate Miss Payne to an extent I'm not obliged to tolerate the dog. And her friends enjoy sufferance as well."

"Where's Mom?" Del asked.

"She awaits you in the music room, Miss Payne. I'll send his nibs along to join you as soon as he's presentably dry."

Scootie grinned out of a cowl of white cotton, enjoying his rubdown.

"We can't stay long," Del told the butler. "We're on the lam from a doll snake rat-quick monster thing. But could we please have coffee and a tray of breakfast pastries?"

"In a trice, Miss Payne."

"You're a dear, Mummingford."

"It's the cross I bear," said Mummingford.

The grand hall, at least a hundred feet long, was floored with highly polished black granite on which their wet rubber-soled shoes squeaked with each step. The white walls were hung with enormous unframed canvases: all abstract art full of motion and color, each piece illuminated precisely to the edges of the canvas by projector lamps in the ceiling, so it seemed as if the art glowed from within. The ceiling was paneled with bands of polished steel alternating with bands of brushed steel. A double cove provided indirect lighting above, and additional indirect lighting flooded out at floor level from a groove in the black-granite baseboard.

Sensing Tommy's amazement, Del said, "Mom built the outside of the house to please the community architectural committee, but inside it's as modern as a spaceship and as Mediterranean as Coca-Cola."

The music room was two-thirds of the way along the main hall, on the left. A black-lacquered door opened onto a room floored with polished white limestone speckled with gracefully curved marine fossils. The sound-baffled ceiling and walls were padded and then upholstered in charcoal-gray fabric, as if this were a recording studio, and indirect lighting was tucked behind the baffles.

The chamber was huge, approximately forty by sixty feet. In the center was a twenty-by-thirty custom carpet with a geometric pattern in half a dozen subtly different shades of taupe and gold. In the center of the carpet were a black leather sofa and four black leather armchairs arranged in a conversational grouping around a solid rectangular-block coffee table veneered with a parquetry of faux-ivory squares.

Although a hundred music lovers could have been seated in the room for a piano recital, no piano was provided. The music—Glenn Miller's "Moonlight Serenade"—didn't issue from a state-of-the-art entertainment system with Surround Sound speakers, either. It came, instead, from what appeared to be a small, table-model, Art Deco radio that stood in the center of the faux-ivory coffee table, in a cone of light from a tightly focused halogen lamp in the ceiling. The tinny and static-spotted quality of the sound suggested that the radio was actually a cassette or CD player loaded with one of those authentic as-recorded-live-on-dance-night-in-the-forties radio programs.

Del's mother sat in one of the chairs, eyes closed, smiling as beatifically as Saint Francis in the limestone carvings around the front door, swaying her head from side to side with the music, keeping time by patting her hands against the arms of the chair. Although she was fifty, she looked at least ten years younger: quite a striking woman, not blond like Del but olive-skinned with jet-black hair, delicate features, and a swanlike neck. She reminded Tommy of the elfin actress in *Breakfast at Tiffany's*, Audrey Hepburn.

When Del lowered the volume on the radio, Mrs. Payne opened her eyes. They were as blue as Del's and even deeper. Her smile widened. "Good heavens, dear, you look like a drowned rat." She rose from the chair and regarded Tommy. "And so do you, young man."

Tommy was surprised to see that Mrs. Payne was wearing an *ao dais*, a flowing silk tunic-and-pants ensemble similar to those that his own mother wore at times.

Del said, "The drowned-rat look is simply the latest thing, very chic."

"You shouldn't joke about such things, darling. The world is ugly enough these days as it is."

"Mom, I'd like you to meet Tommy Phan."

"Pleased to meet you, Mrs. Payne."

Taking his offered hand in both of hers, Del's mother said, "Call me Julia."

"Thank you, Julia. I'm—"

"Or Rosalyn."

"Excuse me?"

"Or Winona."

"Winona?"

"Or even Lilith. They're all names I quite like."

Not sure how to respond to her offer of four names, Tommy said, "That's a beautiful *ao dais* you're wearing."

"Thank you, dear. It is lovely, isn't it? And so comfortable. There's a charming lady in Garden Grove who hand-sews them."

"I think my mother may buy from the same woman."

Del said, "Mom, Tommy is the one."

Julia Rosalyn Winona Lilith Payne—or whatever her name was—raised her eyebrows. "Is he?"

"Absolutely," said Del.

Mrs. Payne let go of Tommy's hand and, oblivious to his wet clothes, embraced him, hugged him tightly, and kissed his cheek. "This is wonderful, just wonderful."

Tommy wasn't sure what was happening.

Releasing him, Mrs. Payne turned to her daughter, and they hugged, laughed, all but jumped up and down like a couple of excited schoolgirls.

"We've had the most wonderful night," Del said.

Her mother said, "Tell me, tell me."

"I set the yacht on fire and crashed it into the Balboa Island sea wall."

Mrs. Payne gasped and put one hand against her breast as if to quiet her heart. "Deliverance, how exciting! You must tell me all about it."

"Tommy rolled his new Corvette."

Wide-eyed, apparently delighted, Mrs. Payne regarded him with what might have been admiration. "Rolled a new Corvette?"

"I didn't plan to," he assured her.

"How many times did you roll it?"

"At least twice."

"And *then*," Del said, "it burst into flames!"

"All this in one night!" Mrs. Payne exclaimed. "Sit down, sit down, I must have all the details."

"We can't stay long," Tommy said. "We've got to keep moving—"

"We'll be safe here for a little while," Del said, plopping into one of the commodious leather armchairs.

As Mrs. Payne returned to her chair, she said, "We should have coffee—or brandy if you need it."

"Mummingford is already bringing coffee and pastries," Del said.

Scootie entered the room and padded directly to Mrs. Payne. She was so petite and the chair was so wide that there was room for both her and the Labrador. The dog curled up with its massive black head in her lap.

"Scootie-wootums have fun too?" Mrs. Payne asked as she petted the mutt. Indicating the radio, she said, "Oh, this is a lovely number." Although the volume was low, she could identify the tune. "Artie Shaw, 'Begin the Beguine.' "

Del said, "I like it too. By the way, Mother, it's not just burning yachts and cars. There's an entity involved."

"An entity? This just gets better and better," said Mrs. Payne. "What sort of entity?"

"Well, I haven't identified it yet, haven't had time, what with all the running and chasing," Del said. "But it started out as a devil doll with a curse note pinned to the hand."

To Tommy, Mrs. Payne said, "This doll was delivered to you?"

"Yes. I—"

"By whom?"

"It was left on my doorstep. I think Vietnamese gangs—"

"And you picked it up and brought it into your house?"

"Yes. I thought—"

Mrs. Payne clucked her tongue and wagged one finger at him. "Dear boy, you shouldn't have brought it into your house. In this sort of situation, the entity can't become animate and do you harm unless you *invite* it across your threshold."

"But it was just a little rag doll—"

"Yes, of course, a little rag doll, but that's not what it is *now*, is it?"

Leaning forward in his chair, agitated, Tommy said, "I'm amazed that you just accept all of this so easily."

"Why wouldn't I?" Mrs. Payne asked, clearly surprised by his statement. "If Del says there's an entity, then I'm sure there's an entity. Del is no fool."

Mummingford entered the music room, pushing a tea cart laden with china, a silver coffee urn, and pastries.

To her mother, Del said, "Tommy suffers from an excess of skepticism. For instance, he doesn't believe in alien abductions."

"They're real," Mrs. Payne assured Tommy with a smile, as though her confirmation of Del's stranger beliefs was all that he needed to embrace them himself.

"He doesn't believe in ghosts," Del said.

"Real," said Mrs. Payne.

"Or lycanthropy."

"Real."

"Or remote viewing."

"Real."

Listening to them made Tommy dizzy. He closed his eyes.

"Though he does believe in Big Foot," Del said teasingly.

"How odd," said Mrs. Payne.

"I do not believe in Big Foot," Tommy corrected.

He could hear the devilment in Del's voice as she said, "Well, that's not what you said earlier."

"Big Foot," said Julia Rosalyn Winona Lilith Payne, "is nothing but tabloid trash."

"Exactly," said Del.

Tommy had to open his eyes to accept a cup of coffee from the apparently imperturbable Mummingford.

From the old-looking radio on the faux-ivory coffee table came an announcer's voice identifying the broadcast as originating live from the fabulous Empire Ballroom, where "Glenn Miller and his big band bring the stars out when they play," followed by a commercial for Lucky Strike cigarettes.

Del said, "If Tommy can stay alive until dawn, then the curse fails, and he's okay. Or at least that's what we think."

"Little more than an hour and a half," said Mrs. Payne. "What do you suppose are his chances of making it?"

"Sixty-forty," Del said.

Flustered, Tommy said, "What? Sixty-forty?"

"Well," Del said, "that's my honest assessment."

"Which is the sixty? Sixty percent chance that I'll be killed, or sixty percent chance that I'll live?"

"That you'll live," Del said brightly.

"I'm not comforted."

"Yes, but we're steadily improving those odds by the minute, sweetheart."

"It's still not good," said Mrs. Payne.

"It's *terrible*," Tommy said, distressed.

"It's just a hunch," Del ventured, "but I don't think Tommy is scheduled for unnatural extraction. He feels as if he has a full-life destiny with a natural departure."

Tommy had no idea what she was talking about.

Addressing him in a reassuring tone, Mrs. Payne said, "Well, Tommy dear, even if the worst were to happen, death isn't final. It's only a transitional phase."

"You're sure of that, are you?"

"Oh, yes. I talk to Ned more nights than not."

"Who?"

"Daddy," Del clarified.

"He appears on the David Letterman show," Mrs. Payne said.

Mummingford passed a silver tray of pastries to Del first, who took a plump cinnamon-pecan roll, and then to Tommy. Although Tommy initially selected a sensible bran muffin, he reconsidered and asked for a chocolate croissant. If he only had an hour and a half to live, worrying about his cholesterol level seemed pointless.

As Mummingford used pastry tongs to transfer the croissant to a plate, Tommy asked Del's mother for a clarification: "Your late husband appears on the David Letterman show?"

"It's a late-night talk show."

"Yes, I know."

"Sometimes David announces a guest, but instead of the movie star or singer or whoever it's supposed to be, my Ned comes out and sits in the guest chair.

Then the whole program freezes, as if time has stopped—David and the audience and the band all frozen in place—and Ned talks to me."

Tommy tasted his chocolate croissant. It was delicious.

"Of course," said Mrs. Payne, "this appears only on my personal TV, not all over the country. I'm the only one who sees Ned."

With a mouthful of croissant, Tommy nodded.

Del's mother said, "Ned always had style. He'd never settle for contacting me through a fake Gypsy medium at a séance or through a Ouija board, nothing as trite and tacky as that."

Tommy tried the coffee. It was lightly flavored with vanilla. Excellent.

"Oh, Mummingford," Del said, "I almost forgot—there's a stolen Ferrari in the driveway."

"What would you like done with it, Miss Payne?"

"Could you have it returned to Balboa Island within the hour? I can tell you exactly where it was parked."

"Yes, Miss Payne. I'll just refresh everyone's coffee and then attend to it."

As Del's mother began feeding pieces of a cruller to Scootie, she said, "What vehicle would you like brought up from the garage, Del?"

Del said, "The way this night's going, whatever we drive is liable to end up on the junk pile. So it shouldn't be one of your most precious cars."

"Nonsense, darling. You should be comfortable."

"Well, I like the Jaguar two plus two."

"It's a lovely car," Mrs. Payne agreed.

"It has the power and maneuverability we need for work like this," said Del.

"I'll have it brought around to the front door at once," Mummingford said.

"But before you do, do you think you could please bring a telephone?" Del asked.

"Certainly, Miss Payne," the butler said, and he departed.

Having finished his croissant, Tommy got up from his chair, went to the tea cart, and selected a cheese Danish.

He had decided to concentrate on eating and not even try to be part of the conversation. Both women made him crazy, and life was too short to let them upset him. In fact, if reliable sources could be believed, there was a forty percent chance that life was very damn short indeed.

Smiling at Del, smiling at her mother, Tommy returned to his chair with the Danish.

From the radio, at reduced volume, issued Glenn Miller's "String of Pearls."

Del's mother said, "I should have had you children change into bathrobes the moment you arrived. Then we could have thrown your clothes in the dryer. They'd be dry and warm by now."

"We'll only get wet again when we leave," Del said.

"No, dear. The rain will be stopping in another four minutes."

Del shrugged. "We'll be fine."

Tommy took a bite of the Danish and looked at his watch.

"Tell me more about the entity," Mrs. Payne said. "What it looks like, what its capabilities are."

"I'm afraid that'll have to wait till later, Mom. I need to use the bathroom quick, and then we'd better run."

"While you're in there, comb your hair, dear. It's kinking up now that it's drying."

Del left the room, and for perhaps ten seconds, Julia Rosalyn Winona Lilith and the big black dog stared at Tommy as he ate the Danish.

Then Mrs. Payne said, "So you're the one."

Tommy swallowed a mouthful of pastry. "What does that mean—the one?"

"Why, of course, dear boy, it means precisely what it says. You're *the one*."

"The one."

"Yes, the one."

"The one. There's something ominous about it."

She seemed genuinely baffled. "Ominous?"

"Sort of like a term that some lost tribe of volcano-worshiping South Sea islanders might use before they throw the virgin into the fiery pit."

Mrs. Payne laughed with obvious delight. "Oh, you *are* precious. A sense of humor quite like Ned's."

"I'm serious."

"That makes it even funnier."

"Tell me about—the one," he insisted.

"Well, of course, Deliverance merely meant that you're the one for her. The *one*. The one she should spend the rest of her life with."

Tommy felt a hot blush rising faster than the mercury in a thermometer bathed with August sunshine.

Evidently Julia Rosalyn Winona Lilith saw the blush, for she said, "My heavens, you are the sweetest young man."

Scootie chuffed as if in agreement.

Blushing so brightly that he was beginning to sweat, Tommy desperately wanted to change the subject. "So you haven't slept since Mud Lake."

Mrs. Payne nodded. "Just south of Tonopah."

"Twenty-seven years with no sleep."

"Almost twenty-eight, since the night that my Deliverance was conceived."

"You must be tired."

"Not at all," she said. "Sleep isn't a necessity for me now. It's a choice, and I simply don't choose to do it, because it's boring."

"What happened at Mud Lake?"

"Didn't Del tell you?"

"No."

"Well," said Mrs. Payne, "then it's certainly not my place to do so. I'll leave it to her, in her own good time."

Mummingford entered the room with a portable telephone, per Del's request, and put it on the coffee table. He retreated without comment. He had to deal with a stolen Ferrari, after all.

Tommy looked at his watch.

"Personally, Tommy dear, I think your chances of living until dawn are a hundred percent."

"Well, if I don't make it, Rosalyn, I'll visit you on the David Letterman show."

"I'd adore that!" she said, and clapped her hands to express her pleasure at the thought.

On the radio, Glenn Miller's big band was playing "American Patrol."

After washing down the last of the cheese Danish with the last of his coffee, Tommy said, "Is this your favorite kind of music?"

"Oh, yes. It's the music that might redeem our planet—if it could be redeemed by music alone."

"But you're a child of the fifties."

"Rock-'n'-roll," she said. "Yes. I love rock-'n'-roll. But this is the music that appeals to the galaxy."

He mulled over those four words: "Appeals to the galaxy."

"Yes. As no other."

"You're so like your daughter," he said.

Beaming, Mrs. Payne said, "I love you too, Tommy."

"So you collect old radio programs."

"Collect?" she asked, baffled.

He indicated the radio on the coffee table. "Is it a cassette player, or are they issuing those collectibles on CDs now?"

"No, dear, we're listening to the original program live."

"Live on tape."

"Just live."

"Glenn Miller died in World War Two."

"Yes," Mrs. Payne said, "in nineteen forty-five. I'm surprised anyone of your age would remember him—or when he died."

"Swing music is so American," Tommy said. "I love everything American, I really do."

"That's one reason you're so strongly drawn to Del," she said happily. "Deliverance is so thoroughly American, so open to possibilities."

"Back to Glenn Miller, if we may. He died more than fifty years ago."

"So sad," Mrs. Payne acknowledged, stroking Scootie.

"Well, then."

She raised her eyebrows. "Oh, I see your confusion."

"Only one small part of it."

"Excuse me, dear?"

"At this point, no one alive is capable of grasping the enormous dimensions of my confusion," Tommy assured her.

"Really? Then perhaps your diet's deficient. You might not be getting enough vitamin B complex."

"Oh?"

"Along with vitamin E," Mrs. Payne explained, "a good B-complex supplement can clarify mental processes."

"I thought you were going to tell me to eat tofu."

"Good for the prostate."

"Glenn Miller," Tommy reminded her, indicating the radio that still swung with "American Patrol."

"Let me clear up this one little confusion," she said. "We're listening to this broadcast live because my radio has transtemporal tuning capabilities."

"Transtemporal."

"Cross-time, yes. Earlier I was listening to Jack Benny live. He was an enormously funny man. No one like him today."

"Who sells radios with transtemporal tuning capabilities, Winona? Sears?"

"Do they? I don't think so. As for how I got *my* little radio, I'll have to let Deliverance explain. It's related to Mud Lake, you know."

"Transtemporal radio," Tommy mused. "I think I prefer to believe in Big Foot."

"You can't possibly," Mrs. Payne said disapprovingly.

"Why not? I now believe in devil dolls and demons."

"Yes, but they're *real*."

Tommy checked his wristwatch again. "It's still raining."

She cocked her head and listened to the faint drumming of the rain on the well-insulated roof of The Great Pile, and Scootie cocked his head as well. After a moment, she said, "Yes, it is. Such a restful sound."

"You told Del the rain would stop in four minutes. You were so precise about it."

"Yes, that's right."

"But it's still raining."

"Four minutes haven't passed yet."

Tommy tapped his watch.

She said, "Dear, your watch is wrong. It's taken a lot of battering tonight."

Tommy held the wristwatch to his ear, listened, and said, "Ticktock."

"Ten seconds yet," she said.

He counted them off, then looked at her and smiled ruefully.

The rain continued to fall.

At fifteen seconds, the rain abruptly stopped.

Tommy's smile faded, and Mrs. Payne's returned.

"You were five seconds off," he said.

"I never claimed to be God, dear."

"What do you claim to be, Lilith?"

She pursed her lips, considering his question, and then said, "Just an ex-ballerina with a considerable amount of enriching and strange experience."

Slumping back in his armchair, Tommy said, "I'm never going to doubt a Payne woman again."

"That's a wise decision, dear."

"What's a wise decision?" Del asked as she returned.

Mrs. Payne said, "He's decided never to doubt a Payne woman."

"Never doubting a Payne woman," Del said, "is not just wise. It's *the* prerequisite for survival."

"Although I keep thinking about the female praying mantis," Tommy said.

"How so?"

"After she mates, she bites the head off her partner and eats him alive."

Mrs. Payne said, "I think you'll discover that Payne women will usually settle for a cup of tea and a scone."

Indicating the portable telephone on the coffee table, Del said, "Did you make the call, Tommy?"

"What call?"

"Your brother."

He had completely forgotten Gi.

Del handed him the phone, and he punched in the number for the back-office line at the New World Saigon Bakery.

Leaning forward in her chair without disturbing Scootie, Mrs. Payne switched off the transtemporal radio, silencing the Glenn Miller band in the middle of "Little Brown Jug."

Gi answered on the second ring, and when he heard Tommy's voice, he said, "I was expecting you to call an hour ago."

"I was delayed by a yacht wreck."

"By what?"

"Have you translated the note?"

Gi Minh hesitated and then said, "Are you still with that blonde?"

"Yes."

"I wish you weren't with her."

Tommy looked at Del and smiled. To Gi, he said, "Well, here I am."

"She's bad news, Tommy."

"More like the comics pages."

"What?"

"If Jeffrey Dahmer were a cartoonist."

Gi was silent. It was the silence of confusion, with which Tommy was too familiar.

Tommy said, "Were you able to translate the note?"

"It didn't dry out as well as I hoped. I can't give you an entire translation of it—but I figured out enough to scare me. It's not any gang that's after you, Tommy."

"Who?"

"I'm not sure. What you've got to do is, you've got to go see Mom right away."

Tommy blinked in surprise and rose from his armchair. His hands were suddenly clammy with the sweat of familial guilt. "Mom?"

"The longer I worked on the note, the more it worried me—"

"Mom?"

"—and finally I called her for some advice."

"You woke Mom?" he asked in disbelief.

"When I told her about the note, as much as I could understand of it, she got scared too."

Pacing nervously, glancing at Del and her mother, Tommy said, "I really didn't want Mom to know about this, Gi."

"She understands the Old World, Tommy, and this thing is more a part of the Old World than it is of this one."

"She'll say I've been drinking whiskey—"

"She's waiting for you, Tommy."

"—like my crazy detective." His mouth went dry. "Waiting for me?"

"You don't have much time, Tommy. I think you better get there as fast as you can. I really think you better. Fast. But don't take the blonde."

"I have to."

"She's bad news, Tommy."

Tommy glanced at Del. She sure didn't *look* like bad news. She had combed her hair. Her smile was sweet. She winked at him.

"Bad news," Gi repeated.

"We've been on this page before, Gi."

Gi sighed. "Well, at least cut Mom a little slack. She's had a terrible day."

"Mine hasn't exactly been a piece of cake."

"Mai eloped."

Mai was their younger sister.

"Eloped?" Tommy said, thunderstruck. "Eloped with whom?"

"A magician."

"What magician?"

Gi sighed. "None of us knew she was dating a magician."

"This is the first *I've* heard she was dating any magician," Tommy said, eager to establish that he could not be accused of complicity in his sister's astounding act of independence.

From her armchair, the ex-ballerina who hadn't slept since Mud Lake said, "A magician—how romantic."

Gi said, "His name is Roland Ironwright."

"Doesn't sound Vietnamese."

"He isn't."

"Oh, God." Tommy could too easily imagine the mood in which his mother would be stewing when he arrived at her doorstep with Del Payne.

Gi said, "He performs in Vegas a lot. He and Mai hopped a plane to Vegas and got married, and Mom only learned about it this evening, didn't tell me about it until I called her a little while ago, so cut her some slack."

Tommy was overwhelmed by remorse. "I should have gone to dinner, had *com tay cam*."

"Go now, Tommy," Gi said. "She might be able to help you. She said *hurry*."

"I love you, Gi."

"Well, sure . . . I love you, Tommy."

"I love Ton and Mai and Mom and Dad, I really do, I love all of you so much . . . but I've got to be free."

"I know, Brother. I know. Listen, I'll call Mom and tell her you're on your way. Now get moving, *you're almost out of time*!"

When Tommy hung up, he saw that Del's mother was blotting tears from the corners of her eyes.

With a tremor in her voice, she said, "This is just so moving. I haven't been so touched since Ned's funeral, when Frank Sinatra gave the eulogy."

Del moved beside her mother's chair and put a hand on the older woman's shoulder. "Now, now. It's okay, Mom."

To Tommy, Mrs. Payne said, "Frank was so eloquent. Wasn't he eloquent, Del?"

"As always," Del said, "he was a class act."

"Even my policemen were moved to tears," Mrs. Payne said. "I had to attend the funeral between these two burly guards, of course, because I was under arrest for murder."

"I understand," Tommy assured her.

"I never held that against them," said Mrs. Payne. "They knew I'd shot Ned through the heart, and they couldn't see it as anything but murder, they were so *blind* to the truth, but everything turned out all right in the end. Anyway, these two dear policemen were so moved by all the lovely things Frank had to say about Ned, and then when he began to sing 'It Was a Very Good Year,' they just broke down and sobbed like babies. I let them share my little pack of Kleenex."

At a loss for comforting words, Tommy could think of nothing to say except: "Such a tragedy, dying so young."

"Oh," said Del's mother, "Ned wasn't all that young. Sixty-three when I shot him."

Fascinated with this peculiar family even as his personal clock of doom ticked rapidly toward the fatal hour, Tommy did some quick mental calculations. "If he died eighteen years ago when Del was ten . . . you would have been thirty-two at the time. And he was sixty-three?"

Nudging Scootie to the floor, rising from her armchair, Julia Rosalyn Winona Lilith said, "It was a May-December romance. I was twenty when we met, and he was over fifty, but from the first moment I saw Ned, I knew he was *the one*. I wasn't your ordinary young girl, Tommy dear. Oh, I was hungry for experience, for knowledge. I wanted to *devour* life. I needed an older man who had been around, who had seen it all, someone who could teach me. Ned was glorious. With Elvis singing 'Blue Hawaii'—the poor dear had a bad cold, but he came to sing anyway—we married at a chapel in Vegas, nineteen hours after we met, and never regretted it for one minute. On our honeymoon we parachuted into the heart of the Campeche jungle on the Yucatán Peninsula with only two sharp knives, a coil of rope, a map, a compass, and a bottle of good red wine, and we made it out safely to civilization in only fifteen days, more madly in love than ever."

"You sure were right," Tommy told Del. "Your mother's a hoot."

Smiling radiantly at her daughter, looking so unlike Tommy's mother in her *ao dais*, Winona said, "Deliverance, did you really say that about me, dear?"

The two women embraced.

Then Tommy hugged Del's mother and said, "I hope you'll invite me over some night to watch the David Letterman show."

"Of course, dear boy. And I hope you'll live long enough to have a chance to see it."

"Now," Del said to Tommy, "it's my turn to meet *your* mother."

Mrs. Payne walked them out of the music room, down the great hall, to the front door.

The Jaguar 2+2 was waiting outside in the now rainless November night.

When Tommy opened the passenger-side door and pulled the seat forward, Scootie romped into the back.

As Del went around to the driver's side, Mrs. Payne called to her daughter from the front door of The Great Pile: "When you bite his head off and eat him alive, try to make it quick and painless. He's such a nice boy."

Tommy locked eyes with Del across the roof of the car.

Del said, "It'll be over before you realize what's happening. I promise."

EIGHT

At the Phan house in Huntington Beach, Tommy's mother waited in the driveway. Although the clouds had begun to shred in the night sky, she wore ankle-high rubber boots, black slacks, a raincoat, and a plastic rain scarf. Her ability to predict the weather was not as impressive as Mrs. Payne's.

Del stayed behind the wheel with the engine running.

Getting out of the Jaguar, Tommy said, "Mom, I don't—"

Interrupting him, she said, "Get in backseat. I sit up front with terrible woman." When he hesitated, she said, "Go, go, foolish boy, less than hour to dawn."

Tommy scrambled into the backseat with Scootie.

When his mother got in beside Del and pulled the passenger door shut, Tommy leaned forward from the back and said, "Mom, I'd like you to meet Deliverance Payne. Del, this—"

Glowering at Del, his mother said, "I don't like you."

Grinning, Del said, "Really? Already, I like you a lot."

"Let's go," Tommy's mother said.

Backing into the street, Del said, "Where?"

"Go left. Just drive, I tell you when turn. Gi say you save Tommy's life."

"She saved my life more than once," Tommy said. "She—"

"Don't think you save my son's life then I like you," Tommy's mother warned Del.

"Earlier, I almost shot him."

"Is true?"

"True," Del confirmed.

"So okay, maybe could like you a little," Tommy's mother grumbled.

Glancing back at Tommy, Del said, "She's a hoot."

"Gi says you total stranger to Tommy."

"Served him dinner maybe ten hours ago but only really met him less than six hours ago," Del confirmed.

"Served dinner?"

"I'm a waitress."

"He eat cheeseburgers?"

"Two of them."

"Stupid boy. No dating?"

"Tommy and me? No, we've never dated."

"Good. Don't. Here, turn right."

"Where are we going?" Tommy asked.

"Hairdresser."

"We're going to the hairdresser? Why?"

"You wait, you see," said his mother. Then to Del: "He bad boy, break your heart."

"Mom!" he said, mortified.

"Can't break my heart if I don't date him," Del said.

"Smart girl."

Scootie squeezed past Tommy and thrust his big head into the front seat, sniffing suspiciously at the new passenger.

Turning in her seat, Tommy's mother met the dog face to face.

Scootie grinned, tongue lolling.

"Don't like dogs," she said. "Dirty animals, always licking. You lick me, lose tongue."

Scootie still grinned at her and slowly eased his head closer, sniffing, surely on the verge of licking.

Baring her teeth at the Labrador, Tommy's mother made a warning sound low in her throat.

Startled, Scootie twitched, drew back, but then bared his teeth and growled in response. His ears flattened against his skull.

Tommy's mother bared her teeth further and issued a growl meaner than the dog's.

Whimpering, Scootie retreated, curling up in a corner of the backseat.

"Turn left next block."

Hoping to ingratiate himself, Tommy said, "Mom, I was so sorry to hear about Mai. What could've gotten into her, running away with a magician?"

Leaning sideways to glower at Tommy in the rearview mirror, she said, "Brother was bad example. Young girl ruined by brother's bad example, future destroyed by brother's bad example."

"Which brother would that be?" Del asked teasingly.

Tommy said, "Mom, that's not fair."

"Yeah," Del said, "Tommy's never run off with a magician." She glanced away from the street, at Tommy. "Er . . . have you, tofu boy?"

Mother Phan said, "Marriage already arranged, future bright, now good Vietnamese boy left without bride."

"An arranged marriage?" Del marveled.

"Nguyen boy, nice boy," said Tommy's mother.

"Chip Nguyen?" Del wondered.

Tommy's mother hissed with disgust. "Not silly detective chases blondes, shoots everyone."

"Nguyen is the Vietnamese equivalent of Smith," Tommy told Del.

"So why didn't you call your detective Chip Smith?"

"I probably should have."

"I'll tell you why you didn't," Del said. "You're proud of your heritage."

"He piss on heritage," Tommy's mother said.

"Mom!"

Tommy was so shocked by her language that his chest tightened, and he had to struggle to draw a breath. She never used foul words. That she had done so now was proof of an anger greater than she had ever displayed before.

Del said, "Actually, Mrs. Phan, you misunderstand Tommy. Family is very important to him. If you'd give him a chance—"

"Did I say don't like you?"

"I believe you mentioned it," Del said.

"More you talk, less I like."

"Mom, I've never seen you be rude to anyone before—anyone not in the family."

"Just watch. Turn left, girl." As Del followed instructions, Tommy's mother let out a quavery sigh of regret. "Boy for Mai not silly Chip Nguyen. This Nguyen Huu Van, family in doughnut business, have many doughnut shops. Perfect for Mai. Could have been many grandchildren pretty as Mai. Now strange magician children."

"Isn't that what it's all about?" Del asked.

"What you say?"

"Strange magician children. If there are three words that sum up what life *should* be all about, it's *strange magician children.* Life shouldn't be too predictable. It should be full of chance and mystery. New people, new ways, new hopes, new dreams, always with respect for the old ways, always built on tradition, but always new. That's what makes life interesting."

"More you talk, less I like."

"Yes, you said."

"But you not listen."

"It's a fault of mine," Del said.

"Not listening."

"No, always talking. I listen but I always talk too."

Tommy curled up in the backseat, in the corner

opposite the dog, aware that he could not compete in this conversation.

His mother said to Del, "Can't listen if talk."

"Bullshit."

"You bad news."

"I'm the weather," Del said.

"What say?"

"Neither good nor bad. Just there."

"Tornado just there. But bad."

"I'd rather be weather than geology," Del said.

"What mean?"

"Better to be a tornado than a mountain of rock."

"Tornado come and go. Mountain always there."

"The mountain is not always there."

"Mountain always here," Mother Phan insisted.

Del shook her head. "Not always."

"Where it go?"

With singular élan, Del said, "The sun explodes, goes nova, and the earth blows away."

"You crazy woman."

"Wait around a billion years and see."

Tommy and Scootie locked eyes. Only minutes ago, he wouldn't have believed that he could ever have felt such a kinship with the Labrador as he felt now.

Del said to Tommy's mother, "And as the mountain blows away, there will be *tornadoes* of fire. The mountain will be gone, but the tornadoes still whirling."

"You the same as damn magician."

"Thank you. Mrs. Phan, it's like the rock-and-scissors game writ large," Del said. "Tornadoes beat rock because tornadoes are *passion*."

"Tornadoes just hot air."

"Cold air."

"Anyway, air."

Glancing at the rearview mirror, Del said, "Hey, guys, we're being followed."

They were on a residential street lined with ficus trees. The houses were neat but modest.

Tommy sat up and peered out the rear window of the teardrop-shaped sports car. Looming behind them was a massive Peterbilt tractor-trailer, like a juggernaut, no more than twenty feet away.

"What's he doing in a residential neighborhood at this hour?" Tommy wondered.

"Killing you," Del said, tramping on the accelerator.

The behemoth of a truck accelerated to match their pace, and the yellow glow of sodium-vapor street-lamps, flickering across its windshield, revealed the portly Samaritan behind the wheel, his face pale and his grin broad, although they were not close enough to see the green of his eyes.

"This can't be happening," Tommy said.

"Is," Del said. "Boy, I wish Mom were here."

"You have mother?" Tommy's mom asked.

"Actually," Del said, "I hatched from an insect egg. I was a mere larva, not a child. You're right, Mrs. Phan—I had no mother."

"You are smart-mouth girl."

"Thank you."

"This is smart-mouth girl," Tommy's mother told him.

Bracing himself for impact, he said, "Yes, I know."

Engine shrieking, the truck rocketed forward and smashed into their rear bumper.

The Jaguar shuddered and weaved along the street. Del fought the steering wheel, which wrenched left and right, but she maintained control.

"You can outrun him," Tommy said. "He's a Peterbilt, for God's sake, and you're a Jaguar."

"He's got the advantage of being a supernatural entity," Del said. "The usual rules of the road don't apply."

The Peterbilt crashed into them again, and the rear bumper of the Jaguar tore away, clanging across the street into the front yard of a Craftsman-style bungalow.

"Next block, turn right," Tommy's mom said.

Accelerating, briefly putting distance between them and the Peterbilt, Del waited until the last possible moment to make the turn. She slid through it, entering the new street back end first, tires screaming and smoking, and the car went into a spin.

With a sharp little yelp better suited to a dog one-quarter his size, Scootie shot off the backseat and tumbled onto the floor.

Tommy thought they were going to roll. It felt like a roll. He was experienced in rolling now and knew what that penultimate angle felt like, just before the roll began, and this sure felt like it.

Under Del's guidance, the Jaguar held the

pavement tenaciously, however, and it shrieked to a shuddering halt as it came out of a complete three-hundred-and-sixty-degree spin.

Not a stupid dog, wanting to avoid being pitched off the seat again, Scootie waited on the floor until Del jammed her foot down on the accelerator. Only after the car rocketed forward did he scramble up beside Tommy.

Looking out the rear window, Tommy saw the Peterbilt braking aggressively on the street they had left. Even the superior driving skills of a supernatural entity—did they have highways in Hell where demons with Los Angeles–area assignments were able to practice?—couldn't finesse the huge truck into making such a sharp and sudden turn. Basic physics still applied. The Samaritan-thing was trying only to bring the vehicle to a stop.

With its tires locked, the Peterbilt shot past the intersection and disappeared into the next block.

Tommy prayed that it would jackknife.

In the front seat, as the Jaguar accelerated to seventy, Mother Phan said, "Girl, you drive like crazy maniac detective in books."

"Thank you," Del said.

Mother Phan withdrew something from her purse.

Tommy couldn't quite see what she held in her hand, but he heard a series of telltale electronic tones. "What're you doing, Mom?"

"Calling ahead."

"What've you got there?"

"Cellular phone," she said blithely.

Astonished, he said, "You own a cellular phone?"

"Why not?"

"I thought cellular phones were for big shots?"

"Not any more. Everybody got one."

"Oh? I thought it was too dangerous to use a phone and drive."

As she finished punching in the number, she explained: "I not driving. Riding."

Del said, "For heaven's sake, Tommy, you sound as if you live in the Middle Ages."

He glanced out the rear window. A full block behind them, the Peterbilt reversed into sight on the street that they had left. It hadn't jackknifed.

Someone must have answered Mother Phan's call, because she identified herself and spoke into the telephone in Vietnamese.

Less than a block and a half behind them, the Peterbilt swung through the intersection.

Tommy consulted his watch. "What time's dawn?"

"I don't know," Del said. "Maybe half an hour, maybe forty minutes."

"Your mom would know to the minute, to the second."

"Probably," Del agreed.

Although Tommy couldn't understand more than an occasional word of what his mother was saying, he had no doubt that she was furious with the person on the other end of the line. He winced at her tone and was relieved that he wasn't on the receiving end of her anger.

Behind them, the Peterbilt was gaining. It had closed the gap to only a block.

Tommy said worriedly, "Del?"

"I see it," she assured him, checking her side mirror and then accelerating even though they were already traveling dangerously fast through this residential neighborhood.

With a final burst of invective in Vietnamese, Tommy's mother switched off the cellular phone. "Stupid woman," she said.

"Give it a rest," Del advised.

"Not you," said Mother Phan. "You bad news, wicked, dangerous, but not stupid."

"Thank you," said Del.

"I mean Quy. Stupid woman."

Tommy said, "Who?"

"Mrs. Quy Trang Dai."

"Who's Quy Trang Dai?"

"Stupid woman."

"Aside from being a stupid woman, who is she?"

"Hairdresser."

Tommy said, "I still don't understand why we're going to the hairdresser."

"You need a trim," Del told him.

The Jaguar engine was roaring so loudly that Mother Phan had to raise her voice to be heard. "She not only hairdresser. She friend. Play mah-jongg with her and other ladies every week, and sometimes bridge."

"We're going for breakfast and a nice game of mah-jongg," Del told Tommy.

Mother Phan said, "Quy my age but different."

"Different how?" Tommy asked.

"Quy so old-fashioned, stuck in ways of Vietnam, can't adjust to new world, never want anything to change."

"Oh, I see, yes," Tommy said. "She's utterly different from you, Mom."

He turned in his seat to peer anxiously out the rear window. The truck was bearing down on them, perhaps two-thirds of a block away.

"Quy," said Mother Phan, "not from Saigon like our family, not born city person. She from sticks, nowhere village on Xan River near borders Laos and Cambodia. All jungle out there on Xan River. Some people there strange, have strange knowledge."

"Sort of like Pittsburgh," Del said.

"What strange knowledge?" Tommy asked.

"Magic. But not magic like stupid Roland Iron-wright pulls rabbits from hats and Mai thinks clever."

"Magic," Tommy said numbly.

"This magic like making potion to win love of girl, making charm to succeed in business. But also worse."

"Worse how?"

"Talking to dead," Mother Phan said ominously, "learning secrets about land of dead, making dead walk and work as slaves."

The Peterbilt was half a block behind them. As it approached, the roar of its engine was growing louder than that of the Jaguar.

Del pushed the Jaguar as hard as she dared, but she continued to lose ground.

Tommy's mother said, "Xan River magic bring spirits from dark underworld, put curse on sorceror's enemies."

"This Xan River is definitely a part of the planet that's under the influence of evil extraterrestrial powers," Del declared.

"Quy Trang Dai know this magic," said Mother Phan. "How to make a dead man dig up out of his grave and kill who told to kill. How to use frog gonads in potion to make enemy's heart and liver melt into mud. How to put curse on woman who sleep with your husband, so she give birth to baby with human head, dog body, and lobster hands."

"And you played mah-jongg with this woman!" Tommy demanded, outraged.

"Sometimes bridge," said Mother Phan.

"But how could you associate with this monster?"

"Be respectful, boy. Quy your elder by many years, earn respect. She no monster. Aside from this stupid thing she do with rag doll, she nice lady."

"She's trying to kill me!"

"Not trying to kill you."

"She *is* trying to kill me."

"Don't shout and be crazy like maniac drunk detective."

"She's trying to kill me!"

"She only trying to scare you so you maybe be more respectful of Vietnamese ways."

Behind them, the Samaritan-thing blew the Peterbilt's air horn: three long blasts, gleefully announcing that it was closing in for the kill.

"Mom, this creature murdered three innocent bystanders already tonight, and it sure as hell *will* kill me if it can."

Tommy's mother sighed regretfully. "Quy Trang Dai not always as good at magic as she think."

"What?"

"Probably make rag doll with one missing ingredient, summon demon from underworld with one wrong word. Mistake."

"Mistake?"

"Everybody make mistake sometime."

Del said, "That's why they make erasers."

"I'll kill this Mrs. Dai, I swear," Tommy announced.

"Don't be stupid," Mother Phan said. "Quy Trang Dai nice lady, you not kill nice lady."

"She is *not* a nice lady, damn it!"

Del said disapprovingly, "Tommy, I've never heard you be so judgmental."

"I'll kill her," Tommy repeated defiantly.

Mother Phan said, "Quy never use magic for herself, not make herself rich with magic, work hard as hairdresser. Only use magic once or twice a year to help others."

"Well, I sure haven't been helped by all this," Tommy said.

"Ah," Del said knowingly, "I see."

Tommy said, "What? What do you see?"

The air horn of the Peterbilt blared again.

To Tommy's mother, Del said, "Are you going to tell him?"

"I don't like you," Mother Phan reminded her.

"You just don't know me well enough yet."

"Never going to know you better."

"Let's do lunch and see how it goes."

Almost blinded by a flash of insight, Tommy blinked fiercely and said, "Mom, good God, did you *ask* this monster, this nutball Dai woman, to make that rag doll?"

"No!" his mother said. She turned to meet his eyes as he leaned forward from the backseat. "Never. You thoughtless son sometimes, won't be doctor, won't work in bakery, head full of stupid dreams, but in your heart you not bad boy, never bad boy."

He was actually touched by what she had said. Over the years she had sparingly administered praise with an eyedropper; therefore, hearing her acknowledge that he was, although thoughtless, not truly an evil boy . . . well, this was like being fed a spoon, a cup, a bowl, of motherly love.

"Quy Trang Dai and other ladies, we play mah-jongg. We play cards. While we play, we talk. Talk about whose son join gang, whose husband faithless. Talk about what children doing, what cute thing grandchildren say. I talk about you, how you become so far from family, from who you are, losing roots, try to be American but never can, going to end up lost."

"I *am* an American," Tommy said.

"Can never be," she assured him, and her eyes were full of love and fear for him.

Tommy was overcome by a terrible sadness. What his mother meant was that *she* could never feel herself to be a complete American, that *she* was lost. Her homeland had been taken from her, and she had been transplanted to a world in which she could never feel entirely native and welcome, even though it was such a glorious land of great plenty and hospitality and freedom. The American dream, which Tommy strove with such passion to experience to the fullest, was achievable for her only to a limited extent. He had arrived on these shores young enough to remake himself entirely; but she would forever hold within her heart the Old World, its pleasures and beauty amplified by time and distance, and this nostalgia was a melancholy spell from which she could never fully awaken. Because she could not become American in her soul, she found it difficult—if not impossible—to believe that her children could be so transformed, and she worried that their aspirations would lead only to disappointment and bitterness.

"I *am* American," Tommy repeated softly.

"Didn't ask stupid Quy Trang Dai to make rag doll. Was her own idea to scare you. I hear about it only one, two hours ago."

"I believe you," Tommy assured her.

"Good boy."

He reached one hand into the front seat.

His mother gripped his hand and squeezed it.

"Good thing I'm not as sentimental as my mother," Del said. "I'd be bawling so hard I couldn't see to drive."

The interior of the Jaguar was filled with the brightness of the headlights from the Peterbilt behind it.

The air horn blared, blared again, and the Jaguar vibrated under the sonic assault.

Tommy didn't have the courage to look back.

"Always worry about you," said Mrs. Phan, raising her voice over the airliner-loud roar of the truck engine. "Never see problem with Mai, sweet Mai, always so quiet, always so obedient. Now we die, and terrible magician in Vegas laugh at stupid old Vietnamese mother and make strange magician babies with ruined daughter."

"Too bad Norman Rockwell isn't alive," Del said. "He could make such a wonderful painting out of this."

"I don't like this woman," Mother Phan told Tommy.

"I know, Mom."

"She bad news. You sure she total stranger?"

"Only met her tonight."

"You not dating her?"

"Never dated."

"Turn left next corner," Mother Phan told Del.

"Are you joking?" Del said.

"Turn left next corner. We almost to house of Quy Trang Dai."

"I have to slow down to make the turn, and if I

slow down, Mrs. Dai's demon is going to run right over us."

"Drive better," Mother Phan advised.

Del glared at her. "Listen, lady, I'm a world-class race-car driver, competed all over the world. No one drives better than I do. Except maybe my mother."

Holding out the cellular phone, Mother Phan said, "Then call mother, hear what she say to do."

Grim-faced, Del said, "Brace yourselves."

Tommy let go of his mother's hand, slid backward in his seat, and fumbled for his safety belt. It was tangled.

Scootie took refuge on the floor in front of his seat, directly behind Del.

Unable to disentangle the belt quickly enough to save himself, Tommy followed the dog's example, huddling-squeezing into the floor space between the front and back seats on his side of the car, to avoid being catapulted into his mother's lap when the ultimate crash came.

Del braked the Jaguar.

The roaring Peterbilt rammed them from behind, not hard, and fell back.

Again Del used the brakes. The tires barked, and Tommy could smell burning rubber.

The Peterbilt rammed them harder than before, and sheet metal screamed, and the Jaguar shuddered as though it would fly apart like a sprung clock, and Tommy thumped his head against the back of the front seat.

The car was so awash in the glow of the truck's

headlights that Tommy could clearly see the Labrador's face across the floor from him. Scootie was grinning.

Del braked again, swung hard to the right, but that was only a feint to lead the Peterbilt in the wrong direction, because the truck couldn't maneuver as quickly as the car. Then she swung sharply to the left, as Mother Phan had instructed.

Tommy couldn't see anything from his dog-level view, but he knew that Del hadn't been able to get entirely out of the truck's path, because as they made the left turn, they were struck again, clipped only at the extreme back end of the vehicle but hit with tremendous force, an impact that made Tommy's ears ring and jarred through every bone, and the Jaguar spun. They went through one full revolution, and then another, perhaps a third, and Tommy felt as though he had been tossed into an industrial-size clothes dryer.

Tires stuttered across the pavement, tires exploded, rubber remnants slapped loudly against fender wells, and steel wheel rims scraped-shrieked across the pavement. Pieces of the car tore free, clattered along the undercarriage, and were gone.

But the Jaguar didn't roll over. It came out of the spin, rattling and pinging, lurching like a hobbled horse, but on all four wheels.

Tommy extracted himself from the cramped floor space between front and back seats, scrambled up, and looked out the rear window.

The dog joined him at the window, ear to ear.

As before, the Peterbilt had overshot the intersection.

"How was *that* for driving?" Del demanded.

Mother Phan said, "You never get insurance again."

Beside Tommy, the Labrador whimpered.

Even Deliverance Payne was not going to be able to coax any speed out of the Jaguar in its current debilitated condition. The sports car chugged forward, loudly rattling and clanking, hissing, pinging, pitching and yawing, spouting steam, hemorrhaging fluids—like one of those rattletrap pickup trucks that comic hillbillies always drive in the movies.

Behind them, the huge Peterbilt reversed into the intersection through which they had just been flung.

"We've got at least two blown tires," Del said, "and the oil pressure is dropping fast."

"Not far," said Tommy's mother. "Garage door be open, you pull in, all safe."

"What garage door?" Del asked.

"Garage door at Quy's house."

"Oh, yes, the hairdresser witch."

"She no witch. Just come from Xan River, learn few things when she was girl."

"Sorry if I caused offense," Del said.

"There, see, two houses ahead on right, lights on. Garage door open, you pull in, Quy Dai close door, all safe."

The demon driver shifted gears, and the Peterbilt pulled into the street behind them. Its headlights swept across the rear window, across Tommy.

Scootie whimpered again. He licked Tommy's face, either to reassure him or to say goodbye.

Facing front, wiping dog slobber off his cheek, Tommy said, "How can I be safe? It's not dawn yet. The thing will see where we've gone."

"Can't follow there," his mother said.

"I'm telling you, it'll drive straight through the house," he predicted.

"No. Quy is one who made doll, called spirit from underworld, so it not allowed hurt her. Can't enter house if Quy Trang Dai herself don't make invitation."

"With all due respect, Mom, I don't think we can count on demons being quite that polite."

"No, your mother's probably right," Del said. "The supernatural world operates on its own laws, rather like we operate under the laws of physics."

As the inside of the car grew bright again from the headlights behind, Tommy said, "If the damn thing drives the damn truck into the damn house and kills me, who do I complain to—Albert Einstein or the pope?"

Del turned right into the driveway, and the car creaked-clanked-clanged, wobbled-rolled-rocked-heaved into the open, lighted garage. When she braked to a stop, the engine coughed and stalled. The rear axle snapped, and the back of the Jaguar crashed to the garage floor.

Behind them the big door rolled down.

Tommy's mother climbed out of the car.

When he followed her, he heard the shrill air

brakes of the Peterbilt. Judging by the sound, the truck had pulled to the curb and stopped in front of the house.

A slender birdlike Vietnamese woman, about the size of a twelve-year-old girl, with a face as sweet as butterscotch pudding, stood at the interior door between the garage and the house. She was wearing a pink jogging suit and athletic shoes.

Mother Phan spoke to this woman briefly in Vietnamese, and then introduced her as Quy Trang Dai.

Mrs. Dai appeared crestfallen when she faced Tommy. "So sorry about mistake. Terrible dumb mistake. Feel like stupid, worthless, ignorant old fool, want to throw myself in pit of river vipers, but have no pit here and no vipers either." Her dark eyes welled with tears. "Want to throw myself in pit so bad."

"Well," Del said to Tommy, "are you going to kill her?"

"Maybe not."

"Wimp."

Outside, the Peterbilt was still idling.

Blinking back her tears, her expression toughening, Mrs. Dai turned to Del, looked her up and down, and said suspiciously, "Who you?"

"A total stranger."

Mrs. Dai raised an eyebrow quizzically at Tommy. "Is true?"

"True," Tommy said.

"Not dating?" asked Quy Trang Dai.

"All I know about him is his name," Del said.

"And she doesn't get that right half the time," Tommy assured Mrs. Dai. He glanced at the big garage door, certain that the truck engine outside would suddenly rev. . . . "Listen, are we really safe here?"

"Safe here. Safer in house but . . . " Mrs. Dai squinted at Del, as though reluctant to grant admittance to this obvious corrupter of Vietnamese male youth.

To Tommy, Del said, "I think I could find some vipers if you'd be willing to dig a pit."

Mother Phan spoke to Quy Trang Dai in Vietnamese.

The hairdresser witch lowered her eyes guiltily and nodded and finally sighed. "Okay. You come inside. But I keep clean house. Is dog broke?"

"He wasn't broken, but I had him fixed," Del said. She winked at Tommy. "Couldn't resist."

Mrs. Dai led them into the house, through the laundry room, kitchen, and dining room.

Tommy noticed that the heels of her running shoes contained those light-emitting diodes that blinked in sequence from right to left, ostensibly a safety feature for the athletically minded who took their exercise at night, though the effect was footgear with a Vegas flair.

In the living room, Mrs. Dai said, "We wait here for dawn. Evil spirit have to go at sunrise, all be fine."

The living room reflected the history of Vietnam as occupied territory: a mix of simple Chinese and

French furniture with two contemporary American upholstered pieces. On the wall over the sofa was a painting of the Sacred Heart of Jesus. In a corner stood a Buddhist shrine; fresh fruit was arranged on the bright red altar, and sticks of incense, one lit, bristled from ceramic holders.

Mrs. Dai sat in an oversize black chinoiserie chair with a padded seat covered in gold-and-white brocade. The chair was so large that the diminutive pink-clad woman appeared even more childlike than ever; her twinkling shoes didn't quite reach the floor.

Taking off her plastic rain scarf but not her coat, Mother Phan settled into a bergère-style chair and sat with her purse on her lap.

Tommy and Del perched on the edge of the sofa, and Scootie sat on the floor in front of them, looking curiously from Mother Phan to Mrs. Dai to Mother Phan again.

Outside, the Peterbilt engine still idled.

Tommy could see part of the truck, all of its running lights aglow, through one of the windows that flanked the front door, but he couldn't see the driver's cab or the Samaritan-thing.

Consulting her wristwatch, Mrs. Dai said, "Twenty-two minutes till dawn, then no one have to worry, everyone happy"—with a wary glance at Mother Phan—"no one angry with friends any more. Anyone like tea?"

Everyone politely declined tea.

"No trouble to make," said Mrs. Dai.

Again, everyone politely declined.

After a brief silence, Del said, "So you were born and raised along the Xan River."

Mrs. Dai brightened. "Oh, is such beautiful land. You been there?"

"No," Del said, "though I've always wanted to go."

"Beautiful, beautiful," Mrs. Dai rhapsodized, clapping her small hands together. "Jungle so green and dark, air heavy as steam and full of smell of growing things, can hardly breathe for stink of growing things, so many flowers and snakes, all red-gold mist in morning, purple mist at twilight, leeches thick and long as hotdogs."

Tommy muttered, "Lovely, lovely, with all the resurrected dead men slaving in the rice paddies."

"Excuse please?" said Mrs. Dai.

Glowering at Tommy, his mother said, "Be respectful."

When Tommy declined to repeat himself, Del said, "Mrs. Dai, when you were a girl, did you ever notice anything strange in the skies over the Xan River?"

"Strange?"

"Strange objects."

"In skies?"

"Disc-shaped craft, perhaps."

Perplexed, Mrs. Dai said, "Dishes in sky?"

Tommy thought he heard something outside. It might have been a truck door closing.

Changing tack slightly, Del said, "In the village where you were raised, Mrs. Dai, were there any legends of short humanoid creatures living in the jungle?"

"Short what?" asked Mrs. Dai.

"About four feet tall, gray skin, bulbous heads, enormous eyes, really *mesmerizing* eyes."

Quy Trang Dai looked at Mother Phan for help.

"She crazy person," Mother Phan explained.

"Eerie lights in the night," Del said, "pulsating lights with an irresistible attraction? Anything like that along the banks of the Xan?"

"Very dark in jungle at night. Very dark in village at night. No electricity."

"In your childhood," Del probed, "do you re-member any periods of missing time, unexplained blackouts, fugue states?"

Nonplussed, Mrs. Dai could only say, "Everyone sure not like nice hot cup of tea?"

No doubt talking to herself but appearing to address Scootie, Del said, "Sure as hell, this Xan River is a primary locus of evil extraterrestrial influence."

Heavy footsteps thudded across the front porch.

Tommy tensed, waited, and when a knock came at the door, he stood bolt upright from the sofa.

"Don't answer door," Mrs. Dai advised.

"Yeah," Del said, "it might be that damn aggres-sive Amway saleswoman."

Scootie crept warily to the front door. He sniffed along the threshold, caught a scent he didn't like, whimpered, and hurried back to Del's side.

The knocking sounded again, louder and more insistent than before.

Raising her voice, Mrs. Dai said, "You can't come in."

Immediately, the demon pounded again, so hard that the door shook and the lock bolt rattled against the striker plate.

"Go away," said Mrs. Dai. To Tommy, she said, "Only eighteen minutes, then everyone happy."

Mother Phan said, "Sit down, Tuong. You just making everyone nervous."

Tommy couldn't take his eyes off the front door—until movement at one of the flanking windows drew his attention. The serpent-eyed fat man peered in at them.

"We don't even have a gun," Tommy worried.

"Don't need gun," Mother Phan said. "Got Quy Trang Dai. Sit down and be patient."

The Samaritan-thing walked to the window on the other side of the front door and peered hungrily at Tommy through that pane. It rapped one knuckle against the glass.

To Del, Tommy repeated, "We don't have a gun."

"We've got Mrs. Dai," Del said. "You can always pick her up by the ankles and use her as a club."

Quy Trang Dai wagged one finger at the Samaritan-thing and said, "I made you, and I tell you go away, so now you *go*."

The demon turned from the window. Its footsteps thudded across the porch and down the front steps.

"There," said Mother Phan, "now sit down, Tuong, and behave."

Trembling, Tommy sat on the sofa. "It really went away?"

"No," said Mrs. Dai. "It going all around house now to see did I forget and leave door or window open."

Tommy bolted up again. "Is there a chance you did?"

"No. I not fool."

"You already made one big mistake," Tommy reminded her.

"Tuong!" Mother Phan gasped, appalled by his rudeness.

"Well," Tommy said, "she did. She made one hell of a mistake, so why not another?"

Pouting, Mrs. Dai said, "One mistake, I have to apologize rest of my life?"

Feeling as if his skull might explode from the pressure of his anxiety, Tommy put his hands to his head. "This is nuts. This can't be happening."

"It happening," Mrs. Dai said.

"It's got to be a nightmare."

To the other women, Del said, "He's just not prepared for this. He doesn't watch *The X-Files*."

"You not watch *X-Files*?" Mrs. Dai asked, astonished.

Shaking her head with dismay, Mother Phan said, "Probably watch junk detective show instead of good educational program."

From elsewhere in the house came the sounds of the Samaritan-thing rapping on windows and testing doorknobs.

Scootie cuddled against Del, and she petted and soothed him.

Mrs. Dai said, "Some rain we have, huh?"

"So early in season too," said Mother Phan.

"Remind me of jungle rain, so heavy."

"We need rain after drought last year."

"Sure no drought this year."

Del said, "Mrs. Dai, in your village in Vietnam, did farmers ever find crop circles, inexplicable depressed patterns in their fields? Or large circular depressions where something might have landed in the rice paddies?"

Leaning forward in her chair, Mother Phan said to Mrs. Dai, "Tuong not want to believe demon rapping window in front of his face, want to think it just bad dream, but then he believe Big Foot real."

"Big Foot?" Mrs. Dai said, and pressed one hand to her lips to stifle a giggle.

The Samaritan-thing stomped up the steps onto the front porch once more. It appeared at the window to the left of the door, eyes fierce and radiant.

Mrs. Dai consulted her wristwatch. "Looking good."

Tommy stood rigid, quivering.

To Mother Phan, Mrs. Dai said, "So sorry about Mai."

"Break mother's heart," said Tommy's mother.

"She live to regret," said Mrs. Dai.

"I try so hard to teach her right."

"She weak, magician clever."

"Tuong make bad example for sister," said Mother Phan.

"My heart ache for you," Mrs. Dai said.

Virtually vibrating with tension, Tommy said, "Can we talk about this later, if there *is* a later?"

From the beast at the window came the piercing, ululant shriek that seemed more like an electronic voice than an animal one.

Getting up from her chinoiserie chair, Mrs. Dai turned to the window, put her hands on her hips, and said, "Stop that, you bad thing. You wake neighbors."

The creature fell silent, but it glared at Mrs. Dai almost as hatefully as it had glared at Tommy.

Abruptly the fat man's moon-round face split up the middle from chin to hairline, as it had when the creature had clambered over the bow railing of the yacht in Newport Harbor. The halves of its countenance peeled apart, green eyes now bulging on the sides of its skull, and out of the gash in the center of its face lashed a score of whip-thin, segmented black tendrils that writhed around a sucking hole crammed with gnashing teeth. As the beast pressed its face to the window, the tendrils slithered frenziedly across the glass.

"You not scare me," Mrs. Dai said disdainfully. "Zip up face and go away."

The writing tendrils withdrew into the skull, and the torn visage re-knit into the face of the fat man—although with the green eyes of the demon.

"You see," Mother Phan said, still sitting complacently with her purse in her lap and her hands on the purse. "Don't need gun when have Quy Trang Dai."

"Impressive," Del agreed.

At the window, its frustration palpable, the Samaritan-thing issued a pleading, needful mewl.

Mrs. Dai took three steps toward the window, lights flashing across the heels of her shoes, and waved at the beast with the backs of her hands. "Shoo," she said impatiently. "Shoo, shoo."

This was more than the Samaritan-thing could tolerate, and it smashed one fat fist through the window.

As shattered glass cascaded into the living room, Mrs. Dai backed up three steps, bumping against the chinoiserie chair, and said, "This not good."

"This not good?" Tommy half shouted. "What do you mean *this not good*?"

Rising from the sofa, Del said, "I think she means we turned down the last cup of tea we're ever going to have a chance to drink."

Mother Phan got up from the *bergère*. She spoke to Quy Trang Dai in rapid Vietnamese.

Keeping her eyes on the demon at the broken window, Mrs. Dai answered in Vietnamese.

Looking distressed at last, Mother Phan said, "Oh, boy."

The tone in which his mother spoke those two words was like an icy finger drawn down his spine.

At the window, the Samaritan-thing at first seemed shocked by its own boldness. This was, after all, the sacred domain of the hairdresser witch who had summoned it from Hell—or from wherever Xan River magicians summoned such creatures. It peered in amazement at the few jagged fragments of glass that still prickled from the window frame, no doubt wondering why it had not instantly been cast back to the sulfurous chambers of the underworld.

Mrs. Dai checked her wristwatch.

Tommy consulted his as well.

Ticktock.

Half snarling, half whining nervously, the Samaritan-thing climbed through the broken window into the living room.

"Better stand together," said Mrs. Dai.

Tommy, Del, and Scootie moved out from behind the coffee table, joining his mother and Mrs. Dai in a tight grouping.

The serpent-eyed fat man no longer wore the hooded raincoat. The fire from the yacht should have burned away all its clothes, but curiously had only singed them, as though its imperviousness to fire extended somewhat to the garments it wore. The black wingtip shoes were badly scuffed and caked with mud. The filthy and rumpled trousers, the equally disheveled and bullet-torn shirt and vest and suit jacket, the acrid smell of smoke that seeped from the creature, combined with its gardenia-white skin and inhuman eyes, gave it all the charm of a walking corpse.

For half a minute or more, the demon stood in indecision and evident uneasiness, perhaps waiting to be punished for violating the sanctity of Mrs. Dai's house.

Ticktock.

Then it shook itself. Its plump hands curled into fists, relaxed, curled into fists. It licked its lips with a fat pink tongue—and it shrieked at them.

The deadline is dawn.

Beyond the windows the sky was still dark— though perhaps more charcoal gray than black.

Ticktock.

Mrs. Dai startled Tommy by raising her left hand to her mouth and savagely biting the meatiest part of her palm, below her thumb, drawing blood. She smacked her bloody hand against his forehead, like a faith healer knocking illness out of a penitent sufferer.

When Tommy started to wipe the blood away, Mrs. Dai said, "No, leave. I safe from demon because I summon into rag doll. Can't harm me. If you smell like me, smell like my blood, it can't know who you really are, think you me, then not harm you, either."

As the Samaritan-thing approached, Mrs. Dai smeared her blood on Del's forehead, on Mother Phan's forehead, and after hesitating only briefly, on Scootie's head as well.

"Be still," she instructed them in an urgent whisper. "Be still, be quiet."

Grumbling, hissing, the creature approached to within a foot of the group. Its fetid breath was repulsive, reeking of dead burnt flesh and curdled milk and rancid onions—as though, in another life, it had eaten hundreds of cheeseburgers and had been plagued with indigestion even in Hell.

With a wet crackling sound, the plump white hands metamorphosed into serrated pincers designed for efficient slashing and rending.

When the radiant green eyes fixed on Tommy's eyes, they seemed to look *through* him, as if the beast were reading his identity on the bar code of his soul.

Tommy remained still. Silent.

The demon sniffed him, not as a snorting pig might revel in the delicious stink of its slops, but as a master viniculturist with an exquisitely sensitive nose might seek to isolate and identify each of the many delicate aromas rising from a glassful of fine Bordeaux.

Hissing, the beast turned to sniff Del, lingering more briefly than it had with Tommy.

Then Mrs. Dai.

Then Mother Phan.

When the creature bent down to sniff Scootie, the Labrador returned the compliment.

Apparently puzzled by finding the scent of the sorceress on all of them, the demon circled the group, grumbling, mumbling to itself in some strange language.

As one, without having to discuss it, Tommy and the three women and the dog shuffled in a circle to keep their blood-smeared faces toward the Samaritan-thing as it prowled for prey.

When they had shuffled all the way around and were back where they had started, the creature focused on Tommy once more. It leaned closer, until their faces were only three inches apart, and it sniffed. Sniffed. Sniffed. With a disgusting squishy sound, the fat man's nose broadened and darkened into a scaly reptilian snout with wide, pug nostrils. It breathed in slowly and deeply, held its breath, exhaled, breathed in even more slowly and deeply than before.

The serpent-eyed thing opened its mouth and shrieked at Tommy, but though his heart raced faster, Tommy neither flinched nor cried out.

At last the demon exhaled its pent-up inhalation, bathing Tommy's face in a gale of foul breath that made him want to spew up the coffee and pastries that he had eaten during the stop at The Great Pile.

The beast shuffled to the *bergère*, where Tommy's mother had been sitting, and knocked her purse to the floor. It settled down in the chair and folded its killing pincers in its lap—and after a moment they metamorphosed into the fat man's hands once more.

Tommy was afraid that his mother would leave the group, pick up her purse, and smack the demon over the head with it. But with uncharacteristic timidity, she remained still and quiet, as Mrs. Dai had instructed.

The hulking Samaritan-thing smacked its lips. It sighed wearily.

The radiant green eyes changed into the ordinary brown eyes of the murdered Samaritan.

The demon looked at its wristwatch.

Ticktock.

Yawning, it blinked at the group standing before it.

The beast bent forward in the *bergère*, seized its right foot with both hands, and brought the foot to its face in a display of impossible double-jointedness. Its mouth cracked open from ear to ear, like the mouth of a crocodile, and it began to stuff its foot and then its heavy leg into its maw.

Tommy glanced at the windows.

Pale pink light spread like a dim blush on the face of the eastern sky.

As if it were not a solid creature but an elaborate origami sculpture, the demon continued to fold itself into itself, growing smaller and smaller still—until, with a shimmer that hid the *how* of the final transformation, it became only a rag doll once more, exactly as it had been when Tommy had found it on his doorstep, a limp-limbed figure of white cotton, with all the black stitches intact.

Pointing at the pink sky beyond the windows, Mrs. Dai said, "Going to be nice day."

NINE

With paper towels and tap water, they had cleaned the blood off their foreheads.

The two Vietnamese women sat at the kitchen table.

After applying a healing poultice that the hairdresser-witch kept in the refrigerator, Mother Phan taped a gauze pad to Mrs. Dai's bitten hand. "You sure not hurt?"

"Fine, fine," said Quy Trang Dai. "Heal fast, no problem."

The rag doll lay on the table.

Tommy couldn't take his eyes off it. "What's in the damn thing?"

"Now?" Mrs. Dai said. "Mostly just sand. Some river mud. Snake blood. Some other things better you not know."

"I want to destroy it."

"Can't hurt you now. Anyway, taking apart is my job," said Mrs. Dai. "Have to do according to rules or magic won't be undone."

"Then take it apart right now."

"Have to wait till noon, sun high, night on other side of world, and then magic be undone."

"That's only logical," Del said.

Getting up from the table, Mrs. Dai said, "Ready for tea now?"

"I want to see it dismembered, everything inside cast to the wind," Tommy said.

"Can't watch," said Mrs. Dai as she took a teakettle from one of the cabinets. "Magic must be done by sorceress alone, no other eyes to see."

"Who says?"

"Dead ancestors of River Xan set rules, not me."

"Sit down, Tuong, stop worry, have tea," said Mother Phan. "You make Mrs. Dai think you not trust her."

Taking Tommy by the arm, Del said, "Could I see you a minute?"

She led him out of the kitchen into the dining room, and Scootie followed them.

Speaking in a whisper, she said, "Don't drink the tea."

"What?"

"Maybe there's more than one way to make a stray son return to the fold."

"What way?"

"A potion, a combination of exotic herbs, a pinch of river mud—who knows?" Del whispered.

Tommy looked back through the open door. In the kitchen, his mother was putting out cookies and slices of cake while Mrs. Dai brewed the tea.

"Maybe," whispered Del, "Mrs. Dai was too enthusiastic about bringing you to your senses and back into the family. Maybe she started out with the drastic approach, the doll, when a nice cup of the right tea would have made more sense."

In the kitchen, Mrs. Dai was putting cups and saucers on the table. The devil doll still lay there, watching the preparations with its cross-stitched eyes.

Tommy stepped into the kitchen and said, "Mom, I think we'd better go now."

Looking up from the cake that she was slicing, Mother Phan said, "Have tea and nibble first, then go."

"No, I want to go now."

"Don't be rude, Tuong. While we have tea and nibble, I call your father. By time we done, he stop by, take us home before he go work at bakery."

"Del and I are leaving now," he insisted.

"No car," she reminded him. "This crazy woman's car just trash in garage."

"The Peterbilt's parked out there at the curb. The engine's still idling."

Mother Phan frowned. "Truck stolen."

"We'll return it," Tommy said.

"What about trash car in garage?" Mrs. Dai asked.

"Mummingford will send someone for it," said Del.

"Who?"

"Tomorrow."

Tommy and Del and Scootie went into the living room, where the glass from the broken window crunched and clinked underfoot.

Mrs. Dai and Mother Phan followed them.

As Tommy unlocked and opened the front door, his mother said, "When I see you again?"

"Soon," he promised, following Del and Scootie onto the porch.

"Come to dinner tonight. We have *com tay cam,* your favorite."

"That sounds good. *Mmmmm,* I can't wait."

Mrs. Dai and Mother Phan stepped onto the porch as well, and the hairdresser said, "Miss Payne, what day your birthday?"

"Christmas Eve."

"Is true?"

Descending the porch steps, Del said, "October thirty-first."

"Which true?" Mrs. Dai asked a little too eagerly.

"July fourth," said Del. And to Tommy, sotto voce, she said, "They always need a birthday to cast the spell."

Moving onto the front steps as Del reached the walkway, Mrs. Dai said, "You have beautiful hair, Miss Payne. I enjoy doing such beautiful hair."

"So you can get a lock of it?" Del wondered as she continued to walk toward the Peterbilt.

"Mrs. Dai is wonderful genius hairdresser," said Mother Phan. "She give you best look ever have."

"I'll call for an appointment," Del promised as she went around the truck to the driver's door.

Tommy opened the passenger door to the truck cab so the dog could spring inside.

His mother and Mrs. Dai stood side by side on the steps of the front porch, the one in black slacks and a white blouse, the other in her pink jogging suit. They waved.

Tommy waved back at them, climbed into the truck cab beside the dog, and pulled the door shut.

Del was already behind the wheel. She put the truck in gear.

When Tommy glanced at the house again, Mrs. Dai and his mother waved at him.

Again he returned the wave.

As Del drove away from the house, Tommy said miserably, "What am I going to do now? I love my mother, I really do, but I'm never going to be a baker or a doctor or any of the things she wants me to be, and I can't spend the rest of my life afraid to drink tea or answer a doorbell."

"It'll be all right, tofu boy."

"It'll never be all right," he disagreed.

"Don't be negative. Negative thinking disturbs the fabric of the cosmos. A little bit of self-indulgent negativity might seem like an innocent pleasure, but it can cause a tornado in Kansas or a blizzard in Pennsylvania."

Scootie licked Tommy's face, and he didn't resist. He knew he was genuinely desperate when he found himself taking comfort from the dog's attentions.

"I know exactly what we need to do," Del said.

"Oh, yeah? What?"

"You've known since we kissed on the carousel."

"What a kiss."

"So for starters, we need to fly to Vegas and get married—if you care to propose to me."

Scootie looked at him expectantly.

Tommy was surprised to hear her offer, but he was not surprised to hear himself say, "Deliverance Payne, daughter of Ned and Julia Rosalyn Winona Lilith, will you marry me?"

"It's going to take a lot more than a doll snake rat-quick little monster thing to stop me."

"You have a beautiful smile," he said.

"You too."

Actually, he wasn't smiling. He was grinning like a fool.

Tommy had expected to catch a commercial flight from John Wayne Airport to Las Vegas, but Del's mother owned a LearJet, which was ready for use on fifteen minutes' notice. Del was a qualified pilot.

"Besides," she said as they walked the last block to the airport from the abandoned Peterbilt, "I think the sooner we tie the knot, the better—in regards to whatever Mrs. Dai may have in mind. Married, we geometrically increase our psychic resources. We have more power to resist."

A few minutes later, as they boarded the private jet, Del said, "Anyway, I want to see if we can beat my mom's record. She married Daddy nineteen hours after she met him."

Studying his watch, calculating, Tommy said, "You served me dinner about . . . twelve hours ago."

"We'll make it. Are you tired, darling?"

"Damn if I don't feel totally rested. And I didn't have a wink of sleep all night."

"You may never need it again," she said. "It's such a waste of time, sleeping."

Tommy sat in the co-pilot's seat, while Scootie lounged in the passenger compartment.

They flew east into the morning sun, where the sky was no longer pink but as blue as Deliverance Payne's eyes.

Their suite at the Mirage Hotel was one of several spacious and lavishly appointed accommodations that were not rented to ordinary customers but were reserved to be provided free to high rollers who regularly gambled fortunes in the casino downstairs. Though neither Del nor Tommy intended to wager one dollar on the tables, the Payne name elicited a response no less generous and effusive than would have been accorded to an Arab prince bearing suitcases full of cash. Eighteen years after his death, Ned Payne remained a legendary poker player, and the hotel management's affection for Del's mother was evident in their numerous enquiries into the state of her health, her current activities, and the likelihood of her coming to visit sometime soon.

Even Scootie was greeted with huzzahs, petted and nuzzled and spoken to in baby talk. In addition to the enormous vases full of fresh flowers that lent their fragrance to each of the seven rooms in the suite, there were strategically placed silver-plated bowls full of dog biscuits.

A clothing store in the hotel shopping arcade sent up two salespeople and carts laden with garments. Within ninety minutes of their arrival, Tommy and Del had showered, shampooed, and selected their wedding outfits.

He wore black tassel loafers, black socks, charcoal-gray slacks, a blue blazer, a white shirt, and a blue-striped tie.

"You look very preppy," Del said approvingly.

She wore white heels, a figure-flattering white silk dress with white lace at the neck and at the cuffs of the long sleeves, and two white orchids in her hair.

"You look like a bride," he said.

"No veil, though."

"Wouldn't want to hide that face," he said.

"You're so sweet."

Just as they were ready to leave the hotel for the chapel, the mayor of Las Vegas arrived with an envelope containing their license. He was a tall, distinguished-looking man with silver hair, attired in an expensive blue suit, wearing a five-carat diamond pinkie ring.

"You dear girl," the mayor said, kissing Del on the forehead, "you are the most glamorous creature I've ever seen. How is Ingrid?"

"She's splendid," Del said.

"She doesn't come to town often enough. Will you tell her that I pine for her?"

"She'll be so pleased to know she's remembered."

"She's more than remembered. She's unforget-table."

Del said, "Well, I'm spilling a secret here, but I'm sure you'll have a chance to tell her yourself."

The mayor embraced Tommy as if they were father and son. "This is a great day, a great day."

"Thank you, sir."

To Del, the mayor said, "Dear, you have arranged a limousine, I presume."

"Yes, it's waiting."

"Then just delay here two minutes so I can pop downstairs and be sure the police escort is ready too."

"You're an absolute jewel," Del said, kissing his cheek.

The mayor departed, and Tommy said, "Who's Ingrid?"

Examining herself in the marble-lined foyer's ornate mirror, Del said, "That's what some people call my mother."

"Of course. Will she be very upset that she wasn't at the wedding?"

"Oh, she's here," Del said happily.

Still capable of surprise, Tommy said, "How?"

"I called her as soon as we arrived, before I show-ered, and she flew up in her other jet."

On the way down in the elevator, Tommy said, "How could you possibly manage to arrange all this so quickly?"

"You took so long selecting your wardrobe," she said, "that I had time to make a few calls."

An enormous black stretch limousine waited in front of the hotel, in the shade of the portico. Mummingford stood beside it. He had flown up from Newport Beach with Ingrid.

"Miss Payne," he said, "may I offer my best wishes for much happiness."

"Thank you, Mummingford."

"Mr. Phan," said the butler, "I offer you my congratulations. You're a fortunate young man."

"Thank you, Mummingford. I think I'm more than fortunate. I'm blessed. And bewildered."

"I myself," said Mummingford, "have functioned in a state of perpetual bewilderment ever since coming to work for Mrs. Payne. Isn't it delightful?"

The Chapel of Everlasting Bliss, one of Las Vegas's more well appointed wedding mills, was bedecked with so many hundreds of red and white roses that Tommy feared an attack of hay fever. He stood by the altar railing, trying not to fidget, smiling stupidly because the place was full of people smiling at him.

Designed primarily to provide a suitable quasi-religious venue to impulsive out-of-state couples who arrived in Vegas either alone or with a few carloads of friends, the chapel seated only sixty people. Even given such short notice of the ceremony, friends of the Payne family filled the pews to capacity, and another thirty stood in the side aisles.

At Tommy's right hand, Roland Ironwright, the magician, said, "Relax. Getting married is a snap. I did it myself eighteen hours ago in this very room."

Accompanied by a nine-piece band, Frank sang, "I've Got the World on a String," as only Frank had ever been able to sing it, while Mrs. Payne gave Del a final once-over in the vestibule at the back of the chapel.

Then the band struck up "Here Comes the Bride."

Scootie entered from the vestibule, carrying a nosegay in his mouth, which he brought to Tommy.

Behind Scootie was Mai, Tommy's sister, radiant as he had never seen her. She carried a white basket full of rose petals, which she sprinkled on the carpet as she advanced.

Del appeared, and everyone seated in the chapel rose to beam at her as she approached the altar.

Somehow Frank managed to ad-lib additional lyrics to "Here Comes the Bride," adding lines like "she looks so groovy, like she stepped out of a movie," without diminishing the beauty and solemnity of the piece. Indeed, if anything, his version enriched the old standard, and he sounded fifty years younger than he was, not like a crooner in the twilight of his life but like a young swinger in the days of the Dorsey Brothers and Duke Ellington.

When Tommy handed the nosegay to Del and took her arm to lead her to the altar, his heart swelled with love.

The minister was mercifully swift in the performance of his sacred duties, and precisely when it was needed, Roland Ironwright cut open a fresh orange and produced the wedding band from the heart of the fruit.

After the minister pronounced them man and wife at 11:34 in the morning, less than eighteen hours after they had first met, Tommy and Deliverance indulged in another kiss of earthshaking power, only the second they had ever shared, and the onlookers applauded joyously.

From his place in front of the band, Frank called out to Del's mother, "Hey, Sheila, you wonderful broad, come up here and do this number with me!"

Del's mother joined him, and they shared a microphone to belt out an up-tempo rendition of "I've Got You Under My Skin," which served as a recessional.

In the receiving line outside, Del reminded everyone about the reception at the grand ballroom of the Mirage at seven o'clock that evening. It promised to be the party of the year.

When the two of them were alone again with Scootie in the back of the limousine, returning to the hotel, Del said to Tommy, "Are you tired yet?"

"I don't understand it, but I feel as if I just woke up from the longest sleep on record. I've got so much energy it's absurd."

"Lovely," she said, snuggling against him.

He put his arm around her, suddenly excited by the warmth of her and by the exquisite perfection with which her supple body molded to his.

"We're not going back to the hotel," she told him.

"What? Why not?"

"I told Mummingford to take us to the airport. We're flying back to Orange County right away."

"But I thought . . . I mean . . . aren't we going to . . . Oh, Del, I want to be alone with you."

"I'm not going to ask you to consummate until you know all of my secrets," she said.

"But I *want* to consummate," he said. "I want to consummate this morning, as soon as possible, right here in the limo!"

"Have you been eating too much tofu?" she asked coquettishly.

"If we go back to Orange County, we'll miss our own party this evening."

"It's less than an hour's flight each way. We have maybe two hours of business when we get there. We'll make it back with time to spare." She put a hand in his lap. "With time to consummate."

In her house on Balboa Peninsula, Del led Tommy upstairs to the studio where she created her paintings.

Canvases were hung on all sides, and others stood in stacks against one wall, at least a hundred altogether. Most of them were exceedingly strange landscapes of places that could never exist in this world, scenes of such stunning beauty that the sight of them brought tears to Tommy's eyes.

"I painted these by remote viewing," she said, "but someday I hope to travel there."

"Where?"

"I'll tell you later."

Eight paintings were different from all the others. They were portraits of Tommy, rendered with a photographic realism equal to that with which the landscapes had been painted.

Blinking in astonishment, he said, "When did you do these?"

"Over the past two years. That's how long I've been having dreams about you. I knew you were the one, my destiny, and then last night you just walked into the restaurant and ordered two cheeseburgers."

The living room in the Phan house in Huntington Beach was remarkably similar to the living room of the Dai house, although the furnishings were somewhat more expensive. A painting of Jesus, revealing His Sacred Heart, hung on one wall, and in a corner was a Buddhist shrine.

Mother Phan sat in her favorite armchair, slack-jawed and pale, having taken the news of the wedding as though she had been hit in the face with a skillet.

Scootie licked one of her hands consolingly, but she didn't seem to be aware of the dog.

Del sat on the sofa with Tommy, holding his hand. "First, Mrs. Phan, I want you to understand that the

Paynes and the Phans could be the most wonderful combination of families imaginable, a tremendous union of talents and forces, and my mother and I are prepared to embrace all of you as our own. I want to be given a chance to love you and Mr. Phan and Tommy's brothers and his sister, and I want all of you to learn to love me."

"You steal my son," said Mother Phan.

"No," Del said, "I stole a Honda and later a Ferrari, and then we borrowed the Peterbilt that the demon stole, but I didn't steal your son. He gave his heart to me of his own free will. Now, before you say anything more that might be rash, that you might later come to regret having said, let me tell you about my mother and me."

"You bad news."

Ignoring the insult, Del said, "Twenty-nine years ago, when my mom and dad were driving from Vegas to a poker tournament in Reno, taking a scenic route, they were abducted by aliens from a lonely stretch of highway near Mud Lake in Nevada."

Gazing at Del, his head ringing like a gong with remembered lines of conversation that had seemed like sheer lunacy when she had spoken them, Tommy said, "South of Tonopah."

"That's right, darling," said Del. To Tommy's mother, she said, "They were taken up to the mothership and examined. They were allowed to remember all of this, you see, because the aliens who abducted them were *good* extraterrestrials. Unfortunately, most of the abductions are perpetrated by evil ETs whose plans for this planet are nefarious in the extreme, which is why they block abductees' memories of what happened."

Mother Phan scowled at Tommy. "You rude to Mrs. Dai, won't even stay for tea, run off and marry *crazy* woman." She discovered Scootie licking her hand, and she shooed him away. "You want lose tongue, you filthy dog?"

"Anyway, in the mothership, hovering above Mud Lake," Del continued, "the aliens took an egg from my mother, sperm from Daddy, added some genetic wizardry of their own, and implanted Mother with an embryo—which was me. I am a starchild, Mrs. Phan, and my mission here is to ferret out damage done by certain other extraterrestrials—which often includes teaching people like Mrs. Dai to perform evil mojo—and set things right. Because of this, I lead an eventful life, and often a lonely one. But at last . . . not lonely any more, because I have Tommy."

"World full of lovely Vietnamese girls," Tommy's mother told him, "and you run away with crackpot maniac blonde."

"When I reached puberty," Del said, "I began to acquire various extraordinary powers, and I suppose I might continue to acquire even more as the years go by."

Tommy said, "So that's what you meant when you said you'd have been able to save your father if he hadn't gotten cancer before you reached puberty."

Squeezing his hand, Del said, "It's all right. Fate is fate. Death *is* just a phase, just a transition between this and a higher existence."

"The David Letterman show."

Grinning, Del said, "I love you, tofu man."

Mother Phan sat as stone-faced as an Easter Island monument.

"And Emmy, the little girl . . . the daughter of the guard at the gatehouse," Tommy said. "You *have* cured her."

"And gave you a massage on the carousel that means you'll never need to sleep again."

He raised one hand to the back of his neck, and as his heart began to race with exhilaration, he remembered the tingle of her fingers as they had probed his weary muscles.

She winked. "Who wants to sleep when we could use all that time to consummate?"

"Don't want you here," said Mother Phan.

Turning to her mother-in-law again, Del said, "When the aliens returned Mom and Daddy to that highway south of Tonopah, they sent along one of their own as a guardian, in the form of a dog."

Tommy would have thought that nothing on earth could have torn his attention away from Del at that moment, but he turned his head to Scootie so fast that he almost gave himself whiplash.

The dog grinned at him.

"Scootie," Del explained, "has greater powers than I do—"

"The flock of birds that distracted the demon," Tommy said.

"—and with your indulgence, Mrs. Phan, I will ask him to give a little demonstration to confirm what I've told you."

"Insane crazy American maniac blond lunatic," Mother Phan insisted.

The Labrador sprang onto the coffee table, ears pricked, tail wagging, and gazed so intently at Mother Phan that she pressed back into her armchair in alarm.

Above the dog's head, a sphere of soft orange light formed in the air. It hung there a moment, but when Scootie twitched one ear, the light spun away from him and whirled around the room. When it passed an open door, the door flew shut. When it passed a closed door, the door flew open. All the windows rose as if flung up by invisible hands, and balmy November air blew into the living room. A clock stopped ticking, unlighted lamps glowed, and the television switched on by itself.

The sphere of light returned to Scootie, hovered over his head for a moment, and then faded away.

Now Tommy knew how Del had started the yacht without keys and how she had hot-wired the Ferrari in two seconds flat.

The black Labrador got off the coffee table and padded to his mistress, putting his head on her lap.

To Tommy's mother, Del said, "We'd like you and Mr. Phan and Tommy's brothers and their wives, all his nieces and nephews, to come to our party tonight in Las Vegas and celebrate our marriage. We can't fit you all in the LearJet, but Mother has leased a 737, which is standing by at the airport right now, and if you hurry, you can all be there with us tonight. It's time for me to quit my job as a waitress and get on with my real work. Tommy and I are going to lead eventful lives, Mrs. Phan, and we'd like all of you to be a part of that."

Tommy couldn't read the wrenching series of emotions that passed across his mother's face.

Having said her piece, Del stroked Scootie, scratched behind his ears, and murmured appreciatively to him: "Oh, him a good fella, him is, my cutie Scootiewootums."

After a while, Mother Phan got up from her chair. She went to the television and turned it off.

She went to the Buddhist shrine in the corner, struck a match, and lit three sticks of incense.

For perhaps two or three minutes, the survivor of Saigon and the South China Sea stood staring at the shrine, inhaling the thin and fragrant smoke.

Del patted Tommy's hand.

At last his mother turned away from the shrine, came to the sofa, and stood over him, scowling. "Tuong, you won't be doctor when want you be doctor, won't be baker when want you be baker, write stories about silly whiskey-drunk detective, won't keep old ways, don't even remember how speak language from Land of Seagull and Fox, buy Corvette and like cheeseburgers better than *com tay cam,* forget your roots, want to be something never can be . . . all bad, all bad. But you make best marriage any boy ever make in history of world, so I guess that got to count for something."

By four-thirty that afternoon, Tommy, Del, and Scootie were back in their suite at the Mirage.

Scootie settled in his bedroom to crunch dog biscuits and watch an old Bogart and Bacall movie on television.

Tommy and Del consummated.

Afterward, she didn't bite his head off and devour him alive.

That evening at the reception, Mr. Sinatra called Mother Phan "a great old broad," Mai danced with her father, Ton got tipsy for the first time in his life, Sheila Ingrid Julia Rosalyn Winona Lilith answered to three other names, and Del whispered to Tommy as they did a fox trot, "This is reality, tofu man, because reality is what we carry in our hearts, and my heart is full of beauty just for you."

A NOTE TO THE READER

Ticktock is a new novel, not a revision of a book originally released under a pen name, as have been some recent paperbacks in my publication schedule. Inevitably, many of you will write to me to inquire why this story appeared initially in paperback without first being published in hardcover. To forestall those letters, I will give you a peek into my—admittedly disordered—mind.

Two and a half years ago, when I finished *Dark Rivers of the Heart*, one of the most intense and arguably most complex books I had ever done, I was exhausted; more to the point, I was shaken by the darkness of the story. I decided that I needed to tackle a project that was considerably lighter in tone.

Over the years, I've become known for mixing different genres of fiction with reckless abandon—suspense and terror and mystery and love story and a little science fiction—changing the mix with every novel. In a number of books—*Watchers, Lightning, The Bad Place, Hideaway, Mr. Murder*, to name a few—I've even blended large measures of humor into the mix, though, according to the common wisdom of modern publishing, this is a sure sales squelcher. These became some of my most successful novels, however, and readers responded to them enthusiastically. Consequently, after *Dark Rivers of the Heart*, I decided to tackle a new and strange mix of genres: the supernatural thriller and the screwball comedy.

Good screwball comedy—exemplified by splendid old movies like *Bringing Up Baby* and *The Philadelphia Story*—is different from all other comedy in that its form is nearly as strict as that of the sonnet. Some basic requirements include the following elements: the male lead must be smart, witty, sensible, but befuddled by the other eccentric characters with whom he becomes involved; the appealing female lead appears to be an airhead but turns out, by the end, to be the wisest of all the characters; she should also be an heiress; she should have an astonishingly eccentric but lovable family; all of the screwball characters should be largely unaware of the way in which they leave the male lead in a state of perpetual confusion; the dialogue should be of a rarefied type that has characters talking at cross purposes and that allows the most outrageous things to be said with convincingly deadpan seriousness; the story should be propelled by surprising character twists and revelations that delight us and that are logical *within the given structure of the story*; and if possible, there ought to be a dog.

When I began *Ticktock* in early 1994, I had fun with it—but then I hit a wall. Something was wrong. I couldn't identify the trouble, so I put the book aside. Instead, I wrote *Intensity,* which turned out to be the scariest and fastest-paced novel I had ever written. Even *Dark Rivers of the Heart* had made room for some humor, if less than usual, but *Intensity* was perhaps (if reviewers can be believed) as unrelenting as a thriller can be, and I finished it with a deep *need* to write something lighter.

When I returned to *Ticktock*, I realized at once what the problem was. The lead character didn't work. He needed to be a Vietnamese-American. You know why if you've read the book before reading this afterword. Suddenly the story flew. As is the tradition with pure screwball comedy, the humorous elements are quiet at first; comic chaos builds slowly through the first third of this supernatural thriller, but then escalates page by page.

The revelations in *Ticktock* left me wide-eyed with wonder as they unfolded, and I came to love the characters—Tommy, Del, their mothers, Scootie the dog—so much that I was dismayed when I reached the final page and couldn't follow their adventures any further, couldn't hear what they would say next. After the darkness and intensity of *Intensity*, writing *Ticktock* buoyed me.

So here are the adventures of Tommy Phan, Del Payne, Scootie, and their families, with the hope that you have as much fun with them as I did.

—DEAN KOONTZ
May 1996

LARGE PRINT EDITIONS

Look for these and other Random House Large Print books at your local bookstore

Ben Artzi-Pelossof, Noa, *In the Name of Sorrow and Hope*
Berendt, John, *Midnight in the Garden of Good and Evil*
Brinkley, David, *David Brinkley*
Byatt, A. S., *Babel Tower*
Crichton, Michael, *The Lost World*
Cruz Smith, Martin, *Rose*
Daly, Rosie, *In the Kitchen with Rosie*
Flagg, Fannie, *Daisy Fay and the Miracle Man*
Flagg, Fannie, *Fried Green Tomatoes at the
        Whistle Stop Cafe*
Follett, Ken, *A Place Called Freedom*
Fulghum, Robert, *From Beginning to End*
Grimes, Martha, *Hotel Paradise*
Hepburn, Katharine, *Me*
Krantz, Judith, *Spring Collection*
Koontz, Dean, *Intensity*
Landers, Ann, *Wake Up and Smell the Coffee!*
Lindbergh, Anne Morrow, *Gift from the Sea*
Mayle, Peter, *Anything Considered*
Michener, James A., *Mexico*
Mother Teresa, *A Simple Path*
Patterson, Richard North, *The Final Judgment*
Phillips, Louis, editor, *The Random House Large Print
        Treasury of Best-Loved Poems*
Pope John Paul II, *Crossing the Threshold of Hope*
Powell, Colin with Joseph E. Persico, *My American
        Journey*
Shaara, Jeff, *Gods and Generals*
Truman, Margaret, *Murder at the National Gallery*
Tyler, Anne, *Ladder of Years*